THE UTOPIA EXPERIMENT

"Mills offers an interesting new premise for action-adventure...[and] rockets the action around the world."
—*Kirkus Reviews*

"Ludlum fans will enjoy the frantic pace and dramatic shifts in plot...Mills's genius is making 'extra-human capabilities' seem not merely possible but almost already available, echoing the prescience of Jules Verne. We are all headed into this brave new world. Here, Mills helps us enjoy the ride while we consider the consequences."
—*Fredericksburg Free Lance-Star* (VA)

"Well-written...This book is a winner."
—**BookReporter.com**

"A fast-paced book with great characters...Mills is a very good writer."
—**Bubblews.com**

THE JANUS REPRISAL

"From the opening sentence that literally starts with a bang, the latest Covert-One novel speeds along at a break-neck pace...Freveletti, who has an amazing talent for action scenes, has written one of the top entries in the

Covert-One series, which has established itself as the best of the numerous series based on Ludlum characters."
—***Booklist***

"Wonderful...Award-winning novelist Freveletti lends her imaginative talents to the Covert-One series with a book that is nearly impossible to put down and moves at the speed of light without pause...[It] races forward with the energy of a super-charged Bourne film."
—**BookReporter.com**

"A fast-moving, well-written thriller."
—***Oklahoman***

"Freveletti turbocharges tension to nonstop levels in this Covert-One thriller."
—***Kirkus Reviews***

"Masterful...The action is quite cinematic, the characters well-drawn, and the plot as tight as they come."
—**CriminalElement.com**

"Exciting...Great read, really well-done, and a great finish."
—**BestsellersWorld.com**

THE ARES DECISION

"The action never flags...Mills nicely integrates relevant military and scientific details into the story line, while his skill at characterization will leave many hoping he'll become a permanent posthumous collaborator with Ludlum."
—***Publishers Weekly***

"A tight and tense page-turner...Mills does the large-scale thriller better than anyone else working the genre today."

—*Booklist*

"Fast-paced and action-filled, with iconic characters and contemporary themes, the story is a stand-alone-worthy entry in the Covert-One series...Fans of Ludlum and Mills thrillers will find *The Ares Decision* right on target."

—*Fredericksburg Free Lance-Star* (VA)

"Plenty of comfort food for those with an appetite for the thriller genre."

—*Kirkus Reviews*

"It should have the dual effect of sustaining interest in the series and moving Mills onto the must-read list of many. If your boat is floated by thriller novels that are set in the real world and have the ability to scare the pants off you, you will absolutely love this one...I can think of no greater compliment than to tell you that portions of the novel made my skin crawl. And I loved every minute of it."

—BookReporter.com

"The pacing and the premise are pure Ludlum."

—WomanAroundTown.com

"Filled with action, intrigue, and a plot that puts the team in a tight spot and their lives in constant danger. The end result is an exciting read."

—TheSunDaily.my

ROBERT LUDLUM'S™

THE UTOPIA EXPERIMENT

A COVERT-ONE NOVEL

SERIES CREATED BY ROBERT LUDLUM
WRITTEN BY KYLE MILLS

GRAND CENTRAL
PUBLISHING

NEW YORK   BOSTON

Copyright © 2013 by Myn Pyn, LLC
All rights reserved. In accordance with the U.S. Copyright Act of 1976, the scanning, uploading, and electronic sharing of any part of this book without the permission of the publisher is unlawful piracy and theft of the author's intellectual property. If you would like to use material from the book (other than for review purposes), prior written permission must be obtained by contacting the publisher at permissions@hbgusa.com. Thank you for your support of the author's rights.

Grand Central Publishing
Hachette Book Group
237 Park Avenue
New York, NY 10017
www.HachetteBookGroup.com

Grand Central Publishing is a division of Hachette Book Group, Inc.
The Grand Central Publishing name and logo is a trademark of Hachette Book Group, Inc.

The Hachette Speakers Bureau provides a wide range of authors for speaking events. To find out more, go to www.hachettespeakersbureau.com or call (866) 376-6591.

The publisher is not responsible for websites (or their content) that are not owned by the publisher.

Printed in the United States of America

Originally published in hardcover by Hachette Book Group
First international mass market edition: September 2013

10 9 8 7 6 5 4 3 2 1
OPM

THE UTOPIA EXPERIMENT

PROLOGUE

Erfurt
East Germany
December 1972

W E'RE RUNNING BEHIND SCHEDULE. I can't be responsible for the weather."

Christian Dresner nodded and continued to gaze through the Trabant's dirty windshield. Outside, everything was hung with ice. Decayed houses glistened on either side of the narrow road, tangled power lines sagged with the weight, and the cobblestones glared blindingly in their headlights.

"We should go directly to the rendezvous," the driver continued nervously. "It's almost midnight."

"You took our money," Dresner said. "Now you'll do the job according to our agreement."

The man leaned over the greasy steering wheel, scowling as he tried to coax a little more speed from the car without losing traction.

A quiet rustle came from the backseat, followed by a voice barely audible over the sickly, communist-made engine. "Christian?"

Dresner twisted around and looked at the thin man clutching a briefcase to his chest. At twenty-six, Gerhard Eichmann was two years his senior, but his physique and manner made him seem perpetually trapped between adolescence and adulthood. Despite that impression, though, he was a brilliant psychologist—something highly valued by Soviet politicians obsessed with controlling every aspect of their people's lives. More important, though, Eichmann was a true friend—a rare treasure in a world full of zealous apparatchiks, secret police, and desperate informants. Perhaps the frail man would be the only friend he would ever have. But it didn't matter. One like him was enough. More than most people could hope for.

"Don't worry, Gerd. Soon, we'll wake up in a warm bed in the West. We'll be free to do what we wish. To become what we wish. I promise you."

Eichmann gave him a weak smile and held the briefcase tighter. It was the only thing they were taking with them, the only thing they possessed of value. It contained records of the research done at a remote facility they'd been all but imprisoned in for the past four years. The currency they would use to start their new lives.

The vehicle slowed and Dresner faced forward again as they started up a winding road, the moderate slope of which quickly proved too steep for the car's bald tires.

He stepped out before they fully stopped, finding his footing on the ice and starting forward as the falling snow swallowed up Eichmann's panicked entreaties.

The building began to reveal itself as the slope leveled— the cracked and faded arches clinging precariously to the facade, the peeling tower that sagged like everything and everyone around it.

A dim light coming from the upper window looked exactly as it had the day he'd been taken away but he averted his gaze, afraid that it would pull him into the past. That the frightened, desperate child he'd been would return and overwhelm him.

The gate he remembered was gone now and he felt his breathing turn shallow as he passed through the empty space where it had been. The swing set still stood, trapped in the frozen mud of the yard along with a teeter-totter snapped in the middle and a set of climbing bars. In his childhood, they'd still had paint clinging to them— patches of bright red and yellow that recalled the days before the war. Before the Soviets. On rare clear afternoons he'd lose himself in their glow, trying to transport himself to a time when children with homes and families clambered over them laughing.

Now even that was gone, swallowed by rust or obscured by the soot from coal fires people used to beat back the cold.

He pulled his coat closer around his neck and walked across the silent yard, stopping at the front door and pounding on it with a bare fist. When there was no reaction, he grabbed the shovel leaning against the railing and used the handle to hammer the unyielding wood. The fog of his breath obscured his vision as he continued to attack the entrance, years of repressed anger, helplessness, and hate resurfacing so easily.

A light came on inside and he stepped back, gripping the shovel in a shaking hand.

But when the door opened, it wasn't the man he'd come for. It was the woman who had seen him off more than fifteen years ago. Her bowl-cut hair and puritan style of dress were unchanged, but now the skin hung loose from her chin and her eyes had trouble focusing.

"Hello Marta."

The recognition came quickly, followed immediately by the fear he had been too consumed to anticipate. Dresner had no desire to inspire that in her and he suddenly felt ashamed. She had never been an evil woman. Just weak. And numb.

He brushed by her, the cold not dissipating at all as he passed in front of a broad staircase leading to the second floor. At its top, the orphans imprisoned there would be hiding in the shadows, just as he had every time an unexpected visitor came. They would be perfectly still, holding their breaths, telling themselves that this time it would be a long-lost parent or cousin or sibling. That it would be someone who would take them away.

He plunged into the darkness, avoiding scattered furniture by memory and starting quietly up the spiral stairs that wound their way up the tower. The door at the top was framed by gray light flickering from the gap around the jamb and he stood in front of it for a few moments, trying to separate the sensation of being there at that moment from being there before.

"What do you want?" he heard from the other side of the door. "You'll get out of here if you know what's good for you!"

Instead, Dresner reached for the knob and went through, feeling the warmth of the kerosene heater that they had all known about and dreamed of. At first, he ignored the bulky, half-dressed man on the sofa and looked around at the room illuminated by the glow of a small black-and-white television. He'd never been inside—

none of them had—and their imaginations had built it into a palace of gold and jewels and candy. In reality, it was just another disintegrating relic of a Germany that no longer existed.

Finally, Dresner's eyes fell on a cane in the corner, still black in places, worn down to bare wood in others. He wondered how much his own back was responsible for the polished gleam of it. And if the broken tip was a relic of the eight-year-old girl who had slipped away in her bed, a victim of a beating she'd received for knocking over an old lamp that had never worked.

"Who—" the man said, pushing himself to his feet with the same anger he'd had so many years ago, but not the same speed or vigor. Recognition wasn't as quick as with Marta.

It was understandable. Dresner's eyes, slightly magnified by thick glasses, were the only things that remained unchanged. The other researchers at the facility had been perplexed when he'd insisted on subjecting himself to many of the same protocols as the athletes they trained. He'd told them it was in the interest of science, but it was a lie. It had been entirely in the interest of this moment. His frail, half-starved body had been replaced with something more fitting for the occasion.

"Christian?" the man said, wet eyes widening as much as the half-empty bottle of vodka sitting on the table would allow.

Dresner nodded silently. Despite so many years planning for this day, he couldn't remember what he was supposed to say.

"You've grown strong." The man thumped his drooping chest. "I made you that way. I made you strong."

For the first time, fear was clearly visible in him. And why not? He was just a broken-down soldier drinking himself to death in a forgotten orphanage. But Dresner had been embraced by the party. He was one of the generation who would show the world the superiority of communism and the Soviet system. He was the future and this old man was part of a distant, irrelevant past.

"Don't worry," Dresner said, walking to the corner where the cane leaned. "I'm not sending the Stasi for you."

"With what your parents did..." the man stammered. "I had to make you ready for the world. To be able to resist the people who would be against you." He paused for a moment and then quickly added. "For something that wasn't your fault."

"And is that what you're still doing?" Dresner said, picking up the worn piece of wood. As with the playground outside, he remembered photographically the condition it had been in when he'd left, and now he ran his hand along every new scratch and gouge, every place where there had been paint that was now polished away. "Making them ready for the world?"

The old man saw it coming, but the years and alcohol had made him slow. The cane cracked across his cheek, causing him to spin and collapse against the grimy arm of the sofa. When it came down again, this time across his back, a low groan escaped him.

Dresner's mind lost its ability to track what his body was doing and he struck again and again. The man slipped to the floor and tried to raise an arm in defense, but the brittle bones in it snapped with the next blow. He soon went motionless, but it didn't matter. Dresner continued to beat him.

Only when his shoulder became too exhausted to rise and fall did he stop, staring blankly down at the body and trying to will his strength to return.

But, in truth, there was nothing left to do. The blood was pooling around the soles of his boots and the man's dead eyes were staring into him as though they could see the terrified child he'd once been.

Dresner dropped the cane and staggered down the stairs, stopping at the bottom where the children had dared to come out of hiding.

He blinked hard, bringing their faces into focus and trying to control his breathing, once again visible in the absence of the kerosene heater.

"I wish I could do more," he said finally. "I will someday. I promise you that."

1

Aᴅɪᴛʏᴀ Zᴀʜɪᴅ ʟᴀʏ ꜰʟᴀᴛ on his stomach behind the long-abandoned stone building, easing past its crumbling edge to scan the village of Sarabat.

The collection of square, dust-colored dwellings was small, even by the standards of this part of rural Afghanistan, and he felt the same shame that his father and his father before him had felt for allowing it to exist. The feud between these people and his own had burned for longer than anyone could remember, though the reason for it had faded with the years. Some said it was over stolen livestock and others a broken promise of marriage. Now it just was.

In truth, it no longer mattered. What did matter, though, was that despite outnumbering these people almost two to one, the fighting always ended in a bloody stalemate that resolved nothing. It was an ongoing humiliation that the elders of his village believed was about to be resolved. Zahid was less certain.

He retreated under cover and closed his eyes, picturing

what he'd seen. Seven people in total were visible: two women, a child, and four men watering their goats at a well built by their good friends the Americans.

The sun was directly overhead and he squinted against it as he searched the walls of the shallow canyon. By now his companions would have completely surrounded the village, but he could find no sign of them. They had become part of the desert.

The anonymous foreigners who had made this moment possible insisted that the raid come now—not under the cover of darkness or even in the shade the cliffs would provide in only a few hours. And it was for this reason that Zahid didn't share the elation of his people at the prospect of wiping these dogs off the face of their land. All he felt was fear and suspicion.

Still, the faceless men had lived up to every agreement they had made. Zahid was holding a new AK-47 they had provided as well as a silenced American hunting rifle that he had used to take down the sentry now lying next to him.

He looked down at the dead man and then propped him against a shattered section of wall. His head easily cleared the top and would offer a reassuring silhouette, keeping the unsuspecting men in the village complacent.

The digital watch on his wrist—also newly provided— didn't read out the time, but a countdown. It would be less than two minutes before it reached zero. Before what could be their final victory began.

Again, Zahid closed his eyes. He had spoken against this. He didn't trust faceless men or their weapons or their money. It smelled like a trap—a CIA trick. But the elders didn't fully understand the new world they lived in. And their hatred for the people of Sarabat burned much hotter than their hatred for an invader that would soon leave in defeat and be forgotten. Like all the others.

He wrapped his hand around his new assault rifle and prayed to Allah for success until he heard the quiet click of his countdown timer reaching zero. His men would be moving now, the younger ones too quickly—driven by adrenaline and the stories of glory they had heard from the day they were born. He was slower to rise, staying low as he approached the village, watching the ridgeline for American soldiers and the sky for attack helicopters. But there was nothing.

The silence was finally broken by the high-pitched scream of a child followed by the familiar roar of automatic rifle fire. A woman was hit from behind as she tried to escape, thrown forward with her arms spread wide, landing in the dirt with the unmistakable stillness of death. One of his own men appeared from behind a building, attempting to sight in on a running villager before a boy of eight on nine knocked his barrel aside. Zahid accelerated to a full run, putting himself on a path to intercept the fleeing man as the boy's skull was crushed by a rifle butt.

His quarry was probably in his mid-twenties, straight and strong, but also seemingly confused as to what to do. He sprinted and then slowed. He looked forward toward his escape route and then back at the massacre taking place in his village. He reached behind him for the ancient rifle on his back but then seemed unable to close his fingers around it.

Zahid stopped and knelt, bringing his AK-47 to his shoulder and squeezing off a careful volley. The disoriented man wavered and then dropped to his knees, staring blankly at the sky. But still he didn't reach for his weapon.

Fearing a trick, Zahid approached cautiously, scanning the empty landscape that stretched out in every direction. Was he being drawn into an ambush? Why would they wait? Why would they let themselves be slaughtered like animals?

He stopped two meters away, keeping the barrel of his new rifle trained on his enemy's unlined face. He was bleeding badly from a wound in his leg and the ground beneath him had gone dark with it. He wouldn't live much longer.

"Why don't you fight?"

He didn't answer, instead focusing on Zahid's face with eyes that contained no hatred or fear. Only emptiness.

"Why don't you fight?" Zahid repeated, glancing behind him as the rate of fire slowed and the screams went silent. The Americans hadn't come. The village of Sarabat was gone from God's vision. After more years than anyone knew, honor had been restored. But how? Why?

"God is great," Zahid said, tightening his finger on the trigger as he turned back to his enemy.

The injured man's brow furrowed and his chin rose until he was staring directly into the intense glare of the Afghan sun. "There is no God."

*   *   *

CLAUDE GÉROUX SWEPT the massive lens north, focusing on one of the last living inhabitants of Sarabat: an old woman trying uselessly to escape a horseman raining blows down on her with a primitive club. Blood spattered across the animal's fur and she fell, covering her head as she was pulled beneath its hooves.

He zoomed out, taking in the entire battlefield—if it could be called that. He'd fought in Congo, Iraq, and Bosnia, to name only a few, and thought he'd witnessed every way a human being could die at the hands of another. But never anything like this.

He turned his lens on one of the attacking force crouching next to the body of yet another armed male villager. They hadn't used those weapons, though. Some had fled, but most had just stood there and allowed themselves and their families to be butchered.

The gunfire went silent and Géroux kept filming for a few seconds more, documenting not the customary pumping fists and elated shouts, but silent confusion as the victorious warriors wandered among the bodies of their fallen enemies.

He finally pulled away from the camera and shut it down, but the recorded images stayed trapped in his mind. They would be added to the others, he knew. The ones he couldn't escape.

2

Las Vegas, Nevada
USA

JON SMITH MADE HIS WAY through the cavernous Las Vegas Convention Center toward a dense knot of people at its heart. The air-conditioning was already drying the sweat that had soaked through the back of his shirt while he was stuck standing in the desert sun. It had never occurred to him that security for the function would be so tight—metal detectors, multiple ID checks, bomb-sniffing dogs. By comparison, the TSA and Secret Service were downright easygoing.

When he reached the crowd, the reason for the over-the-top scrutiny became apparent. It seemed to consist of a Who's Who of the tech industry. He spotted familiar faces from Amazon and Facebook right away. The new CEO of Apple was also there, embroiled in a heated discussion with two gangly young men he didn't recognize but whose presence and spectacular basketball shoes suggested they were probably worth a billion dollars each.

Feeling more than a little out of place, Smith skirted the crowd's edge, examining the hundred or so chairs lined up in front of a stage framed by a twenty-meter-high video monitor. Finally, he reached his objective: an enormous table straining under the weight of an impressive ice sculpture and an even more impressive spread of exotic food items.

His first sample turned out to be a deeply unfortunate combination of dates and caviar, so he headed toward the bar to get something to wash the taste from his mouth.

"Beer," he said to one of the men handling a line of taps that must have been ten meters long.

"My pleasure. We have Fat Tire, Snake River Lager, Sam Adams, Corona—"

Smith held a hand up, certain the man could recite them all but concerned that the flavor of those dates was starting to gain a permanent foothold. "I'll trust your judgment."

The voice of a woman behind him rose above the drone of the crowd. "You look like a Budweiser man to me."

He turned and she planted herself in front of him, red lips crossing pale skin in a broad grin. Mid-twenties, thin but shapely, with a pixie haircut and bangs that she pushed from her eyes to get a better look at him. Her name tag read "Janine Redford/*Wired* Magazine." His, as she had undoubtedly noticed, just read "Jon Smith."

"I've been watching you."

"Me?" he said, accepting the beer and then pushing back through the people mobbing the bar with her in his wake. "Why? I'm not anybody."

She pointed at his name tag. "And you're not afraid to put it in writing."

"Family name. Could have been worse. My father had a falling-out with my uncle Gomer right before I was born."

She seemed unconvinced. "I either know or recognize everyone here. You don't seem to fit."

"No?"

"No. You've got your geeks, your scary business powerhouses, and your skinny, middle-aged Internet gazillionaires..." Her voice trailed off for a moment. "Then there's you."

There was no denying it. His shoulders were a bit too broad, his black hair a little too utilitarian, and his dark skin starting to show damage from sun, wind, ice, and the occasional unavoidable explosion.

"Maybe they sent my invitation by accident?" he said honestly. At this point, it was actually his most credible theory. But why look a gift horse in the mouth? A good quarter of the world would have cut off their pinkie toe to be here. And he was firmly in that twenty-five percent.

She gave him a suspicious little smile and took a sip from her martini glass. "Christian Dresner doesn't make mistakes."

"Okay. Then you tell *me* why I'm here."

"You're military."

"I'm a doctor," he said evasively. "Microbiology. But these days I work with the physically impaired."

"Okay. I'll buy that. But you're a *military* doctor and the impaired people you work with are injured soldiers. No point in denying it. I'm a prodigy at this."

He considered his options for a moment but then just stuck out his hand. "Lieutenant Colonel Jon Smith."

"So does the military know something?" she said, demonstrating a surprisingly firm grip. "Like, for instance, what Dresner's going to roll out today?"

"Not a clue."

Her pouting frown combined with the sagging of her shoulders made it clear she wasn't buying a word he said. When she spoke again, he wasn't sure if it was to him or if she was just thinking out loud. "Dresner's more of a save-the-world kind of guy than a blow-up-the-world guy..."

"And I don't work with weapons, Janine. I really am a doctor. If I'm not here by mistake, my best guess is it's another medical breakthrough. His antibiotics have been really important to us on the battlefield, and retired soldiers are a huge market for his hearing system."

She crinkled up her nose. "My grandpa was an artillery guy in Vietnam and he has one of those hearing aids."

"It's an amazing technology."

"Yeah. I used to shout 'Hi, Gramps!' right in his face and he'd say, 'Oh, about eleven o'clock.' Now he can hear a pin drop in the next room."

People often made the mistake of comparing Dresner's system to Cochlears, but the technology was an order of magnitude more advanced. Dresner had figured out a way to bypass the ear entirely, using a magnetic field to communicate directly with the brain. Children being born today would never even understand the concept of hearing impairment.

She pointed to the left side of her head. "The problem is that he's bald and he's got these two shiny silver receivers screwed right into his wrinkly old skull. I love the guy, but it's disgusting."

"You know the VA will pay to have those painted to match his skin."

"He says the government has better things to do with its money than try to make him look pretty."

Smith raised his glass to the old soldier and took a long pull.

"I think we can both agree that it's not going to be better hearing aids," she continued. "So what then?"

"I can't tell you what it is, but I can tell you what I hope it is. I've been working on developing prosthetics for injured troops and we've made some strides toward allowing people to control them mentally, but the technology is really basic. If there's anyone in the world who could crack that nut, it would be Christian Dresner."

Her eyes crinkled up as she considered the possibility. "We did a story a while back on a monkey that controls this huge mechanical arm with his brain. Doesn't seem to understand it's not his. Creepy."

"I've actually met that monkey," Smith said. "And it is kind of creepy."

She shook her head. "It's not going to be that."

"No? Why not?"

"First of all, because you're the only doctor here—everyone else is straight-up technology. And second, because a few years back Dresner overpaid for a Spanish search start-up that was doing augmented reality for cell phones."

"Like the astronomy app I have on my iPhone? You just hold it up to the sky at night and it shows you the stars behind it with their names. I love that."

She seemed less impressed. "Dresner didn't want the company. He wanted their technology guru. An old hacker named Javier de Galdiano."

"And what's de Galdiano do now?"

"No one really knows. What I *do* know, though, is that Dresner's bought up more than a few hardware companies and patents that would be complementary to what Javier was trying to accomplish at his start-up."

"You know a lot."

"Keeping tabs on what Dresner is doing is pretty much my job. And I'm saying he's getting into computing."

"Seems like a pretty saturated market. These days everything is just a bigger, smaller, or lighter version of something that already exists. Steve Jobs was amazing at taking existing technology and making it useful, but I see Dresner more as someone who's looking to blow people away with something they've never even thought about before. I mean, the guy's completely changed our understanding of how the mind and body communicate. His work in immunology has saved hundreds of thousands of lives and headed off a health disaster that I guarantee was coming. I can't help thinking this is going to be something...amazing."

She hooked an arm through his and tugged him toward the people moving to the seating in front of the stage. "Then let's push through all these geeks and get you into the front row. Maybe we could sit together? I'd feel safer having a military man close. You know, in case the Russians invade."

He grinned and responded in that language as they tried to do an end run around one of Google's founders.

"I'm intrigued. What did you say?"

In fact, it was an old proverb about the benefits of beautiful young women, but he decided to equivocate a bit.

"I said, 'Can you give me directions to the bathroom?' It's the only Russian I know."

"Still, you sold it. And that's what's important."

3

W HAT THE HELL HAPPENED down there?"

Randi Russell swept the helicopter over the village at about 120 meters, passing through the haze created by still-smoldering buildings. She kept her attention on the controls and let the redheaded soldier next to her survey the scene through a set of binoculars. It would have been more practical to just come in lower, but there was a stiff wind blowing upcanyon and she was admittedly not the best pilot in Afghanistan. Truth be told, she might not have been the best pilot at your average Cub Scout meeting.

"What are you seeing, Deuce?"

"Weird shit—so, basically, the same thing I see every day. I vote we head back to base, get a drink, and forget all about this. It's almost happy hour."

Randi risked a look down at the bodies strewn across the sand and the bizarre blooms of blood growing from the tops of about half. Weird shit? Definitely. But not your everyday weird shit.

"I'd like to get a closer look."

The man turned toward her, alarm visible on his face. "Whoa now, girl. You're not going to try to fly low, are you?"

She gave him a withering glance. "I was thinking more about landing."

"Come *on*, Randi. There's not so much as a lizard alive down there and those canyon walls are sniper heaven. Happy hour. I'm buying."

"When did you turn into such an old lady?"

In truth, Lieutenant Deuce Brennan was one of the most talented special forces operatives the U.S. military had ever turned out. She'd been unimpressed by his Howdy Doody looks and frat-boy demeanor when he'd arrived in country, but now used every excuse in the book to make sure he was the one watching her back.

"Look, I love you, Randi. You know I do. You've given me a whole new respect for you useless CIA types. But I'd like to leave here with all my body parts intact one day. And the longer I know you, the less likely that seems."

"Five minutes," she said, slowing to a hover and easing back the power. "Then the margaritas are on me."

It wasn't a bad landing by her standards, though some of the credit went to the soft sand. They jumped out immediately, a bit of an odd couple with him in full combat gear and her in khaki cargo pants and a matching T-shirt.

A scarf hid the short blond hair that made her stand out so badly in this part of the world, and she reached up to make sure none was peeking out as Deuce moved north. His eyes swept smoothly across the shadows thrown by the burned-out buildings that yesterday had been a thriving village mildly sympathetic to America's fading occupation.

Confident that she was covered, Randi started toward the body of a young woman and crouched for a moment, examining the bullet wound in her chest and the fear still frozen into her face.

The next corpse was ten meters away and was an example of what had interested her so much from the air. There was a similar bullet wound in the chest, but the body had been decapitated and in place of the head was a circle of sand stained black by blood.

She moved from body to body, finally drawing her Beretta when she found herself among the blackened buildings. Deuce was visible about a hundred meters away and gave her the thumbs-up. Obviously, he was finding the same thing she was. Death.

Randi ducked through the door of a tiny cube of a house, holding her breath against the stench of burned human flesh and finding two charred bodies in the still-glowing embers. Both had managed to keep their heads and, judging by their size, both were children.

She reemerged into the fresh air and sunlight, continuing her search but finding no break in the pattern. No weapons. Decapitated men. Intact women and children.

She'd been sent there by Fred Klein to investigate what he had characterized—with customary vagueness— as "suspicious mercenary activity."

She saw no evidence of that, though. The attackers had worn traditional local footwear and there were visible gouges from horse hooves—hardly standard merc gear.

That wasn't to say that this was the result of one of the normal rival village skirmishes that had been going on in the area for a thousand years. Beyond the bizarre decapitations, she couldn't make sense of the story told by the tracks of the village's male casualties. A few seemed to have run a short distance but not at the full sprint warranted by the situation. And none showed any evidence that they'd tried to defend themselves or their families. How was that possible for a people who had slapped around everyone from Alexander the Great to the Soviet Union?

A quiet crunch became audible to her right. She spun smoothly, bringing her pistol level with the sound.

"Don't shoot! It's me," Deuce said, appearing from around a mud wall.

She holstered her weapon. "Anything?"

"They must have been taken by surprise," he said with a shake of the head. "Whoever took them out also made off with their weapons and hauled away any of their own casualties. That is, if there were any. I can't find any unaccounted-for blood or footprints of attackers that look like they took a hit."

"You find the heads?"

"Nope."

She let out a long breath and shaded her eyes from the sun sinking in the west. She'd known these people. In fact, she'd convinced the agency to fund a project to get them clean water. They were good Muslims, but had no love for the Taliban.

"Hard to believe that they'd get caught flat-footed like this," Deuce said.

"*Impossible* to believe. They were good fighters and they knew damn well they had enemies—some that go back hundreds of years and some new ones who know they sided with us a few times. There's no way in hell someone just rolled in here and wiped them out."

"Looks to me like that's exactly what happened."

A gunshot sounded and she ducked involuntarily, drawing her weapon and listening to the clang of a round hitting metal.

"Shit!" Deuce said. "It's coming from the south wall of the canyon. They're going for the helicopter!"

Randi slid her back against the sooty building as more shots rang out. The wind was picking up and the sniper could only manage a hit every two or three times but the chopper was pretty much devoid of armor. One lucky hit and they'd have to decide between the humiliation of calling in a rescue and a long, dangerous walk home.

She came to the edge of her cover and strolled across a dirt track to a wall on the other side. The deliberately slow pace had its intended effect and she saw a round kick up dust a meter or so to her right. Hopefully, the sniper would forget about the chopper now that he knew flesh-and-blood targets were on the menu.

"I'm guessing that guy has friends," Deuce shouted. He fired off a volley in the general direction of their attacker, but his weapon wasn't designed for that kind of range. "Word's gonna get out about our visit pretty quick."

Randi pointed at a headless body about halfway between them and the helicopter. "We'll go on my mark. But on the way, we're picking up that body. I want an autopsy."

"An autopsy?" Deuce said incredulously. "I mean, I don't have a medical degree or anything, but I'm pretty sure the cause of death was the bullet in his chest or the fact that his freakin' head is gone!"

"I didn't come all this way to leave empty-handed."

He fired a few additional rounds, more out of frustration than from any hope they would dissuade the sniper trying to zero in on them. "I swear, Randi. Someday, when no one is looking, I'm gonna kill you myself."

4

T RUE TO HER WORD, Janine had gotten them seats four rows from the front. She had a natural pushiness that, combined with her youth and beauty, tended to part a crowd pretty well.

"I wonder if he finally got new glasses," Janine said, putting her hand on Smith's forearm. "We have a pool at the office and it's up to more than five hundred bucks."

Her question was answered a moment later when Christian Dresner strode onto stage and stalked toward the lone lectern at its center. The Coke-bottle glasses he'd been wearing since the eighties were still there, as were the suit and tie that he seemed to have bought around the same time.

The truth was that Dresner looked as out of place as Smith did in this crowd. Not only the clothes, but the graying blond hair worn in such a shaggy, haphazard style that many people believed he cut it himself. In Smith's mind, though, everything seemed carefully calculated to diminish the almost cartoonishly square jaw, the heavy shoulders, and the still-narrow waist. With contacts, a decent tailor, and a coupon to Supercuts he would look like a spectacularly successful Nazi eugenics project.

A light applause erupted and Dresner seemed a little uncomfortable, losing himself for a moment in securing a Bluetooth headset to his ear. In fact, this was only the fourth public appearance in the notoriously shy genius's career.

While comparisons to Steve Jobs had been obvious, Smith had always thought Willy Wonka was a more apt analogy: an odd recluse who suddenly burst on the scene with something incredible and then retreated to the safety of the factory.

"I want to thank you for coming," he said in the slight German accent that he'd never shaken off. "I hope you'll be as excited about my new project as I am."

The screen behind him came to life with an image of a hand holding a device that looked a little like a gray iPhone with no screen.

"Electric cigarette case?" Janine said, nudging Smith in the ribs as a confused murmur rose up around them.

He honestly didn't know. A tiny switch and a blue indicator light were visible on the right side, but other than that it was just a graceful piece of plastic.

Dresner pulled his jacket back and showed an example of the real thing hung on his belt. "I'd like to introduce you to Merge. The next—and maybe final—generation of personal computing devices."

"Oh, God," Janine groaned, actually slapping her forehead. "He's invented the cell phone. And he's carrying it in a holster."

"How many of you out there use augmented reality

systems?" Dresner continued, blissfully unaware of Janine's sarcasm. "You know—astronomy apps, something that tells you how good the restaurant you're standing in front of is...anything."

More than half the audience raised their hands and Smith joined them. Janine just folded her arms across her chest and scowled.

"And how many of you really find them practical?"

His hand dropped along with everyone else's. As much as he loved his $2.99 constellation finder, holding a phone at arm's length and looking past it at the sky wasn't exactly a seamless experience.

"GPS has definitely moved that technology forward, but we're still stuck with an interface that isn't all that much different from the one we had when the first personal computers came out more than thirty years ago. It's that, and not the software, holding the technology back. It's not particularly hard to imagine augmented reality's potential, but almost no one is pursuing it because of the lack of a workable hardware platform. I'm hoping to change that."

He walked back to the lectern. "Let me switch you over to what I see."

The screen behind him faded into a video of the crowd as he scanned across it. Along the left side was a series of semitransparent icons glowing various shades of red and green. Across the top was some general data—that he was connected to the Las Vegas Convention Center wireless network, the temperature inside and outside, as well as a number of abbreviations and numbers that Smith couldn't decipher.

Janine leaned into him again. "That actually looks

pretty good. I tried the Google Glasses prototype and they just have a cheesy head-up display at the top of one of the lenses."

Smith nodded. "I tested a prototype from a British company that projects onto your retina, so it can work with your entire field of vision and create that transparent effect. Great idea but the images were blurry and every time the glasses moved on your face, the image would break up. Maybe Dresner's nailed it."

"I'll admit it's a little cool," she said with a shrug. "But hell if I'm spending the rest of my life walking around in glasses that make me look like I'm using a chain saw."

Dresner looked down from the stage and focused on a man in the second row, his surprised face suddenly filling the screen. "Let's make a phone call. Bob, why don't you stand up?"

He did, looking self-consciously at the crowd behind him. Either he was a damn fine actor, or this wasn't a setup.

"Now, I know that Bob is a good citizen and turned his cell off before he came in. But could I bother you to turn it back on?"

Dresner looked out over his audience again. The phone icon at the edge of the screen expanded and the address book went immediately from names starting with "A" to names starting with "S," finally scrolling to "Stamen, Bob." A moment later, the tinny sound of Blondie's "Call Me" filled the room.

The increasingly nervous-looking man answered and his voice was transmitted through the PA system by Dresner's Merge. "Hello?"

"Hi, Bob. How're things?"

"Good."

Janine leaned forward, squinting at Dresner as he chatted. "How is he controlling those icons and scrolling through the names? Is it tracking his eye movements?"

Smith had been wondering the same thing. "I don't think so. You'd see the screen image moving around. He was looking straight at the crowd when that app opened."

"Maybe this was all set up beforehand. Maybe the system's just in some kind of demonstration mode."

"I don't know. Maybe…"

Dresner pulled out his Bluetooth headset and laid it on the lectern before walking back to center stage. "I've always hated those things. They hurt my ear. How about you, Bob?"

"Um…" Stamen said, missing a few beats as he wrestled with the same thing everyone else was—why was Dresner's voice still being picked up by the PA and why could he still hear the phone call? "I don't like them."

"Exactly! Me neither. So I thought, What if I just had a tiny microphone built into a custom cap that clamps to one of my back teeth? And on top of that, what if I had a much smaller and more sophisticated version of my hearing implants route sound directly to my brain?"

There was complete silence in the auditorium for a few seconds before everyone started talking at once. The tone wasn't necessarily excitement, though. More of an impressed skepticism apparently shared by the young woman sitting next to him.

"Okay, he's definitely into cool nerd territory now, but if you find your Bluetooth so uncomfortable, there are a bunch of companies that will make you a custom earpiece. That's gotta be cheaper and easier than getting a dentist to make something that fits on your tooth and getting studs screwed into your skull."

"I dunno," Smith responded. "I've worked with a lot of people who use Dresner's hearing system and they all say it aches a little for a couple of days and then you forget the studs are even there until they need to be recharged. And he's saying he made them even smaller."

She scowled and leaned back in her chair, arms folded across her chest again. If there was any great truth, it was that her generation was virtually impossible to impress where technology was concerned. They always wanted more.

"Thanks, Bob. I'll talk to you later," Dresner said. The color drained from the phone icon and it tucked itself back into the side of the massive screen.

He started pacing again, the audience following his every move. "I've had terrible vision my entire life and I know I look ridiculous with these huge lenses but I've never been able to get comfortable with contacts."

He took his glasses off and let them hang loosely in his hand. Instead of the screen behind him suddenly tracking the floor, the image of the audience held steady but turned distorted and blurry.

"I don't get it," Janine muttered, but Smith ignored her. He was pretty sure he *did* understand, but he was having a hard time believing what his mind was telling him.

Illegible words appeared across the top of the screen and he concentrated on them as they slowly came into focus.

PROCESSING VISION CORRECTION

Confused silence prevailed as Dresner returned to the lectern and leaned against it. "So then I thought, if I can send sound to my audio cortex, why can't I send images to my visual cortex?"

This time there were no voices at all. The only sound was of a hundred people attacking their cell phones in a desperate effort to be the first to text word of Dresner's new miracle to the world.

5

Marrakech
Morocco

GERHARD EICHMANN SLID his chair farther into the shade and tried again to wave off a shoeshine boy who wouldn't take no for an answer. A few stern Arabic words from a waiter finally got the job done and the boy retreated into the road, dodging the chaotic traffic in search of a less resistant customer.

Despite having lived in Marrakech for more than a decade, Eichmann had never been to this particular outdoor café. Most of the tables were surrounded by local men drinking tea. The only other white faces belonged to a French couple battling the midday heat with bottles of overpriced local beer.

Eichmann nervously examined the people flowing by on the sidewalk, occasionally making eye contact that gave him hope this would soon be over. Every time, though, he ended up watching them hurry off toward the walls of the old city and the crowded markets beyond.

It was the constant motion, the tumult, the mix of

modern and ancient that had convinced him to make
Marrakech his home. It offered anonymity to those who
craved it, without stripping away all the trappings and
conveniences of the civilized world. It allowed him to
be a ghost suspended between the past, present, and future.

A man in a sweat-stained linen shirt and blue slacks
emerged from behind a cart piled with oranges and
jogged onto the sidewalk. This time the eye contact was
more than fleeting.

"Can I join you?" he said, pointing to an empty chair
pushed up against the tiny table. "I twisted my ankle
shopping in the souks."

Eichmann's mouth went so dry, he found it difficult to
respond. "Of...of course. The cobblestones here can be
treacherous."

He hated this—leaving the tiny world he'd so carefully
closed around himself, coming into contact with these
types of men. But he'd been forbidden to use the Internet.
It was too uncontrollable, too populated by clever and curious eyes.

"Do you have it?

The man—Claude Géroux—waved a muscular arm
in the waiter's direction and used French to order a
sparkling water.

"Do you have it?" Eichmann repeated, hiding his fear
but letting his irritation come through. He was scheduled
to leave for North Korea in less than three hours and after
everything he'd gone through to get permission for the
trip, he would not let this meeting delay him.

"Of course," Géroux said, switching to accented
English. "And you?"

"Yes."

The Frenchman didn't display his fear either, but in his case that was likely because he felt none. Why would he? Eichmann knew he looked like exactly what he was: an academic reaching an age when thin became frail and pale became sickly. Géroux would look on him with little more than amusement.

Comfortable that he had the upper hand, the Frenchman casually handed a thumb drive across the table. Eichmann pulled a small laptop from its case and slid the drive into the USB port. After a quick glance to confirm that the only thing behind him was a cracked wall and the feral cat perched on top of it, he entered the agreed-upon password and opened the video file that appeared.

Skipping through the violent footage for a few moments, he felt the strange mix of fascination and revulsion that had become so familiar to him over the last quarter century.

"I didn't think there was anything new under the sun," Géroux said, accepting a bottle of water from the waiter and falling silent until he'd moved on. "They didn't fight back or even try to save themselves. The Afghans always fight. In fact, you could say that it's *all* they do."

Eichmann ignored him, connecting the laptop to the Internet and pulling up a bank account in Yemen.

"Was it the plastic boxes they had strapped to their waists—the ones that were taken from them? Was it drugs?"

Eichmann continued to concentrate on what he was doing, acting as though he hadn't heard. The boxes Géroux was referring to did not contain drugs; nor did they still exist. He had confirmation that they'd been delivered to an obscure military outpost and incinerated more than twelve hours ago.

"It's done," Eichmann said, shutting down the laptop and slamming the lid shut.

Géroux kept his dead eyes on him and took another sip of his water before pulling a smartphone from his pocket. A nearly imperceptible smile broke across his lips as the screen registered the funds transferred into his account.

"You'll have to excuse my curiosity," he said, beginning to rise. "I've fought in many wars, in many places. And this…"

He shook his head and threw down a hundred-dirham note before standing and weaving through the busy tables. Eichmann watched him wade into traffic, jogging athletically past a rusting cab as he made his way toward a median crowded with people waiting for an opportunity to cross the remaining lanes.

He was almost there when a truck piled with mattresses lost control and swerved out of its lane. It crossed into the median, catching him dead center in its grille with enough force that his head shattered the windshield. The entire vehicle listed right as terrified people dove out of the way and oncoming traffic veered onto sidewalks crowded with pedestrians.

Everyone in the café was on their feet, surging toward the accident and then retreating when a pickup slammed into a car parked at the curb. Eichmann, now completely forgotten by everyone around him, stood, fighting off a wave of nausea and slipping the precious flash drive into his pocket.

He stayed close to the wall, clutching his laptop to

his chest until he was able to slip into an empty, urine-scented alleyway. He increased his pace, daring a glance behind him at the frantic people swarming the road and the bloodstained front of the mattress van.

Apparently, Géroux's curiosity had not been excused.

6

Las Vegas, Nevada
USA

CHRISTIAN DRESNER BEAMED from the lectern as the dull click of thumbs on cell phones filled the convention center. Smith didn't have anyone to text since he still had no idea why he was there, so he just sat quietly and tried to wrap his mind around the potential of Dresner's new hardware.

To call it revolutionary was an almost laughable understatement. Smith was one of the few people who had recognized Dresner's hearing aid for what it was: a first hesitant step on the road to changing humanity forever. What made it so new—so extraordinary—was that it had been the first prosthetic that wasn't a wildly imperfect facsimile of what had been lost. Instead, it was an order-of-magnitude improvement over what evolution had spent millions of years creating. In the end, his great accomplishment hadn't been helping impaired people to hear. It had been demonstrating that we were entering a world where Mother Nature could be beaten at her own game.

This step, though, was in no way hesitant. Dresner was

throwing humanity headlong into what could be the next phase of its existence. Where would it go? Where would it stop? Hell, where *should* it stop?

Smith looked over at Janine, but she was completely immersed in her iPhone—a device that had seemed so sophisticated a few minutes ago but now seemed a little like a steam-powered stone tablet.

Having said that, a few critical questions needed to be answered. First, did it really work? Innovative technology was great but if it was hard to use or impractical, it tended to fade pretty quickly. Touchscreens, headsets, and standard voice interfaces already worked pretty well.

The second was about the body modifications. He'd spent his life trying not to be perforated and, with the exception of a few stray bullets and a knife or two, had been fairly successful. Would average people want to have bolts screwed into their skulls for the privilege of getting rid of their smartphones?

He glanced at Janine again, noting the diamond nose stud and the colorful tattoo on her upper arm. There was his answer. The generation after his seemed to look at body modification with the same trepidation he felt when changing his shirt.

The sound of thumbs on plastic died down and Dresner began pacing again, the screen behind him following along as though it were connected to cameras embedded in his retinas. "As all of you know, a piece of hardware is only as useful as the software available for it. In the end, the Merge is just a platform. It's what we're putting on that platform that really interests me. Of course, we have all the basic apps you'd expect: phone, email, social networking, GPS, and the like. But we've also created appli-

cations for the financial services industry and politics—
two areas that are critical to society and I think everyone
agrees need help."

"Oh, God," Janine mumbled, a look of horror over-
coming her youthful features. "He may have invented the
coolest technology since the printing press and he's going
Boy Scout on us."

Dresner seemed to read her mind. "But don't worry.
We've done some fun stuff too."

On screen, the doors of the convention center burst
open and a horde of blood-drenched vampires rushed in.
It was realistic enough to elicit more than a few screams
from the audience as they spun in their chairs to take in
the empty room behind them. When they turned back to
Dresner, he was holding his hand like a gun, happily picking off the ghouls as they charged up the aisle.

"No way!" Janine said, attacking her Twitter account
again. "That's the best thing I've ever seen in my life. And
I once saw George Clooney in a Speedo."

The monsters faded and Dresner looked out over the
slightly ruffled crowd. "The strange truth is that the main
idea here wasn't the hardware—I just needed something
to run the search engine I had in my head." He paused for
a moment, seeming to ponder his next words. "The problem with the Internet—and the world in general—isn't
the *availability* of information, it's that there's *too much*
information. And most of it's nonsense. But what if we
had a way of instantly vetting the quality of what we're
taking in? And I'm not just talking about things we look
up on the 'net, I'm talking about everything around us."

He motioned to Bob Stamen again. "Could you stand
up one more time?"

He did, if a bit reluctantly, and an icon on the screen that looked like a listing wedding cake activated. Suddenly Stamen was surrounded by a hazy green aura, and his name hovered over his head in subtle lettering.

"We've managed to crack the facial recognition problem by hijacking the brain's built-in software for it. So you can see that my new search engine—LayerCake—knows who Bob is and gives him a nice green glow to tell me that he's a good guy. Based on what, you're probably asking. Well, based on everything available in the public record—Wikipedia, news articles, and so on. LayerCake goes through all those things, combines them to some extent with what it knows about my own personal values, and then gives me the benefit of its analysis. Now, why did I pick on Bob? Because he's the very image of the person you want to marry your daughter—he runs a terrific charity, he has no criminal record, he has a perfect credit rating, and so on." Dresner grinned. "Not everyone here would probably get quite that deep a shade of green."

The laughter from the crowd was polite, but also a little nervous. Everyone was obviously pondering the same thing Smith was. What would LayerCake think of them?

The color of the icons running down the left side of the screen now made more sense, too. The stock market icon that had been pale green a few minutes ago darkened perceptibly, undoubtedly reflecting the real-time movement in Dresner Industries' stock price as the texts and tweets of people in the crowd flew around the world. The weather icon went from green on the left to red on the right, probably reflecting the current sunny skies over Las Vegas and the storm front predicted to arrive that night.

"But it doesn't just work on people," Dresner said,

walking back to the podium and looking down at the headset he'd discarded earlier. It had the same warm green glow as Bob Stamen.

"So *why* does LayerCake like this headset? I just said you shouldn't trust the Internet, right?" The icon expanded and a list of hyperlinks appeared: "reviews," "value," "details," and "where to buy." The "reviews" link expanded and a list of sites including Amazon, ConsumerSearch, and CNET came up. The stars were gone, though, and their ratings were displayed through the glow around their logos.

"You'll notice that some of the colors are more transparent than others. That tells you how much data LayerCake has and how authoritative it thinks it is. For instance, it's going to feel pretty good about *Consumer Reports* no matter what. But with Amazon, it's going to take into account the number of reviews and weigh each one based on feedback."

It was a concept with incredible potential. Smith wondered if one day he'd be able to glance at patients and determine how they were doing just by the color of their aura—confident that LayerCake was taking into account everything from the blood workup entered seconds before by a basement lab tech to a related illness that occurred twenty years before.

Dresner put down the headset and strode back to center stage with a hundred sets of eyes locked on him. "Obviously, there's too much to fully explain here today, so the user manual for both the hardware and the software we've developed will be released on our website after the conference. In the meantime, let me open it up to a few questions."

Smith threw his hand in the air, as did every other person in the convention center.

Dresner pointed to a man at the back and a microphone was passed down to him. On screen, a name popped into existence over his head, but it was a neutral color. Dresner had turned off the judgment system, probably to save people the embarrassment of pulsing blood red.

"You used the term 'user manual.' When will you have the approvals you need to release this product to the public?"

"I don't need any approvals, Jeff. The system runs off existing wireless and cellular data networks. The tooth mike is a removable piece of electronics installed by a licensed dentist and the skull implants fall under the existing approvals for our hearing system. The only difference is that instead of two pickups seven millimeters across, you'll have six about half that size. But to answer your question, the Merge will be on sale next week."

Another furious round of texting ensued and the icon for DI's stock price deepened further in color. Smith used everyone's temporary distraction to put his hand up again. He was just a bit slower than a woman in the front row, though.

"Do you have to have the implants for the Merge to work?"

"Absolutely not. We have headsets with built-in electrodes, which we'll include with every unit, but I'll warn you that they look a little strange and both the audio and visual resolution is degraded. Also, it obviously isn't very practical for using with the sleep function."

Hands went up again and Dresner pointed.

"Sleep function?"

"Did I forget to talk about that?" A sly smile spread across his face. "I think some of you are probably aware of the partnership DI has with the sleep research center at Stanford. And with the success we've had in creating a non-pharmaceutical sleep aid that works by manipulating brain waves. Up until now, the machine needed to deliver the therapy's been about the size of a small car, which has left us in a position where we can only provide inpatient care to people with severe disorders. What we needed was a more practical hardware platform and it turns out that the Merge is perfect. I'm sixty-seven years old and I can tell you that I now sleep like I did when I was twelve."

Again, Smith took advantage of the other audience members' obsession with instant communication, and this time it worked. He stood as his distracted seatmates passed the microphone across.

LayerCake immediately tagged him with his name and rank, as well as designating him a medical doctor. For a man who went out of his way to avoid the spotlight, it was a bit disturbing. On the other hand, he was grateful as hell that the judgment system was turned off. That would definitely cross the line into too much information.

"You seem to be able to mentally manipulate the interface's icons. Could this be used to control artificial limbs? And—kind of unrelated—could the Merge be used to cure blindness?"

"Excellent questions!" Dresner said, sounding genuinely excited that someone was interested in aspects of his invention that didn't relate to the billions of dollars it would inevitably rake in. "The short answer on eyesight is yes, absolutely. Assuming normal brain function, two small cameras built into a pair of glasses can transmit excellent binocular vision. Of course, we'll be providing those units free of charge to people in need. With regard to the icons and prosthetics: It's something we're working on. Output has proved to be a tougher problem than input, unfortunately. Control of the icons is still fairly rudimentary—opening, closing, scrolling, and simple selection. So this is going to be something that happens, but on a five- or ten-year horizon."

Hands shot up again, but he waved them off. "Look over the manual and if anything is unclear let us know so we can fix it. Or better yet, buy a Merge next week and try it for yourself."

7

Khost Province
Afghanistan

Y OU! I KNEW IT."

Randi flashed her most innocent smile as Dr. Peter Mailen squinted menacingly at her.

He'd just celebrated his fiftieth birthday but still looked pretty good, with thick, sandy hair and a mustache that he thought made him look like Magnum PI. That probably also explained the Hawaiian shirt peeking from beneath a canvas apron that had faded to the same color gray as the tile walls, but lacked the scattered bullet holes.

"Took you long enough," Randi said. "Did they row you over in a dinghy?"

She skirted past a wall of plastic covering a hole made by a mortar round the week before. The goal was to keep the impromptu morgue cool, but it wasn't working quite well enough to beat back the creeping stench of decay.

"The cargo hold of a plane. Nothing like spending endless hours bouncing around with nothing but ten thousand bottles of water to keep you company."

She shook her head sympathetically and wandered up to a gurney containing a body covered with a blood-stained sheet. "I specifically told them first class."

"I'm a *doctor*, Randi. I work with *live* people." He pointed to the tag wrapped around a toe that was starting to darken from the bacteria working on it. "And while I want to be clear that I'm not an expert in this particular area, the guy on this table doesn't seem to qualify."

"Come on, Pete. You're a genius and I trust you to be discreet. That's why you're here."

His expression softened perceptibly. Mailen had always been a sucker for flattery and beautiful blondes— weaknesses Randi had no qualms about exploiting. Besides, it was true. He really was a genius. The fact that he hated doing something he was so good at was just a nasty twist of fate. And not her problem.

"Tell me what you found out and I promise you more legroom on the way home."

"And a stewardess?"

"Long legs and pouty lips."

Other than a suspicious frown, he didn't move—obviously wanting to display a respectable amount of defiance before caving. She'd flashed another sparkling smile and waited for him to decide when honor had been served. It was the least she could do after dragging him from his cushy gig in DC to a crumbling morgue in the middle of nowhere Afghanistan.

They stared at each other for longer than she would have predicted, but he eventually let out an exasperated breath and whipped back the sheet. The chest cavity of the headless body had been opened up and Randi crinkled her nose as the smell intensified.

"I can't believe you flew me out here for this, Randi. Did they tell you we took fire on the way?"

The story she'd gotten from the pilot was that they'd seen a rocket contrail a good thirty miles away, but she still managed to conjure an expression dripping with empathy.

"I could have been killed," he mumbled to himself as he scanned a pad full of his own illegible handwriting. "Saw my life pass right before my eyes..."

"The body, Pete?" she prompted.

"Well, if you look very closely you'll see that his head is missing and there's a bullet in his chest."

"Everyone's a comedian. Which killed him?"

"The bullet. He was dead when he was decapitated."

"Toxicology?"

"Spotless. Not so much as an aspirin."

"You're sure," she said, still bothered by the strange behavior she'd reconstructed from the battlefield. Killing field, really.

"I wouldn't have said it if I wasn't sure. And why are you so interested in this guy, anyway? It's not like the Afghans have never decapitated anyone before."

"Sure, they'll occasionally hack off a head or three. But this was different. It was every man in the village. And it looks like they didn't try to defend themselves. Not at all."

His irritated expression faded a bit as he pondered that scenario. "How many?"

"Seventy give or take."

"Did you bring me one?"

"A head? No. It looks like they carted them away."

"So this wasn't some kind of ceremonial mass execution. They actually wanted the heads."

"Seems like it, but I don't know why. Maybe they're working on a jihadist promotional video. But something about this feels wrong to me."

"Well, it was obviously incredibly important to them."

"Why do you say that?"

"Because they planned ahead. The spine was sawed through first before they finished the job with a serrated knife. And heads aren't light. Seventy of them would be upward of six hundred pounds."

"How long to saw off a head? Hanging around after doing something like this would be risky."

"Hard to say exactly."

"Is there a body around here that no one's using? And a saw?"

"No, Randi. Besides, we're not talking very long. This wasn't a handsaw. The chipping suggests a powered circular saw."

Randi looked down at the mutilated body and tried to work through what she was being told. "Look, I'm pretty sure I know who's responsible for this—there's a neighboring Taliban village that the people of Sarabat have been going at it with probably since before Jesus. But it's hard to imagine them stopping by the local Sears and buying a battery-powered saw. Last I heard, they didn't even have the electricity to charge it."

"Who knows why people do the things they do," Mailen said with a shrug. "It's a crazy world."

"That's not helpful. Why this? And why now? After a couple thousand years of back-and-forth, the Taliban just roll in with no special weapons and kill everyone without taking a single casualty?"

"Who cares? Pretty soon Afghanistan's just going to

be a bad memory and a few yellowing pages in a history book."

"I need to know, Pete."

"That's easy to say. But how exactly are you going to find out?"

"I figure I'll go ask them."

"Them? You mean the Taliban? I'm not sure they'll be all that happy to see you."

"Maybe not. But this is the kind of thing that keeps me up at night."

Mailen threw the sheet back over the body and began pulling off his apron. "As your doctor, I'd advise you to buy one of those Dresner units instead. I hear they make you sleep like a baby."

8

LIEUTENANT COLONEL JON SMITH pressed the accelerator to the floor, but didn't get much of a reaction from his '68 Triumph. He'd given a lot of time and love to its restoration, but his mechanical skills had never quite lived up to his enthusiasm. The passenger door still had an annoying tendency to fly open when he turned left and the hesitation in the motor seemed to be getting worse now that fall temperatures were descending on the area. Time to swallow a little pride, step away from the tools, and take it to a shop.

He eased back on the gas and slowed to fifty, catching an occasional glimpse of the mist-covered Anacostia River through the trees. To anyone else, that image, the empty road, and the cool air flowing through the window would have been calming. For him, though, it was a drive that usually led to getting shot, stabbed, or thrown off something disconcertingly tall.

He flipped on the radio and used a worn knob to move through the stations. The news was typically depressing and he scanned past it, settling on a morning DJ until the show devolved into something about a juggling stripper. A few more turns took him to NPR and he was surprised to hear a familiar voice emanating from the static-ridden speakers.

"I'm telling you that it's going to be completely trans-formational. Normally I don't like to make predictions but there you go."

It was his new friend from Vegas. Janine Redford.

"So when you say transformational," the interviewer said, not bothering to hide his skepticism. "Are we talking automobile transformational or just iPod transforma-tional."

"We're talking about fire and agriculture transforma-tional."

The interviewer let out a more energetic laugh than was normal for public radio. "When you decide to predict, you really go all-in, don't you, Janine? The Merge just came out. How much time could you possibly have on it?"

In fact, it had been available for just over twenty-six hours. Stores had popped into existence in the world's major cities the week after Dresner's presentation—assembled virtually overnight in spaces rented months before under oppressive secrecy. Smith had driven by the glass-and-neon Merge shop in DC the day before with the idea of stopping in, but the plan had turned out to be a bit naive. The line of potential customers was already wrapped around the block when he got there.

"I got it at a tech industry preview yesterday and have been using it pretty much constantly since then. In fact, I'm using it now."

"You're using it right now?" There was a moment of dead air. "For all of you listening, let me just say that Janine is not wearing a headset."

Smith grinned and turned onto an inconspicuous road that wound down toward the river. It seemed that it hadn't taken Janine long to overcome her youthful cynicism.

"I have to admit that I was resistant at first and I'd be lying if I said there wasn't a little peer pressure involved, but I'm an early adopter at heart."

"And *I* have to admit that they're totally invisible. I can't see them at all."

"The studs? Honestly, the whole thing is kind of a nonevent. They clamp your head into this machine, put some headphones on you so you can't hear the drill, and then it's over."

"No anesthesia?"

"It probably wouldn't be a bad idea to have a couple of cocktails first, but you don't need anything more than that. The whole thing's over in less than three seconds—too fast for you to feel it when it's actually happening. A few hours later it starts to ache a bit but the thing's so amazing, I keep forgetting to take my ibuprofen."

"Did you try the headset before you did it? Are the studs worth it?"

"The headset experience is a little hazy and who wants to walk around with that thing on their head all day? The resolution with the studs is *incredible*. I now have twenty/fifteen vision without the contacts I've been wearing since junior high, and the audio quality is almost a religious experience."

"So you hear through it? You have a mike on you somewhere like the hearing aid?"

"No, I still hear through my ears, unfortunately. But I downloaded my entire music library to it and the clarity is like nothing you've ever heard before."

"Do you have the tooth mike, too?"

"No, I'm using the miniature under-the-collar mike. But I've got a call in to my dentist."

"So what I'm hearing from you is that Dresner's delivered."

"If you tried to take it away from me, I'd beat you to death with a wrench."

"I'll take that as a warning. What about LayerCake?"

Smith eased to a stop in front of a flimsy-looking gate that was actually capable of stopping a fully loaded semi truck driving forty miles an hour. He leaned in close to the windshield and tilted his chin up, letting multiple hidden cameras get a good look.

"I'm still wrapping my mind around that—too much time playing Vampire Armageddon. The basic apps— things like weather and phone and GPS—seem pretty much flawless and the color-coding is incredibly intuitive. My hair dryer burned out yesterday and I was at the store staring at a huge shelf of them when I realized I could just use the Merge. I turned on LayerCake and a couple of seconds later picked the one with the darkest green glow."

"But what about the evaluation of people that everyone's talking about?"

"I'm reserving judgment at this point, but I have to admit that I think it's going to work better than the press is giving it credit for. It's been pretty accurate when I've looked at people I know well and I have to assume that it's just as good for people I don't know. And it's only going to get better as it collects more data and collates user feedback," Janine said.

The gate swung back and Smith pulled into what the sign said was the Anacostia Seagoing Yacht Club. The pleasantly winding asphalt and carefully landscaped berms reinforced that particular piece of fiction, but in fact had been designed to make a straight-on attack impossible. Smith winced as the Triumph scraped over a speed bump and then turned to parallel a dock full of boats that completed the illusion that this was just an extremely exclusive playground for wealthy yacht owners.

"It's a brave new world," the interviewer said, and Smith switched off the radio.

It sure as hell was.

9

Khost Province
Afghanistan

Randi put the helicopter into a steep climb, feeling a jolt of adrenaline when she spotted the shape of a goatherd moving against the dead Afghan landscape. It wasn't the fear of death that caused it, though. It was the fear that something might happen to the chopper.

There were only three in existence and the CIA tended not to hand them out to self-confessed mediocre pilots. The change of heart could only be the result of the quiet involvement of Fred Klein, but still it had been made clear that there would be hell to pay if she brought it back with so much as a scratch.

Neither the animals nor the goatherd so much as glanced at the sky as she passed overhead, reminding her why she'd fallen in love the moment she'd laid eyes on the aircraft. Its blades had a bizarre bat-wing shape that cut rotor slap by more than half; what noise was left was deadened by a web of speakers using the same technology as over-the-counter noise-canceling headphones. The skids and bottom were painted the hazy blue of the

Afghan sky and the top the monotonous tan of the Afghan ground, completing the incredibly effective stealth package.

Of course there were drawbacks. The range was crap and it was a single-seater with a 250-pound capacity. So instead of carrying Deuce to watch her back, she was crammed into the cockpit with a bunch of jerry cans full of fuel. At least they'd make a really big fire if she crashed. Burning alive would be preferable to having to go back to Klein and tell him that she'd left the CIA's multimillion-dollar toy sticking out of a sand dune.

Randi followed an obvious ridgeline, navigating by memory toward the Taliban village of Kot'eh. She was fairly certain they were responsible for the attack on Sarabat and while it didn't seem to bother anyone else, she couldn't shake the image of those headless bodies. She wanted to know what the hell had happened there and, while his motivations were murkier, so did Fred Klein.

It wasn't until she came around the edge of a broad plateau that the smoke became visible—multiple narrow columns rising dead straight for a hundred meters before being ripped apart by the crosswinds she'd been fighting since leaving base.

"Damn," she said, her voice just audible over the hum of the engine and hiss of the state-of-the-art rotors. A tug on the collective took her to maximum altitude—a pathetic two hundred meters off the deck.

In the end, neither the mundane performance specs, the fancy paint job, nor the silence mattered at all. A few passes made it clear that there was nothing left alive in Kot'eh to care about her presence. And while she couldn't say she hadn't considered the possibility that this was what she'd find, the knot in her stomach tightened perceptibly.

She made another arcing pass around the north edge of the village, speaking aloud to herself again. "So what's the brilliant plan now, Randi?"

She answered the question by dipping the chopper's nose toward the rooftops. Just a quick peek. What could possibly go wrong?

It was strange to hear only the sound of the sand battering the glass as she touched down. There was no visible movement outside. She jumped out, leaning over her assault rifle as she ran through the dissipating cloud of dust.

When she made it to clear air, she stood upright and scanned the scene through her scope. To the untrained eye, it would be déjà vu all over again. Just another burning Afghan village strewn with bodies—no different than Sarabat, except that the men were still wearing their heads.

Her eye was far from untrained, though, and it immediately identified stark contrasts. The weapons used against Kot'eh had been far more powerful and destructive than the ubiquitous AK-47. There were gaping wounds in a number of the bodies that were undoubtedly caused by fifty-caliber sniper rounds, buildings displaying RPG damage, and three craters large and well placed enough that they suggested sophisticated light artillery.

The footprints of the offensive force ran the gamut from American and European military-issue boots to sole patterns she didn't recognize—probably commercially available models favored by mercenaries. Even more interesting was that, if followed backward, most just suddenly appeared with two extraordinarily deep impres sions. They'd been dropped, almost certainly at night, and then fanned out in an intricate pattern that suggested serious operators.

Again in contrast with Sarabat, the men in this village had fought. There was no question of that, just as there was no question that their efforts had been completely futile. She counted only three places where bloodstains didn't have a corresponding corpse—attackers that had been wounded and evacuated.

The sun dipped onto the western plateau as she continued her search, finally finding what she was looking for near a charred fence: the body of Farhad Wahidi. They'd had a very tentative relationship, created over a number of years during occasional moments when the interests of the Taliban and CIA converged. She couldn't say that she was sorry to see the fundamentalist son of a bitch dead, but it did make a productive conversation unlikely.

She pushed her sunglasses onto her headscarf and continued to search, staring at the ground as she traced ever-larger concentric circles through the scattered buildings. Occasionally, she'd stumble upon the long-strided tracks of a running Afghan headed toward the edge of the village, and she followed each one to an end that quickly began to feel inevitable: a body with a single, nicely centered round between the shoulder blades.

The light continued to flatten and obscure details that the wind would probably make permanent work of overnight. She was about to give up when she found one last set of footprints coming out of a corral full of blackened livestock. They were awkward at first, suggesting that their author had run crouched, using the panicked animals as cover. After about fifty meters, the stride lengthened and turned east toward boulder-strewn mountains glowing red in the distance.

Three pursuing tracks soon converged, but their configuration was calculated and their pace unhurried. This wasn't a chase initiated in the heat of battle. No, they'd found the track just as she had and were now hunting the escapee like an animal.

Randi looked back at the rising moon. She knew from experience that it would provide plenty of light to track the men and that, in all likelihood, the one person who had the answers she was looking for wouldn't live to see morning. If he wasn't dead already.

Of course, setting out on a nighttime chase meant leaving the chopper. The very thought conjured another surge of adrenaline and the mental image of returning to find it stripped and up on blocks.

"Bad idea," she said, pulling out her sat phone and dialing a number from memory.

A powerful encryption routine delayed the connection for a moment but then Fred Klein's familiar voice came on.

"Did you find anything?"

"Your suspicious mercenary activity. Everyone here is dead."

"So those villagers wipe out Sarabat under suspicious circumstances and then they themselves are wiped out by an unknown mercenary group."

"Seems to me that someone helped them take out Sarabat and now they're covering their tracks. The question is why? Who would care this much about a couple of little villages in the middle of nowhere?"

10

Prince George's County, Maryland
USA

Jon Smith moved deliberately down the hallway, knowing he was being watched from multiple angles. It had been decorated with tasteful rugs and vases full of fresh flowers, but it would take more than the scent of gardenias to make it feel like anything other than what it was: a deadly shooting gallery designed to deal with anyone who might want to penetrate to the inner offices uninvited.

A former special forces operative appeared at the far end and Smith put a hand up—partially in greeting and partially to prove that it was empty. A brief nod was all he got before the man once again faded into the meticulously polished woodwork.

The Covert-One that had been authorized by the president after the Hades virus disaster was in many ways gone now. At first, it hadn't been anything more than a precarious and diffuse organization based entirely on trust—the president's in his lifelong friend Fred Klein, and Klein's in his loose collection of gifted operators around the world.

As it had proved its effectiveness, though, it had grown. Now C1 had a place to call home and even a modest budget—one quietly siphoned from other government agencies without the knowledge of the American people or Congress.

Its very existence was incredibly dangerous for everyone involved—particularly President Sam Adams Castilla. In truth, Smith had initially suspected that cold feet would prevail and the organization would quickly disappear. Unfortunately, the world was becoming increasingly dangerous, politics increasingly bizarre, and the established intel agencies increasingly bloated. The need for a small, nimble organization that could be deployed on a moment's notice grew with every war, rogue nuclear program, and terrorist attack.

Smith entered an outer office dominated by a modular desk topped with five massive monitors. All he could see of the inestimable Maggie Templeton was a wisp of graying blond hair over the top of the one in the center.

He was about to say something when her hand rose and a finger pointed toward an open door in the back wall. He took the hint and headed toward it, tossing his jacket on a sofa that looked like it had never been sat on. Best not to talk to her when she was concentrating.

"So what's going on, Fred?"

Klein stood from behind his far less elaborate desk and took Smith's hand in a firm grip before indicating a chair across from him. In a way, he seemed frozen in time—the receding hairline had stabilized years ago and his eyes never lost their intensity behind wire-rimmed glasses. And while Smith couldn't prove it, he was fairly certain the man was wearing the same suit as the first time they'd met.

"How was the presentation?"

"The what?"

"Las Vegas. The unveiling of the Merge."

So there was the answer to the compelling question of how a purposely obscure army microbiologist had gotten an invitation to a function packed with tech industry billionaires and reporters. Between his relationship with the president and his history at the NSA and CIA, Klein could get just about anything done. He rarely exercised that ability, though, tending to err on the side of not risking exposure unless it was extremely important. Sending a man to graze on imported shrimp at the Las Vegas Convention Center didn't seem to qualify.

"I'm still trying to wrap my mind around it," Smith said.

"So you were impressed? The president wanted the opinion of someone he trusts."

Smith assumed that he meant in regard to the military or intel-gathering potential of the technology, but wasn't entirely sure.

"The claims he made seemed pretty far-fetched, to be honest. But based on the reaction so far, it looks like he's hit a home run with the hardware and LayerCake has a lot of potential—both good and bad. Right now there are only a handful of apps but once independent developers get hold of it, functionality is going to explode."

"So you haven't tried it yourself?"

Smith shook his head. "I haven't been able to get

within a block and a half of the DC store. I thought the lines would die down but according to the news, people are starting to camp out overnight."

"Ah, right. Because it's going to save the world."

"That might be an overstatement."

Klein reached for a pipe, turning it over in his hands before lighting it. "I have to admit that I'm skeptical. It seems like a smartphone with a more convenient interface. That is, if you define 'convenience' as letting someone drill into your skull."

Smith grinned. "You're not really the demographic he's going for, Fred. The truth is that people have been happily using the implants with his hearing system for years. And while I'm with you that it's not going to *save* the world, the Merge—and maybe even more so LayerCake—is going to change it pretty deeply."

"I'm a little old to need a nanny, Jon. And if I did, I'm not sure I'd pick Dresner." The smoke rolled from Klein's mouth before being whisked away by the sophisticated ventilation system. Maggie had no tolerance for second-hand smoke.

"There's no doubt that there are a lot of issues that need to be worked out but there's no way to ignore Layer-Cake's potential. Think about those speed limit signs that tell you how fast you're going. That kind of immediate feedback has been incredibly successful in changing people's behavior. Now consider a hypothetical app that uses brain wave analysis to tell you when you've had too much to drink and puts a little icon in your peripheral vision. That's a powerful piece of data. And then expand that—create an environment where you know that the things you do will bear immediately on the way people see you. That'd make you think twice about your behavior, wouldn't it?"

Klein scowled. "Dresner believes there's a perfect angel in every one of us just dying to get out. I can tell you that isn't my experience."

"I admit it's a little naive. But you could dedicate your life to worse things than trying to make the world a better place. I mean, it's hard to overestimate his contributions, Fred. His work on the way the brain controls the immune system is on its way to wiping out autoimmune diseases. And his new class of antibiotics is making resistance an unpleasant piece of history instead of the looming disaster I guarantee you it was. Then there's his impact on the hearing-impaired, the hundreds of millions of dollars he's pumped into education, the—"

Klein put up a hand, silencing him. "Fine. I'll concede he's on the short list for the Nobel Prize for Medicine and if his apps can actually get our political and financial systems working again, I'll give him the Peace Prize too. But in the meantime, I'm going to stay cynical and ask just what it is we really know about the man."

"Personally? Not much," Smith admitted. "From what I've read, his parents survived a concentration camp and ended up in East Germany. He grew up there and escaped when he was in his twenties."

"That's the public story."

"There's a private story?"

Klein nodded and took a drag on his pipe. "His father was a physicist and his mother was a medical doctor. Both were extremely talented and were put to good use by the Soviets, but then fell out of favor for some reason and ended up in prison. It appears that they were captured trying to escape to the West. Christian, who was six at the time, got sent to an orphanage. Then, a few years later, his own talents were recognized and he was given the opportunity to earn PhDs in biology and neuroscience, which he did by the time he was eighteen. When he got out he went to work for the communists, but we've never been able to determine in what capacity—bioweapons would be a good guess. After a few years, he and a young psychologist named Gerhard Eichmann managed to jump the wall and Dresner went to work for a Munich company that did pharmaceutical research. He proved too unstable, though, and was fired after less than a year. That was 1973. A year later, he'd put together enough private capital to finance a start-up and the rest, as they say, is history."

"Okay," Smith said. "But I still don't understand your interest in all this and how I fit in. You didn't call me to air Steve Jobs's dirty laundry when the iPad came out."

"The iPad doesn't link directly to people's brains and it doesn't constantly gather information to create its own universe of good and evil. If this thing is as indispensable as everyone says, half the industrialized world is going to be hooked up to it within a few years. That gives a man we don't know much about a hell of a lot of power."

"Dresner isn't twenty-four anymore, Fred. Was he unstable at the time? Why wouldn't he be? It sounds like his parents were probably executed and by all reports, those East German orphanages weren't all sunshine and candy canes."

Klein just sat there and pulled on his pipe.

"Come on, Fred. You didn't call me in here to tell

me about Christian Dresner's spotty work history. There's more, isn't there?"

"A bit."

"You have me on the edge of my seat. How did the Merge get on Covert-One's radar?"

"In fact, it's not. You're here today as a soldier."

Smith's brow furrowed. "Okay. You've got my attention."

"Dresner's created a military version of the Merge and he's cooked up some scheme to give the U.S. exclusive rights to it."

Smith couldn't hide his surprise. "A military version? Dresner's never gotten within a mile of creating something that could be used as a weapon. And what does 'exclusive' mean?"

"All I know is that his people contacted the Pentagon and want a meeting. It's really not all that surprising. If Dresner believes that politics and the financial industry are destroying the world and need his supervision, he sure as hell thinks the military does."

"So you figure there are going to be strings attached."

"My guess is that he's somehow angling to try and fix us," Klein responded. "To give us something that will eventually lead us not to fight."

"I'll buy that. And, frankly, if he can pull it off I'll buy him a beer."

"The president doesn't disagree, but he wants to make sure that we understand what we're getting into and that the Merge is used in a way that suits *our* purposes. Not just Dresner's."

"So I still don't understand my role in all this."

"General Montel Pedersen is meeting with the CEO of

Dresner Industries this afternoon and you're going to tag along. You have the combination of scientific and operational backgrounds to understand the technology and Sam trusts your judgment."

Smith winced. "I'm not sure that's a good idea, Fred. Emerging technologies are Pedersen's sphere of influence and he and I aren't fans of one another."

"Really?" Klein said, though it was unlikely this was something he was unaware of. "Why not?"

"Speaking just between us, he's a megalomaniacal half-wit who has a huge say in what cutting-edge technologies get adopted by the military but can barely turn on a computer. On the other hand, he thinks I'm an arrogant jackass who doesn't know his place."

"I won't take sides," Klein said with a barely perceptible smile. "You'll be going as his aide."

"Seriously Fred, I could name three or four really talented people who'd do a great job on this. I don't think the president understands how much this guy despises me."

When Klein spoke again, there was an obvious dismissal in his tone. "Oh, he understands perfectly. He just doesn't care."

11

Outside Baltimore, Maryland
USA

THE COMPLEX HAD THE FEEL of a meticulously white-washed prison from the outside, but once through the gate everything changed. Buildings were widely spaced and partially hidden by landscaping designed to accent the graceful modern architecture. Cars were few and far between, with open-air trolleys ferrying young, casually dressed people through the immaculate, but vaguely Stepford, environment.

It was impossible not to wonder what was going on behind the mirrored windows. Was it a cure for cancer? A sentient machine? Plans for a manned flight to Mars? Or was this just the home of DI's accounting and human resources divisions.

The company had always been incredibly diffuse—facilities like this were spread throughout the world, splitting the work into the bite-sized chunks that their founder preferred. Good science tended to be about the free exchange of ideas and constant peer review. But Dresner's philosophy on development—and so many other things—went against the conventional wisdom. He preferred to break his technical problems down into their most fundamental components and then have them worked on separately by the best people he could find. His job—his genius—was understanding what those basic components were and how to put them together at the end.

Smith got a scowl from a group of people power-walking along a well-tended trail and suddenly regretted not renting a Prius. Who knew that his little Triumph would feel like a diesel-belching semi truck inside the Eden that Dresner had created?

He pretended not to see them and accelerated a bit, following the directions he'd been given to the visitor parking lot. It was hidden behind a stand of pines and the only other car was a generic black sedan with a man in an impeccable army uniform standing next to it.

Smith had made it a point to be fifteen minutes early to avoid just this situation. Obviously, the general had anticipated his move and countered. Round one: Montel Pedersen.

"No uniform, Colonel? Are you embarrassed by it?"

In Smith's extensive experience, tech people didn't respond all that well to the trappings of the military. They didn't seem to differentiate between strolling up in a neat dress uniform and leaping from a tank with a necklace made of human ears. Best to just go with the khakis and a polo.

"My apologies, General."

Pedersen was about fifty, but looked older. His middle had spread enough that it could no longer resist gravity and had collapsed over what was undoubtedly a meticulously polished belt buckle. His hair was cut close where it still existed, accentuating a head that looked a bit like it was melting. He told people he'd been a boxer in his youth and it appeared that he'd lost more than he'd won.

"Let's be clear, Colonel. I have no idea what you're doing here and I never agreed to it. But I didn't have time to do anything about it."

"I understand, sir. I'll do—"

"You'll do *nothing*, including speaking to anyone about what you see here today without my written permission. Is that understood?"

Smith nodded submissively.

Pedersen didn't move for the doors, but instead tried to stare him down. While the general had never been the sharpest tool in the shed, he also wasn't stupid. The sudden appearance of a younger, scientifically more literate soldier at this meeting would undoubtedly make him feel threatened. And making him feel threatened would degrade their relationship even further—something that Smith would have bet good money was impossible.

The truth was that technology was a young man's game and Pedersen's grasp on it became more tenuous every year. Most people who worked for him thought it was a cruel joke that he'd kept his job this long and prayed nightly for him to be put out to pasture. In fact, Smith had already ignored seven messages from Pedersen's staff wondering hopefully if this was the first step in moving him into the general's job.

God forbid.

* * *

Pedersen took the chair at the head of the conference room table and Smith retreated to one halfway down the right side. He was fairly certain that he knew as much as Pedersen: The Merge had some kind of military potential and Dresner wanted to offer it to the United States. Beyond that, everything was completely in the dark. What kind of potential? Had apps been developed similar to the ones for the financial industry and politics? What rights would the U.S. have that other countries didn't?

"Gentlemen. You were early. Sorry to keep you waiting," Craig Bailer said, slipping into the room.

"I appreciate you having us," Pedersen said, shaking the Dresner CEO's hand.

"Always a pleasure to meet with our incredibly well-funded friends from the military," he responded with an easy smile and then stepped around the table to extend a hand to Smith. "Doctor. I'm glad you could make it. Christian appreciated your questions at the presentation. He's very excited about that side of the program and doesn't get to talk about it as much as he'd like. These days all we get is a constant barrage about the release date of our new Facebook app."

Smith just gave a nod and then let the two men sit before settling into his own chair. Bailer was a good two inches taller than his own six feet, with longish gray hair and a tanned face that exuded the same natural healthiness as everything else on the compound. According to a quick bit of research, he had the typical Ivy League background and had made his way around a number of tech firms before settling in as the head of Dresner Industries. Overall, his reputation was as a brilliant businessman with a much better-than-average grasp of the complex products his company produced.

"So what are we actually talking about here?" Pedersen said, deciding to dispense with the expected pleasantries. "There weren't many specifics given when you called this meeting."

"What we're talking about is a military-grade Merge."

"A unique piece of hardware?"

Bailer leaned forward and clasped his hands together on top of the table. "Of course. The commercial version would be too delicate for the application—our primary concerns there were size and weight."

"Are you going to show us a prototype?"

"Oh, more than just a prototype, General. We have a heavily tested and proven design ready to go into full production. Right now there's somewhere around fifty fully functional units for you to take for a test drive."

Pedersen was clearly as intrigued as Smith was, but doing his best to hide it. "Software?"

"We've put together a military operating system built on the same platform as the commercial unit. It's simpler, more robust, and more purpose-driven. Something you can expand on."

"You?" Smith interjected.

Bailer pushed himself back from the table far enough to take in both of his guests. Pedersen was clearly irritated at the sudden inclusion of his new aide.

"The United States will have the exclusive right to develop and use their own proprietary applications and to control weapons systems."

"So no other foreign army will be able to use Merge technology," Pedersen said.

"No other foreign army will be able to use the *military* version. To the degree that other countries can use commercial applications to their advantage on the battlefield— for instance through audiovisual enhancements, GPS, or communications—they'll be able to do so. What they *won't* be able to do is access the military operating system, create military-specific apps, or control weapons."

"And you can guarantee that because your company is going to oversee software development for the Merge?" Smith said, studiously avoiding looking at Pedersen.

"Correct. At the commercial level, we reserve the right to approve or decline any application. If we approve it, we compile it and put it up on the system. Because the Merge's output is so heavily integrated into its user's reality, the interface has to be very carefully designed. Vertigo is a serious problem, and then there are the obvious safety issues. We want to make sure that no one creates, for instance, a YouTube application that can be used while driving a car. With the military, though, that's not as much of a concern. We're confident in your ability to look after the safety of your soldiers."

"So we'll be able to compile and integrate applications without your involvement," Smith continued before Pedersen could jump in.

Bailer shook his head. "We retain the access codes to the operating system. You'll send your applications to us and we'll integrate it into the operating system."

"That seems like a lot of control for us to give up."

Bailer shrugged. "If you're not interested, we certainly understand. But I can tell you right now, these conditions are non-negotiable. Christian isn't going to cede control of his technology. The risks are too great."

"Cost?" Pedersen finally managed to interject, obviously unhappy with being shut out of the conversation.

"With full integration, we're estimating about thirty-five hundred per unit."

The general's brow furrowed as he made a few mental calculations, giving Smith an opportunity to ask another of the thousands of questions bouncing around his head.

"I have to say that I'm surprised by this. Dr. Dresner has never shown any interest at all in military contracting. In fact, I'd go so far as to say he's actively avoided it."

Bailer leaned a little farther back in his chair and nodded thoughtfully. "I can see why you'd think that, but you have to understand that Christian sees America and its military as a force for good. Though admittedly an imperfect and self-interested one. He believes very much in the potential of humanity, but understands that there's evil in the world that needs to be dealt with. In fact, with his background, he probably understands that better than anyone in the room. What he sees here is an opportunity to help the U.S. be a bit more surgical than wiping out an entire Pakistani neighborhood to kill one suspected terrorist or destroying an entire country to depose a single dictator."

"Gentlemen..."

Smith spun in the direction of the familiar voice and saw a screen set into the wall come to life with Christian Dresner's image. "I'm sorry I couldn't be there in person, I hope that Craig is taking good care of you."

"He is," Pedersen acknowledged, but Dresner didn't seem to hear.

"Dr. Smith. I'm a great admirer of your work with prosthetics."

"Thank you. I'm anxious to see how we can integrate the Merge to make them more useful."

"We still have some work to do on that front, but the potential is almost unlimited. As you are a doctor and scientist I know you'll agree that the devil is often in the details. People are so impressed by the integration of the Merge with the human mind, but they have no idea of the incredible challenges presented by complex inputs. Or how much I wanted to include a real-time factual evaluation of what people are saying in conversation but couldn't because of the glacial speed of the cellular data networks."

His eyes became a bit distant as he lost himself for a moment in his own incredible mind. When he spoke again, he seemed to be talking to himself. "And then there's the problem of sarcasm and humor. Absolutely impossible to code for…"

"Maybe you should have just built it to make everybody happy," Smith said, only half joking. "Then no one would care about the details."

An enigmatic expression crossed Dresner's face but then disappeared when Pedersen inserted himself into the exchange.

"I'm interested to learn more about the Merge's offensive capabilities…"

Dresner nodded politely but his eyes suggested that he was already disconnecting from the conversation. "Craig would be able to tell you more about that than I can. I'll excuse myself and let him get on with the demonstration."

Smith chewed his lower lip to hide the anger he felt at Pedersen driving the man away. In truth, though, he wasn't sure that's what had happened. While he was normally fully prepared to blame the general for just about anything, the change in Dresner's demeanor had come not at the question about offensive capability, but at his own comment about happiness.

Pedersen pushed back his chair and stood, looking impatiently down at Craig Bailer. "Did I hear something about a demonstration?"

12

Outside Storuman
Sweden

WHEN HE WAS YOUNG, the darkness had crept up on
him slowly—disguising itself as a passing shadow, using
the constant chaos of his mind as camouflage. Now it attacked without hesitation or pretense, often prompted by
nothing more than an innocuous comment or a brief scent
from a forgotten past. And other times it came for no reason at all.

Christian Dresner stepped out into the sweeping garden, his Merge sensing his position within the compound's walls and shutting down everything but vision
correction. The snow was falling in large, drifting flakes
that absorbed the sound of his footsteps as he weaved
through trees dusted white.

Brushing off a lone bench, he sat and let the cold sink
into him. Behind him, the bunker-like building he'd just
exited stood silent and, in many ways, equally cold. It was
one of a collection of similar structures spread across the
world. How many now? Ten? Fifteen? Maybe it was his
aging mind that kept him from remembering. Or maybe it

was that he felt nothing for any of them. They were less homes than self-appointed prisons meant to make him feel safe. And while he recognized it was probably an illusion, it was at least a comfortable one. In these gardens, for brief, precious moments, he could sometimes make everything outside disappear.

Not today, though. Today, his mind had decided to seize on the stories his long-dead father had told about the concentration camp. About how his initial confusion and fear had faded into a numbness impervious to the death and suffering of others. About how the cruelty of the guards and the desperation of the prisoners eventually became indistinguishable. And finally, about what it was like to watch your humanity slip away.

When Dresner had first heard the stories—at what now seemed like an impossibly young age—his father was still trying to understand what had happened to his people and had been strangely desperate not to place blame. The average German had known nothing of what was happening, he'd said. Only a twisted few were responsible for the evil that had overtaken his country.

He'd believed deeply in the communist ideal and had been proud to use his scientific gifts for the collective good. But then he began to change. The drinking had started, as had long bouts locked alone in the cold, mold-scented basement. He spoke less and less, but when he did, his words no longer forgave. Of course, the German people had been lied to, he would slur beneath the dim light hanging over their rickety kitchen table. But the truth had been right in front of them. They'd just refused to look at it.

And so it had come as no surprise when Christian's parents scooped him up and took him away in the middle of the night. Marxism hadn't delivered the contentment and equality it had promised. Instead, it had become just another weapon to be wielded by men with no conscience— men willing to do whatever was necessary to hold the reins of power.

It wasn't the Nazis, his father had told him as they hid beneath the false floor of a farm truck. It was humanity itself. We were nothing more than hairless monkeys, driven by the same violent urge to survive that had been built into our primitive ancestors.

Of course, they had been captured at the first checkpoint. His father, a man of otherwise extraordinary intellect, had little in the way of guile. The German secret police, on the other hand, was populated by paranoid and sadistic men who understood how to use the dark side of human nature to turn neighbor against neighbor, to create a nearly inescapable web of informants, betrayers, and spies.

He'd never seen his family again. It was only in the last few years that the Stasi records chronicling their fate had surfaced. His father had continued to work under the unveiled threat against the lives of his wife and child, but died after only a few years of being forced to labor eighty-hour weeks. No longer of any particular use, his mother had died of tuberculosis in a Russian gulag, and he had been abandoned to an orphanage in central Germany.

His own intellectual gifts had been identified almost from birth but, as he grew, they became increasingly difficult for the local apparatchiks to ignore. He was eventually transferred to a boarding school where the state could decide whether he could be of use to the great Soviet experiment.

For a short time he, like his father, had been a rabid believer. After years living in violence and squalor as the son of a traitor, he'd seen the bureaucrats enslaving him as saviors, and he'd seen the opportunities they gave him as proof of the egalitarian superiority of communism.

Dresner could still remember the force of his need to belong to something greater than himself. To be understood and respected. To emerge from the shadow of his traitorous family and prove his devotion to the country that had embraced him despite his lineage.

It was a strangely happy—almost ecstatic—time in his life. But it hadn't lasted. The promise of communism gleamed bright and then quickly burned out. Just as his father had promised.

Not long after he escaped, the entire malignancy called the Soviet Union had collapsed. But in many ways, that collapse had made the world even more dangerous. Humanity's evil now churned quietly beneath the surface, growing at a geometric rate, but never coalescing into something tangible enough to fight.

The technology and social mobility that had once held the same promise as communism were again being twisted by a species that would simply not allow itself to live in peace and prosperity. Bizarre ideologies were replacing religion as the opiate of the masses and were being used by politicians to keep the common man off balance. Concentrations in wealth were returning to the corrosive levels of the distant past. Weapons of mass destruction were falling into the hands of fanatics. The world's financial systems had become a boom-and-bust engine that enriched its participants while starving everyone else.

And the trend seemed to be an inescapable downward spiral. The growing choices in media allowed people to retreat from anything that didn't reinforce their own prejudices—creating an increasingly xenophobic population consumed with passion and unencumbered by facts. Wars were being fought over resources that weren't yet scarce, and democracy was deteriorating into nothing more than the tyranny of an ill-informed and superstitious majority.

He'd believed he could change it all. Like so many before him, he'd thought he could perfect humanity. Create a Utopia.

Dresner looked down at the snowflakes melting on the spotted, damaged skin of his hands. With another fifty years he would have succeeded. He would have triumphed where Plato, Marx, and even God himself had failed.

But that dream was dead—a victim of time and the encroaching frailty that he so carefully hid. Now the best he could do was take a place in history among the monsters he despised. It was the only way to give humanity the time it needed to save itself.

13

Khost Province
Afghanistan

RANDI RUSSELL EASED LEFT on the steep slope and leaned against a boulder, making the outline of her body unrecognizable as it melded with the stone. A three-quarter moon was nearly overhead and the hazy streak of the Milky Way cut across the black sky, casting a dull glow over the landscape.

The three men tracking the same fleeing Afghan she was were below, completely invisible in the inky bottom of the canyon. She'd made it to within a hundred meters of them a couple hours ago and spent a few minutes watching and listening. Languages were one of her greatest gifts but she hadn't understood anything she'd heard beyond identifying it as Ukrainian.

Since the Ukrainians weren't part of the coalition forces in Afghanistan, it suggested that these particular gentlemen were mercenaries. And not just any mercenaries. Based on their speed, silence, and equipment, they were highly trained operatives that even she felt compelled to give a wide berth.

So she'd taken the high road, creeping along the steep slope above them, concentrating on not knocking down any rocks that would alert them to her presence. It wasn't the only reason for taking the most precarious possible route, though. In fact, she knew something they didn't. About six months ago, she'd chased an al-Qaeda operative though this same corridor and had made the exact same mistakes the Ukrainians were making now.

The canyon walls steepened consistently as they rose, finally topping out in loose, slightly overhanging cliffs at least fifteen meters high. As a far better-than-average rock climber, she'd concluded that there was no chance of her target escaping that way and focused on keeping her pace quick enough to catch him before the terrain opened up. What she hadn't known at the time—and didn't learn until the terrorist was long gone—was that there was a narrow arch near the top of the canyon's northern wall that went all the way through.

She looked up at the dark cliff band and took advantage of a powerful gust to push on, confident that any rocks she kicked loose would be written off as having been dislodged by the wind.

Randi slowed when things went still again, feeling the cold starting to freeze the sweat trapped between her back and the light pack she was wearing. Her eye picked out a movement twenty meters above and she started for it, worrying less about speed than staying completely silent.

She considered her options as she closed in but, as usual, none was good. Her best bet was the same as it always was—to turn around and get the hell out of there. Discounting that, it was a choice between trying to make contact while she still had room to maneuver, but also a terrific opportunity to fall to her death, and catching the Afghan in the arch where the confined space would neutralize what little advantage she still had.

Option one seemed marginally better. In fact, if she was clever, it might even work.

"Wait," she said in Pashto, muffling the word slightly with her hand.

While she could communicate perfectly well in the language, she hadn't been successful at fully eradicating her accent. Better to communicate in one-word sentences if possible.

The movement visible in front of her stopped abruptly. "Who is that?"

"Adeela," Randi said, picking a woman's name common in the region.

There was a long pause before the man spoke again. "Adeela? How did you escape? Come. Hurry."

Randi slid the sniper rifle down in its sling on her pack. The butt hit her in the back of the legs as she climbed, but the long barrel wouldn't be silhouetted over her head.

Ahead, the man slipped behind a low pile of rocks that had been created to obscure the entrance to the arch and provide a defensive position if it became necessary.

She approached slowly, eyes widening as she tried to penetrate the gloom and pick out the man she was pursuing. There was no way, though. The area behind the wall was so dark, it looked like a gateway to a dead universe.

Heart pounding uncomfortably in her chest, she let her assault rifle hang from its strap and pulled a silenced pistol from the holster on her hip. Stepping behind the wall was like going blind and she tried futilely to pick up a hint of the man she knew was only a meter or so away.

"Adeela," he said quietly. "Are you—"

His eyes were obviously better adjusted and he lunged, but the motion was what Randi needed to pinpoint him. Before he could get hold of her, she had a silencer pressed up under his chin.

"Be calm," she said in Pashto. "I'm not with those men and I had nothing to do with what happened to your village."

"Then who are you?"

"Randi Russell."

She felt him nod through the motion of the gun barrel. "The woman from the CIA."

"That's right. Farhad Wahidi's friend," she said, naming the elder she'd had occasional dealings with.

He let out a bitter laugh that sounded alarmingly loud in the silence. "He did not call you a friend."

"Okay," she said, searching for the correct words to get her thought across. "Occasional convenient acquaintances. Who are you?"

"Zahid. What do you want?"

"I want to know what happened in Sarabat."

"Why should I tell you?"

It was a good question. Her eyes had adapted enough to see his rough outline and she took a step back, lowering the pistol as an act of good faith. "Why shouldn't you?"

He stood there for what seemed like a long time before speaking again. "The men below were with the ones who attacked my village. They killed not only the men but the women and children."

He was in no position to climb onto that particular piece of moral high ground, but she decided that now probably wasn't the time to point this out. "So?"

"I have no weapon. It's why I ran. So I could live to find them. To find them and kill them. Now God has delivered you to me."

"I don't think God had anything to do with this meeting."

"I disagree. He has created an opportunity for both of us to get what we want."

Randi frowned in the darkness. More likely, God was playing one of the cruel jokes he seemed so fond of. The risks of engaging the men below were high even by her standards, but Zahid didn't care. In fact, he likely wanted nothing more than to join his friends in paradise soaked with the blood of men who had killed them. She, on the other hand, just wanted to satisfy her curiosity and retreat to base for a cocktail or ten.

"Fine," she said, holstering her sidearm and handing the Afghan her assault rifle. "But we do it my way."

"I've heard the stories about you, but I believe none of them."

She dropped her pack and unfastened the sniper rifle. "Just another woman, right?"

"These men will not let themselves be distracted by the promise of sex from a whore."

She found a stable surface to set up her rifle and scanned the canyon floor through the starlight scope. "I'm not looking to damage our new friendship with threats, but next time you open your mouth, it better be to tell me about Sarabat."

There was a lengthy silence but finally he spoke. "Our village was attacked from the air and the ground. We killed a few, but they came on us too quickly and with too many weapons. They murdered everyone. I don't know who they were. Not American uniforms. Many different accents and many different weapons."

"You're mistaking me for someone who cares, Zahid. Tell me about Sarabat."

When he didn't answer, she looked up and found him staring up at the stars.

"Do we still have a deal?"

"I said I would tell you if you helped me. You have done nothing."

She returned to the scope and swept the weapon right, stopping when she got to the man bringing up the rear. He was partially obscured from her position and she kept going, finally settling on the point man. He was moving almost directly away from her and she held her breath, centering crosshairs between his shoulder blades and silently counting off the beat of her heart.

A gentle squeeze of the trigger was followed by a less gentle recoil and the earsplitting crack of the round leaving the barrel.

It struck a little low and left but the high-caliber bullet didn't need to be perfectly aimed to tear away a substantial piece of his torso. She didn't bother to watch him go down, instead pulling back as automatic fire erupted from below and began ricocheting off the rocks around them.

"One down," she said, pressing her back against the stone wall. "Now start talking or you're going to be next."

14

Wʜᴇɴ ᴛʜᴇ ᴇʟᴇᴠᴀᴛᴏʀ ᴅᴏᴏʀs ᴏᴘᴇɴᴇᴅ, Craig Bailer ushered them out into an underground facility that was large enough to be almost disorienting. The modest building they'd entered through housed little more than a security desk and a couple of abstract sculptures, but now Smith found himself in a room that was probably two hundred meters long and half as wide, with a ceiling hidden somewhere beyond the steel support grid fifteen meters above.

At the far end was a live jungle guarded by a full-sized tank and various sandbagged machine-gun placements. The extensive computer equipment and personnel that Smith would have expected at a demonstration of a bleeding-edge technology were conspicuously absent as he followed Bailer to a simple table containing two Merges and a couple of laptops.

General Pedersen picked up one of the units and turned it over in his hands. It was slightly larger than the commercial version, with a matte-black exterior displaying a visible carbon-fiber weave. Smith examined the other one, noting that the indicator light was missing, as was the on/off switch and power cable connector. In fact, there was nothing at all that would suggest it was anything but a solid piece of plastic.

"All right," Bailer said, waking up the laptops. "Is it safe to assume that neither of you has used a Merge before?"

They both nodded their heads.

"In our stores, we do demos on how to set them up, but for the most part I'm just going to let you have at it yourself so you can see how simple it is. What I will point out, though, is that the military version of the unit has no connectors at all. That's for two reasons: First, we found connector ports to be responsible for over ninety percent of failures. And second, it's simpler."

"If it's so much better why do the commercial units have a power switch and USB port?" Smith asked. "Cost?"

Bailer gave a bemused shake of his head. "Excellent guess, Doctor, but the reality is much stranger. Our market research suggested that people are comfortable with wired connections and that not having them made the perceived value of the unit less—even though they're completely outdated and serve no real function."

"How do you charge it?" Pedersen asked.

"Dr. Smith? Care to guess?"

He winced perceptibly at the question and considered purposely answering wrong, but his ego wouldn't allow it. "Induction."

"Well done," Bailer said. "There's a small mat that plugs into the wall and you just lay the unit on it. Takes about an hour for a full charge, which in turn will last about twenty-five hours of normal usage. The increased battery size is almost entirely responsible for the additional weight you may have noticed."

"And how does it connect to the computer?" Pedersen asked.

"Standard Bluetooth. But it's only necessary for the initial setup. After that, it stands alone."

He crouched and dug out two military helmets from boxes beneath the table. Both looked more or less government-issue with the exception of elaborate fore-and-aft cameras bolted to the top. "If I could have you put these on and take a place in front of a laptop, we'll get you up and running."

"So the system is built into helmets?" Pedersen said.

"Yes. But only for the purposes of this demonstration. In a combat situation, you'd have to use the head studs."

As he tightened his chin strap and sat, Smith couldn't help feeling a little excitement. Dresner's demonstration, while impressive, had been nothing but a big screen and some interesting parlor tricks. To actually feel a machine-brain link, though, was something he never thought he'd experience in his lifetime.

"Uh, how do you turn it on?" Pedersen said.

"Dr. Smith? You're doing so well. Care to take another shot?"

"I have no idea," he said honestly. That seemed to cheer the general up a bit.

"It couldn't be simpler. Just give it a good shake."

Smith did and the computer screen in front of him immediately recognized the unit, bringing up its serial number and asking if he wanted to enter the setup routine.

"Do I just choose yes?"

Bailer retreated a bit. "No more help from me. I want you to get a feel for what it's going to take to get your people up and running."

Smith clicked through and five images of a tree came up on the screen. The caption asked him to select the sharpest image. He did and what felt a bit like an eye exam continued through a few more screens, asking him to judge color, rotation, and the relative speed of objects. Finally, the word "silver" appeared and he was asked to repeat the word over and over in his mind. A few seconds later, a notification came up that he was done and icons sprang to life in his peripheral vision.

"Whoa," he said, leaning back in his chair and blinking hard.

"It's a little disorienting at first," Bailer explained. "But the effect goes away after a few seconds."

Smith stood and began walking unsteadily forward. The unit, sensing his movement, caused the icons to fade until they were almost invisible. Bailer was right. In less than a minute, his mind had grown accustomed to them.

"General Pedersen? How are you doing?" Bailer asked.

"Done," he said, standing a little too fast and having to steady himself on the table.

Bailer waited for him to regain his balance before starting his pitch. "With the studs, what you see would be quite a bit sharper and will have a more three-dimensional quality. You can manipulate the icons through rudimentary mental commands like 'weather' or 'current location' but it takes a couple of hours to get the hang of it so I'm going to use our demonstration software to run the apps on your units if that's okay."

They both nodded.

"As I said before, this is really just a basic platform. We don't have access to your weapons systems and Christian didn't want to get involved directly in that anyway. But I think you can imagine what the Merge could do if it was, say, linked to a fighter jet's onboard computer. You potentially wouldn't need a canopy or even any physical controls. You could have a full three-hundred-and-sixty-degree view using cameras and all flight and weapons systems controlled mentally. But right now we're going to concentrate on less ambitious applications. Now, if you gentlemen could look down at the jungle and tell me how many combatants you see."

"Two," Pedersen said, squinting to pick out two camouflage-clad mannequins nestled into the trees.

"Dr. Smith?"

"Four. One directly behind the most obvious guy and one pressed up against a tree on the looker's far right."

Bailer's eyes widened slightly. "I'm impressed. No one has ever picked out the fourth man from this distance."

It wasn't surprising. He'd always had a naturally good eye and had spent a fair amount of time putting a fine point on that innate ability. It, among a few other skills he'd picked up over the years, was responsible for him not currently residing in the Arlington Cemetery.

"Let me launch the application that takes feeds from the camera on your helmets."

An icon floating to Smith's right flashed once, but nothing else changed.

"Okay, now I'm going to start layering in different vision protocols. The first is an outline enhancement. For this, the computer uses an algorithm to search for lines that have a potential human or military component and bolds them. The human mind actually does something similar, which is what makes some optical illusions possible. With all due respect to evolution, though, our system is quite a bit more advanced."

Suddenly the visual portions of the four men Smith had spotted were outlined in dull red. More interesting, though, were the things he hadn't seen.

"How many now?"

"Six," Pedersen said, sounding impressed. "And a hidden machine-gun placement."

"All right," Bailer said. "Now we're going to just plain cheat. I'm putting the chlorophyll filter on. This will highlight anything that's not a plant."

"Jesus," Smith heard himself say. Suddenly there weren't six enemy combatants but ten. And at the very back, a tiny section of what looked like a piece of artillery was peeking through the foliage. "Will that work at night?"

"No, it's measuring light absorption. For night we have other solutions." The lights went out, leaving them in the dim glow of artificial stars in the ceiling.

"Here's the light amplification overlay alone."

Everything turned a familiar hazy green. At that level, Smith could only make out the two men Pedersen had originally spotted.

"What do you say we add a little smoke?" Bailer said. A quiet hum filled the room along with a billowing, chemical-smelling cloud that completely obscured the jungle. "Those mannequins are heated to ninety-eight point six degrees, so let's switch to thermal."

The dull green faded and the smoke disappeared. All ten mannequins were visible again, as were the weapons.

"Now everything together."

"Jesus," Smith muttered again. It was almost overkill. The image took on false color with the enemy in red and weapons in blue. Outlines were bolded and the computer was now filling in sections that were obscured. So in a dark, smoke-filled environment, an opposing force might as well hold neon signs that said "shoot me."

Bailer seemed to read his mind and pulled two bizarre-looking assault rifles from beneath the table, handing one to Pedersen and one to him. They weren't anything Smith had seen before—like M16s reimagined by Apple.

"How do you aim it? There's no scope or sights."

Smith suspected he knew the answer, but couldn't bring himself to actually believe it.

"Please put your fingers on the triggers."

He did but nothing happened.

"I think mine isn't working," Pedersen said, obviously having the same problem.

"Point the weapon in the general direction you're looking."

When Smith did, a set of crosshairs appeared at the center of his vision.

"The gun just needs to know its position in three-dimensional space. Where it is relative to your eye doesn't make any difference. Combined with the Merge, it will measure distance and compensate for bullet drop. The only thing you need to worry about is wind and keeping it steady."

Smith held the weapon against his hip and swept it across the jungle, watching the crosshairs projected onto his mind move smoothly from mannequin to mannequin. It felt exactly like a video game.

"Could I fire it around a corner, then?"

"The programming wouldn't be difficult, but it would take some training to counteract the vertigo of having your vision move independent of your physical position."

"And all the systems you're showing us are exclusive to the U.S. military?" Pedersen asked.

"No. We're currently working with Mercedes to integrate the thermal imaging and night vision into their cars. The targeting system, that particular outline enhancement algorithm, and the chlorophyll overlay will be exclusive."

"So it's the helmet cam that makes this work," Pedersen said. "Not my eyes."

"For the most part, yes. We can process the pixels the human eye brings in, but we can't create capability that isn't there, like light amplification or thermal."

"What about the rear-facing camera?" Smith said. "I noticed there's one included in the helmet."

"That's actually just an artifact of earlier research. You might find it interesting, though." He tapped a few commands into the laptop and suddenly Smith's vision went to a full wraparound view. Bailer grabbed both him and Pedersen by the backs of their shirts, steadying them as both nearly fell.

"Some insects handle this view very well, but the human brain can't seem to assimilate it."

He returned to the laptops and Smith's vision went back to forward only. A significant improvement as far as he was concerned.

"We experimented with a semi-transparent rear view similar to a car backup camera, but then abandoned it when we discovered we could generate sensations. Let's assume that you have two of your own men behind you, one right and one left."

A pleasant warmth suddenly spread across the back of Smith's shoulders.

"Now let's say someone unidentified appears behind you."

He felt a sharp prick near his spine.

"There are a lot more possibilities," Bailer said, bringing up the lights and reverting their vision to normal. "Itching, cold, tingling. Each could mean something different. But that's up to you and your people."

"What if someone gets ahold of one from a dead soldier?" Smith said as they removed their helmets and placed them on the table.

"Every brain is unique in the way it communicates with the system, which is why you had to do the initial setup. It would be incredibly disorienting to try to use someone else's unit. Of course, you could set up another layer of security through your military network if it makes you more comfortable, but it would be redundant."

Smith played with toggling through the various icons in his peripheral vision as he listened. He stumbled on one that made his vision zoom in on the tank in front of him and nearly pitched forward over the table.

"So, Dr. Smith? What do you think of our system?"

He didn't answer immediately. The truth was that it was the most fascinating and promising technology he'd ever seen. On the other hand, when something looked too good to be true, it usually was.

"I'm honestly not sure. Ceding so much control to Dr. Dresner doesn't excite me."

"Understandable, but unavoidable."

"And in some ways, it makes me think of da Vinci's military designs."

"Interesting. How so?"

"Great on paper, but not so practical when you're standing knee-deep in the mud with people shooting at you."

15

Hamgyong-Namdo Province
North Korea

THE MIST IS VERY BEAUTIFUL TODAY," the young man said. His Korean accent was clearly audible but not so thick that his words weren't intelligible over the flapping of the jeep's canvas top. No doubt he recognized the importance of his mastery of English in keeping him from living at the edge of starvation like so many of his countrymen.

Gerhard Eichmann nodded absently, and stared out the side window. It really was beautiful. Tall, jagged hills sprang up everywhere around them, emerald green where there was sufficient soil to support life and grayish brown where the rock had been laid bare. Hazy clouds, only a few hundred meters above, threaded through them, being pulled toward the vortex created by a massive waterfall to the west.

It was easy to be lulled into a sense of contentment and peace. But it was there in North Korea that the contrasts nature had created were the starkest. It was a place that demonstrated with heartbreaking clarity the power of a small group of twisted men to create needless destruction and suffering for millions.

The dirt road turned rutted as it detoured around a recent landslide. Eichmann looked past his driver, catching a glimpse of a large facility nestled into a deep canyon. It was normally invisible from the road but the diversion allowed for a brief flash of the fencing and heavily camouflaged roof. His driver, Kyong, suddenly stared straight ahead as though not looking at it could make it cease to exist.

Odd, since two years before he had delivered Eichmann there for a series of meetings relating to the work being done behind its thick walls. Or at least, most of the work being done there. He twisted in his seat as the facility disappeared from sight, trying to pick out the west wing through the trees. Beyond the fact that it was called Division D, he didn't know anything about it. Every query had been politely rebuffed and every request for access flatly denied. At first, he'd thought it was a mistake—one of the many edicts garbled in translation or subverted by the country's dysfunctional bureaucracy. Further investigation, though, proved that assumption to be wrong.

They turned onto a narrow dirt road and wound along it before finally parking at its end. The foot trail that started there, used only very occasionally to transport supplies and personnel, was virtually invisible. Eichmann had been up it once before, though, and vividly remembered the four hours he'd spent struggling along the steep, eroded path.

He stepped from the vehicle and hesitated, looking down at his unsteady legs and the old hiking boots on his feet. There was no point in questioning this excursion now. He had spent three months begging for the opportunity and now here he was—about to personally witness the last, symbolic moment of his life's work.

The beginning of the end to a life that he never could have imagined.

* * *

THE YEARS HAD SETTLED in even harder than Eichmann realized and this time the trip took a full six hours. His exhaustion and the pain from his bleeding feet were so profound that he nearly cried when he saw the first hint of human inhabitation. Not in the form of buildings or roads, but in a bizarre image of farmers tending an expansive rice paddy. From a distance, it looked completely ordinary, deceptively idyllic. As they approached, though, the picture became more complex.

While the tools were typically rudimentary and clothing traditional, the people were anything but. There were Africans, Hispanics, Caucasians, Arabs. Of the few Asians visible, none was Korean, instead having genetic origins in China, Laos, and Japan. Both men and women were represented in equal numbers and all were in their mid-twenties.

Kyong chatted nervously as they passed, ignoring the farmers who had stopped to stare at the strangers approaching their carefully isolated village.

The buildings were typical in design, with simple whitewashed walls and peaked roofs. What made them unique was their large size. There were no families here, only a group of guardians and teachers that had raised the children from infancy according to a rigid protocol Eichmann had designed. Housing was communal with people randomly assigned and reorganized at regular intervals to prevent the formation of overly strong relationships. Interactions with authority figures were limited to avoid favoritism. And outside influences were non-existent. A psychological experiment done with a level of control that the rest of the world's scientists could only dream of.

They entered a building that looked like all the others but was actually a school, and Eichmann followed the hallway toward voices at its end. His boots clacked loudly against the bare floorboards and the moldy scent of Asian wood filled his nostrils. He wanted to remember it all. Every detail.

The girl twisted in her chair when he entered, her wide, pale face registering surprise and terror at the intrusion of an unfamiliar player into her meticulously designed universe.

While it was unlikely that she would remember, she had seen him during his last visit to the village. It was hard to believe that had been seventeen years ago.

The man sitting in front of her said something in a stern voice and she refocused on him as he began reading from a paper on the desk between them.

Despite the fact that she was a blond-haired Caucasian taken as an infant from her home in Romania, the oral examination was being conducted in Korean—the only language she spoke. In fact, the only one she knew existed.

The physical tests, blood workups, MRIs, and CAT scans had already been completed and the data transmitted to Eichmann. This intelligence test and the personality tests to come were the final piece of a puzzle so complex, he wasn't sure he would ever fully understand all its facets.

He settled onto an empty bench, watching the desperate concentration on her face as the test conductor clicked a stopwatch and she began scribbling in the open notebook in front of her.

No reward had been offered to her for excelling on the test, only the promise of severe punishment for failing. The stick without a carrot wasn't an ideal motivator but the incredibly tight controls on the experiment restricted him in this area. Rewards were difficult to provide to people who had no knowledge at all of the outside world. She had no comprehension of, and thus no aspiration to, money or possessions or social status. Food was already adequate, as was housing. Medical care was provided in sufficient quantities to ensure that his carefully designed data set did not shrink unduly over the years.

He had been forced to walk in because neither she nor any of the others was aware of the existence of cars. The only advanced technology she'd seen were the undoubtedly terrifying machines used to test her and the occasional airplane explained away as a kind of bird by the people running the experiment.

Her twin sister, living with adoptive parents in France, experienced a very different world. She had, however, just completed identical testing—though through a much more complex process, and with a cover story created to satisfy her family and the French authorities.

He watched the girl—Eun was her name—and she did the same to him out of the corner of her eye. Undoubtedly, his presence would skew her results slightly, but it didn't matter. The conclusions of the study had been known for a long time. Perhaps even before they'd started down this path.

Maybe he and Christian had just been unable to face it? Perhaps somewhere deep inside them they'd wanted to catch a glimpse of God, to discover that man really was set apart. That humanity would eventually find its way and fulfill its promise.

He smiled sadly. It was hard to believe that they had ever been so young.

16

Khost Province
Central Afghanistan

TRACKING THE MOVEMENTS of both men through the starlight scope was impossible and Randi was forced to jump back and forth between them as Zahid fired uncontrolled bursts in their general direction.

She flattened herself a little more against the ground, ignoring the sharp rocks cutting into her and nursing a grudging respect for the ruthless efficiency of the two remaining mercenaries. They hadn't even bothered to see if the man she'd hit was dead, instead immediately widening their pattern and angling up the steep slope. Both moved with impressive speed and stealth, going from boulder to boulder in carefully coordinated bursts.

She'd counted on them slowing from fatigue as they progressed, but it didn't seem to be happening. Scoring another hit was unlikely and letting this come down to close-quarters fighting was probably not going to go her way. Whoever they were, they were worth whatever they were getting paid.

Zahid rose over the low wall again and fired another

poorly aimed volley. This time the men were ready for it and both leapt from cover with weapons shouldered. Her finger started to move on the trigger of the sniper rifle but then at the last moment, she abandoned it and dragged the Afghan from the path of the bullets spraying through the opening he'd been standing in.

Zahid fought her as the rounds slapped the rock at the back of the small edifice, ricocheting unpredictably. He seemed less concerned that she was using him as a human shield than that she had forced him to retreat instead of facing certain death head-on.

Knowing that the men below would use the opportunity to advance their position, Randi rolled back to her rifle and sighted through the scope again. She fired at the closest target, but the angle wasn't there. The bullet did knock off an impressive chunk of rock half a meter from the Ukrainian's head, though, and that proved enough to get both men to dive for cover.

"Zahid," she whispered. "Are you hit?"

"Not badly."

It was too dark to see much more than the outline of him, but she watched as he teetered and sagged against the cave wall.

"Tell me what happened in Sarabat," she said.

The fact that they had distinctly different definitions of a successful conclusion to this evening was making an already disastrous situation even worse. She wanted to get the information she'd come for and beat a quiet retreat with all her body parts still intact. He, on the other hand, wanted a nice helping of revenge followed by his quota of celestial virgins.

"We were paid," he said as she began scanning the

slope through her scope again. "I don't know who it was and I don't think the elders did either. They gave us new AK-47s and information on where men who guarded Sarabat were. They told us to attack in the middle of the day and that there would be no resistance."

He finally managed to get hold of her assault rifle and fired another burst, unconcerned that there was no visible target.

"Stop doing that!" she whispered harshly. "You're not even getting close and you're going to run us out of ammunition. Why the middle of the day?"

"I don't know," he said, sliding down the rock wall into an awkward seated position. His voice was already starting to lose strength. "I was skeptical, but the money was very good. And it was an opportunity to finally defeat Sarabat after so many years of insults."

She squeezed off a quick shot, kicking up some dust near the boulder the easternmost man was hiding behind. A reminder that they hadn't been forgotten.

As she chambered another round, he burst into view and traversed five meters farther east while his companion sprayed the wall she was lying at the edge of.

They were going to keep spreading out until they could safely pass their position and get the high ground. If that happened, things were going to get really ugly really fast.

"And was what they told you true? Was there no resistance?"

"It was true," he said at a volume that was hard to hear. She wasn't sure if it was his injury or the memory of what had happened in Sarabat.

"The men wouldn't fight. The children and women did. But the men just stood there and died like sheep."

The merc to the east moved again when a gust swirled up enough dust to obscure him. She fired into the cloud, but blew the shot and sent the round spinning off into the darkness.

And that was it. He'd made it far enough that she wouldn't be able to get a bead on him without exposing herself to his teammate. It would probably take him another two minutes to satisfy himself that this was the case and then not much more than another one or two to get above them. She glanced behind her at the blackness of the crack passing through the cliff. There wasn't much more time.

"Why didn't they fight, Zahid?"

"I don't know. It was as if their souls had been taken. I aimed my gun at one of them and he had a good rifle on his back. But he just fell to his knees and looked up at the sky." The Afghan paused, losing himself for a moment. "I praised Allah and he said to me that there was no God."

His voice shook audibly and again she wasn't sure if it was his injury or the weight of the memory. The deaths of Sarabat's innocent women and children would mean little to him. But the abandonment of God—even by an enemy—would be even more disturbing than their bizarre surrender. The only thing etched more deeply into the Afghan identity than combat was faith.

"Why did you take their heads?" she said, trying to catch a glimpse of the man to the west through her scope. He hadn't budged, but it wasn't him she was worried about. At best speed, his partner would nearly be above them.

"We were told to take them by the men who paid us."

"Why?"

"I don't know. They told us that they were never to be found. So we put them in a cave."

"A cave? Where?"

"Ten kilometers to the southeast. In a mountain we call Muhammad's Gate."

She was familiar with that particular geographic feature—three marines had been killed there a few years ago. "There are probably a hundred caves there. Which one?"

"There is only one you can get to from above. The heads were—"

A spray of rounds filled the tiny space and Randi shoved herself away from the wall, rolling awkwardly toward the gap behind her. Adrenaline had her breathing hard by the time she made it inside and she took a quick inventory of her body. Nothing that wouldn't heal.

Even after everything she'd seen, she'd underestimated the speed at which that son of a bitch could take the high ground. Curiosity killed the cat and one day it was going to do the same to her.

The gunfire stopped but this time the deep silence she'd become accustomed to didn't ensue. Instead, she could hear the footfalls of the man approaching from below and the sound of rocks being knocked down as his partner came at them from above.

"Zahid," she whispered. No answer. He had tipped to the side and his head was resting at an unnatural angle on the butt of her M4 carbine. The sniper rifle was still set up at the edge of the wall and that's where it was going to stay. The approaching men would have identified that they'd been attacked with two weapons and if either was missing, they'd know someone else had been there.

Randi reached out and snatched her pack, sliding it back and forth across the marks made by her boots and body in the dust. The sound brought another volley, this time from both directions, forcing her to retreat into the gap. It would have to be enough.

She twisted sideways and dragged her pack along behind her, listening to the footfalls of the two men as they were amplified and distorted by the passageway's acoustics. For a moment it sounded like they were pursuing her but she quickly realized that it was just an illusion. Still, it prompted her to increase her speed, pushing the very edge of what she could do silently. There was a drop-off farther up and she knew her life depended on getting to it before the men reached Zahid's body. The problem was that she couldn't remember the distance.

Ukrainian voices echoed toward her and she used the noise to mask a brief increase in her pace. She couldn't understand the words, but it was likely that they were coordinating the final phase of their assault on the alcove and speculating as to the chances that its occupant was still breathing.

There was a shout and another burst of automatic gunfire and she incorporated them into her running mental video of the two mercs' actions—not difficult because they were almost certainly the exact same ones she'd have taken in their situation.

The man who had staked out the high ground would spray the area as his teammate came in from the east...

The ceiling rose and she stood to the degree she could, breaking into a crouched sprint through the blackness as she continued to mentally play out the scene unfolding behind her.

The approaching man would have good visibility with night-vision goggles, but the position of Zahid's body would initially hide it, making it impossible to make a decent risk assessment. That would slow him down a bit. But only a bit.

The final echoes of gunfire faded and Randi was forced to slow to a pace that allowed her to be completely silent. The Ukrainian would be inching forward now, back against the cliff, listening for movement. He'd come up to the edge of the crack she was moving through and stop. Zahid's foot would come into his field of vision and he'd watch it for a few moments, confirming the strangely unmistakable stillness of death.

Once he was satisfied that the Afghan no longer posed a threat, the merc would turn his attention to the gap. Probably also not a threat, but these were thorough professionals. He wouldn't just stroll past it. No, he'd update his teammate as to the situation and then...

Almost precisely on cue, the shout she was dreading rang out. Randi broke into a full run again as the man stuck his assault rifle into the crack and opened up on full automatic. One bullet passed close enough that she could feel the hot wind from it, another ricocheted off the stone to her right with a deafening ring. And then the ground went out from beneath her.

The landing was less graceful than she'd planned and she pitched forward, slamming headfirst into the ground as more rounds passed over her head.

She remained still, dazed enough that she didn't trust herself to rise in the silence that was once again closing in. Instead, she went back to trying to picture what was happening in the alcove she'd just escaped from. The man would have leapt across the gap and be inching forward again, still keeping his back against the rock wall. A few more seconds...

There was another shout, followed by the rattle of falling rock as the man's teammate started down to him. Zahid had been confirmed dead and, for the moment, they sounded as though they were satisfied that the threat had been neutralized.

Randi pulled herself from the shallow hole and listened for any hint of pursuit as she continued on. The mercenaries had chased and cornered one man and now he was dead. There was no reason for them to think anyone else had been involved—a mistake she herself probably would have made in their position.

Ahead, the darkness took on a hint of gray, but she didn't let it cause her to quicken her pace. It was another interminable five minutes of wondering if they'd empty another clip into the gap before Randi exited onto a steep, moonlight-washed slope.

She immediately started up, wanting to make sure that this time she had the superior position if the men decided to come after her.

After fifteen minutes of lying quietly in the rocks with her silenced Glock on her chest, though, there was still no sign of pursuit.

Finally, she relaxed and redirected her gaze to the sky as she took another inventory of her condition. There was a little blood trickling down her face and she was going to have a nice bruise across her forehead. No big deal. Her right ankle had taken a bit of a beating—nothing that would keep her out of heels, but less than ideal for a five-hour hike that included climbing down a steep, loose mountain in the dark. Particularly with her two Ukrainian friends still out there.

She dug into her pack for her sat phone and began dialing.

"Randi?" Klein said when he came on. "Are you all right? It's my understanding that you're still not back at base."

"I'll live. The last resident of Kot'eh just got taken out by mercs—Ukrainian, I think. Before he died he told me that they were given equipment and intel and paid to go after Sarabat. They were also paid to take their heads and hide them in a cave southeast of here."

"Anything else unusual?"

"He said that the men didn't fight back. The women and children did, but it sounds like the men just stood there."

There was a short pause. "All right. I think this is getting a little beyond the scope of what I have authorization to look into. Let me work on this from my end. Can you get back on your own?"

She looked down the dark slope. "I always do."

17

Near Santiago
Chile

THE ROAD WAS IN EVEN WORSE condition than he expected and Craig Bailer began to regret driving himself. The benefit of a little time to mentally prepare for his meeting had been significantly diminished by crossing no fewer than three streams and a mud bog that had very nearly left him stranded. No place for a man born and bred on the Upper East Side.

A building finally came into view, still distant but unmistakably the one he was looking for. Most of his communication with Christian Dresner was over computer links; the few times they had met face-to-face, it was always at one of these remote bunkers. From the outside, they all looked exactly like miniature versions of the swooping, thick-walled research facilities he'd also strewn across the world. It was like a tic.

Bailer eased up to the gate and, for the first time in his life, was just waved through by one of the highly trained guards Dresner seemed to think were necessary to protect him. From what, no one was sure. Former Israeli and U.S.

special forces seemed like overkill to keep him safe from a world populated mostly with starstruck fanboys.

Interestingly, the apparent lack of rigor didn't reflect an easing of Dresner's obsession with security as much as a simplification of it. The guard's Merge would have instantly confirmed his identity through both facial recognition and an encrypted system that authenticated brain wave patterns. The latter system was one that was being kept under wraps while the public learned to deal with inevitable privacy concerns, but it had incredible potential for making financial fraud and identity theft a thing of the past. Among other things.

His was the only car in evidence as he pulled up to a heavy front door guarded by yet another broad-shouldered man with eyes hidden by dark sunglasses. There was no need for an escort because the layout was exactly the same as it was in the compounds he'd been to in Scandinavia and South Africa. Predictably, the massive garden Bailer entered was created in the familiar Japanese pattern but populated with local plants.

He found Dresner at the back, sitting alone in an intimate conversation pit shaded by a high wall. He stood and they shook hands with warmth that Bailer assumed wasn't felt by either side.

"I appreciate you coming personally, Craig. I feel like our first discussion of this should be done in person. That is to say, I'm very excited to hear what you have for me."

"And I appreciate the invitation, Christian. As always." It was a lie, of course. This was a spectacularly bad time for him to be away from DI's headquarters. A much worse time than Dresner could possibly know.

"Please sit," the old man said, settling back down and

pouring Bailer a glass of water. "And tell me how it's all going."

"Mostly as projected. The stores can't handle the demand for demonstrations, but that's something we anticipated. On the other hand, seventy-three percent of the people who do go through a demonstration, buy."

"And what does that translate to in numbers?"

"After five days of availability, eighty-nine percent of users still are on the headsets but a surprising fifty percent have immediate plans to get implants. That number is trending steeply upward, as people's experiences are almost uniformly positive."

"Age distribution?"

"Not surprisingly, sales are overwhelmingly to people in the twenty-five to thirty-five range. However, adoption among older demographics is on an upward trend that right now looks geometric. The sleep function is probably the most enthusiastically embraced facet of the Merge— I'm not aware of any meaningful negative publicity. I wouldn't be surprised if we see enormous adoption by seniors who use the system only as a sleep aid."

"But for that, we have to overcome the hurdle of convincing people my age to get the implants. The headsets are impractical to sleep in."

"Absolutely. We're starting the process of trying to get Medicare and a number of European health care systems to provide coverage with a doctor's recommendation. If we can get that done, I think we'll see an explosion."

Dresner reached for his glass and leaned back again, contemplating the sunlight reflecting off it. "It's my understanding, then, that we're moving our sales projections upward?"

"No question. By the end of the day today, we'll have sold six hundred and fifty thousand units worldwide. By the end of the quarter, we're projecting just under four million civilian units on the street."

"Military?"

"Impossible to predict at this point. It's my understanding that Colonel Smith, whom you met, is running an initial field test day after tomorrow. He seems to have been given a great deal of influence over whether the military is going to embrace the Merge—more than General Pedersen as near as we can tell."

"As it should be," Dresner said without looking up. "He's far more impressive than the general and appears to be a thoughtful and intelligent man. As such, I can't imagine that he won't recommend full adoption by the American armed forces."

Bailer remained silent.

"Do you disagree, Craig? If so, please speak up."

"No, I think we'll get almost full adoption. But it's only about a million and a half people, Christian. The combined forces of Europe, China, and Russia total five million. If we opened the market—"

Dresner shook his head, silencing the man. "The other militaries will adopt eventually for the data, communications, and vision enhancement. Those will all be significant advantages."

"But not immediate, critical advantages. If we had opened up the ability to use military applications and link to offensive systems we could have created—"

"A new arms race?"

"Yes! We would have had millions of people with unlimited funds climbing over each other to integrate as fast as possible. We could have conservatively doubled our first-year sales."

"And created another military stalemate that benefits no one. That isn't what I want to be remembered for, Craig. The Chinese are insular and self-interested. The Russians are dangerous and unpredictable. The Europeans are useless. And while the Americans have made their mistakes, they've done better than any country in history wielding nearly absolute power. They may be clumsy, but at least they're clumsy in the pursuit of democracy and stability."

"But we need the—"

"Chaos won't help us in the long run."

Bailer fell silent, trying to swallow his anger and calm the nervous energy he always felt when faced with Christian Dresner. The old man was not only still physically imposing in his late sixties, but unquestionably one of the most successful and intellectually powerful forces of the last century. As he aged, though, his naive belief that he could save humanity—through antibiotics, the Merge, charitable donations to education, his bizarre focus on political and financial applications—grew. He'd become oblivious to the fact that humanity didn't want to be saved and that it was precisely this trait that could provide the company either endless opportunity or assured destruction. Dresner was leading them blindly into the latter.

"Chaos can't hurt us, Christian. Because we're dead already."

"I think you're exagger—"

"I'm not exaggerating!" Bailer said, daring to raise his voice. "Even our most optimistic projections aren't enough to save the company, Christian. Our cash reserves are nearly gone and we won't be able to meet expenses and debt payments next month. When we decided to go all-in on this technology, our survival was based on worldwide military contracts. Then you shut us out of the market."

"Craig, we—"

But Bailer kept talking. "Wall Street and the banks are getting nervous. We just rolled out the most transformational technology since the personal computer and our stock only went up a few points. And the pathetic truth is they don't have any idea of the extent of the company's financial problems. If they did, our stock would be trading under a dollar and there'd be a moving truck out front carting away your furniture."

"Are you finished?"

Bailer had never seen anger in Dresner before and he felt a strange twinge of fear. But now wasn't the time to be blinded by the heavenly light so many people saw emanating from The Great Man. "No, I'm not finished, Christian. If we issue stock at the level we would need to in order to save the company, the markets are going to see our weakness and our share prices are going to plummet to the point that a hostile takeover is almost inevitable. If we don't, we're going to have to *court* a takeover to keep from collapsing."

"It's only about money to you," Dresner said, his brief flash of anger turning to disappointment.

"Wake up, Christian! If we're taken over or have to file bankruptcy, you lose not only all your privacy, but all your secrecy. What happens when the world finds out just what it took for you to develop your amazing new technology? What's all your altruism worth then? You can't afford to let that happen. None of us can."

Dresner didn't react other than to turn away and look out over the carefully arranged trees and flowers. The gesture was clear. Bailer had been dismissed.

18

JON SMITH PROPPED HIS bare feet on the coffee table and used a beer to wash down a few more Advil. His television was still propped on a box against the wall and he tilted his head slightly to compensate for its lean.

The subject of the newscast was the mounting tensions with Iran and he flipped the channel, unwilling to even contemplate the idea of ever having to go back there. He'd cross that bridge when he got to it. Hopefully, never.

CNN was running a colorful panel discussion about the national debt and he settled back into the sofa, trying unsuccessfully to get comfortable and regretting letting the saleswoman talk him into the modern design.

What drew him into this particular debate wasn't his passion for government accounting so much as the fact that a tiny icon in his peripheral vision brightened noticeably when he'd surfed to it. The app was called TVMonitor and its function was to vet what was being said on various news programs. Limitations in network speed made it impossible to do real time, but this particular show must have originally aired early enough in the day that LayerCake had had a chance to do its magic.

Smith concentrated on the name of the app and it sprang obediently to life. Craig Bailer had been right. Once you got the hang of it, launching, manipulating, and closing individual modules was surprisingly easy.

TVMonitor glowed green as the host gave a few general numbers and asked a lengthy question about recent budget cut proposals, then took on a reddish hue when a congressman started talking about the relative value of certain changes to Medicare, suggesting they weren't going to be as effective as he claimed. When the subject of the relatively small impact of recent defense cuts came up, it went back to green.

The concept was simple. LayerCake searched objective facts on government sites, Wikipedia, Snopes, and hundreds of others, then compared them with what was being said. If they matched, the TVMonitor icon glowed green. If not, red. Of course, when the discourse turned to something that transcended facts—abortion, for instance—then the personal values of the user would rise in importance. To the degree that facts were stated, though, they would still be vetted.

And what about those personal biases? Smith launched a subsystem of TVMonitor that split the icon. Now the right side was monitoring the brain waves of viewers who had opted in, evaluating their reaction to the debate. He focused on the pulsating colors, fascinated by how poorly coordinated they were. People's reactions seemed completely independent of objective truth. It was something that Dresner hoped his little feedback loop would correct.

These were just the kinds of data the Merge's political

apps fed off and why politicians were adopting them at light speed. The ability to see and react to people's perceptions as well as to see when the system was calling you a liar was an incredibly powerful tool—one that would soon be mandatory for anyone hoping for a successful career as an elected official.

As Smith saw it, the whole thing was one giant psychology experiment. Could Dresner do what he'd set out to do? Not just change the way society functioned, but the way individuals thought and reacted to the world around them? Would people trust LayerCake? Or were they more comfortable wrapped in the warm blanket of their own biases? He himself admitted to harboring a few sacred cows and he wasn't sure how he felt about Dresner going after them—even if he was justified in doing it.

Smith took another pull from his beer, the dull throb in his head subsiding a bit as he surfed through the channels to a Fox panel on the question of the day: privacy issues raised by the Merge. Interestingly, the TVMonitor icon faded. Was it because it hadn't had time to vet this particular show or because of the potential for bias? Was Dresner's search system capable of attacking its creator?

"This is different," a woman on the right said emphatically. "This isn't just about the user opting in, it's about whether the people around that user have. How do we know that the facial recognition software isn't recording everyone we see? What if I'm walking by when you go into a strip club? Or light up a joint? Will that be calculated into your value as a human being? What if I'm shopping next to a woman buying a pregnancy test? Is that information going to be immediately packaged and sold to her health insurer, BabyGear.com, and potential employers? And why not take it one step further? Why not just correlate everything someone sees to how they feel about it using their brain waves? I'm guessing that's something Target and Amazon would be interested in."

"All those things are strictly forbidden in Dresner's licensing agreement," someone interjected.

She laughed. "And of course we can trust him. Don't be evil, right? Unless you can make a billion dollars off it."

"Let it go, Sharon. We're not in the information age anymore, we're in the information overload age. All that stuff is already out there. What we need is some way to sort through it and that's what Dresner's giving us. Better him than someone else as far as I'm concerned."

"Beyond all that," the host said, "what about accuracy? What if I have the same name as a convicted murderer and it gets confused? How is that going to affect the way people see me? Is there a system for fixing those kinds of errors?"

"LayerCake takes into account the quality of the information and is very conservative about how it weights it. But the answer to your question is yes. You can monitor the facts in your profile—there's actually an app for it—and dispute them just like a credit report."

"So what if the facts are right?" the man to the host's right said. "I'm a decent person, but I'm a conservative. I hunt. I'm for the death penalty. I support Republican candidates. Does that mean it's going to paint a pointy tail and horns on me to left-wingers?"

"Dresner can't control people's prejudices," someone else chimed in. "But in the end you'll probably be better off because he's tempering their prejudice with reality."

"I'm not sure I want a machine knowing everything

about me and using that to tell other people what I'm worth."

"Too late. The younger generation doesn't value—or even define—privacy like we do. They don't mind being advertised to and they don't so much as have a cup of coffee without tweeting about it. They *want* to know if the person standing next to them on the train is a Christian who shares their passion for Siamese cats, if they have friends in common, if they're looking for a relationship."

The discussion became increasingly heated and Smith finally hit the "mute" button. It was an impossible situation that didn't turn on right or wrong. Yet another of the growing number of issues that split almost exactly along generational lines. With him right in the middle.

He rose and padded to the bathroom, leaning on the sink and staring at his image in the mirror. The missing hair was a little more obvious than normal because of the military cut and he turned his head, catching the glint of one of the silver studs that had been screwed into his skull that morning. Interestingly, the process had been much quicker and less intrusive than the installation of the tooth mike Bailer had fast-tracked for him. He opened his mouth and pulled back his cheek, but couldn't spot the molar in question with absolute certainty.

He'd considered wearing a headset and throat mike for the field test day after tomorrow, but then dismissed the idea. After all the germ, drug, weapon, and radiation testing American soldiers had been subjected to throughout the years, going in halfway felt oddly dishonorable. And so, like countless others before him, he had been promoted to guinea pig.

Smith hit the light and aimed for his unmade bed, falling into it in the old sweatpants that had been his uniform at home for more than a decade. He reached for the alarm clock out of habit and then stopped, instead laying his Merge on the charging mat spread across his nightstand. When it recognized a power source, the grayed-out icon for the sleep function went active.

The truth was that he didn't sleep that well anymore. In darkness and silence, the past had a way of consuming him—dead friends and enemies, close calls, critical mistakes. Too many of them.

Of course, he'd written himself a prescription for Ambien a number of times, but it always ended up in the garbage. Why, he wasn't entirely sure. Maybe he subconsciously saw it as a sign of weakness. Or maybe he just thought the dead had a right to be heard.

Smith stared at the icon for a few seconds and then activated it, reminding himself that this wasn't about him. It was for king and country.

The interface was typically simple and similar to all the others in the way it used eye movement and simple mental commands. He set the start time on "immediate" and the wake time as six a.m. The app provided a number of advanced functions including the ability to wake up at various times throughout the night, but he left those unchecked and settled back into his pillow.

* * *

SMITH'S EYES SHOT OPEN and he blinked a few times in confusion. The adrenaline rush he normally got when his subconscious mind identified an out-of-place sound was completely absent, as was the grogginess that always accompanied nights weaving in and out of sleep.

He frowned into the darkness, realizing that he'd probably never even fully drifted off. And he knew himself well enough to know that he wasn't going to anytime soon. No, despite all the hype, it looked like he was about to enjoy another night of infomercials for improbable exercise equipment and B horror flicks. Even Christian Dresner couldn't knock it out of the park every time.

A clock icon at the lower right of his vision gained in strength and he squinted at it out of habit despite knowing that his eyes had no role at all in generating the image.

6:00 a.m.

He rolled toward his nightstand and confirmed that his alarm clock read the same. Unable to believe what he was seeing, he went to the window and pushed the curtains back. Outside, the densely packed homes were just beginning to glow with the first hint of sunrise.

"Jesus..." he said aloud.

He hadn't slept like that since he was a kid. And even then he'd remained groggy until he was halfway to the bus stop. Right now, he felt like it was the middle of the day—undoubtedly thanks to the Merge optimizing his brain waves for a state of alertness.

Everyone, himself included, had been confused by Dresner's incorporation of the sleep function into his system. But now it was obvious that it was just another testament to his genius. Even if the Merge didn't do anything else—if it couldn't so much as conjure up a decent game of Pong—anyone over the age of thirty-five who tried it would sell their children to own one.

19

A LIGHT RAIN WAS FALLING on mountains tangled with overgrowth. Harder on his team, Smith knew, but almost perfect for what he had in mind.

The trail—such as it was—had turned to mud, grabbing at his combat boots and splattering his meticulously pressed camo as he worked his way toward a rendezvous site that he knew was 326 meters away. Normally, in this kind of unfamiliar terrain he'd be relying on a soggy map and wondering if all his men were already gathered, but now that seemed like a scene from ancient history.

In addition to distance, the Merge's military training software displayed an arrow pointing him in the right direction, an ETA at current speed, and individual green dots representing his volunteers' positions on an overhead map.

He waded through some wet bushes and came out into a small clearing where five combat-equipped soldiers were huddled beneath a tree trying to stay dry. When he appeared, they gracelessly formed a line and shot off a few awkward salutes.

His SAS friend Peter Howell would have called them "a bit of a motley crew." Of the two women, one was at least thirty pounds overweight and the other just south of her fiftieth birthday. The man to their right was even older and more overweight, with a round, sun-starved face that made him look like exactly what he was: an army lawyer. Next, to him, adjusting a helmet that seemed to swim on his undersized head, was a skinny kid in his mid-twenties who spent his days programming supply logistics systems. And last, but certainly not least, was an active-duty Ranger who was understandably perplexed—and maybe even a little insulted—to have been chosen for this particular team.

"At ease."

It was an impossible order for most of them to follow. Two days before, they'd been plugging away at their desk jobs, blissfully ignorant that Smith was combing through personnel files looking for people who couldn't fight their way out of a paper bag, but who had Merge head studs and tooth mikes installed.

Not surprisingly, General Pedersen had thought he was nuts. And now that he was physically standing in front of the people he'd selected, it seemed that the general might have had a point. In the end, though, this test had the potential to tell him far more than the more obvious course of throwing two equal forces against each other and equipping only one with Merges. Smith had stacked the deck as heavily against Dresner's technology as he could and now they were going to see just what it could overcome.

"I appreciate all of you agreeing to play our little game," he said, knowing that they'd actually had no choice whatsoever.

A few queasy nods.

"My understanding is that you've all been issued military versions of the Merge and that you've familiarized yourselves with them. Is that correct?"

That got a few affirmative mumbles.

"I'm going to repeat myself just this once. Is every one of you the goddamn *world expert* in the use of this system?"

"Yes sir!" the Ranger barked and the group followed suit, finally showing a little life. He'd been right to throw in a combat soldier. If nothing else, he could set an example.

"All right then. That's what I wanted to hear." He pointed to a tall, tangled hill about four kilometers away. "The objective is simple. On top of that is an American flag. We need to get it out of the rain. Any questions?"

His pale attorney—Major Gregory Kent—raised a hesitant hand.

"Yes. Greg." Smith said, deciding to retreat into a little informality after his show of anger. No need to scare these people any more than necessary.

Kent indicated toward five assault rifles stacked in plastic bags. "What are those for?"

"An excellent question. Those fire a laser that can be picked up by the uniform of an opponent and all are equipped with Merge targeting systems."

"Opponent, sir?" the Ranger said, perking up.

"Did I forget to mention that there's a five-man Delta team under orders to stop us?"

Not unexpectedly, his team descended into frightened protests.

Smith held up his hand and they went silent. "If you're hit—and I'm giving you a direct order not to be—the training software in your Merge will evaluate the damage and reduce your effectiveness based on that evaluation."

The fear on the skinny programmer's face faded into cautious curiosity. "How does it do that, sir?"

"If it registers an injury, it'll limit your vision and throw off your equilibrium to mimic your probable condition."

"And if we're dead?" the plump women said. Stacy something. She worked on drones.

"Your vision will go black and your ability to hear will be degraded. Don't panic, though. It's just the Merge projecting a solid color onto your visual cortex. I'll use my simulation leader software to reset your unit when I've had a chance to evaluate the situation. Just sit there and wait until you come back online and then go back to the command tent and get a cup of coffee. Understood?"

A little of the energy had gone out of their response but he decided to ignore it and instead pointed to the older woman whose hand was up. "Yes. Carrie."

"Sir, I think there's been a mistake. With the exception of Corporal Grayson over here, we're not combat people."

Smith nodded. "But you do have Merges. And Delta doesn't."

"I don't see how a fancy cell phone is going to make much of a difference," Kent said. "I represented a Delta guy once. As near as I can tell, if you shoot them it just makes them mad."

Grayson rolled his eyes.

"Look, I'm out here to gather some data on Merge effectiveness," Smith said. "I want that flag, but the only failure here is if you panic or if you don't give one hundred percent every second of this exercise. Is that understood?" No response. *"Is that understood?"*

"Yes sir!"

They all actually managed to say it at the same time. Things were looking up.

"Okay. First things first. I want you to take your Merge unit and throw it in the mud."

No one moved.

"Is there a problem?"

Grayson was first to speak up. "We were told that these are incredibly expensive prototypes and that they were to come back without so much as a scratch."

"Well, those orders have been revised. Now get them into the mud. And stomp on them until I tell you to stop."

The four non-combat soldiers obeyed, but as delicately as possible. Grayson, understanding the point of the exercise, threw himself into the air and slammed his boot down on his unit so hard it completely disappeared into the soft ground.

Smith turned and contemplated their objective, looking for a sign of the enemy while the splashing and stomping went on behind him. It was really just a test of manufacturing consistency, since he'd already performed a much more stringent evaluation of his own unit.

"Okay," he said, putting on an armband that designated him as an observer. "Saddle up."

* * *

CORPORAL GRAYSON HAD TAKEN de facto command of the group and was doing a surprisingly good job of adjusting to the reality of his team's dismal abilities. He kept them on easier terrain and spread out at five-meter intervals.

There was still more than a little bit of tripping, heavy breathing, and panicked drops to the ground, but they were managing to move in the general direction of their objective and no one had yet twisted an ankle or stroked out. A minor miracle as far as Smith was concerned.

He hung back a bit, focusing on a semi-transparent overlay of the battlefield in the right upper corner of his vision. His people were shown as dots in varying shades of green based on their military records—Grayson's was predictably dark and rich, conveying his combat experience and other achievements. The others were significantly lighter, with his skinny programmer semi-translucent.

More interesting, though were the red dots that he was privy to as the leader of this exercise—a Delta ambush that his team was unwittingly strolling into. Smith switched to vision enhancement mode and let the computer automatically calculate the optimal mix of filters as he searched the trees ahead. The thermal imaging blinded him for a moment, confused by the rain, but it immediately faded and left him with primarily the chlorophyll overlay. Combined with outline enhancement and light amplification of the shadows, it allowed him to immediately spot the shape of an arm sticking out from beneath a fallen tree.

But he wasn't the only one.

"Do you see that?" Stacy said quietly over her tooth mike. "What is it? One o'clock."

Incredible. Despite being about as stealthy as a herd of buffalo, they had identified a highly trained, dug-in enemy before they themselves had been spotted.

"Everyone stop and get down," Grayson said. "Nice job, Lieutenant. That's an arm. And we're gonna blow it off. But first we're gonna get a little closer. Everybody move forward real quiet. This isn't a race. There's no such thing as too slow. We're looking for additional targets."

They actually did a good job of staying out of sight, though it turned out there probably *was* such thing as too slow. At the pace they set, they'd overrun the Delta position sometime in January.

"I've got another one," Kent said, his voice sounding shockingly clear over the Merge link. "About eleven o'clock. Next to a small rise."

"I can't see him from here," Grayson responded. "Are you certain?"

"One hundred percent."

Smith pulled up a small window that displayed what the man was seeing. Sure enough, it was another of the Delta team, so smeared with mud that he himself might have walked right past him if he'd only had his naked eye to work with.

"Okay. We're up against a five-man team and we have two of the sons of bitches dead to rights. If we get any closer, we're going to risk being spotted and then all hell is going to break loose. I say we take our shot now. Agreed?"

When everyone came back affirmative, Smith leaned out around the tree he'd taken refuge behind. This was something he had to see.

"Okay, I have the guy at one o'clock—"

"Negative," Smith interjected. "I already know you can hit him, Corporal. Let someone else take the shot."

"Affirmative. Lieutenant. You spotted him, he's all yours."

"But...But I..."

"Relax, Stacy," Smith said. "Just a game, remember."

"Yeah, Lieutenant," Grayson said. "You've got this. Just line the Merge's crosshairs up and tell me when you're ready. Major Kent. I take it you've got a line?"

"My crosshairs are dead center and I'm ready to go."

"Okay, everybody else pull back nice and easy. We're going to go about twenty meters and set up to cover our people's retreat. In the meantime, get a bead on that guy, Lieutenant."

To the degree that it was possible from his position, Smith watched Grayson and two of his team members slither back and find cover that allowed them a clear view of the soldiers left behind.

"You ready Lieutenant?"

"The crosshairs are on his arm. I can't see any more of him."

"That's okay. An M16 round to the arm will ruin anyone's day. Fire on three. One...Two...*Three*."

Both guns flashed and speakers on the sides sounded with the crack of the shot.

And then, predictably, it all hit the fan.

The Delta team, figuring they could terrify the less experienced force, broke cover and charged forward, firing at the two people trying to retreat back to their unit. Smith's software registered a very near miss on his lawyer and he watched Delta's impressive speed and accuracy pulsating bright red as they approached.

Under normal circumstances, it was a sensible strategy. These were not normal circumstances, though.

Carrie and Duane, the computer tech, were shooting wildly, ignoring their targeting system and missing by wide margins. Grayson, however, wasn't so easily rattled. He nailed the lead attacker dead center and was lining up on another when the Delta team recognized that things weren't going their way, dropped, and disappeared behind uneven ground.

When Smith caught up with his team of misfits again, they were huddled against the broad trunk of a tree. All but Grayson were gulping wildly at the air and Smith thought Stacy might actually be in respiratory distress until she grinned and gave him the thumbs-up.

"Okay, now!" Smith said. "So what do you think? Shooting Delta guys is kind of fun, isn't it?"

Based on their expressions, they thought it was.

"So you want to hear the score? Major, you had a kill, congratulations. Lieutenant, unfortunately, you just got a graze, so no appreciable damage."

"Damn!" she said, the disappointment heavy in her voice.

"Don't be too hard on yourself, Lieutenant. That was a low-percentage shot for anyone. And you made your point getting that close."

"What about me, sir?" Grayson asked.

"Dead center of mass."

He pumped a fist in the air.

"So, by my calculations, your first engagement with Delta left your team fully intact, while you scored two kills and a graze. I'd call that a pretty good start to the day."

"So what now?" Duane said. "The rest of those guys aren't going to make the same mistake again."

Grayson nodded. "I think we should sweep northeast, so we can attack the mountain on the least steep side. With those kinds of losses, Delta's going to pull back to a defensive position, and frankly they're going to overestimate us. We can use that."

Based on an overhead image of the battlefield that only Smith could see, Grayson was exactly right. Delta was setting up to keep an extremely professional opponent from climbing the hill, focusing on the steeper southern and western slopes. The east slope had a far less practical entry point but it was probably the only one this group would be able to get up.

The rain started to recede and Smith followed as they moved out again. They passed right by the two "dead" Delta soldiers and he would have loved to see the look on their faces, but the thermal overlay had strengthened to the point that subtlety of expression was obscured.

Grayson had put Stacy, the heavier of the two women, on point. She looked exhausted and he'd obviously decided to sacrifice her if need be. Probably not realistic in real combat but one of those easy calls to make in a training exercise.

"Wait," Smith heard Stacy say quietly over his Merge. "Corporal. Come up here and look at this, please."

Smith stayed where he was, bringing up a window that displayed her unit's input. She was looking at the ground between two trees and, more specifically, a thin blue line running between them.

"Sneaky bastards," he heard Grayson say. "Everybody

step over the trip wire between the rocks. Don't worry, you can't miss it."

Amazing. The tiny wire should have been virtually invisible, but instead there might as well have been a sign with an arrow and "booby trap" written in foot-high letters.

They continued on, finally stopping just before they reached a broad riverbed with only a few inches of water left. It would be just over twenty-five meters of open ground to the trees on the other side.

"Can we get around it?" Duane asked.

Grayson's eyes went distant and flicked around as he pulled up a satellite image of the area and examined it in the air in front of him. "Nope. We have to cross it to get to the base of the hill and there isn't anywhere that's any narrower."

"So what do we do?" the lawyer said.

"We run for it," Grayson said, moving to the edge of cover and scanning the landscape for any sign of the enemy. "You first, Major. Fast as you can."

That turned out not to be all that fast, but he gave it his all and made it to the other side safe. Grayson went with Carrie next, having her start fifty meters downstream to keep their crossing points random. She looked like she was going to make it, when a distant shot sounded.

It was a hit and Smith winced as her Merge reduced her vision and balance by seventy percent, pitching her against the rocks and sending her rolling into what was left of the river. He'd need to talk to someone about attenuating that feature when people were running or in dangerous terrain.

"Stay down!" Grayson shouted, forgetting that his

voice was being projected directly into her mind. Not that
it mattered. The software would reduce the volume to optimal.

Despite his warning, she panicked and tried to get up.
Smith could have shut down her unit and called it a kill,
but decided to instead watch her struggle to her knees and
then fall over again. After one more halfhearted try, she
just lay there panting.

"Sir?" Grayson said and Smith frowned, trying to decide how much he wanted to say. "Seventy percent damage. With attention, she might survive."

"Shit," the Ranger said under his breath. "We need
to deal with this damn sniper. We're in the low ground,
though, and I can't pick him out." He dropped his pack.
"I'm going to go up a tree."

"Hold on," Duane said, showing a flash of confidence
for the first time that day. "I can do that. When I was a
kid, we had these huge cherry trees in our yard. I used to
climb them all the time."

Grayson hesitated for a moment but then gave a short
nod. "And don't come down until you find that shooter."

Smith was a little alarmed when the kid ran to the
tallest tree near them and started into the branches. No
one was supposed to get hurt and he already had a woman
trapped on the riverbank who looked a little worse for the
wear. What he didn't need was this kid falling out of a
tree and breaking his neck.

So he jogged over and started up through the branches
in pursuit. Duane couldn't have weighed much more than
a buck forty. If the wheels fell off, Smith figured he might
actually be able to catch him.

20

Southern New Mexico
USA

CRAIG BAILER GLIDED ALONG the empty rural highway, keeping the rented car's speed steady. Inasmuch as dashboard-mounted GPS units had made maps seem obsolete, the Merge was an even more fundamental leap forward. Even with the limitations of the bare-bones apps included with the first-generation model, the act of driving felt transformed. The road ahead glowed yellow, a color he'd initially opposed because of the obvious Wizard of Oz parallel. He'd been overruled by Javier de Galdiano's tech team, though, due to some technical minutiae about how the brain processed color. And once again, de Galdiano had been right.

More important than the interface, though, was the fact that the images transmitted to his mind were being constantly analyzed and monitored—for children and animals at the edges of the road, for unusual actions or the blind spots of surrounding drivers, as well as constant comparisons to actual and posted speeds. Finally, the sleep function, which worked both ways, subtly manipulated his brain patterns to keep him alert.

It was just a taste of what was to come, though. By next year, Mercedes and a number of other car manufacturers would include compatible cameras with various visual enhancements, as well as links to cruise control, braking, and steering during emergency situations.

That is, if Christian Dresner didn't destroy the company first.

"Call David Tresco," he said aloud in the empty car. Unfortunately, it was still too lengthy a command for the Merge to deal with mentally.

"Cell, home, or office?" came the response in his head.

"Cell."

There were no visual cues at all—most apps and icons were deactivated when the user was behind the wheel—but he could hear the quiet sound of dialing followed by ringing at the other end.

"Where are you?" Tresco said, not bothering to hide his irritation at what he had called "all this clandestine bullshit." It was a judgment that he would be revising very soon.

The yellow path ahead broke right into a solitary gas station.

"I'm about to pull in."

Bailer eased up to the man's SUV, stopping only long enough for him to jump in before accelerating again.

"Okay. I'm here. What's the hell is all this about?"

Tresco was a former oil industry CEO and now was one of Dresner Industries' most influential board members. He was not, however, an easy man to deal with.

"We have some problems that I want to talk to you about."

"I just read through your reports about the rollout. It sounds like we're exceeding projections in every category. And the press has been more positive than any one of us could have hoped—even about the implants. What problems could possibly be important enough to drag me to a gas station in the middle of nowhere on Saturday? My goddamn grandkids are in town."

"The development of the Merge was a lot more expensive and difficult than you're aware of," Bailer said simply.

He didn't take his eyes from the road, but the fact that there was no immediate response suggested that his statement had been enough to put grandchildren out of Tresco's mind. He was not a man accustomed to not having all the facts.

"I don't understand what you're saying to me, Craig."

"We incurred expenses and debt that've been moved to subsidiaries and partnerships all over the globe."

Tresco didn't respond immediately. When he did, he spoke cautiously. "How much debt?"

"Enough to bankrupt the company even if we sell double our projected volume. If we're clever, we might be able to meet our obligations next month. But the month after that, there's no way in hell."

"Why did you keep this from me?" Tresco said, caution turning to fear. "I didn't know anything about it."

"I doubt anyone will believe that."

"Was that a threat, Craig? Are you threatening me?"

Of course, that was exactly what he was doing. But there was no reason to be explicit about it. Tresco was an extremely wealthy man with a carefully crafted and impeccable reputation. He would do whatever was necessary to protect the status he'd spent a lifetime building.

Bailer handed him a tablet and turned onto an even more desolate road that led into the rugged Organ Mountains. Crosswinds buffeted the car, but couldn't be blamed for Tresco's increasingly pale complexion as he scrolled through the graphs and charts.

"How…How did this happen? How could you *let* this happen?"

"I was aware of some of it, but I only recognized the extent about a year ago."

"But Christian—"

"Christian can't be trusted anymore. There was a time when he'd listen to financial realities, but as he's gotten older he's become more and more isolated. He lives in his own world now. A world he believes he can save. And it's causing him to make stupid decisions like focusing on a search system that makes judgments about people, and software that's specific to the financial industry and politicians. It's also caused him to limit our military sales to only a small percentage of soldiers worldwide."

Tresco shut down the tablet and stared out at the dead, rocky hills speeding by. His hand shook visibly as he wiped the sweat from around his mouth.

"We need to move Dresner out, David."

Tresco let out a bitter laugh. "Do you have any idea what that'll do to our stock price?"

"We'll do it quietly. Keep him in place as a figurehead."

"I'm finding it very hard to believe he's going to just give up his position at a company he spent his life building. And how does that help our cash flow? No. We're going to have to look for a partner."

"We can't sell off a significant interest in the company, David."

"Why not?"

"There are things that would come to light..." His voice faded for a moment. "Things that need to stay in the dark."

"The offshore debt?"

"It's not the financial issues, David."

"What then?"

Bailer took in a deep breath and let it out slowly. Even in the confines of the car, it was hard to say these things out loud.

"The human mind is a very complicated piece of engineering. Maybe the most complicated thing we know of. It's difficult to find an adequate substitute for it. When the research started, we used chimps—"

"So what?"

"So, there's only so much you can learn from experimenting on the mind of a monkey. Eventually, we had to move to human subjects."

"I don't understand what you're getting at."

"Some of the tests—particularly the early ones—weren't entirely successful."

Again, Tresco seemed to be struggling to process what he was hearing. "Are you telling me that some of the volunteers were harmed?"

Bailer shook his head, accelerating around a tight curve and looking down the steep slope leading to the valley below. "What I'm telling you is that they weren't volunteers, David. And they were more than harmed."

21

Fort Bragg, North Carolina
USA

Take it easy," Jon Smith said. "You don't want to get spotted."

Above him, Duane was all nervous energy and heavy breathing as he struggled unflaggingly upward. In truth, the wind was moving the branches around enough to obscure all the flailing, but they were more than ten meters from the ground and Smith wasn't anxious to test his theory that he could arrest the kid's fall.

He obeyed, his panting evening out as they continued to rise. Beyond his rifle getting caught a few times, Duane was surprisingly solid. It appeared that tree climbing was like riding a bicycle—once you'd nailed it, no amount of sitting in front of a computer screen was enough to make you forget.

"This looks like a good spot," Smith said when they came to a place where enough of the bright fall leaves had dropped to provide a clear view of the landscape without exposing them. Grayson had tucked the team into cover and the only person visible below was Carrie, still lying in the riverbed. Dresner's training software had immediately degraded her Merge to thirty percent operability, but she was now down to twenty-seven as it simulated her decline in the absence of medical attention. At this point, even if she hadn't been told to stay down, he doubted she'd even have the ability to crawl. For a self-professed pacifist, Christian Dresner could design a hell of a nasty military app.

"Okay, Duane. I know it's hard in this kind of terrain, but think about where you heard the shot come from and what line of sight the sniper would have had to hit Carrie. Then look for..."

His voice faded when he realized that his advice was pointless—instructions on how to start a fire by rubbing two sticks together given to a student with a lighter. The rain had stopped and the Merge was having no problem at all picking up the sniper at a range of just over four hundred meters. There was a pink body-heat plume seeping from the edges of what Smith assumed was a rain poncho scattered with dead foliage. Even more obvious was the enhanced outline of a rifle barrel, which the Merge now also identified by make and model—an enhancement the coding team had just finished. It should have also determined whether they were in range of the weapon but a glitch they hadn't been able to find was causing that data to come up garbage.

"Yeah, I got him," Duane said excitedly. "He's right there!"

"Okay, good job. Anyone else?"

A brief pause. "Not that I can see. Just him."

Smith squinted uselessly, but came up just as empty.

"The others must have pulled back to set up a defensive position closer to the flag."

The young man nodded, his helmet floating on his head a bit. "What do we do?"

The sniper was technically within range of the M16s their training weapons were made to simulate, though only for a good shot lying on firm ground. But what the hell? They were out here to experiment, right?

"Shoot him."

"What? I can't hit him from here. He's like a mile away, sir."

"Then you'll miss him. And if you do, we're going to get the trunk of this tree between him and us, and we're going to very carefully climb to the ground. Him scoring against you is less of a problem than you falling. Understood?"

Duane gave a short, frightened nod as Smith altered the way the young man's Merge treated a hit—disabling the subroutine that would degraded his vision and balance for one that read out the damage percentage only.

"Find a solid position and lean your rifle on a branch. What's your targeting system saying?"

Duane hugged the tree and pressed the side of the weapon against the trunk, which was thick enough to resist the light winds. "The crosshairs have come up and it says he's four hundred and twelve meters away. It's asking for wind direction."

"What do you think? That's because it's such a long shot."

"Pretty much left to right."

"Okay. That's due east. Enter it."

"It's asking for speed."

"And?"

"I don't know. Maybe five miles an hour?"

Smith had significantly more experience judging these kinds of things and decided to cheat a bit. "Why don't you put in seven?"

"Done."

"Okay, Duane. Your team needs to get across that clearing alive. And for them to do that, you need to shoot that son of a bitch. Or at the very least, put the fear of God into him."

"Should I tell them what I'm going to do?" Corporal Grayson's voice suddenly filled their heads. "We're already listening on the open comm. We're ready. Let us know how you do and if we should go."

"Roger," Duane said and then held his breath while he adjusted his aim. It was an odd thing to watch—there was no scope or sights on the weapon, and thus no need for him to look along the barrel.

"Don't jerk the trigger," Smith said. "It's got a nice light pull. Just an easy squeeze when you've got your crosshairs on him."

The artificial sound of the rifle sent the birds sharing the tree into the air and Smith watched the readout in his peripheral vision.

"Jesus . . ."

"It's a hit!" Duane shouted. "Go. Go!"

The sound of the team sprinting across the riverbed drifted up to them as the Delta sniper's combat effectiveness number rolled down to forty-five percent. He lurched from beneath the poncho and, respecting the rules of the game, stumbled along in an awkward retreat. Duane got off another shot, but with the addition of movement into the equation, there was no way he could finish the job. Smith, though, knew that he himself could have easily. Incredible.

As they started to the ground, he tried to concentrate on what he was doing but found himself distracted by the green dots representing two of his team dragging Carrie to the safety of the trees. There was no doubt that it was critical information, but maybe a little too much for his present situation.

On the other hand, the kids who had grown up on video games might be able to handle the varied input better. And every study the military had ever done on women suggested a significantly superior ability to multitask. Yet another thing to add to his endless list of things to explore.

When they hit the ground, they ran immediately to the riverbed and managed to cross with no resistance. With fifty-five percent degradation, their Delta opponent wouldn't attempt a shot that difficult. He'd be retreating toward the flag and help.

When they rejoined their team, all were huddled around Carrie, with the exception of the Ranger, who was crouched behind a tree keeping lookout.

"What do we do with her, Colonel?" Stacy said. "She can't walk."

"This is war," Smith said. "What would you do if we were in Afghanistan?"

They discussed it among themselves and decided one person should stay behind and wait with her for an evac.

"Which one of us?" Gregory Kent asked.

Smith shrugged. "Your call."

Grayson returned to the group, looking impatient.

"We've got these sons of bitches on the run and we need to press the advantage. Who here is the most cooked?"

"I feel good," Duane said, still running on adrenaline.

"I'm tired, but okay," Stacy chimed in, still looking game. Her file had said she was an avid swimmer and it seemed to be serving her well despite the extra pounds.

"Major?" Grayson said, turning his attention to the overweight man sitting in the mud.

He hesitated a moment before speaking. "I'm getting a little old for this kind of thing. I don't know if I'm going to make it up that slope."

Grayson gave a short nod. "No dishonor, sir. Someone needs to stay here and you've already made your kill for the day. Now let's move out."

*　*　*

OKAY, WE'RE HERE," Grayson said, pointing to a laminated map that was still easier to use in a group than the Merge. They'd made it to the base of the eastern slope leading to the flag—not quickly by any stretch of the imagination, but with no injuries. The downside, though, was that the two non-combat soldiers were tired enough that they were stumbling every time they sped up to even a slow jog.

Grayson slid his finger across the wet map. "I'm saying that our injured sniper is here. The terrain above him is too steep to climb in his condition and coming around this way is too far. He's going to dig in as a first line of defense."

"So you think the others have pulled back to the flag?" Stacy said.

He nodded. "And that leaves their forces divided. I say

we take advantage of that. I want you two to move directly up the ridge. Take it easy and stay low. I'm going to swing around behind him through the harder terrain and we'll catch him in a crossfire."

"What about the people above?" Duane asked.

"The rain's coming in and that's going to keep visibility down. I think we'll be okay."

"You think?"

"Combat's like Vegas. There's no sure thing. It's about playing the percentages."

Grayson took off up the steep slope and the other two started along the ridge at the best pace they could manage. The Ranger had been right about the rain: A few heavy drops quickly escalated into a roaring downpour.

Smith took a different route, switching his Merge's frequency to the one being used by Delta.

"Lieutenant Raymond, this is Colonel Smith coming in on your position from the south."

"Understood," came the response.

Grayson had guessed right about his injured opponent but had taken a more cautious route that allowed Smith to beat him. When Smith arrived, he found the unhappy Delta man lying in a shallow depression that was quickly filling with water. Smith lay down next to him, feeling his fatigues finally soak completely through. Fortunately, the temperature was hanging on just north of eighty degrees.

"How's it going?"

Raymond shook his head miserably. He'd been hit in the shoulder and had immobilized the arm by tying it to his torso.

"I figure I'm bleeding out, sir. Twenty-five-meter accuracy at best. Who the hell are these guys?"

"You wouldn't believe me if I told you."

Raymond frowned, undoubtedly believing that he was up against some new black ops team carefully disguised to pass as a typical slice of Midwestern America. He slid forward out of the water a bit, sinking his elbow in the mud and scanning to the east through his scope.

Smith didn't need to rely on anything quite so primitive. Now that he was motionless, he could expand his overhead view of the battlefield. Two green dots were coming slowly up the slope in front of them and another was making slightly better time on the trickier approach behind.

More interesting were the red dots. One, of course, was right next to him, but instead of both of the remaining Delta soldiers protecting the flag, only one was. The other was coming down what must have been a nightmarishly slick gully overhead. They hadn't left their sniper behind just as a first line of defense—they'd left him behind as bait.

"Good luck," Smith said, rolling out of the deepening water and heading for a neutral position where he could get a good view without giving away Raymond's position.

It was raining hard enough now that the imaging system was being supplemented by a beta version of a motion-canceling software that Dresner was developing in conjunction with Mercedes. In the absence of wind gusts, rain droplets tended to fall along a predictable trajectory and at a predictable rate. The software hid everything coming down at that speed, while highlighting motion that didn't fit the pattern. The image it produced was a bit bizarre but, once you got used to it, provided an enormous amount of information.

It took less than a minute for Duane and Stacy to come

into view at about a hundred meters. When they crossed ninety, both dropped suddenly to the ground and aimed their weapons at the Delta man. Amazing. Smith toggled off his vision enhancement and estimated unaided visibility at less than twenty meters.

When he brought his Merge back up he saw his people fire in unison. Both missed, but they got close enough that Raymond got a proximity warning in the form of the hiss of a bullet playing over his earpiece.

He immediately pulled back, going down awkwardly in the water and coming up spitting mud. Smith had linked to the Delta team's comm and he heard Raymond's warning a moment later. "I'm under attack from the east. Can't see anyone but I nearly took another hit. Who the hell *are* these guys?"

The red dot coming down from above started traversing east toward Duane and Stacy as Grayson continued to close from the southwest. Things were about to get interesting.

Smith finally managed to spot the Ranger, his outline appearing and disappearing as the prototype software tried to deal with the wind starting to whip up the slope. The sun broke out of the clouds for a moment, glimmering off the raindrops but improving visibility slightly. It turned out to be just enough for the soldier above. A shot sounded and a moment later Duane's combat effectiveness number spun to zero.

"I...I'm hit...I can't see!" he said, sounding panicked. "I can't see!"

"Calm down," Smith said. "You're going to be black for ten seconds, then your unit's just going to shut down. Stay put until I tell you otherwise."

Stacy fired at the man coming down on her position, but she didn't take time to aim properly. Smith couldn't spot her target but could see that the red dot had stopped and that Stacy's retreat was slow even for her. He assumed that she'd gotten close enough to force the Delta soldier to take cover and was dragging Duane along with her.

"He's dead, Stacy. Get the hell out—"

Another gunshot sounded and her health counter spun to zero. With the advantage of the Merges and their early success, it was easy to forget one critical thing: The men they were up against were off-the-charts good.

He turned toward Grayson as he continued his cautious approach. Lieutenant Raymond was on his back in the water, looking directly in the Ranger's direction but unable to see him calmly raising his dripping rifle. The shot registered center of mass and a few expletives escaped the dead sniper as Grayson rushed the shallow impression and dove in.

Knowing that they were still invisible to the Delta man above, Smith ran over and slipped into the water with the two men.

"Looks like just me left, huh, Colonel?" Grayson's Merge would have taken Stacy's and Duane's icons off the battlefield overview.

"You know how it goes. Things can fall apart in a hurry."

Grayson nodded, propping his rifle on a wet rock at the edge of the indention they were submerged in. "Let's see if we can bring it back to even odds."

Lieutenant Raymond sat silent, futilely searching the rain for what Grayson was aiming at.

The Ranger squeezed off a round and Smith watched the approaching soldier's effectiveness spin to zero.

"Sir?" Grayson said, wanting feedback on the shot.

Smith just shook his head in disbelief. "That's a kill. You're one-on-one now."

22

Near Santiago
Chile

EVERYTHING IN THE ROOM was a perfect white, every inch of wall, ceiling, and floor glowing with the same soft light. The temperature was controlled at exactly seventy-two degrees by radiating panels so that there was no movement of air.

It was his blank canvas—a place that Christian Dresner could quiet his mind enough to think. Or at least that had been the plan.

In the far corner, a fifty-inch computer monitor was built into the wall and a keyboard sat beneath it on a small shelf. Despite their inconspicuous design, they seemed to dominate the room, an archaic intrusion bordering on vulgar. A reminder of his failure to remake the world.

The monitor displayed a ribbon of yellow-tinted road and the dusty, mountainous landscape moving past its edges—a direct feed from Craig Bailer's Merge.

Generally speaking, it was impossible to hack into the units and display their input. The software and bandwidth necessary for that kind of upload would be quickly discovered by a media already obsessed with outdated privacy issues. However, the company-issued units didn't have those constraints, leaving him the ability to provide important players in his world with hardware he could access at the press of a button.

Dresner stood beneath the monitor and watched as Bailer glanced over at David Tresco in the passenger seat and then faced the windshield again to negotiate a treacherous corner. The image seemed hazy and unwieldy, but the use of the monitor had proved necessary when viewing this type of output. Trying to run the images directly into his own visual cortex induced nausea.

He chewed his lower lip thoughtfully. It always came back to vertigo and nausea. The mind had evolved to be very rigid about how it received input. If the information didn't come from the eyes, nose, ears, skin, or tongue, the brain wanted to reject it. Perhaps more youthful adopters would learn to handle the dissonance. The young mind was incredibly adaptable.

The road on screen straightened and the image moved back to Tresco before the limitations of the cellular network carrying the data caused it to freeze. Dresner moved forward a few steps, examining the man's horrified expression for a few seconds before the feed started again.

"You used the North Koreans like lab animals?" he said. "Jesus Christ, Craig. How many died? How many were permanently disabled?"

"I don't know the exact number. It—"

"You don't know the number? My God, it's so many you don't know the number? How could you get involved in something like this? How could Dresner get involved in something like this? He—"

"Why, when, how," Bailer said, the hidden speakers in the wall picking up the increasing volume of his voice. "It doesn't matter anymore. What matters is that it happened and we need to deal with it."

"I didn't know anything about it," Tresco said, trying futilely to calculate a way to save himself. "I wasn't told."

The image kept flicking from the increasingly panicked David Tresco to the winding road ahead.

"Whether you or anyone else on the board knew isn't going to matter, David. If this comes out, no one is going to care about the details of who knew what when. Dresner Industries will collapse, I'll be tried for crimes against humanity, and you'll spend the rest of your life either in prison or fighting to stay out of it. The public will demand its pound of flesh. Whether you're guilty or not won't make any difference at all."

Tresco froze again, but this time it wasn't the network. He seemed paralyzed, staring sightlessly through the windshield at a world he'd taken so much from. A world that now seemed to want it all back.

Bailer returned his attention to the road. "We can fix this."

"Fix it? How could this ever be fixed?"

It was an interesting question and Dresner listened as he turned away from the monitor and focused on the blank white of the wall behind him. The car noise and wind were being filtered out by his own Merge but the audio was still degraded—the result of Bailer continuing to use the primitive structure of his inner ear instead of the microphones that had proved so superior.

"As you know, we have no signed exclusivity agreement with the U.S. military and we've received no payment from them that would obligate us. It's nothing more than a verbal agreement that Dresner made. Another example of him trying to save the world."

"So?"

"I've quietly spoken to the Chinese government and they're willing to use a number of private corporations they control to infuse enough cash for us to cover our short-term obligations. In return, we'll provide them with the same ability to link to offensive weapons that we gave to America."

"And do they know about the Koreans?"

"No. And there's no reason for them to. They aren't buying a controlling stake in the company. They're essentially paying us to abandon our exclusive agreement with—"

Dresner shut off the sound and accessed LayerCake's mapping program, bringing up a satellite image of the area Bailer was driving through. His position came up, as did the position of another car about two kilometers behind.

The man in that car had been following the CEO for two months and Dresner sent him a brief text. One that he'd hoped wouldn't be necessary.

The dots representing the cars began to merge as the chase vehicle accelerated and closed the distance between them. When they appeared to be nearly touching, Dresner turned back to the monitor to once again see through Bailer's eyes. The car was visible in the rearview mirror but Bailer didn't seem to notice, continuing to shift his gaze between the road and Tresco, who was speaking silently on screen. There was no need to turn the sound back on. What the two men had to say was no longer of any importance.

Dresner pulled up an icon that existed only on his unit and could be activated only by commands from his mind. A list of names fanned out and he selected Bailer's, bringing into existence a pulsing "activate" button at the edge of his vision.

He watched for a few more minutes, waiting until Bailer started into a sharp right turn. He would have preferred something more tangible like a rock wall, but the satellite image showed no such obstacles ahead. The curve, and more specifically the steep slope at its edge, would have to do.

23

Fort Bragg, North Carolina
USA

I LIKE THE NEW DIGS," Smith said, entering a room that didn't look much bigger or more luxurious than a storage closet. Maggie Templeton frowned but didn't look up from the laptop she was working on. Without her massive monitors and battleship-bridge of a desk she looked kind of naked.

He'd received orders to immediately report to this forgotten corner of Fort Bragg right after wrapping up his training exercise. The smart money was that it was General Pedersen screwing with him and he was a little shocked to see Covert-One making an appearance outside its Maryland hideaway. Klein—and by extension President Castilla—were clearly taking the Merge seriously.

Maggie thumbed behind her and Smith started obediently toward a doorway with a missing door.

The room he entered was slightly larger, but even more full of junk—stacked folding tables, rusting file cabinets, and even a few old footlockers. Somehow, though, Fred Klein's presence made it all feel like polished mahogany and portraits of George Washington. The man had a way of creating his own gravity.

"I hear you got the flag."

"I was down to my last man, but yeah, we won," Smith said, falling into a rolling chair with a broken wheel.

"So what is your initial impression of the Merge's field capability?"

"Well, I just took out an entire Delta team with one ranger and four noncombat personnel—a couple of whom probably get winded taking out their garbage. I think it's fair to say that my initial impression is positive."

"Then you believe this is something the Defense Department should be putting resources into."

"No question. The advantage in a simple ground-combat scenario where one side has it and the other doesn't is incredible. I proved that today."

"Downsides?"

"Dresner has a fair amount of control. He could decide to walk away from his agreement and start selling it on the open market. Or he could flake out and refuse to let us add apps to the system. Is there anything we can do about that?"

"Probably not," Klein admitted. "My hope was that we'd just be able to crack the encryption and keep that in our back pocket if Dresner tries to shut us out. I gave the NSA one of the prototypes, though, and they don't even know where to start with breaking into it."

Smith nodded. It was basically the same thing his people were telling him. "As far as him opening up sales, it's a risk we have to deal with anyway. Foreign militaries are going to use the commercial version and we're going to have to develop countermeasures. While we're at it, we'll be thinking about how to defend against military versions, in case they ever hit the street. Worst case, we get a significant head start on countries like China. Also, you have to consider that we're focused on unsophisticated opponents right now and it's going to be a huge advantage against those kinds of forces."

Klein leaned back and lit a pipe. The elaborate ventilation system that he had in Maryland was lacking, though, and a moment later Maggie Templeton's shout came through the door. "Smoke!"

He frowned and put it out. "You spoke directly with Dresner, didn't you? What's your take? Assuming he doesn't stab us in the back, how hard is he going to be to work with?"

"It's going to be a constant give-and-take. We're going to lean hard toward defining everything as military-specific and he's going to come up with fifty civilian uses for whatever we propose. The ability to connect directly to weapons is pretty objective, though. That's never going to filter down to the civilian version."

"So your advice is to bend over and take it."

Smith shrugged helplessly. "'Fraid so, Fred. The world keeps moving on whether we like it or not."

"So much for military budget cuts." Klein sighed.

"Tell Treasury to fire up the printing presses because I can personally guarantee you that we're going to want a hundred percent penetration in combat personnel."

"What about the technology itself? Downsides and dangers?"

"Obviously, that's something we need to evaluate, but I don't see many. I can tell you from personal experience that the body modifications are pretty much irrelevant—

a couple of days of discomfort that a few aspirin will knock out. I've talked to a number of top neurologists and they see no real potential for physical or psychological damage. The audio and video signals created by the Merge aren't any different from the ones generated by your eyes and ears. We'll have to guard against soldiers getting overly dependent on it, but that's true of any technology: Guns jam, Humvees break down, planes crash. Basically, it's just a question of what the tech gurus can develop and how practical it will be in the field."

"You mean what *you* can develop."

"Excuse me?"

"You'll be heading up the development of the Merge's military potential."

"Me? I'm a medical doctor, Fred. A microbiologist."

"False modesty doesn't suit you, Jon. You're a gifted leader and an extremely capable scientist with extensive combat experience. Who better?"

"I really don't think this is going to be workable, Fred. General Pedersen will go absolutely ballistic if I end up running this thing."

Klein's expression turned thoughtful. "And yet, the president still doesn't care."

24

Southern New Mexico
USA

SEAN MAHER ACCELERATED to within fifty meters of the Ford in front of him and then slowed to match its speed. Even at that distance, it was impossible to keep it fully in sight as it ducked and twisted through the rocky landscape. A far cry from his home in Ireland, but perfect for the task at hand. The last car had passed in the oncoming lane almost fifteen minutes ago and the wind was starting to gust strongly enough to rock his SUV. No-man's-land.

He'd been told what to expect, but still wasn't fully prepared when it happened. The vehicle had been traveling at exactly the posted speed since he first got a visual and it maintained that monotonous pace as it started into a sharp right-hand curve.

This corner was no different from any of the hundreds of others in the area. This time the Ford veered left, heading toward the steep, unprotected slope at the road's edge. Through the glare coming off the rear window, Maher could see the man in the passenger seat lunge for the wheel.

The vehicle lost traction and the sound of straining rubber rose above the rumble of his engine and the wind. It might have actually stayed on the road had the passenger not panicked and overcorrected. Instead, the rear drifted out over the slope and gravity did the rest.

Maher released the accelerator and let the SUV drift, watching the car drop backward onto the steep grade and pick up speed. It hit a rut near the bottom and rose up on two wheels, teetering precariously before rolling onto its roof.

By the time Maher came to a stop on the shoulder, the Ford had flipped again and come to rest on its wheels with a boulder rammed into the left front quarter panel.

He jumped out and began running as best he could down the loose terrain, looking for movement through glass spiderwebbed by the partially collapsed roof. Nothing obvious. Maybe this was going to be one of those rare instances of easy money.

As he got closer, though, he spotted motion in the passenger seat and was forced to abandon his fantasy of collecting payment with clean hands.

He swung around the trunk and gave the driver's-side door a few hard jerks, only to find it jammed. A rock and his elbow were enough to break out what was left of the safety glass.

As he'd been assured, the driver was dead—staring sightlessly at the ceiling with his head crammed between the pillar and the edge of the seat. Unfortunately, the man in the passenger seat wasn't in the same condition. He was badly dazed but fully conscious, blinking hard and pawing ineffectually at his seat belt.

Maher confirmed that the road above was still empty

and pulled himself through the window frame, using the driver's body for leverage. The surviving passenger finally realized that he wasn't alone and squinted at him, confusion turning to relief.

"Help me get this—"

Instead, Maher grabbed the man's head and slammed it into the side window. He was caught entirely by surprise but quickly began to fight. Not that his resistance was the issue—he was old and weak from the crash. The problem was that the broken safety glass was soft enough to absorb impact.

The dashboard would have been better but the deployed air bags could raise the suspicions of an overzealous medical examiner. Not that it was likely anyone would give two traffic deaths on a treacherous road that much thought, but there was always a chance. And this operation was sloppy enough as it was.

Maher kept at it, breathing hard and working up a sweat as he hammered the man's skull into the glass, dodging fingers clawing weakly at him. His public role as unsuccessful rescuer would look suspect if his skin was found beneath the old man's meticulously buffed nails.

His shoulders burned with fatigue and the sound of his own ragged breathing filled the confined space, but he continued until the man finally slipped into unconsciousness. There was not time to rest, though. Not yet.

He shoved himself back through the window and dropped to the ground, sliding beneath the car to tear through the fuel line with an array of multi-tool implements that wouldn't leave an obvious cut mark. Again, probably unnecessary, but it was impossible to be too thorough in his line of business.

Fuel leaked onto the sun-heated ground and he used a lighter to ignite it. The smoke rose quickly, curling thick and black in the unpredictable winds.

Maher held a sleeve to his face, choking as he retreated to a safe distance. The sound of an engine became audible above and he saw a car pull up behind his rented SUV. A middle-aged couple jumped out and he swore under his breath as he moved back into the smoke and tugged uselessly on the superheated door handle—a quick and extremely painful show for his new audience.

They shouted at him as he retreated, but it was impossible to understand what they were saying. Both were seriously overweight and neither looked capable of getting down the slope. Just to be sure that there would be no futile heroics, though, he let them off the hook by a cautionary wave that indicated he was fine and there was nothing more to be done.

Maher moved back a few more meters as the flames grew, keeping a close watch on the man in the passenger seat through occasional breaks in the smoke. He was consumed without ever regaining consciousness.

25

Khost Province
Afghanistan

RANDI RUSSELL FIRED a quick burst at the Afghan fleeing up the slope, but only managed to kick up a cloud
of shattered rock three meters to his left. It would have
been nice to get lucky, but the real purpose of wasting the
ammo was to give her two teammates time to find cover.

She'd spent the last three months tracking the men
who'd carried out an attack on a CIA outpost. Her normal
zeal for this kind of work had been magnified by her guilt
over being in Sarabat indulging Fred Klein's curiosity instead of watching her colleagues' backs. If she'd been
where she was supposed to be, maybe she could have
stopped it. Maybe her friends wouldn't have died.

Five of the six men responsible were already in the
ground. And the last was less than a football field away.

Behind her, Billy Grant slid on his hip and dropped
into a rocky furrow just deep enough to make him disappear. Deuce had found similar cover and from her position all that was visible of him was the top of his helmet.

It wasn't the normal government-issue headgear she

was familiar with, though. This one was created by a retired SEAL who now made a living building custom racing bicycles. Molded to the owner's head, it bristled with the ever-increasing array of gadgets that fed information to the Merges that had become nearly ubiquitous in active special forces. Apparently, he couldn't churn them out fast enough for the ops guys, who were willing to trade the dismal protection offered by carbon fiber for the weight savings.

Deuce's head didn't move, but his rifle snaked around the side of the boulder he was behind. Randi used her scope to look downrange and watched the Afghan dive to the ground when a round barely missed him. There was no denying that it was an impressive feat. Not only had the shot been incredibly difficult, but Deuce had fired it without breaking cover.

While she would take talent, courage, and character over technology any day, when you combined all four, the results were hard to deny.

Grant hadn't given himself over to the Merge quite as completely. He appeared over the lip of the ditch, sighting pointlessly over his rifle to take advantage of the fact that the target was briefly fixed. A moment later a chunk of the Afghan's left calf was torn away.

His pained cry was clearly audible as he bolted, fumbling something in his hand before leaping awkwardly over the top of a boulder. Both Deuce and Grant were firing now and Randi barely registered another spectacular shot that penetrated the back of the man's thigh right before he disappeared. Instead, she focused on the object he'd dropped as it rolled across the ground.

"Grenade!" she shouted, but neither man heard her over the sound of their weapons.

It exploded well before it reached them, but the force of the blast sent boulders careening down the slope in a cloud of reddish dust. Grant, maybe thirty meters east of her, was in the path of the worst of it. He leapt from the shallow groove but was almost immediately engulfed by the dust.

"Shit!" Randi said in a harsh whisper, trying to will him to reappear. Luck wasn't on their side, though, and when the air cleared she saw the dazed man struggling to reach his rifle with a leg pinned beneath a rock that probably weighed the better part of half a ton.

A shot hit the ground ten meters in front of the trapped soldier and she swore again. With too many bullets in him to go farther, the Afghan had dug in and was going to keep fighting until he bled out.

The next round was closer—four meters short and three right. It wasn't going to take long for him to zero in.

"Deuce—are you all right?" she said, touching her throat mike.

"Fine. But Billy's pinned and my angle on this asshole is crap."

"I need you to keep him busy for me. On my mark. One, two, *three*."

She darted from cover as Deuce let loose a series of controlled bursts upslope. It had been a hastily conceived plan and worked even worse than she expected. The Afghan either didn't care if he took another bullet or recognized the strength of his position. He'd been ready for her to try to get to her injured comrade and a round burned through the air just in front of her face.

There was no going back, though. She let her momentum carry her, charging toward the debris left by the grenade as a round impacted the butt of the rifle on her back, spun her around, and dropped her to the ground.

Deuce's weapon had gone silent in an effort to conserve ammunition and the Afghan used the opportunity to squeeze off another round. Randi tensed, but realized she was no longer the target when the bullet impacted less than a meter short of Billy Grant's right arm. He immediately abandoned his effort to reach his rifle and instead grabbed his blood-soaked thigh in a futile effort to free himself.

There was no question that the Afghan was going to hit him—if not with the next shot, then with the one after that. Randi was only ten meters from her trapped man, but that was ten meters too far in the present situation. And what would she do even if she could reach him? There was no way to free him that didn't involve at least a shovel and maybe a winch.

The next round was even closer and Grant scooted toward the boulder trapping him, contorting his broken leg into a grotesque shape in an effort to get as close as possible.

"Randi!" she heard Deuce say over her earpiece. "The new toy. Can you use it?"

"It got hit when I was running and I'm not sure I can even lift my head without it getting blown off," she said, wiggling out of her body armor and holding it up high enough for Grant to see. He looked like he was on the verge of passing out from the pain but managed a dazed nod.

She threw the heavy vest in his direction and it cartwheeled through the air, landing just behind him. He had barely pulled it in front of his chest when a bullet hit dead center, knocking him back with enough force to elicit an audible grunt. He was still alive, though. The multiple layers had absorbed the majority of the impact.

"Deuce!" Randi shouted. "Get me the hell out of here!"

Grant scooted toward the boulder again and tried to make himself as small as possible behind her vest, but there was still plenty of him exposed. And even if that weren't true, the situation was quickly becoming a disastrous stalemate—a race to see who bled to death first.

"Randi," she heard Deuce say in her earpiece. "I'm going to draw this guy's fire. When I do, run."

"Wait! I didn't mean—"

He ignored her and sprinted from cover as the Afghan opened up on him. Randi bolted from her position with equal speed, running east before dropping to her stomach at the edge of the debris field.

Deuce made it to safety, but his effectiveness would be right around zero unless he could find a way to get to a more strategic piece of ground. She, on the other hand, was finally in a position to assess their situation. The Afghan was about seventy-five meters to the north, lying behind two boulders tipped against each other. The gap between them was low and just large enough to get his rifle through, making him impervious to gunfire from below, but affording him only a narrow field of vision.

She saw a flash and Grant took another hit, rocking backward with the force of the round against her body armor. For a moment, she didn't think he was going to be able to right himself, but he threw a hand back and managed to stabilize before flashing her a courageous grin. His teeth were tinted pink with blood.

There was no way she was going to let him die. She'd lost too many friends already.

Randi dropped her M16 and pulled what Deuce called "the new toy" off her back. There was a fist-sized chunk blown off the butt and she couldn't help wondering what Heckler & Koch was going to charge to fix it. The combination of the XM25's thirty-five-thousand-dollar price tag and thirteen-pound weight had made her consider leaving it at home, but Deuce convince her otherwise. It seemed that his sixth sense for combat had come through again.

Randi was chambering the twenty-five-millimeter digital round when another shot sounded, quickly followed by the now-familiar thud of an impact against Kevlar.

"I think that one cracked a rib," Grant said just loud enough for her to hear. "I would really appreciate it if you'd kill that guy."

"Working on it."

The Afghan didn't have an angle on her so she rose up and sighted through a scope that she prayed hadn't been knocked out of alignment when the butt had been hit.

A laser judged the distance to the boulders the man was hiding behind at seventy-nine meters. Based on the few inches of barrel she could see protruding from the gap, it seemed likely that the rocks were a little less than a meter thick and that he was lying straight out behind them.

She clicked a button near the trigger and added one meter to the range, which would be right around his shoulder blades. Then there was nothing to do but see if the thing was worth the money the CIA had paid for it.

She aimed just over the top of the boulders and squeezed the trigger, feeling the painful jolt of the broken butt against her shoulder. Inside the bullet, a computer calculated the distance it traveled by counting rotations and, at exactly eighty meters, it exploded, sending deadly shrapnel down to earth.

Randi remained motionless, watching the barrel of the gun between the rocks waver and finally tip to the ground.

"Did it work?" Deuce said over her earpiece.

She panned the scope right and saw the telltale pockmarks in the dirt at the correct range, then scanned left and saw more. "Looks good," she said quietly. "But I can't guarantee anything."

"Only one way to find out," Deuce responded and then ran back out into the open, sprinting to his previous position. The Afghan's rifle remained motionless.

"Can you cover me from there, Deuce?"

"No way I can hit him from this position, but I should be able to kick up enough dust to throw off his aim."

"Do it."

She dropped the XM25 and drew her sidearm, running up the slope as Deuce fired repeatedly at the ground in front of the gap the man was aiming through.

She slowed when she got within ten meters, watching her footing and trying to remain silent as she closed on the Afghan's position. At five meters, Deuce stopped firing, concerned about catching her with a ricochet. She held her pistol in front of her, listening to the sudden silence as she edged around the boulders the Afghan was using for cover.

In the end, her weapon wasn't necessary. He lay motionless with his finger still curled around the trigger and his back riddled with the same tiny holes as the ground around him.

26

Central Marrakech
Morocco

GERHARD EICHMANN MOVED nervously through his home, retrieving a leaf from the ancient fountain in his entryway and checking for anything out of place.

He'd restored the derelict riad almost twenty years ago, combining it with two others and leaving most of the rooms open to three interior courtyards. There were no windows to the outside, creating a surprisingly profound sense of privacy and security in a city choked with shops, hawkers, and tourists.

He'd sent Hafeza to visit her family in the mountains and it was the first time in years that she hadn't been there to take care of him. Despite the fact that he'd been in Morocco almost as long as she'd been alive, he was still helpless—with only a rudimentary grasp of French, no Arabic, and a tendency to get lost in the maze of alleyways that tangled the city.

Eichmann pushed through a set of intricately carved wooden doors to confirm that the two chairs he'd set up next to the pool were still shaded and that the ice packed around the champagne hadn't melted. All was in order. Just as it had been the first three times he'd checked.

The thick stone walls still radiated the cold of the night before, but did nothing to keep the perspiration from beading on his forehead as he polished a smudge off the copper facade disguising a much more modern—and secure—door beyond. Where was the key? Had Hafeza moved it when she was cleaning? Would his guest want to enter?

Eichmann took a deep, calming breath. No. There would be no reason. The computers inside were all idle now. They had completed the initial analysis of almost a quarter century of data with no surprises. Further parsing of the information would undoubtedly yield unseen and fascinating details, but would in no way change the over-arching conclusion. The questions posed so long ago had been completely and finally answered.

The bell rang and he rushed to the door, heart pounding as he reached for the massive metal ring centered in it. How long had it been since they'd been face-to-face? Before the fame. Before the billions. Could it be thirty years?

Eichmann pulled the heavy door open and found Christian Dresner standing on the other side. His smile seemed to carry a deep sadness and his skin was looser and more mottled than the television and Internet suggested. Behind him stood two athletic men with earpieces and dark jackets despite the heat. They gave him a brief, suspicious glance before going back to scanning the rooftops and people passing the quiet spur that his door opened onto.

To his surprise, Dresner took a step forward and embraced him. "Gerd. My good friend," he said in the language of their lost youth. "My only friend."

The guards seemed content to stay outside. Eichmann pushed the door closed as Dresner looked around at the carefully preserved architecture. "I remember when you told me you were moving here. I have to admit that I didn't understand it until now. This is truly magnificent, Gerd."

Eichmann nodded self-consciously and led Dresner to the poolside chairs. As his guest sat, Eichmann fumbled with the champagne cork, conscious of Dresner watching him with an enigmatic, barely perceptible smile playing at his lips.

"It's hard to express how good it is to see you, Gerd. I can't believe it's been so long. Sometimes I look back on my life and wonder where I lost control of it. How it could have passed so quickly."

"I'm sorry about the circumstances," Eichmann said, finally getting the cork out and pouring.

"It's not your fault. A good scientist can only follow where the facts lead. I take it your analysis is complete?

"The initial pass. But it's a lifetime's worth of data. There is so much to learn."

"Not the things we wanted to learn, though. And not things that can ever be released to the public."

Eichmann averted his eyes and gave a short, obedient nod. The chiding was gentle but clearly intended. He'd hoped to publish a few properly veiled tidbits in minor psychology journals but, deep down, he'd known it would never be allowed. Anonymity was a small price to pay for the life he'd been allowed to lead. Everything—his quarter-century study, the house he lived in, the food on his table—came from Dresner.

While the academic community would never share in his discoveries, it was enough that he had made them. It was enough to know the truth, even if that truth would die with him.

He finally sat, if a bit stiffly, and held a thumb drive out to Dresner. "My detailed conclusions. And the Afghanistan video. Though I don't know if any of it matters anymore. If it was worth you coming all this way."

Dresner slid the drive into his shirt pocket without bothering to look at it. "That's not why I came. I'm here because, in many ways, my life is coming to a close. There will be no more breakthroughs. No more discoveries. I've done what I can with the time I was given."

Eichmann opened his mouth to protest, but fell silent when his friend held up a hand. "I find myself mired in the past more and more, Gerd. I suppose it's the inevitable nostalgia of old age. I think a great deal about our youth and the dreams we had. I'm here because you're the only person who understands..."

"You've succeeded beyond almost anyone in history, Christian. Sometimes the dreams of young men are just that. Dreams."

"Grand ones, though, eh, Gerd?"

"You underestimate the contribution you've made. LayerCake's feedback loop is a powerful behavioral tool—the ability to immediately determine lies, to see how our actions affect the way other people view us. And that's only the beginning. How can anyone—even you—imagine what will be built on your platform? What it could mean for the world?"

Dresner took a sip of champagne and squinted into the reflection coming off the pool. "I told myself that same thing for years. But now I've come to understand that it's a naive view. My work is no different from anyone else's. Powerful men will find a way to twist it into something that serves their purposes."

"But the Internet can't be controlled. There—"

"It *can* be controlled, Gerd. Everything can. How long will the freedom of information last if it becomes inconvenient to the wrong people?"

"It will be a constant battle," Eichmann agreed. "But not different from the one we've been fighting for millennia. Some people will try to spread the truth and others, lies."

"Eventually the liars and destroyers always win."

Eichmann didn't respond and his old friend seemed content to sip at his drink for a time. It was strange to have him there. The years they'd spent together when they were young didn't seem real anymore. It was hard to associate what he'd become with the much more human figure he'd been in his youth.

"My father was religious for much of his life," Dresner said when he finally spoke again. "Even the concentration camp and the Soviets couldn't take that from him. Slowly, though, he began to question how it could be that we were made in the image of God. Eventually, he came to believe that we were just another of God's animals—no greater or more favored than any other."

He tapped the thumb drive in his pocket. "But it took you to show me that even this was a fantasy."

"You're reading to much into my conclusions, Christian. It would be arrogance to think that my work has allowed either of us to see into the mind of God."

"The mind of God," Dresner repeated quietly. "I've

wasted more than a billion dollars trying to find some spark in us that would prove—or even just suggest—his existence. No, we're nothing more than computers made of meat. And not even well-designed ones at that—ones haphazardly slapped together over millions of years to deal with random environmental changes."

"But ones capable of great...and terrible things."

Dresner shook his head. "Even the most virtuous brain functions are just an illusion created to help our species survive. We don't love our children because of nobility or God. We love them because people who felt compelled to care for their offspring spread their genes more effectively. The illusion of fear makes us avoid dangerous situations. Greed keeps our bellies full. Violence and hate allow us to protect what is ours. Nothing we see or feel is anything more than millions of neurons fabricating a universe that doesn't exist."

Eichmann wasn't sure how to respond. While it was true that Dresner's conclusions were much more drastic than his own, it was also true that he was probably right. Giving up entirely on the idea of reality—accepting that everything was just a chimera created by selective pressures—was a step into a very dark and very lonely abyss. What *was* certain, though, was that humans were creatures much more of instinct than of culture and education.

People were born who they are and little could be done about it. Intelligence, personality, and behavior were largely programmed into every individual at birth.

"And the experiments at the North Korean facility have confirmed your beliefs?" Eichmann said, probing. He'd been indirectly involved in designing the general controls for some of the work done there, but was largely in the dark as to what that work was. Perhaps now he could finally get his old friend to speak of it.

"There are no more questions to answer," Dresner responded, his gaze turning distant. "The facility is being dismantled."

27

H<small>ARDER</small>!" R<small>ANDI</small> <small>SHOUTED</small> over the sound of rotor blades chopping the air behind her. Deuce and the medic threw their full weight on the levers dug in beneath the boulder pinning Billy Grant and raised it a few critical centimeters.

"Sorry about this," she said, grabbing him beneath the shoulders and heaving back. He let out a stifled scream and looked like he was finally going to lose consciousness from the pain, but she managed to get his leg clear before the boulder slammed back into place.

Arterial blood spurting from his leg suggested that they'd done the right thing leaving the stone in place until the evac arrived. Randi dropped to her knees and pressed a hand against the wound while the medic put a tourniquet in place.

"I'll clamp it when we're in the air!" he shouted, indicating for them to lift the injured man. "Now let's get the hell out of here!"

Randi felt the same guilt she always did when one of her people was injured and remained silent as they slid him through the open door of the chopper. The leg would never be the same, assuming the docs were even able to save it. She should have anticipated the grenade. She should have held Billy back...

Deuce jumped in behind the medic and Randi looked up at him for a moment before backing away a few steps.

"Where are you going?" he said. "Get in the chopper!"

She shook her head. "You guys go. I'll find my way back."

"Now, hold on, Randi. We were under orders to get the sons of bitches who attacked your base. And by my count, the asshole behind that rock was the last one."

"Yeah. But there's something else I want to check out."

Deuce rolled his eyes and said something she couldn't hear over the accelerating rotors, then jumped out with his gear.

"Seriously, Deuce—go with Billy. I'll be fine."

He waved at the pilot who immediately lifted the aircraft off the ground and began gaining altitude. They watched it recede into the horizon, not speaking until it was out of sight.

"So what the hell am I doing here, Randi?"

"I said I could handle it."

"Yeah, like I'm going to go back and tell everyone I just left you. If you got killed, I'd never live it down. Now tell me what we're interested in here, because it looks like the middle of nowhere to me."

She didn't respond immediately, instead turning her gaze to a cliff about twenty kilometers away. The sheer rock was pockmarked with tiny caves starting at about the sixty-meter mark and becoming more plentiful above. She focused on the largest and highest of them, finally pointing.

"Remember the survivor from Kot'eh I told you I caught up with?"

"The one you took down outside his village?"

She'd given Deuce—and everyone else—a less-than-honest report about what had happened. When Fred Klein was involved, it was always better to let go of as little information as possible.

"He told me—"

"Hold on. You *talked* to him?"

"Did I not mention that?" she said innocently.

He scowled deeply. "Must have slipped your mind."

"Well, he told me that they put the heads in that top cave."

"Oh, no, no, no. Sarabat again? That was *three months* ago, Randi. Let it go already."

"I did let it go," she said, reattaching the damaged XM25 to her pack and slipping the straps over her shoulders. "But now here we are. I figure it's karma."

"Karma my ass. I don't suppose you've noticed that the sun's going down and the terrain between here and there is pretty much one crappy scree field after another."

"We have about another hour of good light. We'll use it and then hunker down until dawn."

He looked at her like she was a slow child. "Are you kidding? We'll be standing at the mouth of that cave in three hours. Maybe less."

She shook her head. "I left behind my night-vision gear so I could bring the rifle."

He made a show of running a hand through the short hair just below his carbon-fiber helmet. The studs screwed into his skull were clearly visible—colored the matte black that had become fashionable with combat soldiers. "Pull yourself into the twenty-first century, bitch."

She scratched her nose with an extended middle finger. "Then you're on point, Ginger."

*   *   *

IN THE END, Deuce's time estimate was a little on the optimistic side—though Randi had to admit that it was her fault. For one of the first times in her life, she was experiencing what it was like to be the weak link.

They were now standing five meters from the mouth of the cave and the last four hours had been some of the hardest of her life. There was no question that Deuce was younger and stronger, but normally her experience still allowed a slight edge. The addition of his Merge, though, had put an end to that. He'd negotiated the loose, off-camber slopes like it was broad daylight, leaving her to stumble around trying to follow his footsteps in the dim starlight. Thank God the climb from the top of the ridge down to the cave had been easy—a track wide and flat enough for the Taliban to get their carts down. Otherwise, she'd have had to swallow her pride and hold on to him. Or more likely, refused and ended up a lump of broken flesh on the valley floor.

"What's the plan?" Deuce whispered, pulling his rifle in front of his chest.

"I don't see a lot of ways to get fancy. We're just going to have to poke our head in—"

"And see if it gets shot off," he said, finishing her sentence.

"I'll go first," Randi volunteered, removing her pack and fishing out a small flashlight.

"What the hell is that?" Deuce said. It was too dark to read his expression, but she could see the exasperated shaking of his head.

"It's a flashlight. Night vision isn't going to work inside—there's not enough light to amplify."

"Heat?"

"Not going to help keep you from falling in a hole," she said, unwilling to admit that while it wouldn't pick out natural obstacles, thermal imaging would be extremely effective at picking out anyone lying in wait for them. But she wasn't sending him in first. Billy was already down on her watch and if anyone else took a hit in this particular wild-goose chase, it was going to be her.

He brought up a shadowy hand and tapped a small box on the side of his helmet. It wasn't as seamlessly integrated as the other systems, suggesting that it was a new addition. "Active infrared. Invisible to the naked eye— meaning your eye, not mine—and good to about ten meters."

"Look, I don't care about all your electronics, Deuce. I'm going first."

He let out an audible breath. "Bullshit, Randi. But this is the last time I'm wet-nursing you. When we get back to base, you need to hop a transport to Kabul and get Merged up."

She swore quietly under her breath as he started toward the cave. They both knew he was right. Not only would her flashlight be obvious to anyone inside, it would be a dinner bell to the local Taliban.

If she had her way, wars would still be fought with

swords—a weapon of skill that forced you to look in the eye of the people you killed. But the world didn't go backward and now her distrust of overly complex combat technology was endangering not only her, but also the people who counted on her.

Randi pulled her sidearm and inched up behind Deuce, stopping when he held a hand out. She assumed he was running a countdown on his fingers, but she couldn't see them well enough to be sure.

He jerked his head into the cave for a split second and then stood staring into the darkness. She was about to ask him what the hell he was doing, but then realized that he'd taken a heavily enhanced photo and was now examining it in the empty air.

"I think we're good," he said before easing into the cave with her holding on to his shoulder.

"How deep is it?" she said, now completely blind.

"Dunno. Can't see the back. The ground's pretty flat, though. Just stay with me."

It turned out to be larger than she expected and they took multiple turns as they inched along. At first, there was nothing but their quiet footfalls for her senses to key in on, but then she caught a whiff of rotting flesh.

"You getting that?" she said.

"What?"

"You mean that thing doesn't smell for you?"

"Oh, wait. Yeah. Now I'm getting it."

Another two sharp bends and he came to a stop sudden enough to cause her to run into the back of him.

"What?" she whispered in his ear.

"I'm picking up something on heat. Range is twelve meters."

"Human?" she said, gripping her pistol a bit tighter.

"No. It's barely above background temp. Can't really get a shape."

The stench was fairly strong now, suggesting a possibility. "Bacteria create a little heat when they're breaking down flesh. Any chance it's our pile of heads?"

She felt him shrug and then start creeping forward. After a few seconds, he stopped again. "That's them. We've found your goddamn heads."

Randi slipped the flashlight from her pocket and held it up, knowing he'd be able to see it. "If I use this, is it going to screw up your vision?"

"Pull yourself into the—"

"Twenty-first century. I know, I know," Randi said, switching it on.

She was no expert on head piles, but to her calibrated eyeball it looked like all seventy or so adult male inhabitants of Sarabat. The skin of the visible ones had been dried into leather by the mountain air. She knelt, looking into the empty eye sockets of a heavily bearded face staring up at her. The smell and heat must have been coming from deeper in the pile where moisture still existed.

"Come on, Randi. Let's get out of here. It's just a bunch of heads."

She grabbed one by its long hair and shone the flashlight on it. Why were they here? And who paid those mercs to wipe out Kot'eh?

She set the head back down but then saw a strange glint in the hair. When she leaned in for a closer look, her breath caught in her chest.

"Randi, seriously," Deuce said. "I'm leaving before I

throw up. If you're this desperate for a souvenir, why don't you just take one?"

She slipped off her pack and opened the top to dump her non-essential gear.

"Jesus," Deuce whined as she shoved the decaying head inside. "I wasn't serious..."

28

Military Operation
East of the Walapai Test Center

JON SMITH CREPT ALONG the dirt road, eyes moving smoothly from side to side. Ancient-looking mud-brick buildings rose up on either side, most showing signs of years of fighting: arcing bullet holes, gaping RPG hits, and hastily stacked debris from collapses. The people in the street seemed uninterested in the destruction, preferring to focus their suspicious gazes and muttered Dari comments on him and his men.

About ten meters ahead, a horse-drawn cart piled with scrap metal had broken a wheel and was stopped diagonally in his path. Two men in traditional Afghan garb were squatting next to it, examining the damage with a stream of animated commentary.

Smith's Merge failed to recognize the face of either man, but was able to determine that they were Middle Eastern males between sixteen and forty-five years old and therefore gave them the reddish aura of potential threats. A woman standing next to them was also unidentified—not surprising based on the fact that virtually nothing of her was visible behind her burqa—but was given more of a neutral threat rating due to her gender.

The members of his team ahead glowed dark green despite their desert camo and a local coming toward them rated a much paler green—one of the rare locals who had been identified by the Merge's sophisticated facial recognition software and was deemed friendly.

The man spoke as he passed by but Smith didn't hear him in the literal sense of the word. He was wearing earplugs and all sound was being transmitted directly to his auditory cortex via five separate microphones attached to his uniform.

"My horse greets a goat for your life," the mechanical voice said and Smith allowed himself a thin smile. One day the system would accurately translate real-time but for now its interpretation of Dari was for entertainment value only.

In their success column, though, they'd hijacked existing technology to cancel out wind noise, and an app that muted all voices except the one from the person you were looking at was starting to show real promise. On the downside, the directional aspect of the sound coming at him was still almost completely nonexistent. Despite almost two months of work, everything sounded like it came from just ahead and slightly to the right.

Smith scanned left, letting the cameras mounted on his helmet pan over a group of men paying a little too much attention to the American team in their midst. It was broad daylight under a blue sky so most visual enhancement was shut down. The two exceptions—facial recognition and weapon outline enhancement—were coming up empty.

His vision shook when he faced forward again and he gave his chin strap another tug. He'd commandeered the helmet from a Recon Ranger and it had been custom-molded for the Ranger's larger head. Still, it was an amazing piece of gear. If Smith had any say in the matter—and he did—the bicycle mechanic who'd fabricated it would soon be a very wealthy man.

"Right or left, Colonel?" his point man said as they approached a cross street.

Smith expanded a satellite photo hovering in his peripheral vision and checked the layout of the village before responding. "Right."

It would be the fastest way back and Smith had to admit that he'd had about enough of this exercise. The sixty-thousand-dollar seventeen-pound camera perched on his right shoulder seemed to be doing nothing but bending his collarbone. A little more tinkering might make it worth bringing out again but he was going to stick someone else with wearing it.

His man approached the corner and Smith swept left, lifting his rifle to provide cover should it become necessary. He left the satellite image up and watched the green dots that represented his people fan out behind him. Both the smoothness and resolution of the image had been significantly improved from his game of capture-the-flag three months ago. Even more important, though, his mind was growing accustomed to all the input, letting him register the flood of information without taking too much away from the reality around him.

"Rick," he said in a voice that would be virtually inaudible to anyone around him but was easily picked up by his tooth mike. "You're wandering a little far northeast. Tighten it up."

Smith picked up his pace, keeping a line of sight on his point man while examining a section of ground along the edge of the road thirty-two meters away. The heat overlay that had been lurking in the background was now coloring an area about the size and shape of a manhole cover hazy orange, suggesting that the dirt had been churned up recently and was now absorbing sunlight at a slightly different rate than was the ground around it.

His man saw it too and, despite it probably being nothing more than some recently buried garbage, diverted through the increasingly dense crowd of pedestrians.

A tall man in a blue robe came out of a building just past the suspicious patch of dirt and after only a few seconds' delay, started flashing red.

"Terry!" Smith said, raising his rifle and activating his targeting system. "Behind you!"

The soldier spun, but a fraction too late. The man the Merge had identified as a hostile knocked him to the ground before shoving his way through the people packing the street. Smith tried to follow him in his crosshairs, but the crowd started to panic and he couldn't get a clean shot.

"We've got a target running south," Smith said as the man disappeared around a corner. "Everyone behind me backtrack and try to intercept. Terry and I will flush him toward you."

On his overhead display, he saw his people comply as he started running forward.

"You all right?" he said as he came alongside his man.

"Didn't see him in time, sir."

"My fault. Now let's go get him."

The heavy camera on his shoulder was limiting his speed to a fast jog and Terry quickly outpaced him, following the wake their target had left in the terrified throng.

As the street emptied, a hastily coded beta app kicked in and painted a woodpile just ahead of his man fluorescent orange.

"Terry! Trap!"

Too late. The sound of the explosion was heavily filtered by his unit's processors, but the blinding flash wasn't. Smith dove to the ground, causing the massive camera anchored to his shoulder to slam painfully into the side of his flimsy helmet. Visual enhancement kicked on, penetrating the smoke and showing his man and a number of civilians down.

The only thing moving was a hazy human outline coming directly at him. He struggled to get his rifle sighted but when the figure emerged from the smoke, it morphed into a tall, athletic woman wearing jeans and a formfitting black tank top.

She stopped and looked down at him, waving impatiently at the smoke. The tactical overhead view still running in his peripheral vision showed three of his team moving in on his position and another two moving south fast—probably in pursuit of their target. He concentrated on the word "time" and a dim display overlaid the woman's elegantly curved torso.

4:48 p.m.

"All right," he said, struggling to his feet with the shoulder camera teetering on a broken strap. "Let's call it a day."

Bystanders began appearing from the cover they'd fled to and burqas started coming off, revealing women in U.S. Army fatigues and the occasional smaller-than-average man that their system was still failing miserably to identify.

By the time he'd dusted himself off, the only people left on the street were the woman in front of him and Terry, who was still sitting next to the woodpile where the flash grenade had detonated.

"Congratulations," Randi Russell said, pointing at the massive camera on Smith's shoulder. "You may have invented the least practical piece of combat equipment in history."

"It's a spectrum analyzer that can identify explosive residue to about fifty meters. And believe it or not, it actually seems to work."

"Yeah, all fifty pounds of it."

"Seventeen. And we think we can get it down below four, with most of it in your pack."

Her skeptical expression remained for a moment but then she looked around and broke into a dazzling smile. "I gotta hand it to you, Jon. This place is pretty impressive. There's actually a real donkey back there."

"Only the finest when the taxpayer's footing the bill. Simulations are all about the details."

The smoke had cleared and she sniffed at the air. "Doesn't smell right, though. Still smells like Nevada."

Smith considered that for a moment. "You make a good point. I'll work on it."

They looked at each in silence for a few moments before she spoke again. "I'm not sure I like this new world, Jon."

He reached a dirty hand out and brushed back her short blond hair. No studs. "Still holding out?"

"You know me. If I had my way it would be daggers at dawn."

She was only half joking, he knew. The world they lived in was one where you could have world-class skills, the best gear, and near-Olympic-level fitness, only to be killed by a fertilizer bomb built by an illiterate twelve-year-old. It was hard not to romanticize a time when the best man—or woman—won.

"I hear you. But the clock's never going to turn back, Randi."

"Tell me about it. I can't swing a dead cat without hitting someone with one of your little gadgets screwed to their heads."

A typically colorful metaphor but fairly accurate. At the outset, he'd argued passionately that the military didn't have the right to order people to get the Merge body modifications, but his moral stand had turned out to be completely pointless. After seeing what the unit could do, soldiers were lining up to get them.

"We're already at three percent penetration in active combat troops and if Dresner can get production to where it needs to be, forty percent of combat personnel will be Merged up by the end of next year. And that's just military units—soldiers are buying civilian units with their own money because we aren't moving fast enough for them."

"Fortunately for me, the CIA isn't as sold."

Inconspicuous dots appeared on her face as his Merge began mapping it. They'd been talking long enough for LayerCake to determine that she wasn't in its database and to assume he knew her. Later that night, he'd receive a text asking him to put a name to the image the system had created. A text he would delete unanswered.

"They will be soon, Randi. Because of the individuality of brain waves, the security is light-years beyond what you're using in Langley. But enough of that. What is it that you're doing standing in the middle of my training exercise? Last I heard you were in Khost."

"There's something I want to talk to you about. Maybe we could have a drink?"

Most people wouldn't notice, but he'd known her long enough to hear the concern in her voice. And when Randi couldn't completely hide what she was feeling, it was generally something you wanted to pay attention to.

"Deal. But first, you're going to have to help me get this damn camera off."

29

Reno, Nevada
USA

THE BAR WAS CLASSIC RANDI. Out of the way, dark, and sparsely populated—a stale smoke-scented, cracked-black-vinyl-encased facsimile of the ones she haunted in the forgotten corners of the world.

Every male customer immediately turned and followed her with his eyes, something that was impossible not to do. Despite the comically oversized handbag thrown over her shoulder, she carried herself with a mesmerizing, almost predatory grace.

Smith bucked the trend and looked away, casually examining a woman pulling slots next to an overflowing ashtray. The jingle of coins momentarily overpowered the eighties music straining hidden speakers and she joylessly transferred her winnings to a plastic cup.

The men around him suddenly lost interest and he turned back to see Randi disappear into a booth tucked into a shadowed corner of the room.

"Nice place," Smith observed, sliding in next to her. "I have an office, you know. They even gave me a window."

She frowned disinterestedly at his minor victory but he suspected that she felt the same way he did about being there together. Despite a soul-crushing personal history and the tendency for near-death experiences to follow every time they so much as set foot in the same state, they were as close to each other as to anyone. As close as people in their profession could be.

"I guess I forgot to congratulate you on the new job," she said. "I just did a night op with a guy who uses one. As much as I hate to admit it—and you know I do—I was impressed."

"But you're still not sold."

"I've always felt like sticking things I don't understand in my brain isn't a good idea."

"What if I told you that *I* understand it and that it's safe?" he said, picking up a menu lying in the middle of the table and looking at the list of beers.

"I'd say maybe you don't know as much as you think you know."

Smith gave an unsurprised nod and flipped to the wine list. There was only about a two-second delay before LayerCake recognized what he was looking at and flashed dully in his peripheral vision. Curious why, he launched the icon and watched as the *Wine Spectator* ratings of the listed bottles appeared next to their names. How civilized.

"Are you using it now?" Randi asked.

"Yeah."

"Could you turn it off?"

His brow furrowed for a moment and then he shrugged and shut it down. "Okay. It's off. Why?"

Randi scooted close enough to press up against him. "Because I have something I want to show you."

"I'm intrigued."

She unzipped her bag and pulled that something out, setting it on the table in front of him. In the poor light it took his mind a few beats to reconcile what he was seeing.

"Jesus, Randi!" he said in a harsh whisper, twisting around reflexively to look behind him.

Murphy's Law—the principle that seemed to rule his life—was in full effect and a bored-looking young waitress was making a beeline for them through the empty tables.

He must have looked a little panicked, because Randi put a hand on his arm. "Relax, Jon. Don't you ever look at your calendar?"

The young woman arrived at their table jotting on a small tablet. "Can I get you—"

Her voice faltered as she spotted the severed head resting on the cracked Formica. Smith tensed but then a broad smile spread across her face.

"That thing is too cool! Where did you get it?"

"Off the Internet," Randi replied casually.

"The weird musty smell…"

"Comes in a little spray bottle."

"Awesome!"

He was a bit perplexed by the conversation until he remembered Randi's comment about the calendar. He'd been too immersed in his work with the Merge to bother keeping up with holidays. It was October 30. The day before Halloween.

"I'll just have a beer," Randi said. "Don't care what kind."

"Same," Smith agreed.

The girl gave the head one last admiring glance and then returned to the bar. He waited until she was out of earshot before he spoke again.

"What the hell is this? Something for the mantel?" he said.

"Take a closer look."

"Can I turn my Merge back on?"

"No."

A quick glance around him confirmed that no one but the returning waitress was paying any attention at all. He waited for her to slide the beers onto the table and disappear again before pulling the head toward him.

"Looks like the spine was severed with a saw of some kind and then it was left somewhere dry. Skin color and features are a little hard to distinguish with the shrinkage, but based on the hair and the beard, I'd say you found it in Afghanistan."

"Very good. Anything else?"

He kept going over it and was about to say no when the dim light picked up something on the side. He pushed back the matted hair and found himself looking at a Merge stud.

"Christ. They're already smuggling them in?"

She shook her head. "This man died more than three months ago. On July twenty-first."

"You have your dates wrong. The Merge didn't go on the market until after that. Hell, Dresner didn't even make his announcement until the twenty-second."

"I don't have my dates wrong."

If it was anyone else, he would be asking if she was certain, probing for a mistake in her timeline or logic. But this wasn't someone else. It was Randi Russell.

"So you're saying you've had this since July twenty-first?"

She shook her head. "I went to a village on the twenty-second that had been wiped out by the Taliban. All the men had been decapitated and the heads were gone. I finally tracked them down in a cave a few days ago."

"Did they all have studs?" he said, trying to conjure an explanation for what he was hearing. The best thing he could come up with was that someone had snuck into that cave ahead of her and installed studs on a bunch of severed heads. Not particularly high on the plausibility scale.

"I didn't look. That was just the first one I picked up."

The truth was that it didn't really matter. One was as ugly a mystery as a hundred.

"I knew these people, Jon. This village. They were tough sons of bitches and they'd been going at it for centuries with the Taliban who wiped them out. Why did the balance of power suddenly shift?"

Smith considered that for a moment. "Okay...Let's accept for a moment that this Afghan village somehow got hold of Merges before anyone in the developed world and someone is going to great lengths to hide it. Even if they were commercial versions, it should have been to their *advantage*. You've seen how effective they are."

Her expression turned skeptical. "I talked to one of the Taliban who attacked them. He said that the women and children fought but the men didn't. And one who was looking down the barrel of the gun said there was no God."

"Sounds far-fetched, Randi. Maybe your Taliban friend was just trying to insult them after the fact—saying they were cowards with no faith."

Again, she shook her head. "It wasn't bravado. He was shaken by what happened in that village."

Smith moved the head out of sight and leaned back in the booth again. When he looked at her, there was more than just a hint of accusation in her eyes.

"Any ideas, Jon?"

"I know what you're thinking. That the military knew about this before the announcement and we were doing some kind of secret testing on the Afghans that we want covered up."

"The truth is, I've known you a long time and I don't think you'd get involved in something like that. But do you know who originally sent me out to Sarabat?"

"No."

"Fred Klein. And I *haven't* known him for a long time."

Her caution was understandable. She hadn't been working with Covert-One for long, and he'd displayed similar caution himself at first. Since then, though, Klein had proved himself over and over again.

"Here's what I can tell you for certain: I don't know anything about this. And here's what I can tell you almost for certain: Neither does Fred or Montel Pedersen."

She shrugged noncommittally. "Then what happened out there? What would make a group of people who come out of the womb fighting, and who have a piece of gear that even *I* acknowledge is a massive tactical advantage, stand there and get slaughtered? And why did Fred send me out there, then call me off before I went looking for the heads?"

"Maybe they weren't what he was looking for, Randi. Fred keeps a lot of irons in the fire and even I don't know about most of them. As far as the behavior of the people in that village goes, you know what an individual eyewitness account is worth. Maybe we should go talk to a few more of the Taliban who were involved and see if their stories match."

"There are no more. They were wiped off the face of the earth a few days later by a bunch of mercs that no one seems to know anything about. Well, no one but Fred Klein."

Smith took a hesitant pull from his beer. This just kept getting worse. "Drugs? Maybe gas? That could explain the strange behavior."

"Far-fetched since it didn't affect the women and children, but it was a possibility that occurred to me, too. That's why I had an autopsy done."

"And?"

"Clean."

"So I'm guessing that you think they were connected to Merges during the attack and that's what's responsible for the unusual behavior."

"They acted completely opposite of who they are and they had something attached to their brains that shouldn't have been there. It seems like the elephant in the room, don't you think?"

"That's not the way it works, Randi."

"Come on, who do you think you're talking to? It hasn't occurred to you that you could use that thing in the other direction? What about tDSC?"

The program that she was speaking of was the military's experiment with sending a weak electrical current through the brain to enhance the ability to learn new skills. It was an incredibly promising technology that had already allowed them to double the rate of improvement in sharpshooters.

"Okay," he admitted. "We're playing around with a tDSC app. But I can do the same thing with a nine-volt battery and ten dollars' worth of stuff from Home Depot. We're not fundamentally changing someone's personality. We're just improving focus."

"What about the sleep function everyone likes so much? That's affecting the brain and you're not doing it with a bagful of crap from the hardware store."

"You're just optimizing wave functions already built into your brain. And don't forget that you have to be connected to a power source or you'd drain the battery in just a few minutes."

She pushed her beer bottle around the table with her index finger. "I don't know what worries me more, Jon. That you're lying to me, or that you're telling the truth and the head of Merge development for the armed forces doesn't know anything about this."

It was a fair observation. "Let me do some quiet asking around."

"Uh-huh," she said, bringing her lips to her bottle again. "You do that."

30

Morning," Smith mumbled as he stepped into Covert-One's inner offices. He'd been up all night working and didn't bounce back from sleeplessness like he had in his twenties. Of course, he could use his Merge to knock him out at six o'clock tonight and be good as new by morning, but now he felt a little hesitant.

"Everything all right?" Maggie said, peeking out from behind the monitors she was barricaded behind.

He'd caught up with Klein on an encrypted line late last night and it was likely that she hadn't yet been briefed on the conversation. Maggie was the only other person who knew the full extent of the Covert-One operation and she wasn't accustomed to being in the dark.

"Yeah. Randi's got a burr under her saddle..."

"Nothing new there."

He laughed. After years of dancing around, Randi had been brought into the C1 fold only recently. And while she'd already proved her value ten times over, neither Maggie nor Klein had completely figured out how to deal with her. When they did, hopefully they'd teach him.

"It's one of those things that'll probably turn out to be nothing."

"But you're not a hundred percent sure."

"Exactly."

She retreated behind her monitors. "Go on in."

Klein was on the phone when Smith entered, so he just fell into a chair and looked around at the old maps decorating the walls.

"So nothing at all. You're telling me straight, right, JC?"

Smith perked up at the initials. It was what close friends called the director of the CIA.

"...No, no reason," Klein continued. "Okay. Maybe next week? Give me a call."

He hung up the phone and immediately went for his pipe.

"Any whispers?" Smith said.

"Nothing at all. In fact, the silence is deafening. No one seems to know anything about this."

"And you think they're telling the truth?"

Klein couldn't reveal the existence of Covert-One or his working relationship with the president, so he had no authority beyond his history and reputation. And while both carried a fair amount of weight, they didn't preclude the possibility that he was being kept out of the loop.

"I'd say I'm seventy-five percent confident that no one in the intelligence community knows anything about the Merge being used in Afghanistan prior to its release—or even that it existed before Dresner's unveiling."

The skepticism was not only audible in his voice, but

clearly visible in his face. And it wasn't hard to guess why.

"Randi..." Smith said.

Klein's pipe finally caught and he gave it a few hard pulls. "We both know she has a way of grabbing hold of things she can't let go of. And that she's a bit of a technophobe."

Smith shook his head. "I know she can be a pain in the ass, Fred. Probably better than anyone. But if she says that's what happened, that's what happened."

"I appreciate your loyalty, Jon. And let me be clear that I have a lot of admiration for Randi Russell or I wouldn't have sent her out there in the first place. This isn't specifically aimed at her. I wouldn't take this kind of intel on faith if God himself sent it down on stone tablets. Trust but verify, right?"

Smith nodded hesitantly. He wasn't accustomed to questioning Klein, but in this case it seemed justified. "So you didn't send her out there for this—the behavior of the people in Sarabat, the heads..."

Klein didn't respond immediately, obviously considering how much he wanted to reveal. "There seems to be some money bleeding out of the Pentagon. I've been after it for more than a year and still only have a few vague scraps. Whoever's behind it is incredibly thorough at covering his tracks. But we recently found something—a small and very indirect payment to mercenaries who were reported to be operating in that region."

"So this didn't have anything to do with the Merge."

"Not at first. But now I'm concerned. Have you had a chance to examine the head she brought back?"

"I took it to my lab and spent the night looking it over.

Exact time of death is hard to determine at this point but the three months that Randi's telling us is completely plausible."

"What about the studs?"

"They weren't added postmortem, if that's what you're getting at. There's new bone growth around them. I'd say they were installed about a month before death."

Klein set his pipe down. "And the bodies? Can I assume there were no actual Merge units in evidence?"

"Randi said she didn't check all of them, but the few she did—and the one she brought back for autopsy—didn't have units. Someone would have had to remove them. Maybe when they were sawing off their heads."

Klein just nodded, probably thinking the same thing Smith was—that this stank to high heaven of some kind of covert U.S. test. But if it was, who the hell authorized it?

"The way I see it, Fred, is that if we aren't responsible for this, we need to find out who is. I've been working with the Merge for a few months now and my opinion of it has gone nowhere but up. This is going to be a transformational technology, and exclusivity is an important part of that. If someone had access to this thing before us, we have to find out who and what exactly they're doing with it."

"How plausible is it that someone has gotten access to the military version of the operating system?"

"Not. It only runs on our network and the encryption is generations ahead of anything else out there. Plus, I'm the only person who can authorize apps. That means that not only does my password have to be entered, but it has to be entered by my brain pattern."

"What about Dresner himself?"

"It's his system and I haven't been able to figure out a way to shut him out of it."

Klein put his pipe down and let out a long breath. "Who would have ever thought I'd look back fondly on the Cold War? This damn thing's only been out for a few months and we're already worried that it's filtered down to a bunch of goatherders in Afghanistan. Technology cannot be controlled, Jon. Not anymore. And it's going to be our downfall."

Smith nodded sympathetically. "It seems unlikely that Christian Dresner would make an end run around us and hand over this technology to our enemies. He was never obligated to give us the exclusive deal. If he wants to sell it to anyone with a handful of cash, he has every right to do it. No, there are simpler explanations, don't you think?"

The implication was obvious: The United States had a small, beyond-top-secret team who had been involved in some early tests that wouldn't look good in the news-papers.

"Understood," Klein said. "I'll speak with the presi-dent and make sure this particular dark corner isn't one he wants to remain dark. Until then, you're not to continue any inquiries into the matter."

"I assume you're going to tell Randi the same thing?"

"I am. And I expect you to make sure she complies."

Smith let out a short laugh at the idea that he could control Randi Russell. "In that case, sooner might be bet-ter than later for your conversation with Castilla. Randi's not the most patient woman in the world."

31

THE RAIN CAME DOWN HARDER—not quite in solid sheets but in a disorienting rush that blurred the people around him and turned the lake to mist. The words of the priest were overcome by the impact of the drops against umbrellas and Christian Dresner considered it a blessing.

Of course he could use his Merge to compensate for the visual and audio chaos, but why? To hear a stream of meaningless platitudes about a God and a soul that he now knew didn't exist? To hear passages from a two-thousand-year-old book written by ignorant men who needed a deity to explain every clap of thunder and burning bush?

What was left of Craig Bailer's body had been cremated after a cursory autopsy, but it had taken months for the family to put together this modest ceremony. He looked at their faces—the stoic wife, the supportive children, impatient business associates—and wondered about the delay. Was it because no one cared enough to shuffle their schedules? Perhaps they had seen Bailer for what he was: a man obsessed with money and the illusion of personal value it could be used to create. A man eminently replaceable as a business partner, parent, or friend by the thousands just like him.

The priest stepped down and a young man Dresner didn't know took his place. Not that he would have expected to recognize him. He knew very little about Bailer personally. The man had been a convenient tool but, beyond that, of little interest. Not that their impersonal relationship had made killing him—murdering him—any easier. But then, it had been an act of no real importance. Bailer would have died later with all the others anyway. For his sins.

"My father loved it here," the young man said, his voice cutting through the rain in a way that the priest's had not. "When I was a boy, this piece of land only had a little cabin on it and there were other houses surrounding the lake. Over the years, he bought them all up and removed them. He loved the quiet. The beauty of nature."

Dresner frowned imperceptibly. The "cabin" was now a thousand-square-meter monstrosity and the dock they were standing on held a massive speedboat painted a garish red and yellow. The truth was that Bailer had never shown any interest in nature. This was just another trophy.

The family walked in a silent procession to the end of the pier and turned an urn upside down over the water. The wind whipped at the ashes for a moment before they were soaked through and dropped unceremoniously into the lake.

A fitting end to Craig Bailer.

The crowd began to disperse, about half checking their

email on cell phones and the other half doing the same with the subtle pupil jerks that people had taken to calling the Dresner Stare.

He moved against the exodus, people shuffling out of his way with nervous glances as he approached Bailer's wife.

"I'm so sorry, Lori," he said, feeling her tense under his embrace. He was less human than symbol now and people often didn't know how to react to his physical presence.

"I want to thank you for coming," she said as he took her hand. "It would have meant a lot to Craig."

"I considered him one of my closest friends and owe him a great deal. I can't imagine how you and your family must be feeling, but I want you to know that it was a devastating loss for me, too."

She gripped her umbrella tighter, seemingly unsure what to say. "We still don't know what happened, Mr. Dresner. I suppose we never will."

He held out a business card, blank except a single phone number centered on it. "This comes directly to me. If there's anything you need—anything I can help you with—please call."

She accepted the card and this time seemed a bit more relaxed when they embraced. Dresner stood by respectfully as she retreated to the fold of her family and then started up the slope toward the house. A limousine appeared along the muddy road and glided to a stop in front of him.

Dresner pulled the door open, freezing for a moment when he saw a figure sitting next to the heavily tinted window on the opposite side.

"Hello, Christian."

The voice was immediately recognizable and Dresner slipped inside, dropping his dripping umbrella on the floor in front of him. "Very dramatic, James. I've always admired a good entrance."

"You said you wanted to talk and that it was important. I thought I'd take advantage of your rare presence in our country."

The limousine weaved through the people still gathered in front of Bailer's house and Dresner took a seat opposite the man. He had retired years ago as a major in an area of U.S. military intelligence where rank was not necessarily well correlated with power. Now he was in his early seventies, with gray hair still cut in an efficient military style and a gaunt, sun-damaged face that meshed perfectly with a body that was a product of a lifetime in the Marine Corps. The scar that ran from the edge of his starched collar to the underside of his chin completed the image but, ironically, was not a souvenir from combat. According to Dresner's investigators, it was actually the result of a childhood accident.

"Sorry to hear about your CEO. Can I assume that it won't affect the production of military-specific Merges?"

"Your concern is heartwarming."

"Everyone dies, Christian. Even you and me one day."

Dresner looked at the glass separating them from the driver and security man in the passenger seat. It was soundproof, but he still would prefer to have this conversation elsewhere.

"We've run into some cash-flow problems that need to be dealt with in order to keep manufacturing at capacity."

"Cash-flow problems? What kind of cash-flow problems?"

"Nothing that fifty billion dollars won't resolve."

Major James Whitfield sat in silence, nothing registering on his face. It never did.

"It's a temporary shortfall," Dresner continued. "The rollout is actually ahead of projections."

"Whether it's temporary or not is irrelevant. The amount isn't though. We've already given more than a hundred billion to this project."

"And in return, I've agreed to provide America with a number of critical exclusive technologies. Certainly the Merge is more useful than obsolete aircraft carriers and fighter jet prototypes that have trouble getting into the air."

"Do you think I just call the Pentagon and tell them to write a check?" Whitfield said, his voice turning menacing. "Making this kind of money disappear from the defense budget isn't trivial. Even for me."

"Obviously, I could go looking for the money on the open market. I imagine the Chinese government would be interested.

When Whitfield spoke again it was through clenched teeth. "Anything else?"

"In fact, yes."

Dresner pulled up a photo on his Merge and was about to securely transfer it to Whitfield but then remembered the old soldier still refused to adopt the technology. Instead, he was forced to use a laptop lying on the seat next to him.

"What am I looking at?" Whitfield said, accepting the computer and examining the enhanced image.

"The two people sitting in the booth are Randi Russell from the CIA and Lieutenant Colonel Jon Smith, whom you're familiar with."

"What's he holding?" Whitfield asked.

"A severed head that Russell found in Afghanistan."

"Why do I care?"

"Because that particular Afghan was involved in an experiment you paid for almost four months ago. The skull has Merge studs in it."

Still, nothing registered on the former marine's face, but the rise and fall of his chest increased noticeably. "Where did you get this?"

In fact, he had quite a bit more—including photos of Russell actually retrieving the head. He couldn't reveal that, though, without compromising his view into Whitfield's world.

"Smith is in charge of the military's adoption of my technology. It makes sense for me to watch him to the degree practical."

"Why wasn't I told about this experiment?"

"You never seemed interested in this level of detail."

"Christ..." Whitfield said under his breath. "Does anyone at Central Intelligence know about this?"

"I can't say for certain, but I don't think so. She and Smith have a personal relationship—he was engaged to her sister when she became one of the first victims of the Hades virus. It appears that Russell came straight to him because of that history and his position as the director of Merge development. I take it you haven't heard anything through military channels?"

Whitfield shook his head. "If Smith is concerned about this, he hasn't gone up the chain of command with it."

"Then there's still time. Watching Smith is one thing, but dealing with him and a CIA operative is obviously beyond my experience."

"Dealing with? Why the hell were you even following him? This isn't your sphere of influence. If you feel people need watching—and goddamn well if they need 'dealing with'—you come to me."

"I *have* come to you, Major. And I'm expecting you to handle it."

32

Washington, DC
USA

Fred Klein followed an unconcerned Secret Service man toward the president's executive residence. The reason for the casual attitude was that this was a regular occurrence. Klein and the president had been roommates in college and the friendship they'd formed there transcended the world of politics and intelligence that they now lived in. Sam Adams Castilla surrounded himself with the same political creatures that every president was forced to, but he only really trusted the people he'd known before his rise to power. It's how Klein had ended up heading Covert-One and why his virtually unlimited access to America's leader would be the envy of everyone—if they knew about it.

While the two men occasionally met publicly in the Oval Office under the completely reasonable assumption that Castilla would periodically ask his old friend's advice on matters of national security, it was better to keep those meetings to a minimum. Klein, to the degree that it was possible in the information age, felt most comfortable when working from the shadows.

Castilla was sitting on a threadbare sofa that had come with him from the governor's mansion in Santa Fe when his old friend entered. He started to rise, but didn't seem to have the strength. Instead, he grabbed a can of Coors off the coffee table and raised it in greeting.

"Even you wouldn't believe the day I just had, Fred."

Klein had always been suspicious that American presidents started slowly dyeing their hair gray the day they took office—a transition from the youth and energy expected of a candidate to the maturity and gravitas expected of a president. Now he knew. It wasn't dye.

"For me?" Klein said, taking a seat across from him and pointing to a glass of scotch on the table.

"Ardbeg 1975. A gift from the Thai ambassador."

"Is Cassie still out of the country?"

"Touring sugar plantations and eating too much island food. That's the job you want, Fred. First Lady."

Castilla was a brilliant man with an honest streak much wider than most and a reassuring aura of calm that tended to slip when his wife was gone for long periods of time. With so few people he trusted implicitly, he liked to keep them close.

"I'm not sure I'm qualified."

Castilla grinned and drained his beer, pulling another from a dignified-looking oak chest that had been converted to hold ice. "These days it's hard not to start looking forward to building my library, writing a self-serving autobiography, and hitting golf balls. What do you think, Fred? Will you be ready to join me in the pasture when my term's up?"

"I don't play golf," he responded, evading the question.

Castilla let him get away with it. "I assume you aren't here to make sure I'm eating right while my wife is gone. What do you have for me?"

Klein pulled a tablet computer from his portfolio and punched in a password, bringing up a photo of the severed head Randi Russell had found. Castilla looked at it, blanched visibly, and then went back to working on his beer.

"Someone I know?"

"An Afghan from a rural village called Sarabat. Did you see the places on the skull that were circled?"

Castilla nodded. "Dresner's Merge is getting around. We originally thought that Islam's prohibitions against body modification would pretty much shut down adoption in that part of the world, but the effect hasn't been as strong as we thought. Hats off to Dresner's marketing director."

"There's more."

"Why am I not surprised?"

"It appears that the studs in this man's skull were installed more than four months ago."

Castilla's eyes narrowed as he made a few mental calculations. "That was before the Merge was released. Well before."

"That's right."

"Where did you get this, Fred? Is the intel solid?"

"I had Randi Russell looking into a lead on the Pentagon issue. This just fell in her lap. And while I haven't been working directly with her for long, I have a great deal of admiration for her. Also, Jon Smith has corroborated most of her story. I think you and I hold the same opinion of Jon."

"This really isn't what I needed today."

"Sorry, Sam."

"What else do we know?"

"Basically nothing. And that's why I'm here. I need some direction from you as to whether this is something Covert-One should pursue."

"Hell yes, it's something you should pursue. Why wouldn't—" He caught himself and fell silent for a moment. "You think I had something to do with this."

"I'm not here to pass judgment, Sam. You know that. But if this is a government-run test I'm not aware of, it'd be better if we steer clear of it."

"I found out about the Merge the same time the rest of the world did and I found out about the military version the same way you did—from Smith's meeting with Craig Bailer. After I got his report, I met with the CIA and Joint Chiefs to discuss it. They didn't know any more than I did."

"Okay," Klein said in a measured tone. "Then the question we need to answer is how this should be handled. It might make sense to hand it over to the CIA and military intelligence. Keep us out of it."

Castilla settled back in the sofa and stared silently down at the beer in his hand. With Covert-One's involvement always came the risk of exposure.

"I'm telling you straight that I didn't know anything about this, Fred. But there's no guarantee that someone in the military or intelligence community didn't find out before me and decide to do a quiet trial."

Klein nodded. It was a possibility that he himself had

considered. Sometimes things had to be done that the country's politicians didn't want or need to know about.

"If that's the case," Castilla continued. "I have two problems. First, I can't trust the CIA or military to look into this. And second, if it turns out that one of those organizations *was* involved, I don't need a leak before I make a decision about what to do."

"So what I'm hearing is that we should pursue this."

The president nodded. "But we're just gathering information at this point. No action is to be taken without my direct authorization."

33

Near Harpers Ferry, West Virginia
USA

JON SMITH EASED UP on the accelerator and gave in to
his compulsion to confirm on his iPhone that he was still
on the right road. He wasn't sure why, though. The asphalt in front of him glowed dim yellow and a translucent
ETA floated in his peripheral vision. One of the strange
things about the Merge was that the more accustomed you
got to it, the more it faded into the background. Sometimes it was easy to forget it was even there.

The mist was getting worse, hanging in the trees and
threatening to condense into rain. The men he was on
his way to meet were probably gleefully praying for a
deluge—anything to increase the morning's suffering.

Smith had been tagging along with a group of former
and current special forces operatives on their weekend
trail run for years now. The terrain was always brutal, the
pace superhuman, and the competitiveness on the verge
of psychotic.

Two and a half hours of misery that he'd hoped to
avoid by retreating to Nevada, but now his return had

been delayed by Klein's green light. There were no excuses—no kids' birthdays, sick parents, or flooded basements. Even injuries better be backed up with an ugly, emailed X-ray. If you were in town, you showed up.

He flipped off the radio and his thoughts immediately turned to Randi's discovery and what the hell he was going to do about it.

Dresner was the obvious place to start, but access to the great man was extremely limited and U.S. leverage against him virtually non-existent.

Of course, there was Afghanistan, but that would probably turn out to be an even bigger dead end. The locals in question were all in the ground and the region wasn't exactly known for its meticulous record keeping.

Maybe the mercs who had wiped out Kot'eh? Sure, he might be able to find them, but what were they going to say? In all likelihood they had no idea who'd hired them. As long as the price was right, they tended not to worry about those kinds of details.

That left the technology itself. While he was far from convinced that the Afghans' reported odd behavior had anything to do with the Merge—or for that matter even existed—it was an intriguing theory. His team had been so focused on exploiting the Merge's hundreds of obvious capabilities, they hadn't had much time to investigate what they *didn't* know about it.

How was it developed? The human brain was the most complicated thing in the known universe and notoriously difficult to model. Massive testing must have been done but no one thought about that any more than they thought about how their new phone was developed. Was it possible that Dresner had decided to test the military unit in a war zone? Again, doubtful, but not completely out of the question. If the man was anything, he was thorough.

And what about Christian Dresner? Smith had read everything the government and media had on him, which wasn't much. Why would it be? Digging through the trash cans and hacked phones of supermodels and movie stars was a hell of a lot more interesting than putting a microscope on a sixty-odd-year-old recluse who went around trying to make the world a better place. While admittedly intimidating, Dresner slotted in on the sinister scale somewhere between a baby seal and ice cream.

Smith spotted a muddy side road with an old truck waiting to pull out and he checked his iPhone again, confirming that it wasn't his turn despite the fact that the Merge was still painting his path yellow. The trailhead was another 5.4 miles.

Thoughts of Dresner were just reestablishing themselves in his mind when the truck darted out in front of him. Smith slammed on the brakes, but with the slick road and lack of traction control, the rear of the Triumph slid out and bounced off the larger vehicle's front bumper with the heartrending sound of crumpling steel.

He tried to compensate, but what was left of his tires' grip disappeared when he hit the muddy shoulder. A moment later the passenger door slammed into a tree and threw him into what was left of the console he'd spent hours building.

And then all he could hear was the light rain on the crumpled soft top. That is until his own voice drowned it out.

"Son of a bitch!"

He tried to open his door, but didn't succeed until he

rammed a shoulder angrily into it. Leaping out into the mud, he tried to squelch the fantasy of beating the driver of that truck to death with his own arm. Before he could completely eradicate the violent image, though, something moved in the woods about twenty meters to his right.

Smith was using the commercial version of the Merge, so there was no sophisticated outline enhancement, but it didn't matter. He knew the barrel of an M16 when he saw one.

He made a move for the Sig Sauer stashed in the Triumph's glove box, but then froze when a shout rose up behind him.

"Don't!"

He held his arms out non-threateningly and turned back slowly. One gun had become three and all were held by men who appeared to know how to use them.

The sound of a motor became audible up the road and he watched a dark blue Yukon come to a stop next to what was left of his Triumph. The man who stepped out was probably around seventy, with gray, close-cropped hair and a thin but powerful body that would have taken iron discipline to maintain at that age. He moved with military precision and not the mercenary swagger that Smith had learned to immediately recognize. No, this man had served his country as a soldier—probably for his entire career. But what country?

"Colonel," he said with an American accent that answered that particular question. "I'm a great admirer. We all owe you a debt for your work on the Hades virus. And of course, your involvement in Cassandra and Chambord's computer."

He'd listed the operations in a matter-of-fact tone, but they'd clearly been chosen for impact. While some of Smith's role in Hades was in the public record, his involvement with the other two incidents was highly classified.

Smith examined the man as he approached—the intensity of his green eyes, the scar running along the weathered skin beneath his chin, the expression that gave nothing away.

"Walk with me, Colonel," he said, passing by and heading into the trees. A quick glance around confirmed that the armed men were still there. And even if they hadn't been, a physical confrontation with this man, as old as he was, wouldn't be a trivial matter. Better to just play along for now.

"I'm sorry about your car," he said, actually sounding sincere. "It's a beautiful piece of American history."

Smith thought again about the gun safely tucked into what was probably now an inoperable glove box and how, if he survived this, Randi would never let him live it down. How many times had she criticized him for not always bristling with weaponry?

Disconcertingly, the man also seemed to be able to read minds.

"I'd like to talk to you about Randi Russell."

"I'm sorry," Smith responded. "We haven't been properly introduced."

The man's smile had the look of a rare event. "I have to admit I thought it was odd that you were the first person she came to. Your history with her sister and husband seems like it would make your relationship... complicated."

"We've been to therapy," Smith replied, his sarcasm somewhat tempered by the fact that he subconsciously wanted to end the phrase with *sir.* "Can I assume she's getting a similar visit?"

"You cannot. It's my understanding that she's an unreasonable and unpleasant woman. Out of respect for both of you, I'm hoping to keep this civil."

"And what exactly are we talking about here?"

The man didn't reply immediately, instead continuing deeper into the woods. Despite his comment about civility, it was hard not to notice that they kept moving farther and farther from the road.

"We're talking about the severed head Ms. Russell brought back from Afghanistan."

Smith had been prepared to hear just about anything, but that hadn't been on the long list in his head. Still, he managed to keep his expression passive.

"You have an incredible opportunity here, Colonel. The bomb sniffer you're working on could make IEDs an unpleasant memory. The enhanced ability to separate enemy from civilian will give us a real chance to fight insurgencies without turning the locals against us. I'm even confident that you'll get those directional microphones working eventually."

Again, his words were meant less as a compliment and more to showcase his startling access to classified military information.

"I think you're overestimating our advantage," Smith said, probing. "If this thing was already in Afghanistan a month before it was released, I wonder how long until everyone has access to it."

The man stopped and looked directly at him. "No one

else has access to it, Colonel. Just do your job. You're good at it."

They stood there locked in a stare until, to Smith's surprise, the man looked away and started back to the road. "This meeting was a courtesy, Colonel, but you don't want to cross my path again. The next time it won't go as well for you."

34

Near Harpers Ferry, West Virginia
USA

SMITH PULLED HIMSELF CLOSER to the tree, escaping the heavy raindrops exploding against his head, though it wasn't much of an improvement. He'd spent the last two hours bushwhacking to a road running parallel to the one he'd left the Triumph on and had been completely soaked through for most of it.

On the brighter side, there was no way in hell he'd been followed—assuming the man he'd met with was even interested in doing so. More likely, he could be taken at his word. A truce had been called and now it was just a question of whether Smith would honor it—which, of course, he wouldn't.

And that was just about guaranteed to make things interesting going forward. Whoever the man was, he was clearly not someone to be screwed with. Nor someone accustomed to passing out second chances.

Smith heard a car approach and retreated a little farther into the woods. He didn't recognize it when it crested the hill, but it slowed and started hugging the edge of the road when it got close.

Smith darted from cover, timing it so he could grab the handle and jump in before the vehicle came to a full stop. The sudden acceleration nearly caused the door to clip his foot as the driver executed a perfect 180. Engine noise filled the cramped interior and steam rose from the tires as he fumbled with his seat belt.

"You're sure you weren't followed?"

"Don't insult me," Randi Russell said, casually sipping from a Starbucks cup despite their speed and the rain.

He looked around at the shabby upholstery of the nineties Honda for a few seconds, then craned his neck to take in a backseat full of old CDs and dog hair. Not your typical Agency-issue vehicle.

"Did you sweep the car for bugs?" he said.

"Nah. I stole it. Best way if you want to be absolutely sure."

Smith leaned an elbow on the windowsill and rested his wet head against his hand. She'd always had what his grandmother euphemistically called "sticky fingers" when he was a kid. But instead of candy bars and comic books, she tended toward things like Humvees, small aircraft, and cars.

"I really don't need this right now, Randi."

"Don't be such a prude. I got it from long-term airport parking and I'll have it back before the owner ever knows it's gone—detailed and with a full tank of gas. Besides, I believe *you* got *me* out of bed to come save your ass. A little gratitude would be in order."

* * *

CARPET!" MAGGIE TEMPLETON WARNED.

Smith leaned against the doorjamb to remove his muddy running shoes before proceeding into the outer office.

"Towel!"

He grabbed the one folded neatly on top of a safe that served as a filing cabinet, using the thick cotton to catch drips as he made his way toward an open door at the back.

"So you're certain you'd never seen the man before," Klein said by way of greeting.

"Positive." Smith arranged the towel on a chair before carefully lowering himself onto it. Despite the effort, he could hear the metronome-like drip of water falling to the floor.

Randi slipped in with a coffee refill and fell into the chair next to him, taking a hesitant sip as Klein pressed the intercom button next to his phone.

"Star? Could you come in here for a moment?"

She was just a few doors down and appeared a moment later, looking even more impressive than usual. The familiar piercings, tattoos, and black leather boots were all in evidence, but were now accessorizing a rather frilly pink dress. Smith suppressed a smile, suspecting how it must have happened. In the constant battle of wills between her and Klein, the old man had undoubtedly made the mistake of saying something to the effect of "couldn't you just wear a dress?"

Those kinds of exasperated suggestions were pretty much his only recourse, though. A former librarian still in her early thirties, Star was a genius at tracking information—particularly information that hadn't yet made its way to the digital world. She was, in the very real sense of the word, indispensable.

"I need to find someone," Smith said.

"Sure." She acknowledged Randi with a friendly grin. "Name?"

"I don't actually know."

"That's okay. Male or female."

"Male."

"Where does he work?"

"Dunno."

"Where's he live?"

Shrug.

"Do you know where he's from?"

"America. I'm fairly confident about that. Ninety percent."

Her smile began to fade. "I'm probably not going to need a notepad to remember this flood of information, am I?"

"I doubt it."

"Okay, what *can* you tell me?"

"Late sixties to early seventies. Probably retired U.S. military. I'd bet decent money marines—I can smell a jarhead a mile away. Five foot ten, probably a hundred and seventy pounds, only about two of which are fat. Gray military cut, no hair loss."

"Original color? Any hanging on from when he was younger?"

"No."

"Eyes?"

"Green," Smith responded and then ran a finger from his collar to beneath his chin. "And he has an old scar along here."

"Anything else?"

"Nope."

"Well, that should narrow it down to a little over a million people."

Smith smiled easily. "If it was simple, anyone could do it."

"Uh-huh. When do you need it?"

He opened his mouth to respond but she held up a hand and retreated through the door. "Never mind. I already know what you're going to say."

Randi watched her disappear around the corner before speaking. "I have to admit that I'm looking forward to seeing what she finds out. It sounds like he had you dead to rights and didn't take the opportunity. Why? Has he figured out a way to use you? Is he trying to convince you he's something he's not? That you're on the same side? Does he really think you'll give up just because he trashed your car and had some thugs point guns at you?"

"I can answer one of those questions," Klein said.

Randi turned to him. "Which?"

"He's not trying to portray himself as someone he's not."

Klein slid two pieces of paper across his desk, one meant for each of them. Smith took his and leaned over it, trying to stay ahead of the drops splattering across the text as he read. It was an immediate transfer to the Amundsen-Scott research station to relieve the current doctor. He had to rack his brain for a few moments to come up with the location of the facility.

"What's yours say?" he asked Randi.

"I'm being reassigned—effective immediately—as an advisor to a rebel group in Yemen."

"Sounds cushy."

"Really? What's yours?"

"South Pole."

"Antarctica," Randi said, a hint of admiration crossing her face. "Well, we've learned two things about your new friend: He has a hell of a lot of juice and a certain amount of style."

"A little too much of both for my taste," Klein said.

"Can we assume you'll do your magic and make these transfers go away?" Smith said.

Klein looked uncharacteristically doubtful.

"Fred?"

"I'm working on it but it's not a simple matter."

"You're saying that I might be moving into my bunk in Antarctica in a couple of days?"

"Could be worse," Randi said. "You could be barricaded in an apartment with a bunch of lonely Yemeni freedom fighters."

Klein frowned. "I haven't been able to determine how these transfers were done and on whose authority. What I'm finding is the same kind of maze that I leave when I get you your indefinite leaves of absence." He paused for a moment. "Look, I don't want you to worry about this. I'm going to get it done but, as always, I have to do it in a way that doesn't expose Covert-One or the president."

"And in the meantime?"

"In the meantime, I need you to figure out what we're into here. We have a slight advantage in that whoever this man is, he thinks he understands the limitations of your resources as an army scientist and CIA operative. Based on what we've seen so far, though, he isn't going to be fooled for long."

35

East of Chiang Mai
Thailand

N<small>OW THAT WE'VE HAD A CHANCE</small> to get together and analyze numbers for first quarter," Chris Mandrake, Dresner Industries' acting CEO, started, "I'm happy to say that we've had to increase our sales estimates for a third time."

Dresner was sitting motionless, concentrating on the live feed from the meeting as it was transmitted directly to his mind. The app, submitted by a group of students from MIT, calculated size of known objects like chairs and coffee cups, then scaled the image using that information. The room Dresner was in had completely dissolved, replaced with a crowded boardroom half a world away.

As stunning as the software was, though, he'd been forced to send the industrious students a rejection. The interface allowed the user to stand and take a few steps before the image faded—too dangerous for the general public. But within the confines of his Thai compound, it was a joy.

"In-store demonstrations have declined significantly, but we've learned that it's really a function of the positive word of mouth the Merge has been getting. Feedback is fairly consistent in the under-forty demographic—they want to buy. Cost has overtaken concern over the head studs as the primary barrier to purchase. In fact, stud integration continues to be well above our initial projections. We're already at almost fifty percent and I feel confident that by the end of the first year, we'll see eighty-five percent of experienced users integrated. Tooth microphones are running much lower due to the fact that the procedure has to be done by a qualified dentist and because the collar microphones work fairly well. As people go in for checkups, though, we're expecting to see those numbers come up."

"What about the older demographics?" someone said.

"The trend continues to move heavily toward adoption. Our campaign highlighting vision correction and the sleep function has been even more effective than we'd hoped. We're also prioritizing developers whose apps target that market, per Mr. Dresner."

There were some quiet murmurs, but no protests that rose to a level of being intelligible. His insistence on expending so many resources trying to capture people over fifty had met with significant resistance for financial reasons, but there was more to the Merge than making money. Much, much more.

"How many units are up and running right now?" a woman he'd swear was actually in the room with him asked.

"Usage varies over the course of the day, but our peak to date is four point two million worldwide. Interestingly, the variation in the number of Merges online over a given twenty-four-hour period is flattening very quickly. People are discovering that there's no reason not to use the sleep system, even if it's just for the alarm clock function. That's another thing that's driving head stud adoption, particularly in older users: Sleeping with the headset just isn't practical."

"Satisfaction levels?"

"Stratospheric. About one percent of people simply can't adapt to the input and we're giving full refunds on those units. Of course, we also have a small number of people with head stud problems—the occasional infections that we expected. Non-specific complaints like excessive pain have been significantly lower than we projected—probably because of the general satisfaction with the technology."

"Military adoption?"

"Colonel Smith has authored a number of evaluations and all are glowing to say the least. It's my understanding that he compared the Merge to the stirrup as a transformational technology. There are already over thirty thousand U.S. soldiers online, many with commercial units they purchased personally. The military has committed to a quarter million Merges with the eventual goal of full penetration."

"The *American* military," someone pointed out.

Mandrake nodded. "The remaining world governments are also testing and all have acknowledged the military benefits of the commercial version. But we don't know yet how that's going to translate into sales."

More quiet mutters from the board. No one liked the exclusive deal, Dresner knew, and he privately agreed. In the end, though, there had been little choice. The admittedly formidable James Whitfield had contacted him years ago when the group he led had somehow become aware of the technology Dresner was developing.

Progress had been slow due to financial constraints, and the major's ability to quietly redirect Pentagon resources had given the project a new life. Of course, as was true with all deals with the devil, there had been a price: A military version would be simultaneously created and the United States would be given sole rights to it.

While problematic, the situation was hardly fatal. It was the U.S. military—not the Chinese, Russians, or even Muslim-led armies—that prompted fear and instability in the world. America spent nearly as much as the rest of the world combined on weapons, it started and fought pointless, protracted wars, it bombed innocents from airborne robots, and it forced the rest of the world to waste trillions to prevent a single country from being the only one with the ability to effectively use violence.

"The remaining militaries will adopt," Dresner said, speaking for the first time since the meeting started. "Penetration will just be slower."

"I agree," Mandrake said, obviously wanting his new position to become permanent. "Soldiers worldwide are adopting at about the same rate as civilians and they're largely being permitted to use the units at work. Going into combat without the Merge's commercial vision and audio enhancement just isn't going to be practical for much longer. And as other apps like language translation and communications are released, the consumer version will become even more advantageous."

"So all good news," Dresner said.

"Not entirely," Mandrake admitted. "We're still getting bad press over some aspects of LayerCake's judgment system. With regard to products and services it's enormously popular, but judgment of *people* is getting a fair amount of pushback. No one's really complaining about its accuracy, but we're adding an entirely new privacy issue to the hundreds out there already."

"I'm concerned about this," someone at the table said. "LayerCake is already causing us problems and we're only running it at about fifty percent of its true capability. Not to mention the fact that we've set it to lean toward the positive, right?"

"Correct," Mandrake said. "It's obviously still in beta and until we have enough data on individual Merge users to tailor the system to their particular values, we have Javier running essentially a light version."

"And when we do turn the thing on full-guns? Is this something people really want or is the system going to be providing us a little too much information for our own good? And that's leaving aside our legal vulnerability."

Dresner nodded thoughtfully, but it was really just for show. In truth, the public system was running at a far smaller fraction of its actual capability than the board knew—probably closer to twenty percent. Thanks to the brilliant former hacker Javier de Galdiano, LayerCake's heavily firewalled core had almost limitless access to social networking sites, financial information, websites visited, and products purchased—among a host of other critical data points. De Galdiano considered it nothing more than a control—something to compare the results of their public system to in order to create an algorithm that could mimic the less ethical—indeed illegal—central system. In reality, it was the foundation for everything Dresner had spent so many years planning.

"I think this is something we're just going to have to allow to unfold," Dresner said. "We're about to begin a new marketing campaign revolving around people who have been harmed by misinformation on the Internet— people who have been confused with others with the same name, victims of identity theft, people who have been unfairly attacked through social media and other means. The message is that the information is already out there and that LayerCake will make it much more difficult to game or misuse. Let's not forget that we're only three months into this. Considering the revolutionary nature of the technology, it's going surprisingly smoothly."

Mandrake nodded his agreement. "We've had an extremely positive reaction from the focus groups who've seen the ads. I think the momentum is with us and it's just going to get more powerful. Now let's move on to finance, where the news gets even better. The surprise retirement of some of our debt yesterday has driven our stock prices up past four hundred dollars a share for the first time."

The life-sized images of the people in front of him glazed over with greed, causing Dresner's interest in the meeting to fade. It had been Whitfield's money, of course, and based on the speed with which he was able to deliver, he had almost certainly anticipated the request. Once again, he'd demonstrated a level of cleverness that would undoubtedly become dangerous in the future. But not yet. At this point, he was still useful.

"I must leave you," Dresner said. "I think we have every reason to be proud of the Merge's success and to continue to expect great things."

He shut down his feed and replaced it with a set of projections from the marketing department. Graphs rose more than three meters high in front of him and he leaned back in the soft leather chair to study them.

Sales projections had been increased to thirty-three million units worldwide by the end of the first twelve months and eighty-four million at the end of the two-year window he was interested in.

Dresner switched views to a set of bar graphs showing Merge units broken down by country. The United States had the best penetration, followed by Western Europe. Sales were also substantial in China, primarily due to the sheer size of the market. Russia was lagging, though the technology was being adopted by its politicians, soldiers, and industrialists—the most important people to him. The Muslim world was one of their weakest markets due to poverty and Islamic prohibitions. His people continued to create Koran apps, court imams, and refine their Arabic-language offerings, though, and the effort appeared to be showing some reward.

He switched views again, reconfiguring the charts in a way that could only be done from his personal Merge. A block of red began rising from the bottom of the bar graphs, representing the people LayerCake's core processors deemed destructive to society: corrupt politicians, the swelling ranks of financial industry robber barons, criminals, warmongers, and twisted religious leaders, to name only a few of the categories.

It was an ugly view of humanity, with the red portion of the charts rising to almost twenty-four percent—just shy of one and a half million people. Of course, it was also a skewed view. The method of his product's rollout, which confused so many, had been designed to target those who victimized society.

With every passing year, technology magnified the destructive forces available to the ruling class and brought humanity closer to causing its own end. It was only a matter of time before greed combined with waning resources and ideological fanaticism to wipe out billions of innocents while those responsible profited.

He couldn't let that happen. Not now. Not when humanity was so close to perfecting itself.

Dresner switched to another view, projecting the growth of deleterious individuals using his system. When it reached six million—the tipping point he'd calculated would bring the world back from the brink—he would activate the subsystem that killed Craig Bailer. In an instant, the world's militaries would be decimated. Politics and the financial industry would be cleansed of corruption and all-consuming greed. Religious leaders whipping their followers into violent frenzies would finally get an opportunity to discover that their gods existed only in their own minds. For the first time in millennia, the human race would be free.

It would be devastating, of course. All power vacuums—particularly ones of unprecedented size and suddenness—were. But society would quickly knit itself back together and recognize the opportunity offered by the eradication of its parasites and sociopaths.

Not that he was entirely naive. The destructive role vacated by the dead would be soon filled—it was the nature of the smart apes they were so closely related to. But those malignant players wouldn't be capable of re-imposing their stranglehold on the planet. No, the advanced technologies that had proved so dangerous would finally fulfill their promise of transforming the human race. The destroyers would return, but they would be too late.

36

**Near Washington Circle, District of Columbia
USA**

Jon Smith twisted around and scooped a handful of
CDs from the filthy backseat. "How long are you keeping
the car?" he said flipping through them and recognizing
precisely none. The dull whistle of wind coming through
the gaps in the windows was probably preferable to whoever Psycho Charger was.

"The owner gets back on Thursday," Randi said.

She didn't much care for technology, but there was no
questioning her grudging mastery of it. She'd undoubtedly strolled through the Dulles long-term parking lot
running plates against TSA and airline databases to determine the travel plans of each vehicle's owner.

"Marty's house is probably only another fifteen minutes unless we hit traffic," she added. "Don't you think
you should call him?"

Smith sighed quietly. He had been friends with Martin
Zellerbach since high school, but it was an incredibly ex-
hausting relationship. While Marty was a stunning genius

when it came to all things digital, he was the victim of a long list of mental illnesses that combined to make him about as easy to deal with as a bored toddler on a sugar high.

Eighty percent of the fistfights Smith had been in as a kid—and one hundred percent of the high school suspensions—were the result of either protecting Marty from someone he'd insulted or trying to cover up some bizarre prank he'd pulled. His old friend never intended to harm anyone, but it was impossible not to sympathize with the anger he could inspire in others.

Smith grudgingly retrieved his phone and dialed, taking a deep breath and trying to reach the necessary Zen-like state of patience.

"What do you want?"

Marty's greeting wasn't intended to be impolite—it was simply the obvious question in light of the fact that Smith didn't make a lot of purely social calls to him.

"For you to take a look at something."

"What?" he said, the curiosity audible in his voice. The problems that Smith brought him in the past had nearly gotten him killed on a few occasions, but there was no denying that they were interesting.

"Maybe we could talk in person? We're on our way."

"We?"

"Randi's with me."

"Randi? She's with you right now? And you're coming to my house?"

"She insisted. Been dying to see you."

Randi took her eyes off the road long enough to give him the same withering stare her sister used to, but he ignored it.

"She said that?" There was a pause that seemed long even for him. "How long until you're here?"

"Less than fifteen."

Another silence.

"So Jon. Are you wearing old clothes by any chance?"

It was an odd question, but Smith was used to odd questions from his old friend. "Muddy running clothes. She's in jeans and a sweatshirt."

"Are the jeans tight?"

"Focus, Marty."

"Do you have guns?"

"What?"

"It's a simple question."

"Are you taking your meds?"

"Yes."

Smith looked over at Randi. "Do we have guns? Mine's still in the glove box of the Triumph."

The roll of her eyes suggested it was a stupid question.

"Yes."

"Extra clips?"

"I have no doubt."

"Bring them."

"You're sure you're okay?"

"Fine. I just need your help with something. Call it the cost of my inestimable services."

"Can't I just pay your fee?"

"No."

The line went dead.

* * *

Pₐᵣₖ HERE," SMITH SAID. "Let's not get too close."

Randi pulled to the curb of the quiet street and they continued on foot, quickly covering the remaining two hundred meters to a gate protecting Zellerbach's driveway. Out of habit, neither stood in front of it, instead ducking behind a sign that read, "Private property—keep out. No trespassing. No soliciting. No collectors. Go Away."

"Marty, it's us," Smith said, holding down the intercom button. "Open the gate."

No response.

"Marty! Open the damn gate."

Nothing.

"Shit," Smith muttered.

What the hell was going on? The intercom wasn't broken—Marty was physically unable to tolerate electronics that weren't state of the art and in perfect operating condition.

"Do you think there's a problem?" Randi said. "Is this why he told us to bring guns?"

Smith shrugged and then let out a long breath—something he did a lot when Marty was involved. "We're going to have to go in."

"I have a better idea. Let's call the police and let them do it."

Her reluctance was understandable. Marty cherished his privacy enough to spend a fair amount of time and money on custom security measures that included air horns, stink bombs, and the dreaded fish catapult. It was the latter that had finally caused UPS, FedEx, and the post office to stop serving his address.

Smith just shook his head miserably and began climbing over the tall hedge that acted as a surprisingly effective fence. He dropped into an untended flower bed on the other side and waited a disconcertingly long time before Randi landed gracefully next to him.

Pulling the Glock she'd lent him, he examined the expansive yard and confirmed that it was exactly as he remembered: half dead and half overgrown into a jungle-like mess. Apparently Marty hadn't been able to coerce his gardeners to come back either.

"House looks fine," Randi observed. "No broken windows. No damage to the door that I can see from here."

Smith nodded. "You go left. I'll go straight."

He'd made it less than four meters when a mechanical whirring became audible just in front of him. His heart sank when he saw a potted plant start to flip backward on a hinge. If it was the catapult, Marty was going to wish he'd never been born.

It wasn't. Instead of rubber tubing and out-of-date seafood, the mechanism in front of him had two serious-looking barrels sticking through heavy steel armor.

"Jesus!" he shouted and hit the ground just as one of them opened up.

He rolled immediately to his feet and sprinted left, seeing Randi firing uselessly at the mechanical bunker that was, thank God, just a little too slow to track him.

It quickly lost interest in him and targeted Randi, who broke into a run only to be hit with a fire hose that took her feet out from under her. She was obviously dazed and just lay there in the mud as Smith angled toward her, diving when he was still a meter and a half away. He landed harder on top of her than he'd planned, but his momentum was enough to roll them both behind a tree. The staccato bark of the gun when silent as it lost line of sight on its targets.

"Are you okay?"

She choked and a stream of water flowed from her mouth. "I...I told you we should let the police handle this."

"Look, I don't know what's going on or who the hell installed real weapons, but we need to find out without getting any cops killed."

She gestured toward a large concrete planter halfway between them and the front door. "If you can keep the bunker busy, maybe I could make it to there."

The planter looked new and a little out of place. "Too obvious."

"Drawing us in?"

He nodded. "I think I can outrun the gun. I'm going to go back the way I came and when I do, you go for the east side of the house. See if you can get in though one of the windows."

"On three," she agreed.

They burst from cover in unison, the crunch of their footsteps immediately drowned out by the gun opening up again. Smith was right about being able to outrun it, but only barely and only at a full sprint. He passed behind a small stand of trees and came to a section of the yard that looked suspiciously healthy and well laid out.

When he tried to stop he discovered that his suspicion was well founded. The plants were fake, resting on a slick sheet of plastic hidden beneath a thin layer of mulch. He landed on his back and slid uncontrollably toward a dense bush that almost certainly contained something unpleasant.

The knife Randi had insisted on giving him was sheathed on his forearm and he rolled onto his stomach, slamming it through the plastic with enough force to bring him to a stop next to a tiered fountain full of green sludge.

With no other option, he took cover behind it, tensing as he waited for it to blow up, tip over on him, or fly away. When none of those things happened, he risked a quick peek around its edge at Randi, who was still trying to get to the edge of the house.

She had what looked like an open line and her hesitant pace suggested that he wasn't the only one who thought it was too easy. It looked like she was going to make it right up to the moment when she suddenly disappeared into the earth.

"Randi!"

No answer.

Smith grabbed a faded lawn gnome and threw it into the open. When the machine gun started tracking it, he slipped around the fountain and leapt over a rusting wheelbarrow in an effort to get to her.

He was less than halfway there when a familiar mechanical whirring started at his two o'clock. This time, there was nowhere to hide. The roar of the second gun filled his ears just before an impact sent him headlong into the dirt.

He reached for his chest and his hand came away bright red. Dead center of mass. He closed his eyes and the breath escaped him.

He'd always known that one day Marty would be the death of him.

Randi Russell stood on the mattresses stacked at the bottom of the concrete-lined pit and looked at the steel doors that had closed above her. She'd heard a second machine gun come online a few seconds after she'd fallen but now everything was silent.

"Jon!" she shouted. "Jon! Can you hear me?"

It wasn't Smith who answered, though. Instead, a section of wall next to her slid aside, exposing a computer monitor with Marty's Zellerbach's disembodied face centered in it.

"Randi! How could you possibly still look so hot after all that? Is there no limit to your sexiness?"

"Marty?"

"I should have known I couldn't sucker you with the planter. You wouldn't believe the thing I built back there. It's based on an orb spider's—"

She rushed the screen and slammed her hands on both sides, trying to ignore the half-drowned, mud-splattered reflection in the glass. "I'm going to kill you, Marty. And that's not a figure of speech. I am actually going to *murder* you and then hide your body somewhere no one will ever find it."

"What?" he said, sounding genuinely surprised by her anger. "You do this for a living. Would I get mad if you asked me to fix your router?"

"Where's Jon? Is he okay?"

"Oh, he's just lying there milking it…Wait. No, he's up now. Hmmm. He looks a little pissed, too."

"You were shooting at him with a machine gun, Marty!"

"Don't be so melodramatic. The right barrel had blanks in it and the left one's a paintball gun. Man, you guys are pretty quick. I'm going to have to replace the turret motors with something more powerful. Or maybe it's just the rain we've been having. Some rust could have gotten in there and—"

"Marty..." she said, trying to sound calm through clenched teeth.

"What exactly was it that you didn't like about the planter, Randi? What if I made it a statue? Maybe me on a horse. That would be—"

"Shut up, Marty! Shut up, shut up! And get me the hell out of here!"

37

JAMES WHITFIELD SAT IN THE windowless room at the back of his house, illumination coming only from a small lamp hovering over his desk.

Arrogance.

With age was supposed to come wisdom, and for the most part it had. But now he'd made grave, and uncharacteristically amateurish, mistakes. Not only had he drawn conclusions with insufficient facts, he'd erred on the side of underestimating an opponent instead of the other way around. In his younger years battling the KGB, he'd be dead. A fate that would have been richly deserved.

The clock on his laptop ticked over to four p.m. and before he could even reach out, a quiet ring emanated from it. Another example of the captain's unflagging efficiency.

"Yes," he said, picking up the heavily encrypted line.

"Did you receive the file I had couriered to you, sir?"

"I did."

"You know we use the Internet to transmit—"

"I'm aware of that, Captain. Thank you. Now, what have you found out about the transfers?"

"Not as much as we'd hoped. I have been able to confirm that both are on hold."

"Why?"

"Smith reported a concussion from a car accident this morning."

Whitfield would have actually allowed himself an admiring smile if the situation weren't so dire. Had that simply been a convenient excuse or was the army scientist sticking his middle finger in the air?

"And Russell?"

"Some sort of disciplinary action. Obviously, our eyes aren't as sharp inside the Agency."

Disciplinary action. He himself might not have thought of that. Credible in that it was something that could crop up suddenly, would prevent reassignment, and also was entirely fitting with her work history. Clever. Clever enough to make him break a sweat.

"Keep me informed, Captain. There are no details too trivial."

"I understand, sir."

Whitfield severed the connection and reached into an open safe to retrieve the file on Smith, ignoring for the moment the much thinner one on Russell. His wife started a vacuum cleaner somewhere in the house but the comforting sense of normalcy that it usually provided didn't come. Not today.

He spread the contents across his desk in neat stacks—not something that could be done with the computer files the captain was constantly trying to get him to use. There was something about seeing it all laid out that helped him think. Though he recognized that his was the last generation harboring such a bias.

Lieutenant Colonel Smith's record was spotless. He had performed admirably as a front-line doctor in virtually every hot spot on the planet and later had become one of the army's top virus hunters. It seemed generally agreed on that he was borderline brilliant in the realm of science and, more interesting, just as capable in combat. On no fewer than two occasions, he had taken command of the special forces team he'd been embedded with as a doctor and the experienced operators had fallen in behind him without question.

If he had any weakness, it was that he wasn't terribly good at hiding the fact that he believed himself to be the smartest man in the room. It was an attitude that tended not to be particularly appreciated by one's superiors, but one that Whitfield could sympathize with. And in Smith's defense, it appeared that he generally *was* the smartest man in the room.

In truth, if he had been aware of the existence of Lieutenant Colonel Jon Smith, Whitfield would have seriously considered recruiting him. The problem was that he suspected someone had beat him to it.

Many of Smith's exploits were easily explained on the surface. The Hades virus had been very much within his sphere of influence. And his involvement with DNA computers could—tenuously—account for his actions in France. Even his participation in investigations in Russia and Africa tracked to a bioterror angle. But upon deeper analysis, disturbing questions surfaced. Actual orders were hard to come by and it seemed that he had been on mysterious leaves of absence during a number of those episodes.

Just as strange was his on-again-off-again partnership with Peter Howell. Not that anyone wouldn't want the former SAS/MI6 man watching their back, but he was a retired foreign agent. The U.S. military had its own people for these types of operations.

And finally, there was the stalling of the transfers his contacts inside the army and CIA had orchestrated.

The obvious explanation was that Smith, and possibly Russell, had a power base outside the organizations they were publicly affiliated with. A power base that was in no way trivial.

Whitfield continued to shuffle through the papers for another ten minutes, but finally had to admit that the answers weren't there. Only dangerous hints and impenetrable shadows.

Revealing himself had been stupid. He'd been understandably reluctant to move against two patriots who had served their country so admirably. It seemed reasonable to believe that his conversation with Smith, combined with the transfers, would convince the scientist that he had inadvertently tread on ground well beyond his pay grade. As far as Russell was concerned, she was even easier. Embroil her in the Yemeni resistance and she'd forget all about this. That woman just liked to fight.

Now, though, he was paralyzed until he could gain a deeper understanding of the situation and players. Any blind action on his part could have serious and unpredictable repercussions.

Patience was the only available course of action. He'd have to be content to watch and wait. It wouldn't last, though. Soon he would have to act and deal with the blowback as best he could.

38

JON, YOU LOOK TERRIBLE. But you, Randi...you are a vision, as always."

Marty Zellerbach was standing in the doorway, his pale, puffy head and hands the only thing emerging from a shimmering red tracksuit. Undoubtedly, his finest regalia in honor of Randi's visit.

He turned and headed back into the house, indicating for them to follow. "Try not to get the rug dirty, if you wouldn't mind. It's new."

Randi pantomimed strangling him from behind and Smith grinned as he examined the side of his friend's head. He spotted the telltale glimmer of studs when they passed beneath a light.

Not that he was surprised—Zellerbach was a lifelong technology addict. There was very little of interest that he hadn't bought and disassembled. In high school, his room had been piled with the carcasses of everything from Atari game consoles, to Rubik's cubes, to VCRs. It was precisely this tendency, along with his two PhDs, that made him perfect for the job.

They entered a room in the back dominated by an enormous worktable and an even more enormous Cray computer.

Zellerbach dropped into the only chair and left them to lean against the back wall. "Now, why is it you're here?"

Smith pointed to a Merge disassembled on the table. "That."

His response came out in one long rush. "Isn't it *incredible*? I mean, I knew Christian Dresner was a genius, but he always seemed to waste it on boring things like antibiotics and hearing aids. Who would have thought he had this in him? I've already got four apps in to Dresner for approval, but I haven't heard back yet. One's particularly sweet. It lets you—"

"What do you know about it, Marty?"

"The Merge? What do you mean?"

"You've taken it apart. What did you learn?"

"Oh, that. They sent me one for free because of my tech blog. Thought I'd have a closer look."

"And?" Smith said, trying not to let his exasperation show. As he suspected, Zellerbach was just about due for another dose of his meds and was starting to lose focus. He'd get increasingly manic until he took a pill that would then cause him to descend into sluggishness. It was the brief span between those extremes when his incredible mental horsepower really shined.

"You tell me, Jon. Rumor has it that you're running the military's development program."

Smith frowned deeply. Was there anyone on the planet

who didn't have that particular piece of classified information? "And where did you hear that?"

"If the military doesn't want people on their networks they should do a better job of securing them."

Smith just let that go. "What about the Merge? Can it be hacked?"

"If you were to give me the encryption codes."

"I don't have them."

"Come on. After everything I've done for you, you're going to stand there and lie to my face?"

"Scout's honor, Marty. I don't need Dresner's approval to upload software but I can't get into the operating system."

Zellerbach couldn't hide his disappointment. "In that case, it can't be done."

"You've told me a hundred times that there's no such thing as a completely secure computer."

"But this is different," he whined. "You don't just have to come up with the password—and it isn't going to be his birthday or his dog's name—you'd have to mimic the way his brain communicates that password to the system. And he's the only person who knows the language the brain speaks."

"Catch-22," Randi said.

"Exactly. In order to access the system you'd have to know so much about it you wouldn't need to access it."

None of this was any real surprise. Smith's own people, as well as the NSA's brain trust, had told him exactly the same thing.

"You're sure the military doesn't have access and you're just not telling me, Jon? I can keep a secret. And I have some other app ideas that Dresner's gonna be a dick about. You know, with the right camera, you could see everyone naked—like those glasses in the comic books when we were kids. Tell me *that's* not a moneymaker."

"You're already rich," Randi pointed out.

"True. Would you like to come out on my yacht? I have a bikini in mind for you that would—"

"You don't have a yacht."

"But I do have the bikini."

She gave him a stern look that hid a smile. "Let's see if we can focus on the task at hand, shall we?"

He shrugged. "There *is* no task at hand."

"So, you're telling me that no one has hijacked this system."

"Hijacked it? No way. Not without Dresner's direct involvement. And if he's involved, that's not really hijacking, is it?"

It always circled back to Dresner. Did he know the asshole who totaled the Triumph? And if so, what exactly was their relationship?

"Can it affect your mind?" Randi said.

"That's *all* it does—makes you hear and see things that aren't really there. Icons, maps, music…"

"What I mean is, could it, for instance, make a soldier not defend himself? Could it turn a very religious person into an atheist?"

Zellerbach's brow knitted. "I'm not sure what you're asking."

"Simple question, Marty."

He pondered it for a moment. "I mean, I could code something that made everyone who attacked you look like your mother. That might make you less likely to fight back. Not sure how you'd turn someone into an atheist."

"I've talked to a few neurologists about this," Smith said. "And they all tell me it's pretty far-fetched. There is evidence that religiosity and the propensity for violence have a genetic component. And they have been able to manipulate it in a crude way using magnetic waves, but it takes a lot of power and the effect is pretty unpredictable."

"Maybe someone's figured it out. I'm guessing that if we asked your neurologist friends a few months ago about projecting Angry Birds onto my visual cortex they'd have said no chance in hell."

"Touché."

Marty shook his head. "It's possible, but really unlikely. Even if you could figure out how to do it, the magnetic fields you're talking about would take so much juice. Seriously, if you were eating breakfast, you'd be in danger of your spoon flying up and sticking to your head. That's just physics. Ever wonder why you have to have the unit plugged in for the sleep function? Power. And sleep is light-years easier than changing someone's personality."

"So you're saying there's no way to affect someone like that."

Another shrug. "You could make people dizzy and nauseous. That'd make them not want to fight or go to church."

"Yeah," Smith said. "But if the Merge really started screwing with you—made you sick, changed your personality, or whatever—why wouldn't you just turn it off?"

"Someone could disable the switch."

"Sure," Marty said. "But there wouldn't be anything stopping you from taking it off and walking out of range.

Or hitting it with a hammer. Or throwing it in a pool. Or—"

"I get the point, Marty. Thank you. What about something permanent?"

"You think Christian Dresner is trying to give us brain damage?" he said, squinting a bit as he examined Randi. "Why are you asking all this stuff?"

Smith wasn't prepared to tell him about Afghanistan and that reticence made this line of questioning less effective than it could be. Science was about the free exchange of ideas and he always seemed to be in the position of having to hide something.

"We're just brainstorming here. We'd like to make sure we cover all the angles before we hand it out to our entire military."

Marty didn't seem entirely convinced. "The short answer to Randi's question is no. Doing physical damage to the brain would take still more power. Even if you suddenly emptied an entire Merge battery into one skull implant, it'd just give you a nasty shock and confuse you for a few seconds."

"Very brief, very weak electroshock therapy," Smith agreed.

"Maybe our question needs to be broader," Randi said. "Marty, is there *any way* you could use this thing to do mischief?"

It was a beautifully phrased challenge. Marty's job, his passion—in fact all he really ever thought about—was new ways to do mischief. And in light of that, his answer was surprising.

"Not without getting Dresner to approve apps that he'd never get behind in a million years."

"I can't believe you're so easily defeated."

Another nicely phrased challenge. Smith decided to reinforce it. "He's right, Randi. It's a tough problem. Maybe we should go see that kid from Anonymous. I hear he's—"

"I didn't say I wouldn't look into it! Did I? *Did I?* I don't think so."

"Well, we—"

"Look, there are a few things in the Merge hardware that I don't completely understand," Marty said, suddenly desperate to prove his superiority over his Anonymous nemesis. "I assume they're future upgrade paths or maybe something to do with battery management. But if they're not being used, maybe they're not locked down by the operating system. It's possible I could get control of them. And I've only been thinking about this for less than half an hour! You can't expect me to work that fast! No one can!"

"That's the Marty I know and love," Randi said. "So here's your assignment, Marty. Make that thing do something evil."

* * *

THE DOOR BEHIND THEM closed and both Smith and Randi immediately slowed, looking around the quiet yard for any sign of the security systems they'd tangled with on the way in.

"You don't think he'd…"

Smith shook his head. "I think even Marty knows better."

She nodded, but let him take point in case the fish catapult should suddenly appear. "What now?"

"Dresner," Smith responded. "If Marty and my people are right, no one does anything without his approval."

"They could have missed something."

"Maybe. But just between you and me, we've thrown everything we have at this and come up completely empty."

"Looking to cut Dresner out of the loop?"

Smith shrugged. "Not specifically, but it makes sense for us to have as much control over our system as we can. You can't be too careful."

"Do you think Dresner's responsible for what happened in Afghanistan?"

"Based on everything I know about him, it seems far-fetched. But it's worth looking into."

"What about the guy who wrecked the Triumph?"

"Hopefully, Star's making some progress. But if not, I have some ideas of my own on that subject."

They made it to the gate and were both relieved to be through it and back out on the street. Damp and muddy, yes. But not picking smelt out of their hair.

"Then we're off to Germany," Randi said.

"Germany? Why?"

"Because I have a friend there that I think can help."

39

Berlin
Germany

I⊤ WAS A PART OF BERLIN that Smith had never been to—
old warehouses and dirty streets lit by security lights that
came to life as their car drifted by. Randi, on the other
hand, seemed to know where she was going, so he leaned
back and closed his eyes.

The car came to a stop and he jerked upright, not sure
if he'd been asleep or not. "Are we there?"

"It's about three blocks west," Randi said. "I didn't
want to park right out front."

She hadn't provided a great deal of detail on who they
were going to see, only that the man's name was Johannes
and that he might have some records they would find
useful.

When Smith stepped out, though, the area didn't look
terribly promising. She'd parked in front of a boarded-up
building and it was dark enough that he stumbled a bit as
he jogged up alongside her.

"I thought they moved the Stasi Records Office over
by Checkpoint Charlie," Smith said as they continued

along the empty street. The frigid wind was funneling between the buildings and through his light jacket, but at least the forecasted downpour hadn't materialized.

"Johannes doesn't exactly work for the BStU," she said using the German acronym. "He's more of a private consultant."

The euphemism was classic CIA—entirely ambiguous, yet vaguely official sounding.

"Private consultant," Smith muttered. "More likely former Stasi."

"Why devolve into labels?" she responded with a wry smile. "Aren't we all just people in the end?"

"Christ..."

East Germany's secret police had the dubious honor of being the most paranoid organization in history. At its peak, it had employed over a hundred thousand people to watch over a population of only sixteen million. According to some calculations, spying on its own citizens had been East Germany's largest industry.

When it became clear that the wall was coming down, the Stasi started shoveling their literally billions of pages of documents into shredders and incinerators. And when those broke down, they cut them up. And when they ran out of scissors, they ripped them by hand. Eventually, the country's citizens figured out what was happening and began storming the Stasi buildings, taking control of the records and keeping any more from being destroyed. Now they were housed on the BStU's endless expanse of shelves, waiting to be organized, deciphered, and disseminated.

The building they finally came to looked as abandoned as the one they'd parked next to. A rap on a steel portal that looked like navy surplus, though, caused an immediate reaction. A bulb hidden in the jamb came to life and lit their faces for a moment before the door opened and they were motioned inside.

"I'm Konrad," the young man said, glancing out at the empty street before closing them in with the throw of a heavy deadbolt. "Johannes's assistant."

Smith and Randi nodded politely but declined to introduce themselves. It seemed to be a custom that the German was used to and he led them down a narrow corridor to a much more modern-looking door—this one complete with a retinal scanner and keypad that he made use of.

When it slid back on quiet motors, Konrad stepped aside. Smith was initially a little hesitant to enter but his reticence faded when Randi strolled casually through in front of him.

"Darling!" the man rushing toward them said. He had a narrow head with a few wisps of gray hair still clinging to it and a spherical torso that suggested a lengthy love affair with sausage and beer.

"Johannes. It's been too long," Randi said, switching to German.

They embraced, but Smith barely noticed, instead looking in awe at the room around them. It was probably twenty meters high and seventy-five square, filled with teetering shelves that rose almost to the ceiling. Every inch was covered with some kind of crate, box, or garbage bag stuffed to the point of overflowing.

What little open floor existed was dominated by four huge machines that were a steampunk kluge of copper funnels, conveyor belts, and exposed electric cables.

What they did or whether they were even functional, Smith could only guess.

"Colonel!" Johannes said, offering his thick hand. "What do you think of my little recycling center?"

"Impressive. Where did you get all this?"

"Oh, a bit here and a tad there. When East Germany began to fail, I understood that it was time to embrace capitalism. To become a Westerner, yes? But what did I know? What could I do? And then it came to me. I knew the Stasi. I knew the files."

"The important ones," Smith added.

"Just so. The rabble became bold very quickly, but I had three weeks before they gained control. And in that time, I managed to spirit away the documents you see around you. To keep them out of their hands and the hands of the BStU."

Smith tried to calculate how many tiny pieces of shredded paper they were surrounded by. A hundred billion? A hundred trillion?

"Seems like intact files would have been easier."

He laughed. "Never pay for an intact file, my good Colonel. The Stasi shredded the most important things first. That is where the valuable information is contained."

"And is that what the machines are for?"

"Exactly! My son built them for me." His expression transformed into one of pride. "I know that every parent says this, but he is a very fine young man. And a brilliant engineer."

"So the machines can put it all back together?"

"We used to do it by hand. Unbelievably time-consuming and tedious work. But now we pour the scraps in these machines. They create three-D images of each piece and send the data to my computers. There they are reassembled like a puzzle."

"Seems like it would have been expensive to develop and build machines like that."

"Well, I do provide the fruits of my labor to select clients. And they've been very generous."

Smith didn't doubt it. Individuals, newspapers, politicians, intelligence agencies—even academics—still had a great deal of interest in what had gone on behind the Iron Curtain. Hell, even if Johannes just used what he found for simple blackmail, he wouldn't exactly be wondering where his next meal was coming from.

"The CIA got in on the ground floor," Randi said. "And in return for our early support, we get a peek at anything interesting he turns up."

"And what is it you're interested in today, my dear?"

"Christian Dresner."

His jovial expression turned to one of caution. "He has done very well for himself."

"Have you had requests for files relating to him before?" Smith asked.

"Of course. Many."

"And have you fulfilled them?"

The German shook his head. "Dresner is a powerful man and I suspect has the resources to discover where they came from."

"But you have something?" Randi said. "You have the Stasi records on him?"

"Yes."

"What's in them?"

He hesitated. "I know this goes without saying, but I'd ask you to be very discreet."

"As always, Johannes."

He sighed quietly. "There is a great deal of information. The Stasi were fanatics for recording every detail of people's lives—particularly ones they considered important or subversive. Can you give me an idea of what you would like to know?"

"What did he do for the Soviets?" Smith said. "Bioweapons research?"

"Not at all. At the time, you'll remember that the East Germans were quite dominant in athletics..."

"He doped athletes?" Randi said, surprised.

"Doped them, created training programs for them, studied their physiology. Along with a young psychologist named Gerhard Eichmann, Dresner is largely responsible for East Germany's success during that period."

"I was expecting something a little more sinister," Randi said, sounding a bit disappointed.

Again, Johannes seemed to speak with reluctance. "You might be surprised, dear. The Soviets were very committed to their athletic program. Like the Nazis, they saw it as a way to showcase their superiority. Many of these people were experimented on in ways that would never be allowed now. And not only adults. Often gifted children were taken from their families, separated into test groups, and subjected to different programs to judge which was best. Between the strain, the unproven drugs, and the psychological abuse—brainwashing you would say—many didn't survive. And the ones who did were never the same."

Smith kept his face impassive, unsure how to feel about what he was hearing. In fairness, the young Christian Dresner wouldn't have known anything other than the communist machine that dominated every aspect of his life. And when he'd finally come to understand what he was doing, he'd escaped and devoted the rest of his life to making the world a better place.

"Gerhard Eichmann," Randi said. "He's the one who escaped with Dresner, right?"

The German nodded. "Theirs was a very close friendship. No evidence exists that either ever informed on the other. A rare thing in a country where everyone was on the Stasi payroll in some way or another."

"It must have been tough for two people who were so important to get over the wall," Smith said. "I'm surprised it went so smoothly."

"Not entirely smoothly. On the way out, Dresner went to the orphanage where he was raised in order to face the man who ran it."

"Face?" Randi said.

"More accurately, beat to death with a cane."

They both must have looked a bit shocked, because Johannes seemed to feel compelled to elaborate.

"He was a cruel man, you must understand. The abuse the children suffered at his hands was truly horrible. It was a fitting end, I think."

Smith remembered what Klein had told him about Dresner—the fact that he'd been too mentally unstable to hold a job after his escape. In light of this hidden history, it wasn't surprising. What would it be like to grow up like that and then suddenly have your position changed from victim to victimizer? When he'd looked into the faces of the children he was experimenting on, had he seen his own?

"What about Eichmann," Randi said. "Do you have files on him, too?"

"Of course," Johannes said, turning toward the back of the cavernous building. "If you would follow me to the terminals, we can begin sorting through the information you're interested in."

* * *

His phone rang and Konrad picked up immediately, speaking softly, though he knew that nothing said in his office could be heard in the warehouse. "Did you receive the photos I sent?"

"I did," the electronically altered voice on the other end responded.

He'd been contacted by the anonymous man only a few weeks after he'd taken the job with Johannes. The request had been simple: Notify him if anyone should ever come asking about Christian Dresner.

Konrad had initially refused, but when the subject of payment was raised, his resistance had faded. Three million euros for a simple phone call.

He'd begun to wonder if he would ever have an opportunity to actually earn the money he'd been paid, but then a few minutes ago, a subtle alarm on his computer had sounded. Christian Dresner's name had been entered into their network's search function.

"Are they alone?" the voice said.

"I think so, but I can't be sure. They arrived on foot. I never saw a car."

The line went dead.

40

Berlin
Germany

THE WIND HAD DIED DOWN and, while there were no stars visible, the rain still seemed to be holding off. Smith and Randi stayed in the center of the empty road, taking a different route back to their car. It was quiet enough that they could hear Johannes throwing the dead-bolt on his door and Smith felt a little regret at the sound. He could have spent the next ten years in that place exploring the secret history of the Cold War. And of Christian Dresner.

Randi finally managed to connect with Star and he leaned in toward her phone as they walked.

"Hey, Randi. How's Germany?"

"Cold. I need you to find someone for me. Gerhard Eichmann. He escaped East Germany with Dresner back in the seventies."

"An actual name! I like working with you better than Jon."

"That hurts," Smith said loud enough for her to hear. "But since you bring it up, how's that going?"

"Don't be sad, Jon! You know I love you. But as far as how it's going, I'm not sure yet."

Out of the corner of his left eye, Smith spotted a shadow moving between two buildings. It was probably just a stray cat or loose awning, but he immediately began scanning both sides of the street. "You better hurry. I have a plan and I might just beat you to it."

"I'm not worried."

He spotted what looked like a human shape around the side of a van rusting away in an alley just ahead. Randi gave an almost imperceptible nod to indicate that she saw it, too.

Once again, he was missing the Merge that he was becoming increasingly reluctant to use. It was a little frightening how quickly he'd become reliant on it.

"Careful, Star," Randi said, still speaking casually. "He's a lot brighter than he looks."

In the end, he didn't need sophisticated vision enhancement. Two men emerged from the shadows and ran into the street in front of them as two more closed from the sides. A quick glance back confirmed what he already intuitively knew. One more behind.

"Gotta dash," Randi said into the phone. "Talk later."

"Looks like five total," Smith said quietly.

"Yeah, but they all look like morons."

It was a fair observation. Each had either extremely close-cropped hair or a shaved head. Neck and face tattoos complemented heavy jackets and boots with jeans partially rolled up. At least one swastika was visible—on a silver chain hanging around one man's neck.

They kept moving forward, not stopping until they were a meter or two from the men blocking their path.

The ones coming in from the sides didn't seem to be in a hurry and the one in back had slowed to a crawl, giving himself room to intercept if they should make a break for it.

The question was what exactly was happening. Was this just bad luck—the not-so-surprising result of wandering around a bad neighborhood at an hour when the skinheads were just heading home to sleep it off? Or was it something more?

"I'd suggest you move on, son," Smith said in German. "We don't have anywhere near enough money to make this worth your while."

The one on the right, probably no more than midtwenties, seemed to hesitate. He was undoubtedly accustomed to generating a lot more fear in the couples he mugged. The one on the left just stared hungrily at them with wet eyes reflecting the glow of a security light behind them.

"Maybe there's more money in this than you have in your wallet. And I think we will enjoy the woman very much," the nervous one said, then glanced behind him at a car parked at the edge of the intersection. Smith had noticed it earlier, but until now hadn't seen the figure standing in front of it.

With the question of whether this was just an unfortunate coincidence answered, it was probably time to move on to just how they were going to stay alive.

"I can guarantee you that she won't be as fun as you think."

The men at three and nine o'clock stopped a few paces away and the footsteps behind went silent at what Smith estimated to be five meters. It was a practiced pattern designed to deal with bolting prey—almost certainly perfected over a number of years of petty muggings.

"What do they want?" Randi said in Russian, feigning terror and checking the faces around them for comprehension. The Soviets hadn't controlled the country since before these men were born and it appeared that none of them could understand the language of their former masters.

Smith responded soothingly in the same language, reaching out and giving her hand a reassuring squeeze. "The one to my left is probably seventeen and the one behind is too far to do much quickly."

"Surprise is on our side," she said, making her words sound like panicked babble. "But once they move in, we've got problems. I say we take out the leader and Crazy Eyes. That might be enough to make the others decide the paycheck isn't big enough."

"Speak German!" the one she'd dubbed "Crazy Eyes" shouted.

"She doesn't know how," Smith said, again trying to sound soothing. He wanted to find a way out of this without killing anyone. They were young and had no idea what they were into. The problem was that flying commercial had left them with no guns and Randi was right about the dangers of letting them attack first. "Now, I'm asking you again. Move on."

They all laughed—the humorless braying of young men who enjoyed violence when they were confident in their superior position.

"Or what?" their leader said. "Are you are going to kill us?"

"Probably."

More laughter, but the man who had spoken didn't join in. He was a little older than the others and didn't seem quite as stupid.

"You're going to get us killed with all this hand wringing," Randi said, no longer bothering to play the role of frightened woman. "Crazy Eyes goes first. Their ringleader's yours."

"Wait! We might be able—"

But she didn't wait. She reached behind her for the six-inch knife she'd brought in her checked luggage and with an underhand flick of her wrist sent it spinning through the air. Smith recognized that it was too late to stop this and launched himself forward.

The speed of her action and dim light made it impossible to follow the weapon, forcing him to make a few quick assumptions. The chest was the easiest target but getting good penetration would be almost impossible at this range. No, Randi would take the riskier approach. She always did.

Smith was already reaching for Crazy Eyes's neck when the knife passed by and lodged there. Dead center, but her rotation was off a bit. Not so much that it didn't penetrate a good inch into his windpipe, though.

Shouts rose up around them, but he barely heard, concentrating on getting hold of the knife's hilt before the others could process what was happening. Smith drove it in the remaining five inches before yanking it out and spinning, building enough momentum to ram it deep into the lead man's stomach.

Randi was already running toward the car in the intersection when Smith pulled the blade and followed. The young man wouldn't die, which was a good thing, but really just an ancillary benefit. Stomach wounds were nasty and had a tendency to demoralize everyone around.

Smith had made it only ten meters when the expected wailing started from the wounded man, but so did the pursuing footsteps. When he looked back, all three of the uninjured men were chasing at a full sprint. Apparently concern for one's comrades wasn't one of this group's virtues.

He ducked a wrench thrown by the man in the lead, but focused on the one who had stopped to dig a hand desperately into his jacket.

"Gun!"

Randi kept going, but crouched and began zigzagging as the first shot sounded. Smith did the same, daring another quick look back to confirm that they were holding the gap to their pursuers. Youth, adrenaline, and rage couldn't quite overcome the disadvantage of too many cigarettes and heavy boots.

Ahead, Smith could hear the sickly sound of a starter motor as the man who had been watching tried to get his engine to fire. Randi was pulling ahead and he said a silent prayer that she would just run past the car and into the darkness.

As usual, though, his prayer was ignored. Another bullet passed by and Smith crouched lower as Randi ran full-speed into the side of the car, slamming an elbow into the driver's-side window. It was old enough that safety glass hadn't been an option and it shattered all over the man as he tried to jerk away.

Smith collided with the rear quarter panel as Randi threw open the door and dragged the man onto the pavement.

All three of their pursuers were almost on top of them and Smith tossed her the knife. She pulled the man to his feet and pressed the crimson blade up under his chin. Hopefully, they cared about him more than the friends they'd left bleeding on the pavement.

The three skidded to a stop a couple meters away. The one with the gun tried to get a bead on Randi, who was hidden behind the bulky older man.

"You have a knife," one of them said. "We have a gun."

By way of response, Randi pressed harder with the weapon they were so unimpressed with, breaking the skin under the chin of the man she was holding.

"Stop," the man said, slurring a bit because he couldn't move his jaw without being cut deeper. "If I'm dead, none of you gets paid."

At this point, it seemed unlikely that any of them were going to get paid anyway, but none of the remaining three was smart enough to realize it.

"Get out of here," Smith said.

None moved.

"Get the hell out of here!" he shouted. "Run!"

They finally did, heading back up the road, right past their fallen comrades, and into the gloom.

Randi shoved the man behind the wheel and slid into the backseat while Smith ran to the other side and dropped into the passenger seat.

"Drive," Randi said and the man twisted the key. This time the engine caught.

He looked terrified as they pulled onto the empty street and accelerated into darkness deep enough to resist his dirty headlights.

"Where'd the money to pay those assholes come from?" Randi said.

"I don't know."

"Cut his finger off, Jon."

"No! I swear to you. I got a text asking me to do this. The money was wired from an offshore account."

"When did you get the text?"

"A few hours ago."

"How many hours."

"I don't know. Four?"

"Shit," Randi said, pulling out her phone and dialing. It rang a few times but, to her obvious relief, was eventually picked up. Johannes's tinny voice was clearly audible in the confines of the car.

"Randi? Is everything all right?"

"Are you still at the warehouse?"

"Yes."

"Someone knows we were there. They—"

"Yes, I was afraid of that."

"What? Why?"

"Konrad. He made an unauthorized phone call, but I don't know to whom. When I questioned him about it, he tried to kill me. Can you imagine? After everything I've done for him? I'm afraid I had to shoot him."

"Thanks for the warning," she said sarcastically.

"And thank you for coming here and ending my life as I know it."

"Look, I'm going to send some people—"

"No, you've already done quite enough. The first thing I did when I started this business was make preparations for my retirement. Good-bye, Randi. We won't see each other again."

She severed the connection and leaned up between the seats. "Why does this son of a bitch still have ten fingers?"

He began to protest in panicked, rapid-fire German again, but Smith tuned him out. The man's age, dull eyes, and cheap suit suggested that he was nobody—a former low-level Stasi agent who used the endless supply of neo-Nazi idiots to make a buck. Whoever they were up against wasn't stupid enough to reveal their identity to him.

Smith's foot bumped something under the seat and he pulled out a small bag stuffed with euros. He handed it back to Randi, who immediately started counting.

"I'm a little insulted at the amount," she said. "But it's definitely enough to get us upgraded to first class with a little left over for a decent dinner in Frankfurt."

"That's not your money!" the man sputtered, eyes widening enough to suggest that he'd already committed the funds to men who expected those kinds of commitments to be honored.

Smith shrugged. "Then maybe you should try asking her to give it back."

41

Near Salihorsk
Belarus

JAMES WHITFIELD STEPPED THROUGH the door already
suspecting what he would find. He'd been to three of
Dresner's compounds in the past and found them to be
virtually identical. This was no exception.

The layout of the garden was familiar, though it was
populated mostly with native plants that could survive
the local climate. It was barely fifty degrees but the high
walls kept out the breeze and the sun was directly overhead, beating down on him as he walked along a stone
pathway.

The governments of the world loved Dresner for
spreading his wealth—setting up homes, research centers, and manufacturing plants in its every corner. And
while there may have been some altruistic ancillary benefit, Whitfield had come to learn that Dresner's primary
motivator was paranoia.

Not that this was particularly hard to understand after
what the Nazis and Soviets had done to him and his family. While Whitfield's career had provided more than a

few glimpses into the dark side of human nature, Dresner had stared right into the abyss.

So now he moved from one heavily secured compound to the next, never staying in one place long enough to be located, communicating remotely, and meeting almost no one face-to-face. Unfortunately for him, though, no matter how remote his hidden sanctuaries were, they couldn't be fully separated from the world he so feared.

Whitfield finally spotted Dresner near the center of the garden, staring into a small pond as though it held some kind of secret. If anything, his recent success seemed to have aged him even more. His shoulders were a little rounder and his face a little more slack than it had been before. Perhaps he wouldn't live much longer—a situation that had both dangers and benefits.

"Why the hell did you move against Smith and Russell?" Whitfield said angrily "I said I was handling it."

Dresner looked up slowly, examining him as he approached "But you didn't, Major. You *warned* them. And then you tried to transfer them. Now they've appeared in Germany to go through my Stasi records."

Dresner always knew too much for his own good. Whitfield wasn't so naive as to believe that the man wasn't using his almost limitless resources to watch every potential threat. It was only when he tried to *act* that the situation became dangerous.

"And was sending a group of criminal half-wits after them productive?"

"It will appear to be nothing more than a failed mugging."

Whitfield didn't respond immediately. He'd cleaned up most of the mess. All the men involved in the attack were now dead and Johannes Thalberg had himself burned his warehouse before disappearing. For now, the loose end that he represented would have to be tolerated. The man had undoubtedly been planning his escape for his entire career and would be unlikely to make waves that could end up drowning him.

What was really worrying Whitfield was the glimpse of Christian Dresner he'd never seen before: a man who would hire neo-Nazis—the ideological progeny of the very people who had tortured his parents—to murder two people endangering his attempt to reshape the future. Many men throughout history had decided that their vision was important enough to justify any action. All had been absolutely certain that they were right. And all had turned out to be incredibly dangerous.

Whitfield concentrated on keeping his voice calm. As unstable as Dresner was, his technology was exceeding all expectations as a weapons system and America's continued control over it was essential. "Both Russell and Smith have proven over and over again to be very hard to kill. I'm also concerned that they have a power base beyond the military or CIA."

"Then it seems you need to redouble your efforts to get rid of not only them, but the people behind them."

Whitfield stiffened. "Careful, Christian. I don't take orders from you. In fact, if it weren't for me, your company would have collapsed years ago and you'd be tinkering in a basement in Leipzig. This is my sphere of influence. Back off."

Dresner stared down into the water again, looking past the reflection of the man in front of him. The good major's confusion was understandable. He had the illusion that he was creating a military superpower that would last for centuries. Thus, he needed to take the long view—to examine the repercussions of every action.

Dresner, on the other hand, had a much shorter horizon. Adoption of the Merge continued to be above projections, making his two-year horizon entirely realistic. But the continued presence of Smith and Russell had the potential to threaten even that short time frame.

"If our relationship and the details of development become public, it isn't just me and my company that are at stake, Major. Your involvement and the involvement of the Pentagon will almost certainly come to the surface. Something that, I think you agree, your country can't afford."

"Getting rid of them isn't as simple as—"

"It *is* simple, Major! If you're right and someone is pulling Smith and Russell's strings, perhaps they'll reveal themselves when the two of them are gone. But one way or another, their investigation has to stop."

Dresner took a deep breath and let his expression soften. "I understand that they're both honorable and courageous people. And I understand that Smith will be difficult to replace in his capacity as the military's director of development for the Merge. But we have to weigh what's at stake for your country and the rest of the world against the lives of two people. How many American soldiers and indigenous civilians has my technology already saved? I suspect it's more than two."

Whitfield didn't respond immediately and Dresner was satisfied to wait.

"Stay out of this, Christian. I told you that I'm taking care of it."

Dresner nodded. "And I'm watching."

42

Damn," Smith said, throwing the forty-five-year-old Naval Academy yearbook in the backseat with all the others.

"Nothing?"

Randi was piloting the car along the winding, tree-lined road at an unusually careful pace, her eyes flicking to the empty rearview mirror every few seconds.

"Nada," he said, snapping off the reading light next to the visor. "But then I've only been through the navy books. And he's a lot older now. Maybe I wouldn't recognize him."

"Or maybe he didn't go to Annapolis."

It was certainly a possibility. The guy who was responsible for the condition of his Triumph reeked of military academy, but now Smith had to consider that his normally unfailing instinct for fellow soldiers might have abandoned him. Hopefully, Star was having better luck.

"Home sweet home," Randi said, pointing to a modern wood-sided house barely visible through the trees. She pulled into the gravel driveway and Smith stepped out, grabbing his duffel and pausing for a moment to admire the property. The setting sun was giving the tasteful land-scaping a pleasant glow and glinting off spotless win-dows. It was hard to believe that, until recently, the house had been nothing but a pile of charred wood and ashes—an unfortunate consequence of an attempt on Randi's life by a young Afghan assassin.

"Quite a change from the old cabin."

"Fred gave me a blank check to rebuild. I think he feels guilty about putting me out for bait. I still feel that impact when I lift stuff."

She walked to the front door and opened a hidden panel, punching a lengthy code into the keypad beneath. It was a strangely elaborate security system given the setting. Not exactly a high crime area and there wasn't another house in sight.

The interior was even more impressive and Smith wan-dered through, admiring the workmanship and finally stopping to examine the custom kitchen cabinets. "Those would look good in my new place. What kind of wood is it?"

"Dunno. I flew some guys in from Norway to do them."

"Seriously?"

"Hell yes. That body armor wasn't as miraculous as Fred made it out to be. Did I mention that my goddamn back still hurts when I lift things? Now go put your stuff in the back bedroom. The one on the left."

He did as instructed, nearly throwing his well-traveled duffel on the bed before realizing that the linens probably cost more than he made in a week. Best not to give Randi the company credit card after getting her shot between the shoulder blades.

Klein's loss was their gain, though. After the Triumph episode and what had happened in Germany, this out-of-the-way cabin had seemed like a better idea than going to his place. It was the vacation home of one of Randi's college roommates who let her crash there on the rare occasion she was in the States. Not that it would be impossible for someone to find, but at least they'd have to work harder than opening a phone book and looking under "S."

"I thought you said the woman who owns this place is pissed at you," he said coming back out into the living room and selecting the more comfortable looking of the two sofas. "That she blames you for starting the fire that burned the place down?"

"She is and she does. Apparently, there was a bunch of old photos and some toys her kids played with when they were babies here. People can be so sentimental. I mean this place is ten times nicer than the old one and she didn't have to pay a dime for it. But do I get a thank-you? No. All I hear is how she's all broken up because she lost a few headless Barbies."

He glanced down at the massive fossil of a prehistoric fish in the center of the stone coffee table. "Couldn't get a *T. rex*?"

"Back-ordered," she said, handing him a glass of whiskey before dropping into the opposite sofa.

He took a sip and leaned his head back into the cushion, registering something that his exhausted mind had missed when they'd entered. The place looked and smelled completely unlived in.

"We don't have permission to be here, do we?"

She didn't answer.

"Randi?"

"Define permission."

"Christ," he mumbled as he propped his feet on the arm of the sofa—being careful not to let his dirty loafers touch the leather. It felt good to lie down. Even in a stolen house.

The cell phone in his pocket buzzed and the tone told him it was an encrypted text from Covert-One. He pulled it out and punched in his password. It was amazing how clunky and outdated the device felt compared with the Merge he'd left at home.

"It's from Star," he said.

There were no words, just a black-and-white picture of a young Naval Academy cadet with a familiar scar rising from the collar of his dress uniform. A second image had him digitally aged to around seventy.

Even without Photoshop, there would have been no doubt. It was him.

"Son of a bitch," he said, shaking his head in admiration.

"What?"

"She found him," he said as he dialed.

Star picked up on the first ring. The smugness in her voice was thick and obviously intentional. "Why, hello there, Jon."

"Okay. How did you do it?"

"Child's play. A forty-three-year-old Naval Academy yearbook."

"Uh-uh. No way. I looked through that one. The picture you sent wasn't there."

"And where did you get your copy of the book?" she said, clearly enjoying herself.

"You can just order them online. I had it FedExed."

"What did they teach you in all those years of higher education, Jon? The devil is always in the details. I used original books from people who'd graduated in those years."

He let that process for a moment. "Are you telling me this guy's picture has been removed from the current version?"

"That's *exactly* what I'm telling you. Books are living things, Jon. They don't just—"

The line went silent.

"What? Say that again, Star. You're breaking up."

He lost the connection and started to try to call her back but when he looked down at his phone, it indicated no signal. A moment later the power went out and left them sitting in the dim glow bleeding through the west windows.

The darkness lasted only a moment before a backup generator came on but the comfort provided by the return of electric light faded with the sound of shattering glass and a grenade bouncing across the wood floor.

43

THE EIGHT-BY-TEN PHOTOGRAPH was centered on the desk when Fred Klein walked into his office. He didn't bother to sit, instead examining the digitally aged face looking up at him. The scar on his neck pegged him as the man who had threatened Smith, but there was something else. Something in the eyes, the severe turn of the mouth. He was certain he'd seen the face before.

Klein flipped the picture but there was no further information on the back. Only a note from Star scrawled in the corner: "Found him!!!!!!!" followed by a number of smiley faces and a few hearts shaded with a red Magic Marker.

He grimaced and took a sip from the steaming cup in his hand. For a long time he'd thought she did these things just to irritate him but now he knew it wasn't true. And even if it was, it wouldn't have mattered. When you managed to find someone with her level of talent, you learned that the tattoos, the bizarre piercings, and even the glittery hearts punctuating her reports were things you just had to let go.

"Star!" he shouted, knowing his voice would carry the short distance to her office. When she didn't come running, he leaned his head around the door. Before he could call her again, though, Maggie tapped one of her many computer screens. "Quit yelling, Fred. She's dialing out to Jon."

Klein let out a long breath but didn't immediately move. Finally, he slipped out of his office and began the reluctant but all-too-familiar trudge down the hall.

By careful design, his visits to her office were infrequent. He hated everything about it: The grinding music played at elevator volume. The plastic dolls, old records, and commemorative plates that covered nearly every surface. And then there were the framed pictures of her with men—all very famous, she assured him—who looked like they had just been released from prison.

Star held up a finger when he appeared in her doorway but she seemed to be looking right through him. It was an increasingly common phenomenon known as the Dresner Stare. Cell phones had been annoying enough, but at least you knew when people were using them. Now there was no way to tell what someone was seeing when they looked at you.

"Damn," she muttered and then pushed the intercom button on the phone at the edge of her desk. "Maggie? I had a perfect connection with Jon and it just went dead. Now I'm rolling to his voicemail. Do you think you can get him?"

"He's with Randi," Maggie responded over the speaker. "Hold on. Let me give her a try."

Finally, Star's eyes seemed to focus and she smiled pleasantly. "What can I do for you, Mr. Klein?"

He held up the photo he'd found on his desk. "Who is this?"

"Pretty impressive, huh? All I had was a vague description and it's only been..."

"Too much information."

"Sorry. He's a former military intelligence guy. Name's Whitfield."

Klein felt a dull rush of adrenaline in the pit of his stomach. "Major James Whitfield?"

"Yeah. Do you know him?"

He didn't answer, instead dropping the photo and rushing back to Maggie Templeton's desk. "Have you been able to get Jon yet?"

She shook her head. "He's still rolling over. And I can't get Randi's cell either."

"What about a landline?"

"There is one at the cabin but it seems to be out of service." She tapped a few commands into her keyboard. "I'm not sure what the problem is. The cell tower servicing the area seems to be online and they normally get good signal..."

"Shit!"

Maggie looked up at him with alarm as he ran to the safe and began digging through it. Klein rarely swore. And he *never* ran.

"Get a team to where Randi's staying," he said. "Now!"

"A team?" Maggie responded. "What do you mean? What kind of team?"

"Anyone and everyone we can get with whatever weapons they can put their hands on."

"But we don't have any people available, Fred. Kate's on the East Coast, but she's in Philadelphia right now. And you just sent Darren to Kazakhstan."

"Then we'll pull from our security detail. Tell Jason to bring the helicopter."

"Here? You want him to bring it here?"

"Just do it!"

She dialed and then held her hand over the phone's mouthpiece. "Fred!" she said, starting to sound a little panicked. "What in God's name are you looking for?"

"My gun."

"Gun? What are you going to do with a gun?"

He found it at the back under some files and checked the clip while rushing back down the hallway. "Just bring in the helicopter! And get Jon on the damn phone!"

"What do you want me to tell him if I do?" she shouted after him.

"Tell him to try to hold out. Help is on the way."

44

Outside of Washington, DC
USA

THE GRENADE HADN'T EXPLODED, which turned out
to be a mixed blessing. Instead, it was rolling across
an imported Oriental carpet spewing a bluish gas that
Smith couldn't identify. He held his breath and squinted
in an effort to protect his eyes as Randi launched herself
around and over furniture with customary athleticism.
He had no idea where she was going, but she seemed to
have a plan, so he followed with lungs already starting to
burn. If it was a nerve agent, one breath was all it would
take.

They made it to the hallway at the back of the house
and Smith ducked when a sighting laser came through the
window and diffused in the haze. Randi bounced off the
doorjamb leading to the room she'd claimed when they
arrived and immediately dropped, sliding across the polished floorboards until she slammed against the wall between the two east-facing windows. Smith hit the ground,
too, staying out of the reddish beam probing above him
while Randi pulled the shades. With the windows safely

covered, she got to her feet again and ran for a small walk-in closet, grabbing his collar as she passed and dragging him along with her.

Despite the cramped fit—and the fact that even children considered closets too obvious a place to hide—she slammed the door behind them. Smith dropped to his knees in the darkness, ripping clothes from the wall and stuffing them in the crack beneath the door. If the gas was just some kind of an irritant or anesthetic, it might help. If not, there was probably already enough in the closet to kill them. And worse, now they'd cornered themselves. Had she taken a breath? Was her judgment compromised?

There was a muffled crack of wood and suddenly the closet was bathed in the dim glow of a keypad similar to the one next to the front door. Randi's eyes were bulging a bit from lack of oxygen as she punched a code into it.

Was it a panic button that signaled the alarm company? Had she sucked in enough gas to think a bunch of rent-a-cops were going to come riding to their rescue?

It turned out that he'd once again underestimated her obsessive thoroughness and well-justified paranoia. Instead of connecting them to ADT, the entire wall slid silently back to revealing a room of about the same size as the closet, illuminated with red emergency lighting. He crawled in after her and she slammed an open hand against a large red button. The door slid shut and Smith felt a cold breeze as a fan came to life and began flushing the tiny space with outside air. His vision was blurring from lack of oxygen and he could see Randi's chest starting to convulse as her body tried to force her to breathe, but they just stared at each other. Both wanted to let as much gas as possible clear but, even with people trying to kill them, there was no denying that it was also a competition.

No more than five seconds passed before the breath exploded from Randi. He lasted another two before they were both desperately sucking in air that might kill them.

There was a slight chemical odor that he couldn't place but it was probably just coming off their clothes and seemed to have no effect. It took almost a full thirty seconds before he could pull himself to his feet and look around.

A short laugh was all he could get out.

Most of the back wall was hung with combat equipment—everything from gas masks to assault rifles to knives. There was even a crossbow. Smith wasn't quite sure what she intended to do with that.

"I told you I spared no expense," she said, pulling her shirt over her head and starting to unbutton her pants. Feeling inexplicably uncomfortable, he turned toward a bank of video monitors while she donned the camo fatigues neatly folded on a shelf.

"Does your friend know about this?"

"To be completely honest, I may have forgotten to mention it."

In the reflection off a monitor, he saw her finish dressing and reach for an HK416 assault rifle suspended above a row of communications equipment. A moment later he spotted movement on the top left screen.

"We've got a man coming for the back door. Looks like he's getting cover from someone in the trees on the west side. I can't see anyone in front, but I think we can be sure there's at least one man watching the north and east aspects. Okay, the man in back is kicking the door...He's in."

Despite the remaining haze in the rest of the house, Smith could make out the details that mattered. The man was wearing all black and his helmet was a familiar custom carbon-fiber rig bristling with electronics that he not only recognized, but had helped design. The rifle was an M4 carbine with a Merge-linked targeting system.

"Shit..."

"What?" she said, pulling two throat mikes off the wall and handing him one.

"They're Merged up. Military-issue."

"What the hell, Jon? Are you guys selling those things at Walmart?"

Smith didn't respond, instead inserting an earpiece that now felt like the technological equivalent of a plastic cup with a string attached.

The man moved through the gloom with complete confidence, using an efficient pattern that would make it impossible for anyone to get by him.

"He knows the layout of the house. Is there any way he could have found out about this room?"

Randi shook her head. "Not unless he notices that the closet and powder room are a little smaller than they were on the architectural drawings. A friend did it for me."

"He's headed for the bedroom...Okay, he's in."

They watched the man sweep his rifle smoothly around the small space and then turn. His teammates outside would undoubtedly be following his progress with an overhead map application, probably superimposed onto the house's floor plan.

"He's coming our way."

Smith grabbed a silenced pistol from the wall when the man threw the closet door open, but Randi put a hand on his wrist.

"Half-inch steel," she explained. "Even if he somehow figures out we're in here, it'll take a lot more than what he's carrying to get through."

The man backed into the center of the room again, standing next to the bed as he reported. A microphone picked up his voice, but Smith had designed the military version of the Merge to pick up very low-level speech and he had to strain to hear.

"The house is clear. Any activity out there?" Pause. "Damn. Well, we know they didn't leave. Let's burn it."

"Oh, no, no, no," Randi said, leaning over to the monitors as the man pulled off a small pack and begin digging through it. "Tina will *kill* me."

"Let's worry about her later," Smith said. "Can we survive the fire?"

"No way. Basically we've got the steel, a little insulation for sound, and some drywall. One outside source for air, but it's just a normal duct that connects to the roof."

"Then we've got to get out of here. If we move fast, maybe we can take him out and get to the window—"

"Where they'll be waiting for us with all that supercharged infrared targeting crap you seem to be handing out at parties."

"You have a better idea?"

She pointed to a small wheel in the ceiling that looked like a submarine hatch mechanism. "That leads to the attic. According to the blueprints, though, the only way in or out is with a ladder on the back deck. There's a little door about three meters up."

She stepped up onto a stool that seemed to have been purpose-built and began opening the hatch while Smith selected a Swedish-made submachine gun from the wall. When he turned back to her, the hatch was open and she was pulling herself up into it.

He followed. Once he was safely through, she went to the door she'd described and quietly moved an old pair of skis out of the way.

"The guy covering the back looked like he was about forty degrees to our left at the edge of the trees. Call it twenty meters out. We should have the element of surprise, but it's not going to last long. The Merge will lock on and the dark isn't going to help you. This is a daylight fight to them."

She pointed to a brass knob on the door and then walked to the back of the attic. "You pull it. I'll go through first. Ready?"

He grabbed hold of it and nodded hesitantly. Normally, he preferred to put a little more thought into these kinds of things but there was no time.

"Don't land on the grill when you go," she said. "It cost five grand."

Randi sprinted at the door and he jerked it open at the last possible moment, hearing the roar of her assault rifle as she launched herself into the air. He went through a moment later, seeing her hit the deck and roll into the overgrown grass beyond.

Flashes from the east immediately started tracking her as she sprinted for the cover of the woods. Despite her warning, Smith clipped the grill with his ankle on the way down and landed hard on his side, slamming a shoulder into the unforgiving wood planks.

By the time he'd struggled to his feet, Randi was in the trees firing controlled bursts at the men mobilizing against them. He ran toward her, but at a slower pace than he would have liked. The damage to his ankle caused it to want to collapse every time he approached a full sprint.

Smith held the compact weapon behind him, spraying blindly and trying to coax a little more speed from his awkward gait. Cover was only ten meters ahead, but with Merge-equipped men behind him, it would likely prove to be ten meters too far.

45

Damnit!" Smith said in a harsh whisper.

The bullet went well wide of him, but it barely missed Randi, slicing through the branches only inches from her left shoulder. She cut right, nearly losing her balance on the soft earth as she tried to put a tree between her and the shooter.

His ankle was in bad shape and combined with the weak moonlight penetrating the trees, his progress had slowed to an unsteady jog. They'd made it farther than he'd expected into the wilderness but their pursuers were gaining ground fast.

Smith turned and fired at a fading flash behind them, but when he did, his ankle finally gave out. He splayed out on the ground and a moment later a bullet that should have found its mark passed overhead.

Randi came back for him, pulling him to his feet and taking some of his body weight as they hobbled down a slippery bank toward a stream turned black by the moonlight. They dropped to their stomachs in the mud and searched behind them, but there was only the dark outline of the forest. The three men were still coming—of that there was no doubt. But they'd gone silent.

"Damn!" she said, so quietly that he barely heard despite the fact that they were lying nearly on top of each other.

Her frustration was understandable. He'd played a similar game countless times over the past months. Their opponents had heat detection, light amplification, outline enhancement, targeting, and a host of other military-specific apps. What he had was a thin polo shirt, a swelling ankle, and a pair of slick-soled penny loafers.

"I can't keep up," he said, lips brushing Randi's ear in an attempt to defeat their pursuer's audio enhancement. It would be canceling out the sound of the wind and the brook behind them, searching for any noise that could be human-generated. "I hit your damn barbecue on the way down. But even if I hadn't, we're outmatched."

She spoke equally softly. "Are you suggesting we surrender?"

That wouldn't end well. But neither would their current non-strategy. The fact that their attackers hadn't appeared and taken them out might suggest caution on their part. Or it could just mean that they were taking the time to flank them and would soon be coming in from all sides.

"No," he said, looking at the water behind them as an idea started to form. "But we're not going to win a fair fight with these three."

"I'm all for making it an unfair fight if you've got something figured out."

He pointed at a dense row of bushes to their right. "Go for those. When you get through them, head north."

Even in the dim light he could see her skepticism. "Bullshit. You're going to sacrifice yourself so I can get away."

He shook his head. "I don't like you that much. Keep your earpiece in. If you don't hear from me in five, you're not going to. If you do hear from me, do everything I tell you to the letter. Now give me your knife."

She handed it to him but clearly wasn't happy about the plan. Alternatives were hard to come by, though, and a moment later she was slithering into the bushes.

Despite her skill, the branches moved enough to be picked up by their pursuers' motion detection overlay, but still there was silence. No doubt they didn't want to give away their positions until they had a high-percentage shot.

Smith lowered his head and waited. Thirty seconds. A minute. Finally, he heard the rustle of branches at eleven o'clock.

The cold was already seeping into him but he ignored it and slid slowly toward the stream. The quiet gurgle as he entered it would be filtered out as background noise by the Merge worn by the men bearing down on him. One of the units' few weaknesses.

The water was cold enough that his chest caught when he tried to breathe. A moment of concentration allowed him to get in enough air to go under, and he gripped a partially submerged sapling to keep himself hovering just inches beneath the surface.

A shadow passed near the bank and he watched it, trying to calculate how much time he had before hypothermia set in. Not until long after he'd drown or been shot, most likely. How comforting.

The water's uniform temperature would fool the Merge's heat detection and the reflection of the moonlight would dazzle the night vision, making the stream a complete blank to the man creeping slowly past it. As expected, he didn't consider the water at all—another example of the Merge-induced overconfidence that he himself had fallen prey to on more than a few occasions.

There wasn't much time. He wasn't as desperate for air as he had been back in Randi's safe room, but he wasn't far off. The man crouched to get a closer look at the tracks in the mud. There would be no better chance.

Smith slipped smoothly out of the water and managed to grab the man before his Merge could make sense of the sound. His hands were numb but the oxygen flooding his lungs cleared his head enough to recall the education that Star thought was so wasted on him. Killing the man would immediately register on his teammate's Merges. He had to be more skillful than that.

Smith barely managed to clamp a hand over the man's mouth before he felt himself being pushed toward the water. As they toppled, he inserted the thin blade into the back of the struggling man's neck, severing nerves he hadn't thought about since medical school.

They hit the ground in unison and Smith wrapped his legs around the man's waist, holding him tightly as his body jerked wildly and then went limp. A quick check of his pulse confirmed that it was still strong and racing, but that wouldn't last long. He was completely paralyzed and that paralysis extended to the muscles that controlled respiration. The clock was ticking as he suffocated.

Smith searched beneath the man's camo shirt and confirmed what he already knew: that the Merge he was using was military-issue. And ironically, that was what just might save them.

His fingers had been compromised by the cold but he still managed to get the unit off the man's belt and crawl out of range of his head studs. He paused for a moment, trying to prepare himself before contacting the unit with his own skin and dropping onto his stomach in the mud.

As far as he knew, he was the only person who had any significant experience trying to use units set up for other people—experiments that had been necessary to see what would happen if the enemy gained access to one from a dead or injured soldier.

The research had been done only in an effort to be thorough—a U.S. Merge would be unusable by the enemy due to the fact that, beyond being indescribably unpleasant, the military network wouldn't recognize their brain wave signature and would therefore deny access. He *was* on the army grid, though. In fact, he more or less controlled it.

The nausea started immediately, growing in strength as the Merge tried to link up with an unfamiliar mind. He knew from experience that this imperfect connection was possible. It would cause a momentary hesitation on the man's teammates' units and then somewhat garbled data that would look like a network issue.

After fifteen seconds, his vision swam sickeningly and the only thing keeping him from throwing up was the near hypothermia. His record for staying connected like this was thirty-nine seconds and it had involved some of the worst suffering he'd ever endured. This time, though, that wasn't going to be anywhere near long enough.

Something flickered in his peripheral vision and a moment later distorted lettering confirmed his identity as "Lt. Col. Jon Smith" and gave him a level of access that only he and perhaps Dresner had.

Two distorted green dots appeared on an overhead of the battlefield, displaying the position of the paralyzed man's teammates. There was a flash from one of them that represented rounds fired, but he could barely hear the shots over the metallic screech caused by the computer trying to funnel improperly encoded signals to his auditory cortex.

Using the menus was incredibly difficult, but he managed to shut down the voice port and press a hand to his throat mike.

"Randi...Are you...Are you still alive?"

"Barely," came the nearly unintelligible response. "If I show so much as a thumbnail, these sons of bitches damn near shoot it off."

Another flash came from one of the dots on his overhead and he heard her swear angrily.

"Are you hit?"

"Just a graze. But next time they're going to kill me. I can't see shit and they see everything. If you've got a plan, sometime in the next ten seconds would be good."

"Where's...Where's the guy who just shot at you?" he said, sliding partially into the frigid water again to push back the nausea. He figured he was over thirty-nine seconds now and the suffering just kept intensifying.

"North by northeast about fifty meters."

That gave him a good idea of her relative position.

"Okay. You have—"

He vomited violently, trying unsuccessfully to do it quietly.

"Jon? Jon? Are you there?"

"Yeah. You have another one coming in on you from... Wait. No. He heard me. He's turning my way."

"Can you handle him?"

"No," he said, struggling to pull up the military simulation application. It became impossible to keep his head up and his face went down in the mud. Was he breathing? He couldn't tell anymore.

The muffled sound of gunfire filtered through to him but he ignored it, concentrating on activating the training exercise system. It hesitated a few seconds but then launched, making him the default exercise leader.

According to the overhead, the man was bearing down on him fast while the other held his position looking for a line on Randi.

Smith tried to slide farther into the water, but couldn't control his body anymore. How long had it been. A minute? More? Could he die from doing this? Would he even care at this point?

The approaching man slowed and he heard a garbled voice—undoubtedly he was calling to his companion, confused as to what he was doing stopped by the streambank and the erratic output of his unit.

"Randi... On my mark, break cover and go straight at the guy shooting at you. Then turn west and keep going full speed. You'll run right into the guy coming my way."

"Are you nuts?" came her unsurprising reply. "I've already been grazed once. I can't—"

"Do what I say!" he choked out as he highlighted both the men's icons and told the network that they'd been killed in the exercise. Their Merges temporarily blinded and deafened them to simulate their deaths.

"Now! Go!"

Randi Russell heard, but didn't comply. Smith sounded completely out of it and the bastard tracking her would be incapable of missing the kind of target he was asking her to present.

"Go!" he shouted again and this time she did, taking a leap of faith into the open. She ran full-speed in the direction of the shooter, teeth grinding against each other as she waited for the inevitable round that would kill her.

Instead, she found the shooter on his knees reaching desperately for something behind him on his belt. Figuring that there was no point in looking a gift horse in the mouth, she fired two rounds center of mass and another into the man's face as she passed. Smith had once again pulled a rabbit from his hat.

It took only a few seconds to come up on the second man, who was also on his knees, but with his Merge in his hand. He heaved it into the woods and was bringing his rifle around when she fired a shot that penetrated his lightweight helmet and tore away most of the top of his head.

"Both men are down!" she said into her throat mike, adjusting her trajectory to take her toward the stream.

"Jon?"

She burst through the bushes, immediately sweeping her rifle toward a camo-clad man lying on his side at the edge of the water. The knife sticking out of his neck suggested he was no longer a threat and she ran to Smith, who was lying half submerged in the stream.

"Jon?" she said, grabbing the back of his hair and pulling his face out of a pool of vomit. No response.

When she rolled him on his back, his eyes fluttered open and she saw the Merge he was holding against his stomach. He tried to throw it, like the man she'd just killed, but it only went about six inches. She picked it up and hurled it into the trees.

"Jon? Jon!" His skin was dead-white and freezing cold to the touch. "Talk to me. Are you hit?"

He shook his head weakly as the sound of a helicopter became audible. Randi grabbed him by the hands and began dragging him to cover, but didn't make it before the chopper came overhead and a powerful spotlight illuminated them.

She released him and swung her rifle into the blinding glare, but then stopped when an amplified voice overpowered the beat of the rotors. "Randi! Hold your fire!"

The copter swung in a slow arc, looking for a place to land, and she dropped to her knees, taking Smith's head in her lap. "Hang on, Jon. The cavalry's here."

46

Alexandria, Virginia
USA

No SIR. WE DON'T HAVE details yet on how it happened."

James Whitfield sat in the office at the back of his home, staring into the darkness as he listened over an encrypted line.

"Davis was killed and we lost communication with Craighead over the course of a few seconds," his man continued. "Miller's Merge started sending garbled data right before that and then went offline. We're trying to make sense of that now."

Whitfield didn't respond. Had he made the same mistake again? Had he underestimated his adversaries? No. Smith and Russell had repeatedly proven themselves in the field and he'd responded to that with overwhelming force: three well-armed, Merged-up special forces operatives benefiting from the element of surprise.

"So they both survived?" he said finally.

"It appears that way, sir. A helicopter touched down on top of Miller's last known position. It was on the ground for less than five minutes and we believe picked up Smith and Russell, as well as our people."

"You believe?"

"Our man on the ground has confirmed that they're all gone, but he didn't personally witness the transfer."

"And where did the helicopter go?"

"We weren't prepared to track an aircraft. I hope to have that information soon."

"We don't have the luxury of hoping, Captain. Call Andrews and get surveillance planes in the air."

"That's going to be difficult, sir."

"I don't care if it's difficult," Whitfield said, momentarily losing control of the volume of his voice. "Do whatever you have to do and find that goddamn chopper."

"Sir, we could expose—"

"No more excuses, Captain! Get those planes in the air."

Whitfield broke the connection and threw his headset into the wall. This was a complete, unmitigated disaster. If Miller and Craighead were still alive, they'd hold out for a while, but eventually would talk. They wouldn't know anything more than the fact that they'd been sent to take out two people involved with a homegrown terrorist network, but if the right questions were asked, the carefully crafted anonymity of Whitfield's Pentagon contacts could begin to show cracks.

How had they defeated his men? Where had the helicopter come from? But most important, who were these bastards?

47

Is a little goddamn hot water too much to ask?"
Smith said, unable to control his mounting frustration as
he ran the faucet over his numb hands. The only heat and
light in the dilapidated farmhouse came from the flames
crackling in a woodstove that looked like it hadn't been
used since the turn of the century.

"Come over by the fire," Randi said, throwing a threadbare blanket she'd found over his shoulders and pulling
him toward the living room. Fred Klein slid a low stool—
the only piece of furniture in the house—toward the stove
and Smith lowered himself carefully onto it.

"Sorry about the accommodations," Klein said as
Randi knelt and rubbed Smith's back vigorously, trying to
get the blood circulating. "It's not the Four Seasons, but
it's on its own hundred acres and owned by a fictitious
mining company that can't be traced to us. If you need
medical attention we can bring someone in."

Smith shook his head, fighting off another of the endless waves of nausea that refused to subside. "My body

temperature's coming back up and there's nothing you can do about the effects of the Merge but wait them out." He paused. "Thanks for coming for us, Fred. I know the risk you're taking."

"I don't think you have much to thank me for. Too little too late."

Smith just stared into the flames in front of him. While he'd always admired Klein's patriotism and intellect, the retired spook wasn't exactly a spring chicken and had very little direct experience with ops. Smith had always assumed that in this type of situation he and Randi would be sacrificed—an unfortunate fact of life that he understood and could live with. But seeing Klein standing there with a gun bulging in his jacket put the man in an entirely a new light. Smith's already enormous respect for him grew just a little more.

Klein's phone beeped and he seemed grateful to be able to divert his attention to it. Randi took the opportunity to stoke the fire, trying not to look worried while Smith watched her in his peripheral vision.

"All right," Klein said, stuffing his phone back in his pocket after a brief conversation that consisted mostly of worried grunts on his end. "We have a positive ID on all three men."

"Mercs?" Randi said.

He shook his head. "Active military. Two SEALs, one special ops marine."

"What the hell were they doing at my friend's cabin?"

"No one seems to know. The SEALs are posted to Afghanistan and the marine is an advisor in Iraq. I'm guessing they were supposed to be on their way back by now with no one the wiser."

"They didn't just fly to the States on their own," Smith said. "Someone gave the order."

"James Whitfield," Klein said.

"Who?"

"He's a retired military intelligence officer who consults for an organization that lobbies on behalf of the military. I think you're familiar with him, Jon. Gray hair, scar on his neck?"

"What do you mean by 'lobbying for the military'?" Randi said. "You mean he's in the pocket of defense contractors?"

"No, actually. While he's definitely been involved in making sure that our soldiers are well equipped, he's also supported serious cuts in unnecessary bases and weapons systems. His goal is to make the military stronger, but also cheaper and more efficient—something that hasn't won him many friends in Congress and the military industrial complex. I've only met him in passing, but I have to admit that I've always been an admirer."

"Well, I can tell you that those guys weren't trying to lobby us," Randi said.

Klein crossed his arms and leaned against the wall behind him. "I think there's a good chance that Whitfield is the one behind the money disappearing from the Pentagon. It just never occurred to me to look at him. I was focused on criminal activity—someone embezzling or a contractor covering up a failing project. Not someone diverting money to fund an organization looking to *help* the military."

Smith finally turned away from the fire. His hands were thawing to the point that numbness was giving way to pain. "Am I the only one here who thinks it sounds a lot like you're describing yourself? Whitfield sounds like your mirror image. Some kind of evil counterpart."

Klein considered that for a moment. "Counterpart? Possibly. Evil? I'm not sure. There's nothing I know of in his background to suggest he's anything but an incredibly patriotic and competent former soldier."

"It's a hazy line, isn't it?" Smith said. "Doing what you believe is right without any real authority. Killing people from the edges of democracy . . ."

"We save lives," Randi said, sounding a little indignant.

"Maybe he does, too," Smith responded. "Maybe he sees the importance of the Merge to our soldiers and thinks we're poking our noses into places that could jeopardize that."

"At this point, his motivations are irrelevant," Klein said. "What we know is that the man is smart, motivated, and well connected. Your transfers didn't work only because Whitfield had no way of knowing about my involvement—"

"And we aren't dead because I'm one of the only people who really understands the control and command structure of the Merge's military operating system." Smith thumbed toward Randi, who was adjusting the blanket around his shoulders. "And of course because of the paranoia level of certain CIA operatives."

"Miscalculations I myself might have made," Klein admitted. "But I wouldn't make them again. And neither will he."

"Can we get him off our backs?" Randi said.

"I honestly don't know. It's a dangerous fight for us to get into."

"Particularly in light of the glass house we live in," Smith said.

"Exactly. Going toe-to-toe with Whitfield could shine a very bright light into places that need to stay dark."

"And where does that leave us?" Randi said.

"Our primary concern is the proliferation of the military version of the Merge. We need to understand how those Afghans got those head studs and what they were doing with them. Secondarily, we need to look into the behavioral issues that you're concerned about and the possibility that the Merge has capabilities we're not aware of or that it can be subverted in ways we don't understand."

"But what's Whitfield's angle?" Randi said.

"If I had to bet money, I'd say that he somehow got early access to the military units and what happened in Afghanistan was some kind of pre-release test."

"Maybe," Smith said. "But maybe not. We found out that Christian Dresner was part of the athletics program in East Germany."

"Athletics? I don't follow," Klein said.

"He has a history of experimenting on humans."

"You think he could be behind what happened there?"

"The human brain is very different from a rat brain or even a chimp brain. I'd never given it a lot of thought until now but in order to get his system to integrate with the mind, there would have had to be a fair amount of direct experimentation."

Klein nodded, obviously seeing where he was headed. "But where are all the early test subjects? I've never heard anyone talking about being involved in those kinds of trials."

"And let's not forget Craig Bailer," Randi said. "It's possible that his death was just a coincidence, but now I'm starting to doubt it."

"Do we have any information on that?" Smith asked.

"Apparently his car missed a turn and rolled down an embankment. The bodies were badly burned, so information is shaky. Based on Bailer's lungs, he was dead before the fire started, but there was no obvious trauma. Best bet is a heart attack. The passenger—a member of Dresner Industries' board—appears to have been knocked unconscious and died in the fire. No obvious evidence of foul play."

"Doesn't mean there wasn't any," Randi pointed out.

"No it doesn't," Klein admitted. "Any thoughts on how to proceed?"

"Get our hands on Dresner?" Randi said.

"That's not going to happen," Klein said. "Beyond his obvious wealth and connections to more world leaders than I can count, he's a German national who tends to move constantly between compounds set up all over the world. I'm not sure I could even find him, let alone get you access to him."

"What about the psychologist he escaped East Germany with?" Randi said.

"Gerhard Eichmann?" Klein said. "You think he might be involved?"

"We Googled him on the way back from Germany," Smith said. "He worked for a few years after making it to the West and then pretty much disappeared. A guy that brilliant should be at a top university or at least have a trail of publications in academic journals. Instead, there's nothing."

"And you think he was working on the Merge project?"

"He wouldn't be a bad guy to have around if you wanted to integrate machine and mind."

"Any idea where he is?" Klein said.

"Maybe Morocco, but we need Star to do some digging."

Klein nodded. "We have to move fast on this. I've managed to postpone both your transfers but doing any more could generate tracks that I can't cover. Talk to Eichmann and see what you can find out. But—and I want to be very clear on this—you're not to take any direct action without my authorization. For now, we're just gathering intel."

"What about Whitfield?" Randi said.

"I'll see what I can do to keep him off you, but I can't promise anything. My advice is to watch your back."

His phone rang and he pulled it from his jacket again. "Yes? ETA? Okay, I'll be ready.

"Time for me to go," he said. "We need to get the chopper in and out of here before the sun comes up. Good luck."

48

Marrakech
Morocco

Jon Smith narrowly dodged a moped coming up behind him and then watched it weaving aggressively through the people packed into the alley. Overhead, tarps had been hung to keep out the sun but seemed more effective at holding in the heat, enveloping him in humidity scented with sweat, urine, and cooking meat. Along the sides of the narrow corridor, shops sold everything from food to clothing to hand-carved doors, supplied by an endless procession of animal-drawn carts.

Despite his dark complexion and hair, Smith had no hope of passing for Moroccan so he'd opted for the baseball hat, camera, and khakis of the inexperienced tourist. Randi, shuffling along behind him, had disappeared into a chador that revealed only her eyes.

This time, they'd traveled by private jet, giving him a chance to get some sleep. Despite that, he still wasn't fully recovered from the episode in the woods. His ankle had turned out to be much less of a problem than he'd anticipated but his use of Corporal Jeff Miller's Merge had taken a lasting toll. Network records put his total connect time at a minute thirty-two. It was a record that would undoubtedly stand for a very long time.

He adjusted his sunglasses and pulled the brim of his hat down a bit, searching for people using Merges and finding only one tourist busy negotiating for a set of silver earrings. Dresner's invention had gone from being a miracle to a threat with amazing speed—something that was more depressing than surprising. How many times had humankind made the mistake of thinking it could control complex technology? Anticipate how it would be used? How it could be subverted.

Was it possible that every Merge on the planet was searching for his face? Hell, had he already been tagged with a GPS coordinate?

Randi pulled ahead and turned down an empty side street with him close behind. Feral cats watched from a high wall as they skirted along it, finally stopping in front of a massive wood-and-copper door.

Star had tracked Eichmann down almost before their jet's wheels left the ground. He led a private life, but didn't seem to be making any special effort at anonymity. Who would be interested in an aging psychologist living out his golden years in sunny Morocco?

Randi, instead of immediately going to work on the lock like he was accustomed to, just stood there staring down at it. Smith glanced back at the narrow alley to confirm they were still alone.

"Problem?"

"What the hell am I supposed to do with this?"

"Your usual magic. Didn't you once tell me there wasn't a lock on the planet you couldn't open?"

"This thing's probably three hundred years old. What do I look like? Some kind of lock historian?

"So laser-cut keys, computer encryption, thumbprint activation—all a piece of cake to you. But this bucket of rust has stopped you dead."

She shrugged. "Maybe we should just knock?"

Smith scowled and jerked a finger toward the mouth of the alley. Randi retraced their steps and peeked around the corner, giving him a thumbs-up, but with an urgency that suggested faster would be better than slower.

Smith grabbed a pipe running down the wall and began going up it hand-over-hand, keeping his eye on the rusty straps holding it to the stone. A few pulled out as he passed, but it held long enough to get him to the roof. He crept across it until he was at the inside edge, looking down onto three interconnected courtyards two stories below.

There was a passage below him protected only by a meter-high railing and he swung off the roof, landing on an elaborately tiled floor and nearly falling over the back of a sofa that made up one side of a conversation nook.

He pulled the pistol from his waistband and listened to something that sounded like pans banging downstairs. Beyond that, though, the massive riad-style house was silent. His initial urge was to go straight for the noise, but instead he decided to carry out a systematic search from the top down that would hopefully minimize surprises.

The floor he was on turned out to contain little more than three unused bedrooms. A winding stone staircase took him to the ground floor and he moved in the opposite direction of the noise through interior courtyards dominated by orange-tree-shaded fountains and a lap pool.

Hinges were all well oiled and he carefully opened every door, finding dens, bathrooms, storage areas, and two bedrooms that looked a bit more lived-in. The last door turned out to be the most interesting. Closed, it looked like all the others. When opened, though, it revealed not a room but another door—thick steel and with a high-tech lock that would be more to Randi's liking.

He backtracked to the entry and eased the front entrance open. Randi immediately slipped inside and he signaled toward the kitchen. A Glock appeared from her chador and she took point, stopping in the archway at the end of the hall. Smith moved up behind her and saw a young woman arranging food on a silver tray. Lunch. But for whom?

The Glock disappeared again, replaced by a roll of duct tape. It was another reason she loved this particular disguise—the hardware and weapons store she could carry with no one the wiser.

He hung back as she slipped up behind the girl and clamped a hand over her mouth. Randi spoke soothing Arabic as she eased the terrified girl to the floor and began going to work with the tape.

He'd have helped, but since Muslim women were particularly resistant to being pawed by strange men, he padded over to the tray and began grazing on olives and hummus. It took only a few seconds for the girl to be completely silenced and immobilized—barely enough time for him to drizzle a little honey into a bowl of yogurt.

Randi whispered a few more reassuring words into the girl's ear before standing and turning toward him. "Am I disturbing your lunch?"

"You should try this. She must make it herself."

Randi let out an impatient breath and headed back toward the archway. He followed, but took the bowl and spoon with him.

"Check out the door to your left," he said when he caught up.

She opened it and, spotting the second door inside, dropped to her knees to insert a key-shaped card with what looked like circuits imprinted on it. Less than thirty seconds after connecting it to her iPhone, the mechanical bolt slid obediently back.

"Good thing it wasn't secured by a rope with a knot in it," he commented. "We'd have been here all day."

She scowled as they entered a small room packed with books, papers, and computer equipment. Randi took the chair in front of the terminal and stuck a thumb drive in the USB port while he browsed the hundreds of German and English titles on psychology and neurology.

"Damn!" Randi muttered.

"Problems again?"

"His encryption isn't anything I've run into before."

Smith came to a table stacked with loose papers and began scanning the statistical analyses, graphs, and endless columns of data. He finally dug up a partially completed abstract written in German and used it as a key to figure out the abbreviations on a poster-sized collection of charts.

"I don't think I'm going to get anywhere, Jon. If we want in to this thing, we're going to have to pile it on a donkey and take it with us."

"Uh-huh," he said absently, continuing to dig through the papers on the table.

"Do you have something?"

"I'm not really sure. This looks like a long-term study of behavior and intelligence. The subjects were all adopted at birth..."

"And this is interesting to me how?"

He didn't respond, continuing to try to decipher what he was reading but finding it increasingly hard to believe. Where would Eichmann have gotten this kind of data? While it was vaguely possible that he would be able to track thousands of cross-cultural adoptions, it seemed like every aspect of the children's lives—from education to nutrition to parenting—had been meticulously controlled. Admittedly, the study design was impeccable, but it was also wildly unethical and completely illegal. And then there was the astronomical cost of micromanaging and recording every aspect of people's lives over the better part of a quarter century.

"Jon? Are you—"

Randi went silent when the sound of a key being inserted in the massive lock on the front entrance floated in to them.

She made it into the courtyard first and he ran after her, skidding into the entryway just as the heavy door was swinging open. He pressed himself against the wall and watched a frail-looking man cross the threshold.

"Hafeza?" he said in heavily accented French. "Where are you?"

Randi slipped up behind him and pressed her pistol against the back of his head. "She's indisposed."

Smith stepped out of hiding and the man froze. He didn't look like much of a threat—more like a composite of every aging professor he'd ever had in college and medical school.

"Gerhard Eichmann?"

"Who are you?" he said, the confusion on his face deepening. Home invasions weren't unheard of in Marrakech but camera-toting tourists and women in traditional dress generally weren't the perpetrators. "What do you want?"

"Just to talk," Smith said, taking him by the arm and leading him toward the office they'd broken into.

"Where is Hafeza? What have you done with her?"

"She's fine," Randi answered, still covering him from behind.

He stopped short when he saw the open door, but Smith dragged him through. Once inside, Eichmann broke free and ran to the obviously rifled-through papers on the table. "You have no right to look at these! They are of no interest to you!"

"Don't rush to judgment," Smith said. "My field is microbiology but I read my share of behavioral studies in school. Children from all over the world, primarily poor countries that don't keep very good records and are amenable to bribes. Identical twins, fraternal twins, siblings, all split up, often adopted by foreigners with very different backgrounds. And all completely ignorant that you were pulling the strings."

"They . . . they weren't harmed," Eichmann stammered.

"Please, Doctor. You *stole* these children. You separated them from their families, you shipped them all over the world through bogus adoption agencies—"

"They had better lives! Girls taken from rural China where they aren't valued were given to parents in Europe and—"

"But you're a better scientist than that, aren't you?"

Smith said, snatching a stack of papers off the table and holding them up. "If you're going to do that, you'd also need to take the children from wealthy people in industrialized countries and ship them off to third-world orphanages. You'd want to see if the effects on behavior and intelligence go both ways—you'd want to do brain scans to see what effects things like starvation and abuse have…"

"No," the man said, but then he didn't seem to know how to continue. "I—"

"Just like the old days in East Germany, right, Doctor? How do you build a perfect athlete? You test the limits of pain. You experiment with dangerous drugs. You see how hard someone can train before they drop dead. No point in letting morality and human decency get in the way of science."

"Enough!" Randi interjected. "Can't we just shoot him in the knee and make him give us the password to his computer? If I wanted to hear about the thousandth study on why Johnny can't read, I'd watch the Discovery Channel."

Smith ignored Eichmann's terrified reaction. "You're right, Randi. There *are* a lot of studies. But most aren't worth the paper they're printed on. Most researchers wouldn't be willing to do what it would take to control all the variables. And even if they were, they wouldn't have the resources. Which brings me to an interesting question. Who would be willing to spend tens of millions of dollars on a study that can never be published?"

Randi perked up at that. "Dresner."

"Christian?" Eichmann said, a little too quickly. "That's insane. Why would he—"

The old man fell silent and began to back away when Randi aimed her pistol at his leg. "Don't insult our intelligence."

Smith was taken by surprise when the old man made a break for the door. He was forced to dive, just missing the back of the German's shirt before landing hard on the marble floor.

"Stop!" Randi shouted, her foot landing firmly in the small of Smith's back as she started to chase. Just as she came even with the doorjamb, though, the crack of a shot from above echoed off the stone walls. Eichmann went down, sliding uncontrolled across the smooth tile as Randi started firing at the rooftop.

49

JAMES WHITFIELD SNATCHED the phone off his night-stand and silenced it before glancing at his wife in bed next to him. She'd never slept particularly well and it was something that had gotten worse as she aged. Bad luck that she'd spent the last thirty-five years married to a man whose job never ended.

Instead of bolting awake and scowling at him by the glow of the alarm clock, she kept breathing in the same relaxed rhythm. She'd initially been reluctant to get the head studs but now told anyone who would listen that it was the smartest thing she'd ever done. Dresner's Merge really was a miracle.

The encrypted text displayed in the phone's window was typically brief and ambiguous: "At your convenience."

Whitfield slipped on a bathrobe and navigated the dark hallway by memory, entering his small office and closing the door behind him. A gentle tap on his key-board woke the computer and he put on a headset before bringing up a heavily secured link to the man who had contacted him.

"Sorry to bother you at this hour, sir."

Unlike his wife, Whitfield had spent the night staring at the ceiling, running through endless—and pointless—worst-case scenarios relating to the Smith-Russell situation. If there was relevant information to be had, this would be a very welcome interruption.

"Do you have something on the helicopter, Captain?"

"Yes sir. If you hadn't called in the surveillance planes, we would have lost it. And even so we were the beneficiaries of a lot of luck."

"You were able to track it then?"

"We were. It landed on a vacant farm in West Virginia."

"Owned by whom?"

"A maze of offshore corporations that I can almost guarantee you will lead nowhere."

"A CIA safe house?"

"Not according to our sources, sir."

Whitfield didn't immediately respond. It wasn't military intelligence and it wasn't the Agency. Who else would have a property like this available for an army physician and a CIA operative normally stationed overseas?

"Go on, Captain."

"The helicopter left the farm and landed in a clearing in the mountains, where it was met by a single four-wheel-drive vehicle. It was on the ground for a short period of time before it took off again and returned to the farmhouse."

"What was the purpose of the flight to the mountains?"

"To unload cargo."

"What cargo?"

"Our men. They were buried in extremely well-camouflaged sites. Two were shot and one died of a knife wound to the back of the neck. We've extracted their bodies and transported them to the crematorium."

Whitfield took a deep breath and let it out slowly. When dedicated, talented men died in the field, it wasn't their failure. It was a failure of leadership. In this case, his leadership.

"I assume provisions are being made for their families?"

"Yes sir. Through the normal charities."

"Cover stories?"

"In process. There won't be any problems."

There won't be any problems, Whitfield repeated in his mind. More and more, it seemed that's all there were.

"What happened at the farmhouse in West Virginia?"

"Three people got out of the chopper and went inside. The helicopter returned just before dawn and picked up a single passenger. It flew to the end of a dirt road about a hundred and thirty miles southwest of DC. One man disembarked and got into a Yukon XL. We didn't have capacity to follow both, so we chose the car."

"And?"

"We got lucky. After about an hour, it went into a tunnel and a decoy came out. The surveillance plane picked up the heat signature of the colder engine or we'd have fallen for it. Ten minutes later the original vehicle continued on to DC. One man eventually got out and entered the Metro, where we lost him."

"You lost him? How is that lucky?"

"We got a photo from an ATM camera as he was entering the station. We've cleaned it up, but the resolution and angle still aren't ideal. It should be good enough for an ID and we're working on that. I'm transmitting it to you now."

"What about the farm?" Whitfield said as the photo decrypted pixel by pixel on his screen.

"Empty. Dense trees come right up to the south porch and we're guessing that Russell and Smith went out on foot and got picked up somewhere."

Whitfield turned and stared into the darkness. He was being outmaneuvered at every turn—a situation he was very much unaccustomed to. There were no excuses for this. With three men down, he had accomplished nothing but to expose himself.

"Sir? Has the file I sent come through?"

Whitfield redirected his gaze to the grainy photo of a man walking head-down through scattered pedestrian traffic. The collar of his suit was turned up, obscuring the lower part of his jaw, but there was still something familiar in the large forehead, the receding hairline, the long, slightly hunched stride.

"We're estimating him at about five-ten or -eleven, sir. Probably in his early sixties, with..."

But Whitfield was no longer listening. A jolt of adrenaline surged through him and he reached a shaking hand out to eradicate all evidence of the photo from his hard drive.

"There's no way to know what train he got on," the captain continued. "We got the security camera footage but there was some unknown problem with the video. We're trying to get something useful from it but—"

"You won't be able to get anything useful," Whitfield said.

"Sir?"

"I want you to listen to me very carefully, Captain. You are to permanently destroy all copies of this photo and all records of your investigation into the man in it."

"I don't understand, sir. I—"

"Then let me be perfectly clear. There is to be no evidence that any of this ever happened. You and everyone else involved are never to speak of it—or even think about it—again. Do you have any questions?"

"No sir. Your orders are clear."

"Do it now, Captain."

Whitfield severed the connection and wiped a hand across the perspiration forming on his upper lip.

Fred Klein.

It explained a great deal, but in the worst way possible. Of all the people in the world he could have found himself pitted against, Klein was one of the most dangerous. And, if he guessed correctly, also one of the best connected. While Whitfield's own power base was quietly centered at the Pentagon, it was almost certain that Klein's was currently occupying the Oval Office.

50

Marrakech
Morocco

JON SMITH SPRINTED INTO the courtyard while Randi fired upward from the cover of the balcony above her. A bullet impacted only inches from the prone Gerhard Eichmann's head, kicking up a spray of shattered marble.

The near miss broke him from his stupor and he rolled to his knees, trying to crawl beneath the leafy branches of an orange tree next to him. Psychological cover at best.

Another shot from above slammed into the floor and Smith grabbed the elderly scientist under the arm, jerking him to his feet and dragging him into the house's entry. Randi came in a moment later, her momentum carrying her into an ancient sideboard and knocking an undoubtedly priceless vase to the floor.

Eichmann jerked at the sound of it shattering, then grabbed Smith's shoulder with adrenaline-fueled strength. "They were shooting at *me*!" he said in panicked German. "Not at you! At me!"

"That's because they aren't after me," Smith said, crouching and ripping open the leg of Eichmann's pants to get at the bullet wound. "They know we're talking to you and they want you silenced."

"No...I don't believe..."

"How is he?" Randi said. "Because I'm almost out and if that guy comes down the stairs with a full clip we're going to be screwed."

"Just a scratch," Smith answered, standing again. "Dr. Eichmann. Is there another way out of here? We can't get caught in that alley with a shooter above us."

"No...Yes! There's a servants' door that leads to the main street. We haven't used it in years, though. I don't—"

"Take us to it," Randi said when the sound of cautious footsteps reached them from the stairwell. "Now!"

He led them through the kitchen and Smith shoved him forward when he tried to stop next to his immobilized cook. They passed through a curtain at the back and down a narrow passage lined with food and kitchen utensils before coming to a thick wooden door.

It was dead-bolted with a rusted but extremely sturdy-looking iron bar. Even using both hands and a foot against the jamb, it took Smith a good thirty seconds to break it free.

"This leads out to the pedestrian shopping street?" Randi said, pressing her back to the wall and looking down the narrow hallway for signs of pursuit.

Eichmann nodded.

"We'll want to get off it as soon as we can. Is the closest branch left or right?"

"Left. Yes, next to a jewelry stall. Twenty meters at the most."

Smith nodded and glanced at Randi, who took a position by the door. "On three."

He counted down and shoved the door open. Randi went first, hiding her gun beneath her chador and pulling Eichmann along with her. Smith followed, staying a few paces back as they integrated themselves into the shoppers and tourists jammed into the souk.

They'd made it almost halfway to the jewelry stall Eichmann mentioned when a shot sounded from above. There was no way to identify the impact point because of the crowd's sudden, violent reaction. Deafening screams rose up as everyone scattered in different directions. A motor scooter hit a cart cooking chestnuts a few meters away and Smith found himself being pushed away from the side street that was their objective. Randi's disguise was a little too good and he lost sight of her as he fought his way back to the outer wall of Eichmann's house.

Smith flattened himself against the stone, edging along it in an effort not to be trampled by the people running past. He finally reached the door they'd come through and wedged his fingers into the crack between it and the jamb—there was no outside handle.

Finally, he managed to get it open and slipped inside before slamming the bolt home again. The woman in the kitchen let out a muffled scream as he ran past and started up the winding stairs.

When he broke back out into the blinding sunlight, he immediately spotted a man disassembling a rifle on the north edge of the roof.

"Jesus, Eric," Smith said, slowing to a walk. "You actually hit him."

The man shrugged and stuffed the stock of his weapon in a canvas sack. "You said to make it convincing, mate. He looked convinced to me."

51

Marrakech
Morocco

JON SMITH HAD BEEN LOST at least eight times in the last hour—only six of which were on purpose. But now he felt confident enough that he wasn't being followed to emerge from the maze of souks onto an open road.

Taxi drivers slowed as they drove by but he waved them off and kept moving along the sidewalk, avoiding eye contact with the people he passed. Sirens were still audible as the police and military responded to the shooting, but that was more than three kilometers east now.

He came to an innocuous door on a street dedicated to the sale of scrap metal and gave a complex knock calculated to sound clandestine. A moment later the door swung open and he stepped into the dim interior of an apartment he'd found on the Internet. It looked just like a safe house should: dilapidated and austere with curtains tucked carefully around the lone window.

"Is he all right?"

"Nothing serious," Randi said, continuing to stand next to the door with her gun drawn while Eichmann sat frozen in a chair. Most of his right pant leg was cut off and a makeshift bandage was wound around his thigh.

"Were you followed?" she asked, already knowing the answer but wanting to milk the illusion of imminent danger.

He shook his head. "I don't think so. But we probably shouldn't stay long."

"I don't understand," Eichmann said, exhaustion and fear clear in his voice. "Who are you?"

"We're the people keeping you alive," Randi said.

"You're American. Do you work for the government?"

Smith took a seat across the small dining table from the scientist. "I'm Dr. Jon Smith."

The immediate recognition wasn't surprising. Eichmann would know the name of the man in charge of the U.S. military's Merge program.

"Why are you here? What do you want from me?"

"We're here because the Merge was used in Afghanistan before its official release."

Eichmann was an academic, not a spy—something that was obvious in the way his every thought played out across his face. He knew about Afghanistan and was terrified that Smith did too.

"Yesterday, someone leaked that I'm looking into what happened there," Smith lied. "And that I knew about you. We were concerned for your safety and came as fast as we could. Good thing we did."

"Leaked?" Eichmann said. "Leaked to whom?"

Smith leaned back in his chair. "Christian Dresner."

"I...I don't understand," he said, but again his face gave him away. He understood perfectly.

"There's a lot of money on the table, Doctor. Not to

mention Dresner's entire legacy. If it were to become public that he was involved in these kinds of experiments..."

"But we're...We've been..." the aging scientist stammered, suddenly incapable of getting a sentence out. His hesitation suggested that Smith had guessed right. Dresner *was* involved.

"What happened in Sarabat?" Randi said, getting impatient.

When Eichmann didn't answer, she reached for the knob of the door and opened it. "I don't have time for this. If you don't want to talk, get out."

"What?" the German said. "But—"

"But your old friend will have you killed?" she said. "That's right, Gerd. He will. In fact, I doubt you'll last two hours without our protection."

When he didn't move, she closed the door again. "I believe we were talking about Afghanistan?"

Again, Eichmann didn't respond. He was clearly having a hard time processing the seismic shift in his universe—that his benefactor and oldest friend was now a mortal enemy.

"He's a different man than he was when you escaped the Soviets," Smith prompted. "Wealth, power, fame. Those things can change you."

The German nodded numbly. "I'm nothing. Nothing compared with him."

"Why didn't the people in Sarabat fight back?" Randi said, but Smith subtly waved her off. He wanted to give the good cop some stage time.

"Doctor?"

Eichmann stared at the floor for a few seconds and then looked up to meet his eye. "It was the dream."

"What dream? What were you trying to do? Influence people's behavior?"

"Christian just wanted to help. After everything that happened to him—the Nazis, the Soviets—he realized that our primitive instincts were combining with modern technology, media, and politics to destroy us. He wanted to change that."

"I remember that he spent hundreds of millions of dollars on educational research," Smith said. "But that was more than thirty years ago."

Eichmann licked his lips nervously. "Yes. We set up charter schools all over the world and educated tens of thousands of children for free. What wasn't clear to the public was that the students were carefully chosen. Randomized."

"So that you could test various educational theories," Smith said. "Year-round school, separating boys and girls, classroom size, home intervention..."

"We tried them all. Every teaching technique and idea that had ever been conceived."

"And it was a huge success. I learned about it in college."

The German shook his head. "No. We made it look that way by choosing what data we released. The truth is that different educational techniques have almost no effect on intelligence and behavior. And what little impact they do have disappears in adulthood. But he didn't believe it. Neither of us did. School and parenting virtually useless? The majority of our destiny written at birth? How could this be true?"

"So you created the study that I saw back at your house."

"Christian decided we needed to try more drastic interventions—and to get the remaining cultural noise out of the data."

The old man fell silent and Smith walked to the sink to get him a glass of water. "We're not here to judge you, Dr. Eichmann. We're here because the U.S. military needs to understand the technology it's going to be relying on for the next hundred years. We're not people who like surprises."

Eichmann accepted the glass and took a hesitant sip from it. "As I'm sure you surmised, we took children from all over the world."

"Took?" Randi said, but then fell silent when Smith shot her an angry glance.

"Some parents are willing to accept money, others are open to the promise that their children will be given opportunities they wouldn't have otherwise. Hospital workers are amenable to mixing up paperwork for the right price. And sometimes it's as simple as directing and facilitating adoptions."

In his peripheral vision, Smith could see Randi's horrified expression turn to anger. And as a human being, he understood completely. But as a scientist, he couldn't help being intrigued.

"So you created a perfectly controlled behavioral study."

"The first—and almost certainly last—in history. We put children from poor or abusive backgrounds into ideal environments, we put children from privileged backgrounds into brothels and on the street. We split up fraternal and identical twins. We even populated an isolated village in North Korea with children from all over the world and controlled every aspect of their life and up-bringing."

"Gathering data the whole time."

"We had various ways of giving parents and children personality and IQ tests—through school, extracurricular activities, job interviews, and the like. We looked at every aspect of life outcomes and I just recently finished a comprehensive analysis of all the data. Though, in truth, we've known what we would discover for a long time."

"And what was that?"

"Our minds are just sophisticated computers. Some are very powerful, others aren't. And all come with pre-existing software. A child of wealthy, highly intelligent Chinese parents taken at birth and put on the street in Cambodia will retain an IQ and personality closely re-lated to the birth parents she never met. The reason par-enting and education techniques change constantly with no real effect on society is because they don't matter. Who we will become is largely determined before we're born."

Smith thought about his own parents, trying to calcu-late the effect of the environment they'd provided. The truth was that his intelligence had been recognized at a very early age despite the fact that they hadn't been par-ticularly interventionist on that front. And both had been horrified when he joined the military.

"So the real purpose of the Merge isn't augmented reality," Randi said, making an unconvincing effort to mimic Smith's calm, friendly tone. "It's to change the way the human mind works. The men in Sarabat lost their faith and didn't fight back because the Merge destroyed that part of their brain—"

"No!" Eichmann responded. "It doesn't destroy anything. It just regulates brain waves. And the unit we used there is very different from the one you're familiar with—much larger, with enormous rates of power consumption. Our hope was that we could—"

"Strip us of who we are?" Randi said, finishing his sentence.

For the first time, Eichmann met her eye. He was a scientist first and foremost, and his fear was starting to be overshadowed by the subject matter. It was something Smith understood and he was unashamedly hanging on the man's every word. It appeared that Dresner's brilliance and ambition went well beyond anything anyone had ever imagined. Unfortunately, so did his insanity.

"Who we are?" the German said. "We aren't *anyone*. You're a calculating machine made of meat. A neurotic, violent, depressive computing device. Where do you think love comes from? God? Don't be absurd. It's an illusion created by natural selection. People who felt compelled to protect their family had more children survive than people who didn't and they passed on that trait. But there's a dark side to those survival instincts: greed, cruelty, bigotry. All emotions are like this—strategies for either spreading our genes or stopping others from spreading theirs. Together, they create the illusion that we exist. That we have consciousness."

It was a fascinating theory, but not one Smith was fully willing to accept. "If an illusion is perfect enough, though, it *is* real."

"Exactly!" Eichmann said. "But what if we could manipulate that illusion and change the perverse Darwinist incentives that control our species? What if we could dull the drive for self-interest and increase the pleasure of giving? What if we could provide the happiness that so many have harmed themselves and others for but never really achieved?"

"Make everyone Christian Dresner's robot," Randi said. "Take away our free will."

"You're wrong!" he said, actually slamming a hand down onto the table. "There *is* no free will. Evolution has imprisoned us. Consider the trivial example of diet: We crave fatty, sugary foods that used to be important to our survival but now kill us. It isn't our *will* to eat those foods. Quite the opposite. It's an artifact of programming written a million years ago without our knowledge or permission. What if we could change it? *That* is free will. What we have now is slavery."

Randi opened her mouth to speak, but the old man cut her off. "We would have forced no one. If you want to remain angry and unfulfilled, searching for relief from drugs or violence or sex or money, that would be your choice."

Smith's head was spinning. His work in medicine had convinced him that over the next fifty years the line between man and machine would become increasingly blurry. But he'd always thought in physical terms: prostheses, artificial organs. Dresner's ideas weren't so confined. He wanted to reinvent humanity. To perfect it.

"And this is something you can actually *do*," Smith said, stunned. "You proved that in Afghanistan. All you need is a more efficient power supply."

"No," Eichmann admitted as his manic energy faded. "Even without the battery issues, it was a complete failure. Behavioral control had bizarre side effects and massive inconsistencies among individuals. And the real-world environment just made them worse. Perhaps Christian learned something from the experiment that could help him but I doubt it. If he had another half century, he might be able to produce something usable. But he doesn't. Neither of us do."

"What *Christian* learned? You weren't involved?

"I analyzed the data downloaded from the Afghan units as well as the video of the villagers' behavior. But my area of expertise is narrow and I'm not involved in many of the technical aspects. Most of the major research is done in North Korea and I have very little access to that. I've only been to that facility twice, and there's an entire wing I'm barred from."

Smith chewed thoughtfully on his lower lip. A moment ago he had been more or less satisfied that he had everything he needed to write his report. Of course, the president and Dresner would have to sit down and hash out exactly what had happened and what capabilities existed that hadn't been made public, but that wasn't his problem.

Now, though, he wasn't so sure. It wasn't a surprise to him that North Korea had been used as a location for a testing facility—it was a country largely hidden from the rest of the world, with a government desperate for hard currency and an expendable population. But now he had to wonder if the North Koreans could have gained access to the military operating system. And even if they hadn't, what was going on in the facility that Dresner wouldn't even discuss with his oldest friend? Was his research more advanced than Eichmann knew? Was he developing some completely new capability?

"Tell me more about the North Korean facility," Smith said.

The German scientist shrugged. "My understanding is that it's in the process of being dismantled. In the coming weeks, it will cease to exist."

Smith chewed a little harder on his lip. So whatever Dresner was doing there, it appeared that he'd finished and wanted the evidence wiped from the face of the earth.

"Do you have contacts there?"

"At the facility? Of course. I've worked with the director on a number of projects."

"Do you have a way of getting in touch with him?"

"I have his private number," Eichmann said, starting to sound a bit suspicious. "Why?"

"Call it. Tell him you're on your way with two assistants."

"What? I have no authority to go there. Christian has always—"

"Tell him Dresner wants you to check up on the dismantling of the facility," Randi said.

"What if he calls and checks? What if we get there and he knows we aren't authorized? No. I won't do it."

Smith pointed to the door. "Then best of luck to you."

52

Limpopo
South Africa

CHRISTIAN DRESNER SHIFTED in his chair and the image before him immediately became translucent, showing the details of the room beyond. It was the second version of MIT's movie app and the safety features had been improved to the point that it was nearly ready for release.

He settled in again and the image darkened, transporting him to the Afghan village of Sarabat just as it was attacked. Women fought desperately, children screamed in terror, livestock bolted. And the men did nothing.

It took barely fifteen minutes to turn a village full of people going about the mundane business of life into a battlefield strewn with bleeding corpses and cheering victors. He'd always thought the study of the past was a bizarre avocation. What use were dates and names and details when a short video like this one could encompass the entirety of human history so completely?

Of course, this scene was set apart somewhat by the Merge prototypes worn by Sarabat's adult males. Convincing them to use the bulky units had been almost as difficult as developing them, but eventually the villagers had been won over by money, weapons, and the obvious combat benefits of the system. Of course, when the attack came, the software they'd become accustomed to had been shut down in favor of something much more interesting.

Despite its incredible sophistication, though, the application had been the same abject failure in the real world as in the lab. Test subjects derived no happiness or pleasure from the inputs—only confusion and a profound loss of identity.

Above all things, the human brain was an exercise in pointless complexity. It had been modified countless times over millions of years, adding a new function or hijacking an old one for a new purpose in reaction to the constantly changing demands of survival. Now it generated an endless maze of carefully crafted delusions, barely resolved dissonance, and outright lies. A maze that he had failed over and over again to negotiate.

If religiosity was taken away, a profound sense of loneliness was generated—along with an inexplicable degradation in the test subject's ability to count above the number three. If the propensity toward violence was taken away, empathy was paradoxically compromised. But even those were trivial matters compared with the much more individual concepts of happiness and well-being. For every person who derived contentment from love and peace, another derived it from hate and conflict.

And though he had failed miserably to realize his dream, he had started something that would be taken up by the next generation, building momentum that could never be stopped. It would begin slowly and innocuously, probably with the Merge being used to treat serious mental illnesses like depression and schizophrenia. Or maybe by replacing the illicit narcotics trade with much less harmful lines of code that generated the same effect. These first steps would be necessarily crude, but they'd lead inexorably to a day when humanity would be free to take the path of reason, enlightenment, and peace.

Dresner shut down the Afghan video and brought up a set of graphs depicting Merge adoption. Ninety thousand new units were being sold every day and, because of his targeted marketing strategies, a large percentage of those sales were to people LayerCake deemed dangerous to society.

He refocused on a small icon in his peripheral vision. The gray-and-black human outline appeared only on his unit and had been inspired by the images of civilians vaporized in Hiroshima. A reminder of the seriousness of his undertaking.

It accessed a simple subsystem that he'd built into every unit disguised as battery management hardware and unused upgrade paths. The Merge didn't have enough power to directly harm anyone, even if fully discharged over a short period of time. What it could do, though, was create a feedback loop in the area of the brain that controlled heart function. He'd learned early in development that if he mimicked the signal the heart sent to the brain to indicate that it was beating, the brain would stop sending the commands for it to continue doing so. With less power than it took to run a simple gaming app, the user's heart would simply stop.

A phone icon began to pulse at the edge of his vision and Dresner's brow furrowed. It was a private number only a select few had and unscheduled calls never came in on it. Perhaps it was Craig Bailer's wife taking him up on his offer to help?

He activated it but discovered that it wasn't a grieving widow looking for closure. It was the director of the North Korean facility.

"Hello?" he said hesitantly.

"Dr. Dresner. This is Dr. Nang. We are dismantling the facility per your instructions. Do you have concerns?"

"Should I? Why are you calling me about this?"

"Dr. Eichmann and his two assistants are due to arrive in a few hours for their review of our progress. We never talked about that kind of oversight and I can assure you that it isn't necessary. We're attending to this in the same way we've attended to all your requests over the years."

Dresner felt his breath catch in his chest. Two assistants?

"Do you want me to give them access to Division D? In the past, Dr. Eichmann—"

"No!" Dresner said immediately, trying to work through what he was hearing. The only plausible explanation was that Smith and Russell had discovered the connection between himself and Eichmann and had somehow coerced the man into talking. How much did they know? What had they discovered?

He took a deep breath that shook audibly as it escaped from his lungs. He needed to calm down and think. Eichmann knew about the long-term studies and about Afghanistan, but little more. It was likely the limits of his knowledge about the North Korean facility that had prompted the two Americans to investigate further. But why just the two of them? Were the other intelligence agencies working through other channels? No. He'd have heard if they were. Was it possible that they were acting on their own?

"I'll call you with further instructions," Dresner said, severing the connection and immediately dialing James Whitfield. For the first time, there was no answer.

He dialed again, anger quickly turning to fury. Whitfield always picked up by the second ring. The only explanation was that he was avoiding the call, unwilling to admit to another failure. The graphs still hovered in front of him. Only three and a quarter million people were online—a fraction of what he had planned. Projections suggested nearly full adoption by the malignant elements in the political, financial, and military complex within two years. In order to change the world on the fundamental level necessary to allow it to survive, he needed time. The blow he was going to strike against those people had to be fatal.

He dialed again and this time Whitfield answered.

"Yes."

"Gerd Eichmann is on his way to the Korean facility with what he says are two assistants."

"Why is this important to me?"

"Because I authorized none of this. Could these two assistants be Smith and Russell? Is it possible that they're still alive?"

There was a long pause before Whitfield answered. "I sent three Merge-equipped special ops people—an overwhelming force. We're not sure what happened yet, but it appears that Smith managed to get hold of one of the men's units and use it against them."

Dresner wiped at the sweat starting on his upper lip

while he considered what he was being told. Smith had root access to the combat simulation software. Could he have used that?

"It was my understanding that it was impossible to use someone else's unit," Whitfield continued.

For all intents and purposes, it was. The suffering Smith must have endured and the will it would have taken to manipulate the icons were almost unimaginable. Yet another confirmation of just how dangerous the man was.

"Why wasn't I told they survived?"

"Because I'm taking care of it."

"All evidence to the contrary, Major."

"By the end of the day, this will all be a non-issue. You have my word."

"Your personal guarantees are less reassuring than they once were."

"I'm warning you, Christian. Leave this alone. I'm taking care of it."

"Then we'll talk later today. And I expect full disclosure. If you can't resolve this issue, I *will* protect myself. Make no mistake about that."

Dresner severed the connection and shut down the graphs hanging in the air. Mocking him.

He could no long trust anything Whitfield said. The soldier had too many conflicting loyalties: his country, his comrades-in-arms, his outdated fantasy of battlefield honor. Of course, Dresner had always known their paths would diverge, but he'd hoped it wouldn't happen this quickly. There was no choice now but to take control of the situation and deal with the backlash as best he could.

He dialed another private number, this one in Pyong-yang. As usual, General Park let the phone ring endlessly—

a display of his importance and the incalculable value of his time.

"Yes, Dresner. What is it?" finally came the accented voice.

"We need to move up the timetable for the sterilization of the facility."

"Dismantling not finished. Still many scientists and equipment on the site."

"Three people are on their way there. A German and two Americans. I want them captured."

"I see. And if capture is impossible?"

It was a question he was prepared for, but not one he wanted to consider. He needed to know what Smith and Russell had discovered and who they had told. And then there was the entirely different matter of Gerd.

"If capture is impossible," he said, reluctantly. "Then killed."

"This will all be very expensive."

It was always about money—the hard currency that kept North Korea's elite inner circle in luxury and power while their people starved.

On the brighter side, the country's entire hierarchy had adopted the Merge in a showy display of their technological sophistication. In fact, this call was being handled by Park's personal unit.

"How much?"

"Fifty million."

On top of all the other money he'd paid, it was an outrageous sum. But there was little point in arguing.

"Agreed."

"Then I will take your request to our leader as soon as possible."

"As soon as possible? For fifty million dollars, I expect this to be handled immediately."

"He has a country to run. By comparison, your problems are unimportant."

Dresner fought to swallow his anger. "I appreciate your considering my request."

"Of course," Park responded. "And now I have other matters to attend to."

The line went dead and Dresner put his Merge in standby mode, looking around the empty room with no alterations or enhancements.

Would Park succeed in capturing them and wiping away all evidence of the facility? And even if he did, would it be enough? Dresner needed time to reach the tipping point—the critical level at which the people leading the planet to its destruction couldn't be seamlessly replaced. But where exactly was that point? He'd calculated two years, but what if he couldn't wait that long? What if his hand was forced? Would it be enough?

53

Above the Hamgyong-Namdo Province
North Korea

Dr. Eichmann!" Smith shouted from the back of the anonymous Learjet they'd flown from Morocco. "Don't bother her when she's trying to land."

The German, who was standing in the cockpit door, looked back fearfully and then started down the aisle. Instead of taking one of the seats closer to the front, he dropped awkwardly into the one facing Smith and strapped himself in.

"We shouldn't be here. This is North Korea. They—"

"This isn't anything new. You've been here before."

"With Christian's permission and protection! The military controls this place. We have no authority here without him."

"You're going to have to calm down, Doctor. People can smell fear. If we act like we're here with Dresner's blessing, no one will have any reason to question that."

Eichmann looked unconvinced, which wasn't surprising. He wasn't a stupid man. In truth, they were very much working without a net. There was no way to know what security protocols were in place or how much direct communication the Koreans had with Dresner. They could very easily be walking into a summary execution and unmarked grave. But what alternative did they have? If the dismantling of the facility was already under way, going through the nearly nonexistent political channels between Pyongyang and Washington was guaranteed to fail.

Randi swung the plane in a slow arc and Smith looked out the window, admiring the lush mountainscape for a moment before focusing on the narrow airstrip. On the bright side, the massive military force and SAMs that he'd half expected weren't in evidence. But then, maybe they just wanted to take them alive.

"Is this how it looked when you've come in the past?" he said, pointing to a single open jeep parked next to the ribbon of asphalt. "Do you see anything that looks unusual?"

The German squinted out the window and shook his head. "That's Kyong. He always picks me up."

"Is he armed?"

"We should turn around. We can still—"

"We're not turning around," Smith said. "After this is over, you're going to live out a very comfortable retirement under another identity. But now it's time to focus. Is he armed?"

"Never that I've seen," Eichmann said shaking his head miserably. "He isn't a scientist or a soldier. He was born near here and speaks very good English, which makes him an ideal escort."

Randi touched down without her normal drama and shut down the engines as Smith opened the door. He peeked out and saw nothing but the young Korean jogging toward the plane waving.

"What do you think?" Randi said, coming out of the cockpit and sliding a .32 beneath her light jacket.

"Looks okay."

She indicated toward the door. "Age before beauty."

Smith unfolded the steps and went cautiously down them with Eichmann close behind. As terrified as the elderly scientist was of the locals, he didn't seem particularly excited about being left alone with Randi either.

"Dr. Eichmann!" the young Korean said, rushing up and offering his hand. "It's good to see you again so soon."

"Hello, Kyong. I'd like to introduce you to my associate..." He hesitated and Smith covered.

"Dr. Smith." He indicated behind him, seeing no reason to bother with aliases at this point. "And this is Dr. Russell."

Kyong gave them a quick nod and then started toward the jeep. "Please, if you'll follow me."

Temperatures were in the mid-fifties, but the sun was hot in the cloudless sky. There was no humidity and no pollution, just clear air and snow-topped emerald hills in every direction. A deceptively peaceful scene.

Smith slipped into the passenger seat, forcing Eichmann into the back with Randi, where he couldn't cause any trouble. They took off at a casual pace with Kyong skillfully negotiating the uneven dirt road while Smith watched the trees for signs that they were headed into a trap.

Nothing but a few colorful birds, a distant waterfall, and a constant flow of small talk from their driver.

They came out of the trees after about fifteen minutes and began angling toward an enormous complex built near the shore of a small lake. A chain-link fence surrounded the entire campus but they didn't slow as they passed through the open gate. The regular army guard seemed interested in them only insofar as it gave him an excuse to snap off a crisp salute.

The activity Smith had noted during their approach was even more frantic up close. Trucks of every type and size were coming in empty, being loaded, and then heading for the gate. What Eichmann had told them about the place being shut down was apparently true. But more than that, it looked like it was being completely dismantled. To the west, windows were being carefully removed and three men were carrying out a security desk that looked like it had been cut from the floor.

They pulled up to what appeared to be the main entrance—so far untouched by the demolition crews crawling over the rest of the facility—and Smith jumped out. A military flatbed rumbled by with a massive tarp pulled tight over its load. The shapes bulging beneath it were unmistakable: bodies.

Smith followed the vehicle with his eyes as it moved away, spotting a single hand peeking out from beneath the canvas. At first he thought it was covered with dust, but then he realized the color was natural. The body wasn't Asian, but African or possibly East Indian.

"Dr. Eichmann!" came a thickly accented voice behind him. Smith turned to see an older Korean man in an immaculate lab coat come through the glass doors. "I'm so pleased to see you again."

Introductions between them and the facility's director

went fairly smoothly, with Eichmann's queasy expression and weak voice easily written off to jet lag and turbulence on the way in.

Dr. Nang led them inside, where they found still more gaunt workmen using hand tools to tear out everything that had even a remote chance of being recycled: drywall, insulation, plumbing. Even the floor. In a country where labor was virtually free but materials were at a premium, they would undoubtedly strip everything right down to the ground.

"As you can see we're on schedule with closing the facility," Nang said, leading them down a long corridor lined with empty doorways labeled in Korean. Smith looked into each one, finding rooms of various sizes with little left in them beyond the odd IV pole and the marks left by beds long since scavenged.

"Most of the equipment is being sent to other government research facilities," Nang continued. "And about eighty percent of the personnel have already been reassigned."

They passed a large space that still had a few things in it. Oddly, playground equipment.

"What was here?" Randi said, breaking her promise to let him do the talking.

"It was part of our childhood behavior modification effort."

"Where are they?" she said, ignoring an angry glance from Smith.

"Some were released back to their families but the most severely impaired had to be euthanized," he said casually. "Between the drug therapies and surgeries, many wouldn't have been productive in their villages. We had a great deal of success, though—it's unfortunate we're abandoning this area of research. The brain grafts between subjects created significant changes in intelligence and behavior. And our experiments using chimp tissue were fascinating."

"Chimp tissue?" she said, the horror on her face now visible enough that it would be impossible for Nang to miss if he were to turn around. Smith fell back a bit and grabbed her arm in a grip calculated to be painful.

"We actually were able to generate some simian behavior in a few of the children. Of course, rejection happened very quickly, even with our strongest immunosuppressive drugs. A shame. Did you read the report?"

Eichmann had drifted so far from Randi that he was nearly sliding against the left wall as they walked.

"I did. Fascinating work," Smith said. When he looked over at Randi, her face had become a death mask. It was an expression he'd seen before.

"We've gained a great deal of knowledge that could be useful to Mr. Dresner if I could continue the research. We're on the verge of a number of breakthroughs."

Undoubtedly Nang was interested in a job and a ticket out of North Korea—something Smith could take advantage of.

"Mr. Dresner is very impressed with your work here and agrees that there are some aspects that might be worth further investigation. Now, how is the dismantling of Division D progressing?"

"According to schedule," Nang said. "Everything is either on time or ahead."

"Obviously, D is extremely important to Mr. Dresner. He wants it specifically included in our report."

Nang nodded a vague acknowledgment. "Unfortunately, I don't have permission to allow you into that area. I assure you, though. There are no problems."

"You understand that we're Mr. Dresner's representatives," Smith said, deciding to push a bit. They were already in the middle of North Korea with no official authority or backup. How much worse could it get?

"I would need direct authorization."

Randi pushed past and, before Smith could react, shoved her pistol into the back of Nang's head. "How's this for authorization?"

"Damnit, Randi," Smith said, looking behind them. There was no one else in the corridor and the only evidence of the security cameras that had once been there was a few wires hanging from the ceiling. But there was no way to know when someone was going to come strolling around the corner.

Randi seemed to read his mind and pushed Nang through a door to their right. Eichmann looked like he was going to bolt or pass out but Smith grabbed him before he could do either.

By the time they made it into the large, dormitory-style bathroom Randi was drowning Nang in one of the few remaining toilets. Smith yanked her back, allowing the terrified scientist to twist around and raise his hands defensively as he crammed himself farther into the stall.

"Division D," Smith said, looking down on him.

"I can't get you in there!"

"You're the director of the facility," Randi said, coming for him again, but being blocked by Smith's outstretched arm.

"I don't have authority over security—the military answers directly to the government. I'm just a researcher."

Smith frowned. It was almost certainly true. The North Korean government was obsessed with security. Orders would come from central authority—maybe the supreme leader himself.

Smith grabbed the man and pulled him to his feet. "What kind of work went on there?"

He remained silent.

"Listen to me, you don't want to—"

Randi came around him and slammed the butt of her .32 into the side of Nang's head, knocking the man from his grip.

"Randi! For God's sake—"

She jumped on top of the fallen academic and pressed the barrel of the gun against his forehead. "Did you hear him, Jon? Were you listening? He experimented on children's brains and then executed them. *Children!*"

Eichmann had apparently reached his limit and ran for the door. Smith barely managed to get hold of him before he could dart into the hallway. This was getting out of hand fast.

"Tell us what you did in Division D," Randi said, grinding the gun into the prone man's head.

He remained silent, staring her directly in her eyes. It wasn't courage, Smith knew. It was just that the threat she posed wasn't as great as the one posed by his own government. She could kill him. Maybe even torture him. But she couldn't get to his family.

Randi pulled the hammer back on the gun and Smith was about to intercede when Eichmann spoke.

"Wait!"

They both looked at him as he backed slowly toward the wall.

"Do you know something?" Randi said. "Because I'd talk fast if I were you."

"I don't *know* anything. But I suspect."

"What?" Smith said.

"The research related to autonomic brain functions— something that's beyond my expertise. Lower functions like balance and respiration."

Randi actually laughed. "So they're downright *proud* of sticking monkey brains into kids' skulls but they're too ashamed to admit that they were looking into breathing? You'd better do better than that, Doc—"

A deep thud sounded and the entire building shook around them. Smith ran to the door, yanking it open and looking into a hallway billowing with dust. The second impact was closer and completely unmistakable. A bomb.

"Randi! Come on! Let's get the hell out of here!"

He grabbed Eichmann and they ran back the way they'd come with the old man stumbling along behind. When Smith looked back, he saw that Randi was in the hall but with a much less cooperative prisoner. Nang used his momentum and superior weight to break free, turning and running deeper into the complex while she lined her sights up on his receding back.

The next blast almost knocked the fleeing scientist off his feet and part of the ceiling caved in, ruining her aim but undoubtedly crushing her target. She seemed to think justice had been done and began running toward Smith.

The dust was getting thick enough to choke on when she grabbed Eichmann's other arm and they began rushing toward the exit. The workmen they'd passed on the way in were all down, lying amid the rubble—some dead, others trying to get up. The frequency of the blasts increased and Smith nearly pitched onto his face when the floor dropped six inches beneath them.

The doors they'd entered through weren't far ahead, but he wasn't sure bursting out into the open was a good idea. The explosions didn't seem to be from demolition charges. They were coming from outside.

"Do you have any ideas?" he shouted, his voice barely audible over the noise.

"Get the hell out of here?" Randi came back.

"How?"

"The jeep."

She released the German and sprinted ahead, leaping through the shattered glass door. It was unlikely that Kyong would be out there waiting for them, but she seemed to have a plan, which was more than he could say for himself.

He and Eichmann passed through the doors a bit more cautiously and immediately stopped when a tank swiveled its turret toward them.

The round passed over their heads and took out what was left of the wing's main wall. Puffs of smoke on a ridge to the west became visible and were quickly followed by the inevitable mortar blasts behind them. Two more tanks were coming in, crushing the chain-link fence and then stopping so as not to put themselves in range of friendly fire.

With the fence down, armored troop carriers appeared, speeding into the compound and unloading men armed with weapons designed for serious destruction: flame-throwers, handheld rocket launchers, and bandoliers hung with grenades.

Smith pulled Eichmann left, following Randi as she jumped into the back of the jeep that was miraculously still there. And so was Kyong—desperately searching the floorboards for something.

Smith threw the German into the back next to Randi and then slid into the passenger seat as she leaned forward and held out a set of ignition keys.

"Looking for these?"

54

FRED KLEIN SLIPPED THROUGH the door to the White House's private residence and saw the president in his usual position on the sofa. He was about to greet Castilla by his first name but then spotted the top of a man's head protruding over the back of a broad leather chair.

Castilla had personally called him about an emergency—not a word the almost preternaturally calm man often used. Klein had assumed that it was a Covert-One matter, but those meetings were always one-on-one affairs explained away as two old friends getting together to talk about old times.

"Mr. President," he said respectfully, closing the door behind him.

Castilla didn't rise, but the man in the chair did. When he turned, it took all of Klein's discipline to keep his expression impassive. Major James Whitfield.

"I'm not sure if you two have ever actually met," Castilla said. "But I assume that introductions aren't necessary."

Neither man spoke as Klein walked to his usual chair, mind working through every possible explanation for the man's presence.

"Jim here called me because he thought it was time for us to put our cards on the table," Castilla said.

"I thought he already did that at Randi Russell's cabin," Klein countered.

Whitfield mulled his response for a few seconds. "And now three good men are dead."

"But not a certain army doctor and CIA operative."

The anger and suspicion on Castilla's face wasn't anything new—he was the leader of the free world. What had changed was that Klein couldn't be sure it wasn't aimed at him.

"Enough," the president said. "Major, you told me you wanted to have a frank discussion. Well, let's do it. You have the floor."

"Thank you, sir." Again, he hesitated, but his resolve was clear when he locked eyes with Klein. "As I think you've become aware, I run an organization that protects the interests of the military and ensures the country is as well defended as it can be. We operate on similar unstable legal ground as your group—which is why I'm willing to admit any of this."

"Mutually assured destruction," Klein said.

"I hope not, Fred—we're on the same side. But I don't have to tell you that it's a difficult business. In going through the background of your Jon Smith, I can see that you've been forced to make tough decisions. And like me, you've probably made a few mistakes along the way."

Over the last few days, Klein had gathered a substantial dossier on the retired soldier, piecing together a probable history of his organization and making connections between him and the Pentagon officials supporting him. But it seemed that Whitfield had been similarly occupied and equally successful. The questions were, what did he want and how could they get out of this particular standoff without tearing the country apart?

"All right," the president said. "I think we all understand the position we're in. Now, what do you know about Merges in Sarabat?"

Klein was relieved that Castilla hadn't mentioned North Korea or Morocco. Apparently, he wasn't prepared to lay their *entire* hand on the table. Would Whitfield hedge similarly?

"It was a military field test done by Dresner prior to releasing the unit. I don't know the exact details because I'm not a scientist and this is just one of hundreds of experiments and tests that we helped fund during development."

"So you've known about this technology for a long time," Castilla said. "Much longer than we have."

Whitfield nodded. "I became aware of it almost twenty years ago when it was a skunkworks project in one of Dresner's subsidiaries. The research looked promising and the military applications were obvious."

"Obvious enough for you to support it through black funding from the Pentagon."

"It wasn't a project that was far enough along to get the government funding it needed. There was less than a fifty-fifty chance that Dresner could pull it off. And he wouldn't accept public funding from the military anyway. In the end, I persuaded him that it was the only way he was going to get his dream financed and that we'd keep it completely out of the public eye."

"And in return, he would create a military version and give us exclusive rights to it," Castilla said.

"That's exactly right, sir."

"At a high cost, though. People died in Afghanistan. Women and children."

Whitfield gave a jerky nod. "Two Afghan villages were unfortunately wiped out. But neither my organization nor any branch of the U.S. government was directly involved in that or with any other experiments."

The suspicion on Castilla's face deepened. "Other experiments?"

"Yes," Whitfield admitted. "There have been extensive experiments on humans in North Korea as well as large-scale, but less intrusive, long-term studies on children worldwide."

Klein was initially surprised by the man's forthrightness, but after a moment's thought he understood. The damage was already done and everyone in this room lived in far too fragile a glass house to start throwing stones.

Castilla lost a few shades of color. "The North Koreans?"

"Yes sir. But I want to stress that the technology was developed in a very compartmentalized manner. They have no access to it. The facility was focused on—"

"Providing an endless supply of guinea pigs," Castilla said, finishing his sentence.

"Initially, I wasn't aware of Dresner's unorthodox research methods—"

"Unorthodox?"

Whitfield pretended not to hear. "Unfortunately, the

complexity of the human mind can't be replicated by animals or computers. Again, I want to stress that we kept a great deal of distance between us and those activities."

"But you didn't discourage them."

He shook his head. "Your own Jon Smith will tell you that the Merge has already saved more soldiers' and civilians' lives than died in Kot'eh and Sarabat. And we're not just talking about the military system. When the Merge is integrated into things like automobiles and commercial planes, more people will be saved worldwide in a few months than—"

"So the end justifies just about anything: human experimentation, the military making decisions without political authority—"

"With the only goal being keeping the country safe," Whitfield said.

"But that's how it always starts, doesn't it?" Castilla said, standing and beginning to pace around the room. Once again, Klein felt sorry for the man. Power could be intoxicating, but having no higher authority to turn to— being the final word—had a way of slowly crushing men of conscience.

Finally, the president turned back toward them and stared directly at Whitfield. "I want you to give Fred all the information you have on every dime you've siphoned off. I want his assessment of the chances it could be discovered by some outside party."

Klein shifted uncomfortably in his chair. He'd done a great deal for his old friend, but getting involved in this might be a bridge too far. "Sam..."

Castilla cut him off, keeping his eyes locked on the former marine. "I want to be clear here. I don't condone any of this and I wish to God that it had never happened. But the Merge can't be uninvented and the major has been very clever at tying my hands. Dresner Industries is a multinational corporation headed by an incredibly popular and powerful German citizen. The North Koreans will deny everything like they always do. And I don't think anyone questions how important this technology is to our soldiers."

"But..." Klein started.

"But what, Fred? What do you want me to do? Let it come out that a faction inside the Pentagon has been funding human experiments? And what about me? Should I say I knew about it all along and give our enemies the PR coup of the century? Or should I say I didn't know anything about it and make the world wonder who really has control of the deadliest fighting force in history?"

He was right, Klein knew. Any weakening of America's stabilizing influence on the world had the potential to create chaos. And at the same time as America's reputation was going down in flames, so would Dresner and his exclusivity deal with the U.S. military. The people who had been killed in the development of the Merge weren't coming back. Tossing a few million more on their funeral pyre would help no one.

"I'd welcome a second set of eyes," Whitfield said. "Particularly Fred's. I think he'll be satisfied that we've done everything possible to obscure this and that the few loose ends left are being tied up. The remains that Russell found have been destroyed and the North Korean facility is being sterilized."

"What do you mean sterilized?" Klein said.

"It's been in the process of being dismantled for some time and it's my understanding that the timetable has been moved up. By tomorrow, there will be nothing left but rubble."

Castilla gave a curt nod that was obviously intended to be a dismissal. "Then I suggest you start working on Fred's briefing, Major."

Whitfield stood and disappeared through the door at the back without another word.

"What the hell," Klein said as soon as it clicked closed. "I have people in North Korea."

"Then pull them out. From now on your organization's investigation into this is going to be limited to making sure that Whitfield hasn't missed anything—that a thousand years from now, this thing still won't have seen the light of day. And don't start with your moral indignation. I don't give a shit."

"It seems like you don't give a shit about anything anymore, Sam. Why would you blindside me like that?"

"Blindside *you*? My office gets a call from a former high-level intelligence officer saying he wants to talk to me about Fred Klein's investigation into the use of the Merge in Sarabat and I blindside *you*?"

He threw a hand out and heaved a lamp onto the floor. The sound of shattering porcelain caused a Secret Service man to burst in but then quickly retreat when the normally serene Castilla pointed at the door and shouted "Out!"

Klein waited until they were alone again before he spoke. "Can I assume that Whitfield found a way to track me when I tried to stop him from assassinating Jon and Randi?"

"Brilliant! But a little late. What the hell were you thinking, flying in there like that?"

"I understand that secrecy is a priority, Sam. But my people are not expendable. If that's what you're after, I suggest you start looking for my replacement."

For a moment, the president looked like he was going to throw something else, but instead he just let out a long stream of expletives. When he was done, he seemed to have regained some of his familiar calm.

"The son of a bitch put spy planes in the air and still only IDed you by blind luck. That's the other reason he was here. He took a huge risk sending those birds up and now it's starting to bite him in the ass. He needs me to smooth things over."

"If there had been time, Sam, I'd have contacted you about going in."

Castilla gave a familiar wave of his hand, indicating that the storm was over. "And I'd have authorized it. You're right. Your people aren't expendable. But god-damn if my tit isn't caught in a wringer now."

"Are you sure you want to cover this thing up, Sam? Is it the right decision?"

He laughed bitterly. "I make a hundred decisions a day and there's never been a single one that I was sure of. Look, Fred. Even with all our problems, America is a bright light in a dark world. I can't express to you how important it is that we stay that way."

"So that's the final word."

Castilla nodded. "This country has a closet where we permanently store our skeletons—some so ugly even you don't know about them. And that's where this is going. Understood?"

55

Hamgyong-Namdo Province
North Korea

A SECOND BLAST FROM THE TANK caused Smith to duck behind the dashboard, though he knew it wouldn't do much good. Fortunately, the round went wide, passing through the doors they'd escaped from and taking out most of the front of the facility. Apparently, someone had decided they wanted it gone. Now.

The jeep fishtailed and Smith searched for a seat belt that turned out not to exist. He'd originally assumed he'd have to take over driving, but Kyong seemed to know every pothole, ditch, and rock on the compound. The Korean turned off the dirt road and headed across a field of tangled ground cover toward a section of fence that had been crushed by an armored troop carrier.

It didn't take long for the men pouring from the back of the vehicle to spot them and begin swinging rifles in their direction. That was less worrying, though, than the fact that the vehicle's driver was starting to back across the opening in the fence to block their path.

"Shiiiiiiiiiiit!" he heard Randi shout from the back

as Kyong aimed at the shrinking gap leading to what may or may not have been freedom. Smith slid down in his seat as a few of the soldiers managed to bring their weapons to bear and individual shots became audible over the explosions behind. Their driver didn't seem to notice, though, and just stared straight ahead as he struggled to keep the jeep under control on the uneven ground.

They were jerked hard to the left when the truck's rear bumper slammed into their rear quarter panel, but then they were across the fence line. Smith stayed down, preparing to take over if Kyong was hit and not rising again until he calculated they were out of range.

A quick glance back confirmed that Randi was still upright, looking surprised to be alive. Eichmann had crammed himself onto the floorboard behind the driver's seat and was now struggling to get free. Beyond, the troop carrier was accelerating in their direction with soldiers running alongside, grabbing hold of anything that would let them join the chase.

Kyong threw the jeep right and headed toward a dirt track cutting through the trees in front of them. Their jet was in the other direction, but so were the majority of the tanks. Best to give them a wide berth.

They made it to the main road, but the slightly smoother surface didn't seem to be translating into speed. Smith looked past Eichmann, who had finally managed to untangle himself, and saw the troop carrier gaining.

"Can't this thing go any faster?" Smith shouted

"No," was the only reply.

The Korean seemed to have gone through a profound transformation. The friendly helpfulness was gone, replaced not by panic or despair—but by anger. Maybe even hate.

Not that being chased by the North Korean army wouldn't ruin anyone's mood, but this was something more. The change was so complete, Smith had to wonder if this was the real man and the dutiful guide was nothing more than a meticulously crafted character.

"Is there any way off this road?" Smith said. "Onto terrain that will give us an advantage over the truck?"

"No," Kyong said flatly. "We will be caught."

The satellite phone in Smith's pocket vibrated and he pulled it out, punching in his password when he saw that the text was encrypted. Even under the circumstances, it was impossible not to laugh when he read it.

"What?" Randi said from the back.

"Fred says we should get out. That it isn't safe to be here."

"Nice timing."

"We can't be captured!" Eichmann said in a panicked voice. "They'll call Christian and find out we—"

"Shut up!" Randi screamed and punched the man in the side of the head with alarming force. "You *knew* about this place! You knew what they were doing here. And you just sat there and collected data. Don't talk. Do you understand me? Next time you open your mouth, I'm going to kill you!"

The German was too dazed to respond and instead teetered precariously toward the edge of the open jeep.

"Calm down!" Smith said.

She turned her angry gaze on him. "You shut up too."

Knowing that there was no point in fighting this battle, he gestured toward the vehicle behind them. "It's going to catch us. And when it does, it's going to ram us. The road's too narrow for us to do anything about it."

"Then we need to slow it down," Randi shouted, barely audible over the wind and the roar of the approaching troop carrier's engine.

"The tires are made in North Korea. Maybe they aren't run-flat. Do you think you could hit one with your Beretta?"

She shook her head. "I have a better plan."

Eichmann had shaken off the effects of the blow to the head, but he wasn't prepared when Randi grabbed him by the front of his jacket. And neither was Smith. By the time he managed to throw a hand out, the scientist was already over the gate and dropping into the road.

"Goddamnit, Randi!" he shouted, watching the old man rag-doll in the dirt.

"What?" she challenged. "He was a sadistic bastard who didn't have anything else to tell us. I made him useful again."

It was hard to argue—particularly when the truck skidded to a stop in front of the man and soldiers began streaming out. She'd bought them some time. Now he just had to figure out what to do with it.

When he turned back in his seat, Kyong was staring at him. The anger on his face had turned to confusion.

"But you were with him," he said. "You worked for him."

Smith didn't initially respond but then decided that this was no time to be clever. He might as well come clean and see what happened.

"We forced him to bring us here. We wanted to investigate what was happening at that facility."

378 Robert Ludlum and Kyle Mills

"Then you're American agents?"

Smith nodded as the dirt road they were on turned steep and winding, improving their odds against the personnel carrier. What wasn't going to help them, though, was the familiar green shape rising over a crest about a kilometer ahead.

"Tank!" he shouted.

At first, the driver didn't react, but then the jeep he'd insisted was at full speed started to accelerate. To their left, Smith spotted a double track leading into the trees and assumed they were headed for it.

That wasn't the case, though, and Kyong sped by, continuing on a collision course with the tank.

"Did you see that?" Randi said from the back. "We could have gotten off there!"

"No!" the Korean said forcefully. "We might be able to make it! If they stay stopped behind us to pick up Dr. Eichmann and we can get to the river bottom..."

Another path, this time to the right, became visible ahead and Smith felt Randi grab him by the back of the neck.

"He's probably secret police," she said, bringing her lips close to his ear. "Who else would they send to escort foreign nationals? He's going to drive us right into that goddamn tank!"

She was probably right. But where did all these side roads go? For all he knew, they petered out after a hundred meters. Add to that the fact that neither of them spoke Korean, they stood out like sore thumbs, and they were in the most clamped-down police state on the planet. It was time to gamble.

He managed a weak shrug and Randi released him,

falling back in her seat as they started down a steep hill toward a dry riverbed. Fifty meters before they got to it, Kyong slammed on the brakes and spun the wheel.

"Hold on!" he shouted, crashing into the trees to their right.

Smith put a hand up to protect his face, but in less than a second they were through. Trees that had looked dense a moment before turned out to be a row of saplings planted only a meter deep.

"Come on!" Kyong shouted as he slid the vehicle to a stop and leapt from it. "Help me!"

Still not sure what had just happened, Smith and Randi jumped out and began helping him push the trees and bushes they'd broken upright again. The sound of explosions and mortar fire was still audible in the distance, but it was quickly being drowned out by the rumble of the tank bearing down on them.

"Hurry!" Kyong said. "It's coming!"

A moment later Smith saw a flash of it going through the riverbed. There was no way to know if the man protruding from the top had seen them go in, but they were about to find out. He helped Randi prop up a bush with a rotting log and then hit the ground. The vibration from the tank sank into his chest as Kyong dropped between them and closed his eyes.

56

CHRISTIAN DRESNER SAT in the back of his private plane—a 737 that his growing security detail had insisted on—and watched the black SUV approach through the rain. Another meeting—another altercation—that he didn't want to be involved in. It was more of his increasing sense of disconnect from the world and the people in it. His time was fading while for so many others it was just beginning. In some ways, he wished he could be part of the future, could see what was to come. Other times, he just felt tired.

As he watched a man in a gray coat emerge from the vehicle, a phone icon in the colors of the North Korean flag appeared in his peripheral vision. He picked up immediately.

"Yes?"

"Mr. Dresner?" came the thickly accented voice. Not General Park's. His assistant's. The man he used when a failure needed to be reported.

"What's happened?"

"The facility has been completely destroyed."

"Destroyed? You mean dismantled."

"Our leader sent the military and they accomplished their goal with magnificent efficiency."

"You used the military?" Dresner said, turning away from the window and trying to control the anger welling up inside him. Even in the North Korean hinterlands, that kind of action wouldn't escape the American intelligence community. Once again the North Korean leadership had proved itself to be a tantrum-prone child trying to display its power and relevance.

"And the people I wanted captured?"

"We have the German."

Dresner found himself unable to respond. Was it possible? Was it possible that a military force sufficient to destroy a fifty-thousand-square-meter bunker had managed to let Smith and Russell escape? That all they had accomplished was to trap a single aging scientist?

He glanced through the window beside him and saw James Whitfield stride through the rain as though he wasn't aware of it.

"And the others?"

"They escaped in a jeep. Our leader is extremely busy, but you will be honored to know that he is giving this his personal attention. We expect to have them in a short time."

"You expect—" Dresner started, but the man cut him off.

"You must excuse me. I have things to attend to. We will contact you when the situation changes."

The line went dead and Dresner pushed himself to his feet, stalking to the empty rear of the plane and entering the elaborate bathroom there. He stood over the sink staring into the mirror, trying to construct the facade of control that would be necessary for his meeting with Whitfield. He constantly tried to remind himself of the seriousness of the path he'd taken but sometimes it was impossible not to be overwhelmed by the emotional satisfaction of knowing that one day soon, the world would be free of men like the ones who ran North Korea.

Perhaps his carefully laid plans to disappear after all this would be unnecessary. There were literally billions of people in the world who would thank him for what he'd done and some might even offer him asylum. The starving, oppressed population of North Korea would certainly have no reason to do anything but laud his actions.

He heard the door in the side of the plane open and took a deep, cleansing breath. His resources inside the CIA and army could find no extraordinary power base behind the two Americans, but questions remained—particularly about Smith. His history was especially murky.

The danger they posed could not be underestimated. In all likelihood, the North Koreans would put an end to this. They were two whites at the center of a manhunt by a regime whose only area of competence was making people disappear. But he would be foolish to count on it. Smith and Russell had proved their resourcefulness too many times.

When he emerged, Whitfield was already sitting at the small conference table in the center of the plane. He didn't speak until Dresner had taken a seat across from him.

"It's my understanding that the North Korean facility has been leveled. In as obvious a way as possible."

"And it's my understanding that Smith and Russell

were there at the time. They've now escaped into the countryside."

No surprise registered on Whitfield's face but it was impossible to know if it was because he'd already known of their presence in Korea or if it was a result of the mask he wore so comfortably.

"They're no longer a threat."

"Are you saying they're dead?"

"I'm saying that they're no longer a threat."

"And I should just leave it at that?"

"Yes."

"You must think I'm much more trusting than I am, Major. I have no idea how involved the CIA or military intelligence is in their actions but it's impossible to believe that they're working alone. The time when you could just make pronouncements and have me accept them has been over for quite a while. Your record doesn't warrant that kind of confidence."

Whitfield just stared at him and Dresner settled back to return the stare. It was a childish battle of wills, he knew, but not one he would permit himself to lose. There was too much at stake.

"The CIA and military intelligence aren't involved," Whitfield said finally. "This was isolated to Randi Russell and Jon Smith. She has a history of going out on her own and she recruited Smith because of their personal history and his position working on the Merge."

"How can you be certain they haven't told anyone about their suspicions? And if they're still alive, how do we know that they won't continue their investigation?"

Again, he didn't immediately answer. And again Dresner waited him out.

"Because I spoke to the president."

"Excuse me?"

"Smith and Russell are notoriously hard to deal with and this was escalating out of control. I met with the president and told him everything."

"What do you mean 'everything'?" Dresner said, trying to keep the shock from reading on his face.

"I mean how the Merge was developed and about my involvement in its financing."

Dresner tried to process what he was hearing, beating back the growing sensation of panic as Whitfield continued.

"For obvious reasons, Castilla agreed that none of this can ever see the light of day. He's personally going to call off Smith and Russell and I'm coordinating with him to make certain that every aspect of this is permanently swept under the rug."

As dangerous as the situation was, what Whitfield was saying rang true. Castilla's motivations were clear here: He wanted to remain in the White House and he wanted the American military to dominate the world. Ironic how much the politician would risk to protect a device that had been designed to destroy the very malignant power structure he sat atop.

"I'm not confident in Russell," Dresner said finally.

"Explain."

"Don't play stupid, Major. Smith is a good soldier. He can be counted on to follow orders. But her past paints a very different picture."

Whitfield's expression lost its enigmatic neutrality for long enough to make it obvious that he was sympathetic to that particular concern.

"It's my understanding that you have a relationship with the political leaders in North Korea."

Dresner nodded.

"Well, I don't. As long as they're in Asia, I have neither the ability to protect them nor the responsibility to do so."

The message was clear. He was unwilling to have anything to do with the killing, but if they never returned, it would be simpler for everyone. A modern Pontius Pilate.

"Are we through?" Whitfield said.

"I think so."

The former marine stood and headed for the front of the plane. Dresner watched him exit into the heavy rain and kept watching until the SUV disappeared. A moment later the calming rumble of the jet engines spooling up filled the cabin.

Nothing that could be confused with serenity came to him, but the fear that had been building subsided a bit. In all likelihood, Russell and Smith would never leave North Korea. But even if they did, it was probable that they could be controlled—at least for the time frame important to him.

It was conceivable that his position had just been strengthened—that instead of worrying about being discovered, he would now be able to operate under the protective umbrella not only of Whitfield's organization, but of the White House itself. Perhaps the two-year window he'd planned on could be extended to three, possibly even five years. What if he could delay activation until there were a billion users? Two billion? And over that time, how much more sophisticated would LayerCake become at targeting those responsible for the unnecessary suffering of humanity and everything humanity touched?

Grand dreams. But probably no more than that. Jon Smith and Randi Russell had motivations that were much more complex than the powerful men they answered to and it made them unpredictable.

They would have to be dealt with. Until he had seen their dead bodies, he would not be safe.

57

Hamgyong-Namdo Province
North Korea

KYONG HADN'T SAID A WORD since the tank had passed, leaving them with lungs full of diesel smoke and a glimmer of hope that they might survive. Admittedly a faint glimmer, but a glimmer nonetheless.

They walked up the overgrown dirt road with Randi and Smith keeping watch on the dense trees encroaching from either side. A startled water deer had caused a brief panic about a half a kilometer back, but since then everything had been quiet.

"That tank will have reached Eichmann and the troop carrier by now," Randi said. "They'll know we got off the road somewhere."

The Korean, a few paces ahead, didn't acknowledge that he'd heard. He clearly still didn't fully trust them. And after what they'd seen at that facility, it was hard to blame him.

"The soldiers won't know about this road," he said finally. "It hasn't appeared on a map since many of them were children."

"Where does it lead?" Randi said.

The Korean's gait slowed a bit, suggesting that it was a more difficult question than it seemed. "To nowhere."

She wasn't willing to leave it at that. "Roads that people go to this much trouble to hide *always* lead somewhere."

Kyong picked up his pace and Randi gave Smith a quizzical look. The message was clear—they knew nothing about this man and it was hardly a stretch to think he could be leading them into a trap. But he hadn't yet and alternatives were limited. On their own, it was unlikely they'd last long.

She frowned at his noncommittal shrug, jamming her hands in the pockets of her jacket and starting to watch the trees again.

It was another fifteen minutes before Kyong came to a stop at the edge of a rolling, open meadow where the road dead-ended. Smith squinted into the sunlight, looking for something that distinguished it from every other rolling, open meadow in the area, but came up empty. He pulled out his satellite phone and looked down at the screen again, confirming that there was still no signal. It was likely that the North Koreans had started jamming and that the text from Fred had skidded in under the wire.

"This was my village," Kyong said. "I was born here. So were my parents and my grandparents. We were farmers. Very poor like all the workers in my country. Twenty years ago, the complex opened. They paid a little money to people willing to go there. A little bit of food."

"Go there?" Smith said, noting the interesting turn of phrase. "You mean 'work there'?"

Kyong shook his head. "The old people went first. They couldn't farm anymore but they wanted to contribute. My grandmother never returned. My grandfather came back blinded, though there was nothing wrong with his eyes. When the weather turned bad, the crops failed and more of our people went there. I was small then, but I still remember. We were starving."

"I don't mean to question you," Randi said. "But are you sure we're in the right place?"

It was a valid question. There was no trace of irrigation ditches or crop rows. No paths or home foundations. If Kyong was telling the truth, someone had done a hell of a job of wiping his birthplace off the map.

Their skepticism must have shown because the Korean started east toward the trees. "Come. I'll show you."

He crashed into the dense forest with them lagging a bit behind, scanning the shadows for troops and secret police. When they finally caught up, they found Kyong standing in front of a tiny house with the remnants of white paint still clinging to rough-hewn boards. The glass was still intact in the only window, so Smith rubbed the dirt from it and peered into the gloomy interior. It looked like the people had just walked out and never come back. There was a sewing machine with a piece of cloth in it, metal cups on a makeshift table, a small bed left unmade. All that gave away the passage of time was the thick layer of dust and a few empty animal nests.

He stepped back, listening for a moment to the chirp of birds and wind-rustling leaves. The bomb blasts were silent now and Smith wondered if it was over. If the facility was a corpse-ridden pile of rubble.

He turned back to Kyong. "Do you know what Division D was?"

By way of an answer, the Korean started walking again, motioning for them to follow.

It was less than a minute before they came upon the first mounds, their size and shape making it impossible to mistake them for anything but the unmarked graves they were. As they continued, the mounds grew in width: couples buried together. Then they expanded into what looked like whole families. A few of the graves had wooden markers with fading Korean lettering, but most of these people would face eternity in anonymity.

Kyong pulled a flowering vine from one of the markers, looking down at it with a mix of sadness and anger. "I'm the only one left. The only one who remembers."

"What do you remember?" Randi prompted.

"When the people stopped returning or were brought back to us dead, we no longer volunteered to go. Starvation was better. After that, they just took us. The trucks would come at night. Parents would stay in their homes and send their children to hide in the forest until the soldiers were gone. The worst time was going back to your house. Not knowing if anyone would be there."

He paused for a moment, lost in the past. "Eventually, I was the only one left. And they came for me too. But I knew the area and I had an ability with languages so I survived—but only if I worked for the people who destroyed everything I ever knew."

"When you buried the bodies," Smith said. "Did you look at them? What killed them?"

"Some had shaved heads and scars. Some had little holes in their skull that we didn't understand. Others had nothing. They were just dead."

Kyong swept an arm around the improvised graveyard. "This is what you're looking for, Dr. Smith. This is Division D."

58

Hamgyong-Namdo Province
North Korea

ARE YOU ALL RIGHT, KYONG?" Jon Smith said.

The Korean nodded weakly, using the question as an opportunity to bend at the waist and take in a few deep, ragged breaths.

They'd been forced into the wilderness when the military's search intensified and foot soldiers had been deployed to find where they'd turned off the road. According to Kyong, there was a large village twenty kilometers to the east where his last surviving relative—an aging aunt—lived. In the plus column, she apparently had no love for the government and would probably be willing to help to the degree she could. In the negative column, fifteen of the twenty kilometers were through a rocky, overgrown mountain range devoid of trails.

The Korean started up the steep slope again, staying close to a stream flowing from the snow line in order to avoid the tangled foliage on either side. Randi gave him an optimistic grin that turned to an expression of deep concern once he'd passed.

"We're less than ten kilometers into this," she said quietly to Smith. "And we haven't even gotten to the hard terrain yet."

She was right, and it wasn't just their less-than-athletic guide. Anticipating trouble, he and Randi had worn versatile shoes and jackets, but they weren't suitable for a multiday expedition into the middle of nowhere. Their primary goal had been to pass for scientists, and showing up in full combat regalia would have looked a little suspicious.

The sun was starting to sink toward the horizon and the warmth of the day was already starting to fade. With the altitude they were gaining, he guessed that temperatures would dip well below freezing before sunrise.

So no gloves, no hats, no food. No ability to build a fire with the army tracking them. And a team member who was completely unsuited to this kind of work.

The rumble of a jet engine became audible and both he and Randi slipped into the trees as a Chinese-made attack aircraft swept low a few kilometers to the west. There was no need to warn Kyong to do the same. Staying clear of the government was hardwired into him.

When the sound of the plane faded, Smith switched on his satellite phone again.

"Anything?" Randi said, not sounding particularly hopeful.

He shook his head. "Still no signal. If they're jamming, we might be able to get something when we make it over the peak. But I don't know how extensive their capability is. I've never operated here. You?"

"Nope."

"It probably doesn't even matter. Fred's well connected around the world, but North Korea's a black hole."

"I'll bet your Merge would work," she said sarcastically. "Too bad you left it at home."

"Don't start, okay?"

He squinted down the slope and at the distant clearing that had once contained Kyong's village. Something seemed to move, but it was impossible to be sure. At this distance, vehicles would be visible but individual men in camo wouldn't. Had the Koreans found the entrance to the road? Did they know they'd been there?

What he wouldn't give for a pair of binoculars. A sandwich. A rifle. And, despite Randi's chiding, a little audiovisual enhancement wouldn't be a bad thing either.

"What do you think was going on in Division D?" she said as they started along the stream again.

"Dunno. Might just be another aspect of the development of the technology."

"Then why not tell Eichmann about it? It wasn't like that son of a bitch was squeamish about turning people into guinea pigs."

"I don't know that either," he said, deciding to return a little of her sarcasm from earlier. "But it's going to be hard to ask him, isn't it?"

"Bullshit. I saved our asses back there and that old man wouldn't have made it five steps up this mountain."

They walked in silence for a few minutes before Randi spoke again. "Why does something like this happen every time we see each other? I'm starting to think we should each pick a hemisphere and stay there."

"Probably not a bad idea."

The foliage started to encroach on the edge of the

stream and Kyong was no longer visible ahead. He wasn't hard to track, though. His thrashing would be audible for hundreds of meters in every direction and his trail of broken branches and muddy footprints would damn near be visible from space. Worse, though, was that Smith had underestimated the drop in temperature when the sun dipped below the horizon. Kyong would stay warm as long as he could keep moving but his trail was starting to wander. It was doubtful that they had much more than an hour before he collapsed from exhaustion.

Smith passed Randi and came up behind the man, watching him with admiration. He might not be fit, but he could sure as hell suffer.

A few hundred meters ahead, a cliff rose above the foliage and the area around the base looked relatively flat and dry. The glow of the sunset was still powerful enough to illuminate the fog of Kyong's breath, but it wouldn't be long before the unfamiliar terrain would become too dangerous even for Randi and himself.

He glanced back at her. "Dig in up there?"

"Looks good."

When they arrived in the tiny clearing, Randi took off her jacket and held it out to the Korean.

He shook his head. "It's yours. I'm fine."

Randi smiled and pointed to a natural furrow slanting northwest. "Don't be too hasty. I need you to do something for me. Walk up that for about fifteen minutes and then turn around and come back. Don't step out of the groove, though. You'll get lost."

He looked scared but, to his credit, just took the jacket and set out.

They watched him for a moment and then began gathering sticks and leaves, piling them next to the tangle of bushes and vines growing along the base of the cliff. When they had a reasonable supply, Smith began constructing a small lean-to—less than a meter high and barely wide enough to accommodate the three of them. With the frame finished, he covered the outside with dirt and leaves, then crisscrossed it with the vines growing around it. Randi weaved together a makeshift hatch out of the same materials while he finished up by stuffing the interior with grass and moss.

"What do you think?" Smith said, standing and dusting himself off.

"I'd probably walk by it. Particularly once it gets completely dark."

They heard Kyong's stumbling footfalls coming from above and Smith jogged over to help the exhausted Korean down a steep section of rock.

"You made it," he said, throwing the man's arm over his shoulders and half carrying him to the open side of the lean-to. "Now's the reward. A good night's sleep."

"In there?"

"Yup. Just wiggle in feetfirst. You'll be fine."

He looked skeptical, but did as he was told, struggling to worm his way into the tight space through all the debris stuffed into it.

"Will this be warm enough?" he asked as Smith squeezed in next to him. "It can snow here this time of year."

"It's not as good as a nice down sleeping bag—"

"Or a room at the Four Seasons," Randi chimed in.

"But we'll survive."

It was a tight fit, which was the plan, and once Randi

pulled the cover she'd made closed, it started warming up noticeably. Smith closed his eyes, forcing his mind to shut off. They had too few options to bother going over. What he needed now was some sleep. Tomorrow was going to be harder. A lot harder.

* * *

SMITH'S EYES CAME OPEN and for a moment he was confused where he was. It didn't take long for the sticks and leaves jabbing at his face to remind him, though. Why was it that he couldn't occasionally wake up in his own bed to find that the day before had been nothing but a particularly ugly nightmare? Like normal people.

He wasn't sure why he'd awoken—probably the cold or the rock in the small of his back—but there was no sunlight filtering through to him so he closed his eyes again. Before he could drift off, though, a quiet crunching and the snap of a twig brought him fully alert.

The wind? Maybe an animal?

Again, his luck just wasn't that good. Quiet Korean voices became audible and he felt Kyong shift next to him.

Smith grabbed the man's wrist, giving it a reassuring squeeze as the voices closed in. The Korean started to tremble with fear as the men outside stopped only a few paces away. Smith increased the pressure on Kyong's wrist and assumed that Randi was doing the same from the other side. If they stayed cool, they might get out of this.

The men didn't pause for long, moving away again after less than a minute to follow the trail Kyong had left leading up the gully. Smith calculated that it would take them about ten minutes to get to where it dead-ended, maybe a minute of confusion, and then another five to double-time it back. The three of them would make a break for it as soon as the men were safely out of earshot.

Again, though, his luck wasn't that good. Whoever the tracker was had real talent. The sound of them had barely faded when they turned and began running back in the direction of the clearing. Kyong tensed again, this time completely locking up in terror. It was impossible not to be sympathetic after what had happened to his family. Men like the ones approaching had taken everything from him.

Soon, the voices were all around. Smith couldn't understand them, but Kyong could and he began to fidget. A flashlight came on outside and swept over them.

Don't do it . . .

But Kyong had finally reached his limit. He jerked upright, bursting from the delicate lean-to and bolting in the wrong direction. Surprised shouts rose up as the Korean ran straight into the cliff, bounced off, and fell backward over a log.

Randi didn't even have time to reach for her weapon before no less than five guns were pointed at them. Orders were shouted in Korean and, though unintelligible, it seemed likely that they wanted their new captives to raise their hands and stand.

They were forced to more open ground with the guns still on them, some only a few inches from their heads. Running would almost certainly get them shot before they made it more than a few steps. And even if they did managed to slip away, what then?

A man emerged from the darkness and came to a stop directly in front of Smith. Based on the nervous deference the others gave him as he reached into his jacket, he was in command.

Instead of the expected gun, he produced a phone and held it out. His accent was thick, but the English still decipherable: "Call your boss."

Smith just stood there. Did they still think he worked for Dresner? And if so, how could he take advantage of their confusion?

His inaction elicited a frustrated huff from the man and he began dialing the phone himself.

"Take," he said, holding it out again.

Smith did, and listened to the ringing on the other end. Apparently, they had a way through the military's jamming.

He was still trying to formulate some kind of plan when a familiar voice came on.

"Go ahead."

"Fred?"

"Jon! Are you and Randi all right?"

The men lowered their guns and backed into the woods to take up perimeter positions. Randi didn't seem sure what was happening but took the opportunity to kneel next to Kyong and examine the gash in his head.

"We're fine. I should have known you'd be connected here."

"The resistance movement is small and not very well organized, but there were a few people I could call on. They'll do their best for you, but no guarantees. North Korea runs by its own set of rules and I'm afraid none of them favor you getting out."

59

Prince George's County, Maryland
USA

"Y OU TWO LOOK AWFUL!" Maggie Templeton said, actually standing up from behind her monitors to give them an apprehensive once-over.

"The aftermath of being smuggled across North Korea," Randi said. "On foot, in boats, hidden in oil drums, on flatbeds..."

"And don't forget under half a ton of rice on that horse-drawn cart," Smith added.

"How could I? I still have grains stuck in places I'm not sure they're ever going to come out of."

It had taken the better part of two weeks, but they'd finally made it over the Chinese border, where Randi's language skills and Covert-One's contacts were a hell of a lot more useful.

Fred Klein appeared in his doorway and motioned them inside, taking the unusual added step of closing the door behind them.

"Sit," he said, apparently deciding to dispense with any niceties about being happy they weren't dead.

"We got into the facility before they destroyed it," Randi told him, ignoring the invitation. "The scale of the human testing is worse—"

"Sit!" Klein repeated and she fell into a defiant silence, but not a chair.

Smith, on the other hand, did as he was told. Randi hadn't worked with Klein long enough to know how out of character his tone was and to be concerned by it.

"Your investigation has ended."

"What?" Randi said.

"Was I unclear?"

Smith shifted uncomfortably. After what he'd seen, even *he* would have a hard time taking that order at face value. The chances of Randi just nodding submissively were hovering around zero. When you signed on with her, you got the skills but you didn't get the obedient soldier.

"Yes," she said. "You were unclear."

Based on Klein's expression, he'd anticipated the pushback. Whether he was starting to regret bringing Randi into the fold was less obvious.

"Whitfield identified me at your cabin and went to the president. The three of us had a meeting and decided to…" He paused for a moment, considering his phrasing. "De-escalate the situation."

"A meeting?" Randi said, the volume of her voice rising. "You had a *meeting*? Do you have any idea what we found in Korea? What they were doing to those people?"

"This isn't my call to make, Randi. But the consensus is that America needs the technology and the only people looking for skeletons in Dresner's closet are you and Jon."

"So we're supposed to just walk away from people

who've been murdered, tortured, and experimented on because Jon and his soldier buddies need a new toy to play with?"

Smith passively examined an antique globe by the back wall while she stalked out and slammed the door. A string of muffled expletives was audible for a few moments as she headed for the exit—undoubtedly to drive off in the car they'd come in. Stranded again.

Klein finally took a seat behind his desk, and the two men stared at each other. Smith was the first to break the silence.

"There was something called Division D at that facility, Fred. All we know about it is that a lot of the test subjects there died. Even Eichmann—"

"I don't want to hear it, Jon."

Smith ignored him. "My concern is that this was something separate from the normal development research. Something that could bite us in the ass."

"The investigation is over," Klein repeated.

"Because Castilla is worried about his legacy?"

"Don't try to channel Randi's outrage. You know better."

Smith let out a long breath and tried to figure out a way to get through. "Our military is getting reliant on the Merge faster than even I expected. Actually, 'reliant' isn't even the right word. Addicted. How can I get comfortable continuing to integrate a technology that I don't fully understand? A hell of a lot of blood and treasure was expended in Division D, Fred. And even Dresner's closest friend and collaborator didn't know why."

Klein didn't react.

"Authorize me to continue to quietly pursue this, Fred.

I'll convince Randi to walk away. This will just be between you, me, and the president. Then we can make a decision with a full set of facts."

Klein didn't seem sure how much to say. "You're not bringing up any points that I didn't already discuss with the president, Jon. This is over. We're shut down."

"What about Whitfield? What does he know?"

Klein stood in a way that was clearly a dismissal. "I'm going to say this one more time. We're not asking those kinds of questions anymore. We're not even authorized to speak about it among ourselves. Any data—anything you've written down or recorded—is to be destroyed. By the end of the day, I want there to be no record that any of this ever happened."

"Fred, we—"

"I'm not sure you understand how difficult it was to get you out of North Korea and how involved with that operation the president was," Klein said, cutting him off. "We've compromised some of our best eyes in that country and now have to get them and their families out. Castilla could have left you there to rot, Jon. Are you going to make him regret his decision?"

Smith didn't answer.

"I want to hear you say it, Colonel. I want to hear you say that you're clear on your orders."

"I'm clear. But what about Randi?"

"I'm making her your responsibility. My hands are tied here, Jon. If you can't handle her, I'll be forced to."

Smith didn't know exactly what that meant, but he was certain he didn't want to find out.

"I'll take care of it."

Klein nodded solemnly. "See that you do."

60

Outside of Pyongyang
North Korea

CHRISTIAN DRESNER FOLLOWED SILENTLY, a darkness he hadn't felt since the night of his escape from the East threatening to overwhelm him. The concrete-and-steel bunker of a building was empty except for the occasional guard, whose only purpose seemed to be to snap to attention when he and the aging Korean general came into view. None of this was as he had instructed. Whatever this building's original purpose, it now felt like the dungeon it was.

On his way there, he had flown over the facility in Hamgyong and confirmed that its destruction, while unnecessarily public, had been entirely thorough. Even the rubble created by the military's heavy-handed action was nearly gone—to be recycled into a project proclaiming the enduring glory of Kim Jong Il.

The immediate eradication of the facility had been a difficult decision. The human cost was much higher than it would have been under the more measured dismantling he'd planned before his hand was forced. North Korea had become an ironic microcosm for his situation—a reminder of not only *why* what he was doing was so necessary, but also of the gravity of that undertaking.

Left to its own devices, the country's malignant government would continue to starve its people by diverting resources to the task of staying in power. But when those resources dwindled, they would have no choice but to turn to their nuclear arsenal. Millions of their own people would die, as would countless innocents in the greater region. All for a handful of twisted men like the one in front of him.

Dresner could never allow himself to forget the blood on his own hands, though. The people who had died at that facility weren't part of North Korea's sadistic ruling elite. They were blameless victims who he had sacrificed so that others could live and prosper.

General Park stopped next to a heavy steel door and turned toward Dresner. His skin hung loosely, contrasting with the heavily starched uniform weighted down with meaningless medals and a polished sidearm. He didn't speak, but his dull eyes flicked toward the door, making it clear that they had reached their destination.

Dresner's anger intensified as the bolt was thrown back and he entered. The cell was probably no more than three meters square with an open toilet, a cot, and a single chair where Gerhard Eichmann sat. Park had undoubtedly gone out of his way to defy his wishes that his friend be made as comfortable as possible until he arrived.

When Eichmann looked up, the fear in his eyes was replaced by relief, hope, and even joy. All illusions spun by the computer in his head, of course, but no less powerful for not being real. And neither was the deep sense of melancholy he himself felt.

"I'm so sorry, Gerd. They weren't supposed to put you here. I came as soon as I could."

He crossed the tiny room to help his friend overcome the cast on his leg and rise to his feet. When Eichmann looked into his face, though, some of the fear had returned.

"You tried to kill me, Christian."

"In Morocco?" Dresner smiled sadly. "No. It was Smith and Russell. They did it to turn you against me. To trick you into bringing them here."

Eichmann broke away and stumbled backward, trying to think through what he was hearing. By the time Dresner reached out to steady him, it was clear from his face that he realized it was the truth.

"I...I'm sorry, Christian."

"I know."

"They found the data for the study. And they know what was done here. Everything except Division D."

Dresner retrieved a set of crutches leaning against the wall and held them out. "Let's go, Gerd."

"Go? We're leaving?"

"Of course. My jet is waiting. We'll be home soon."

"Home," Eichmann repeated. "But that's where they found me. I can't go back unless they're gone. Are they? Do you know what's happened to them?"

In fact, Dresner didn't. They'd escaped into the mountains and the military had mounted a massive—and thus far fruitless—hunt for them. While it seemed impossible that they would be able to avoid capture, both had proved their resourcefulness too many times to make any other assumption. And that left him relying on Castilla's anxiousness to end their investigation. Far from certain, but more likely than Smith and Russell allowing themselves to be caught. Powerful men were easy to predict and even easier to manipulate. Castilla would protect his beloved country. And he would protect himself.

"Not Morocco," Dresner said, opening the door to the cell and standing aside so Eichmann could hobble through. "Somewhere else. Somewhere no one will be able to bother you again."

Dresner watched his oldest—only—friend struggle up the hallway, unable to keep the memories from intruding on his mind: Their first meeting at East Germany's Olympic training facility. The delicate beginnings of trust as they tested each other with increasingly unequivocal admissions of their disillusionment. And finally their escape.

The corridor was so long it seemed to stretch into infinity. No guards were present and the only sound came from the confused rhythm of their footsteps and breathing. Dresner put a hand on Park's shoulder and then pointed to his holster. Understanding came quickly, as would be expected for a man like him.

The Korean pulled his sidearm and held it out as they walked. Dresner took it with no outward demonstration of the hesitation he felt, no acknowledgment of the terrifying weight of it in his hand.

He had done so many horrible things and there were so many more to come. None had touched him personally, though. And that was hypocrisy.

Dresner raised the gun to the back of his friend's head. He wouldn't feel any pain. None of them would. The computer that made him who he was would just turn off. Forever.

The sound echoed through the confines of the concrete passage, and blood splashed hot across Dresner's face. He let the gun fall next to his friend's body as he once again told himself that there had been no choice. That Eichmann was a weak link in the chain he'd spent the better part of half a century forging. And while it was all true, it did nothing to diminish the profound sense of emptiness he felt. For the first time since he'd been dropped in front of the orphanage in Erfurt, he was truly alone.

61

J ON SMITH PULLED THE CHEESECAKE he'd bought from its box and limped into his living room with it and a newly opened bottle of whiskey. The new sofa was a bit of a monument to form over function, but exhaustion had a way of making just about anything comfortable.

He took a large bite from the edge of the cake, feeling it settle uncomfortably on top of half the Taco Bell menu. He'd dropped more than ten pounds in the last two weeks—weight his already spare body couldn't afford to do without.

The slap of bare feet became audible and he lay back in the cushions, closing his eyes and listening to Randi drop into the chair across from him.

"Nice place," she said, pouring herself a drink. "Looks like a picture from a catalog."

"And the cabin doesn't?"

"Yeah, but not a Kmart catalog."

There was no denying that the place she stayed in was

a lot nicer and had the added benefit of being nearly as well armed as a *Ticonderoga*-class cruiser. Too bad it was full of workmen trying to get the smell of gas out.

"You gonna eat that pie, Jon?"

"Help yourself."

She gnawed noisily on it for a few moments before speaking through a full mouth. "So what now?"

It was a question he'd known was coming. In some ways Randi Russell was a complete loose cannon, but in others she was infinitely predictable.

"Back to work for the both of us."

The silence that ensued seemed a little angry and he kept his eyes closed, avoiding confirming that impression. What did she have to complain about? She'd go back to Afghanistan or Yemen or Iraq and lose herself in her life again. He had no such luxury.

Tomorrow, he would go back to integrating the Merge into the U.S. military, not entirely sure of its full capabilities, its security, or the purpose of the mysterious Division D. And worse, he'd know how the technology was developed. It was strange how his life had come to be built around the motto "The end justifies the means"—a philosophy he didn't really subscribe to.

Maybe it was time to leave this life behind. There were a number of universities after him, including one in Cape Town that had all kinds of interesting possibilities. Let someone else save the world.

His phone started ringing and he ignored it, knowing it would be Marty for the fifth time that hour. Right now, the idea of talking to the manic computer wizard was about as appealing as a brick to the side of the head.

"Who keeps calling?" Randi asked.

"A guy I play racquetball with."

She tried to sip calmly at her drink but started fidgeting noticeably. "So you're just going back to work?"

"After I shake off the hangover I'm working on, yes. I'm going back to my life. We both are."

"Your life passing out Merges to our soldiers."

"Yes. Maybe. I don't know. Maybe that Antarctica post is still available. Who would have ever thought that it would sound attractive? Or maybe a leave of absence. A real one this time. I have a friend setting up an expedition to Borneo to look for a new butterfly species. He needs a team doctor."

"Butterflies?" she said. "That's an interesting mental picture."

Another silence stretched out between them.

"This is bullshit," Randi said finally.

"Here we go."

"Fred's getting played and you know it. By Whitfield, by Dresner, by the president..."

"Trust me, Randi. Fred Klein doesn't get played. He knows what's happening. He just doesn't feel he can do anything about it."

"So we're going to let our military—and the rest of the world—get completely reliant on a technology that was secretly developed using human test subjects. What could possibly go wrong?"

"We're done, Randi. We have direct orders to walk away."

"Orders from Fred."

"Yes."

"Covert-One doesn't exist, Jon. And orders from an organization that doesn't exist aren't binding."

This just wasn't a conversation he wanted to have. His phone rang again and he reached for it, hoping for a diversion. But it was just Marty for the sixth time.

"Man," Randi said. "Your friend must really like racquetball."

"Nuts for it."

A moment later a different ringtone sounded, this time from the kitchen. Randi's.

Her eyebrows rose a bit and she crossed the room to answer it. Smith only half listened to her side of the conversation, already knowing what would be said.

"Really? You've been trying to get in touch with him all night?"

She sat down again and switched to speaker.

"Over and over!" Marty Zellerbach said. "His phone is on and has signal and I know he's there because the last three times, he declined the call."

She glared at him.

"Jon?" Zellerbach said. "Are you there? Why aren't you answering your phone?"

"Because I'm tired, Marty. I'm dead tired."

"But there's something I need to talk to you about."

"What is it?" Randi said.

"I don't really want to say on an open line. It's about that stuff you wanted me to look into. You know. With the thing?"

"Forget it," Smith said. "Job's over. Bill me."

"I don't want to bill you, Jon. I want to talk to you."

"Email me the invoice, Marty. Put what you've got to say in the comment section. Or better yet, don't."

"But this is *important*," he whined. "Forget payment. It's free."

He reached over to disconnect the call but Randi snatched the phone off the coffee table. "I'd love to meet with you, Marty. When and where?"

*   *   *

MAJOR JAMES WHITFIELD sat in his dark office listening to the voice of Martin Zellerbach.

"My place, Randi. Now. Yesterday. A year ago. Just get here."

"I'm on my way."

"What about Jon?"

"I honestly don't know."

The connection went dead and Whitfield leaned back in his chair. With Klein involved, it had been too dangerous to contact his friends at the NSA to get bugs on Smith's and Russell's phones. Fortunately, he also had people at AT&T who had been able to feed the unencrypted calls in real time.

He reached for his keyboard and brought up the now-archaic Google homepage, searching on the name "Martin Zellerbach." LayerCake would undoubtedly have better-organized information, but it was impossible to know if Dresner was watching.

Wikipedia had a picture of a muscular, shirtless Zellerbach that looked suspiciously like it was taken from the cover of a romance novel. The text gave detailed accounts of his role in the defeat of the Nazi Germany, his improbably acrobatic sexual escapades with the entire cast of *America's Next Top Model*, and his defeat of Chuck Norris in a bare-knuckles tournament. The fight was accompanied by a surprisingly convincing video and seemed to have taken place in the bar from *Star Wars*.

Impressively, every other link he clicked on corroborated those events.

Convinced he was getting nowhere, Whitfield dialed his organization's tech guru and waited impatiently for him to pick up.

"Yes sir. What can I do for you?"

"I need you to get me some reliable information on a Martin Joseph Zellerbach. I ran an Internet search and came up with junk."

"Marty Zellerbach? I don't need to do a search, sir."

"You know him?"

"Not personally. But I know *of* him. Everybody does."

"Well, I'm not everybody. What have you got?"

"Marty's a hacker—maybe *the* hacker. Reclusive and pretty crazy, though. From an online perspective, not a man to be screwed with. The last guy who crossed him has spent the last five years living off the grid in Indonesia because it's the only place he can get any peace."

"Thank you, Lieutenant," Whitfield said, severing the connection. A tech expert. Not exactly a surprise.

He looked at Jon Smith's military record sitting on his desk but didn't reach for it. There was no need. He was an honorable soldier who could normally be counted on to follow orders. The problem was Russell. And now an unstable hacker with a massive and entirely fabricated online presence.

It was clear that the control he thought he'd regained was nothing more than an illusion. If the situation continued on its current trajectory, it could end up beyond even Castilla's power to rein in.

What had Zellerbach found? And more important, had he released information about his discovery to the Internet? Because once that door was opened, there was no shutting it again.

Whitfield let out a long, angry breath. He'd actually started to believe that he'd be able to get out of this without the blood of two American patriots on his hands.

A card with Castilla's direct number was on his desk, but he pushed it aside. This wasn't a situation that could be solved by political hand wringing and Fred Klein could be counted on to do everything in his considerable power to protect his people. The time had come to put an end to this.

Whitfield dialed another number. This one was picked up on the first ring.

"Sir?"

"I need a team."

"Target?"

"Three. Jon Smith and Randi Russell. The third is a computer tech named Martin Zellerbach."

"Yes sir."

There was a worrying, but understandable, excitement in the man's voice. Payback for what had happened to his comrades.

"I'll be directing the operation personally."

"Sir?"

The NSA had taken the position that the Merge's encryption was uncrackable, but he couldn't help wondering if Zellerbach had found a way in. Dresner's control over his technology was an ongoing problem that Whitfield would be very pleased to resolve.

"You heard me. And Zellerbach is to be taken alive for questioning."

"What about Smith and Russell?"

He let out another long breath, this one quiet enough not to be picked up by the microphone. "They're to be eliminated."

62

JON SMITH LAGGED FARTHER and farther behind Randi as they moved along the dark sidewalk. She slowed and finally was forced to stop in order for him to catch up.

"What's wrong with you? My grandmother moves faster."

"I don't want to be here, Randi."

"Quit being such a Boy Scout. It's getting on my nerves."

"We're going off the map here. Beyond this point, there be dragons."

"You're overreacting."

"I'm so not sure. Fred told me to walk away from this and to make sure you do the same. I know him, Randi. And I can tell you he was serious."

"You need to be more creative, Jon. Think of it this way: We sicced Marty on this before we got those orders and he called us with something before we could tell him to stand down. All we're doing here is debriefing him and making sure whatever he's found is permanently buried. Isn't that exactly what Fred would want us to do?"

Of course, he'd already considered—and rehearsed—that precise rationalization. Its plausibility, combined with his burning curiosity and loyalty to Randi, was the only reason he'd come this far.

They stopped in front of Zellerbach's gate and this time it swung open without them having to use the call button. Smith hung back, letting Randi take a hesitant step inside while he waited for the stink bombs and fish to fly. When nothing happened, he reluctantly followed.

The front door opened, and Marty scanned his property nervously while they squeezed by.

"What took you so long?" he said, pushing the door closed and activating a high-tech dead bolt.

"Jon's been sulking," Randi said.

It was impossible to know if Zellerbach heard her response. He just turned and started for his office in the rushed waddle that Smith remembered so well from high school. Back then, it meant he'd pissed someone off and needed protection. What it meant now was a mystery.

The Merge that had been disassembled on the table was still in pieces, but now bristling with countless wires that led to the Cray in the corner. It looked a little like something out of a Frankenstein movie—though Zellerbach was more Igor than Victor.

"What did you find?" Smith said, anxious to get this over with.

"I'm not sure."

"Are you kidding? You got me all the way out here to tell me you're not sure?"

"What's gotten in your bonnet?" Zellerbach said.

"Ignore him," Randi said. "Tell us the story."

"Well . . . I figured out a way to trigger something."

"Something?"

His expression was as familiar as his odd gait. He was trying to figure out how to explain something to the slow kids. They'd been friends for a long time, but suddenly Smith remembered why it was that people always wanted to kick his ass.

"Okay . . ." he started. "There are certain parts in this thing—small stuff spread out all over the place—that no one's been able to figure out. What everyone agrees on, though, is that they never activate no matter what app you use."

"Twenty-eight of them," Smith said.

"That's right! How did you know?"

"My team's been over that thing with a fine-tooth comb, Marty. We talked to Dresner and he says most are upgrade paths and a few relate to a power cell he's developing. So thanks, but we've got it covered. Can we go now?"

"No. Because Dresner is lying. They don't have anything to do with batteries or upgrades. They work together as a whole—kind of like a hardwired piece of software."

"Hardwired software?" Randi said. "Isn't that contradictory?"

"Not really. All software does is tell hardware what to do. It sends a little electric pulse that, say, turns on your computer's speakers. Or causes your modem to upload something to the Internet. This is the same thing. If you send each of the twenty-eight components just the right signal, they launch all at once and act in unison."

"It seems like if that was the case, my people would have triggered it by now."

Zellerbach shook his head. "The problem is that each component needs a slightly different signal. Think of it this way: You've got a safe with twenty-eight keyholes. You need twenty-eight keys, right? But more than that, you need to know what order to turn them in and how far to turn each one down to the tenth of a millimeter."

"There would be an almost infinite number of combinations," Randi said.

"Tell me about it. Took me ten days to finally hit on it."

"If there are really that many possibilities, ten days wouldn't be anywhere near enough time. Even with your Cray."

Zellerbach looked at the floor and chewed his lower lip for a moment. "I have to admit that I had to borrow some other people's computer power."

"Other people?"

"Well...I figure you don't care about the Chinese government, but I did accidentally crash Amazon. Twice if you want to be technical about it. And you said you were in a hurry, so I maybe didn't cover my tracks as well as I normally would..."

"Are you saying they could trace the crashes to you?" Smith said.

"Not if you were to smooth it over."

"We'll take care of it," Randi said before Smith could find a blunt object to hit him with. "So what happens when you give it the right signals?"

"The twenty-eight individual components run for eighteen seconds and then it goes back to its normal mode."

"Why? What's it do?"

"Dunno. Without Dresner's knowledge of how the Merge communicates with the brain, there's no way to simulate the outcome. The only option would be to just stick it on your head and turn it on."

63

Near Dupont Circle, Washington, DC
USA

JON SMITH SIFTED THROUGH the piles of dirty dishes, selecting the only glass clean enough to see through and filling it from the sink. He leaned against the counter, staring vacantly at a wall of yellowing pizza boxes as he considered what Zellerbach had said.

Was the discovery real or just another delusion? His mild clinical paranoia had caused all kinds of problems in the past, including a lengthy episode when he thought people were putting poisonous spiders in his locker. When it came to computers and technology, though, his vision tended to be a hell of a lot clearer. Crystal, in fact.

Randi appeared in the doorway and leaned against the jamb. "So what now, boss?"

"I don't know," Smith admitted.

"The cat's just about all the way out of the bag. I'm not sure we can stuff it back in."

She was right. There was no way that Zellerbach was going to just let this go. All his other psychological issues paled in comparison with his obsession over intellectual closure. Left unresolved, this mystery would slowly drive him into a frenzy and eventually make it out onto the Internet.

"We're going to have to call Fred, Randi."

She shook her head. "What if he orders us to drop it again? What do we do with Marty?"

Smith took a sip of his water, trying to overcome the growing dryness from his mouth. It was the million-dollar question: *What do we do with Marty?*

Once again, he'd inadvertently put his friend in danger. But this time that danger came from the people he worked for. Both Klein and the president were good men, but they had responsibilities that far outweighed one reclusive, unstable computer hacker. What lengths would they go to in order to make sure none of this ever saw the light of day?

"Look, I want to know what this is as much as you," Smith admitted. "But if Marty can't figure out a way to do a simulation, my people certainly won't be able to."

"He said we should test it out on his neighbor who keeps calling the cops on him."

"That may not be an ideal plan."

She shrugged. "Probably not. But we need *something*. A vague report of a bunch of doodads moving at the same time isn't all that compelling. It's going to be too easy for Fred to walk away from."

He took another sip from the dirty glass. "The head of my tech team is a good man who'll back me. If I tell him to take credit for the discovery, then it becomes a military issue."

"An issue you're dead-ended on. Marty can't figure out a way to simulate it and neither could Dresner if the graves in North Korea are any indication."

"You're suggesting we try to get to the man himself?"

"That seems a lot like jumping into a pool without checking if there's water in it. He went through a lot of trouble to hide something in this system and he hasn't historically been a big fan of the military."

"You think it could be something dangerous?"

"I don't know. Maybe we should ask the people in Division D. Oh, yeah, we can't. They're all dead."

Once again, she was right. His loyalty to the president and admiration for Dresner were preventing him from staring at this thing clear-eyed. The bottom line was that they needed to know what that hidden system did so they could take it to Klein. And they needed to know now.

"I guess I'm going to have to volunteer then," Smith said, "We'll test it on me."

"Always the selfless hero," Randi replied, digging in her pocket for a quarter. "Tell you what. We'll flip for it."

She was about to toss the coin when something that sounded like an air raid siren started wailing through the house. A moment later a sultry woman's voice came over hidden speakers. "Intruder alert, Marty. Intruder alert."

They ran back into Zellerbach's office and found him staring into a monitor displaying multiple feeds from cameras on his property.

"Do you know who they are?" he said in a shaking voice.

A man had come over the hedge next to the gate and another two were over on what appeared to be the south side. One more was already moving toward a gazebo rotting away at the back of the house. The cameras' light amplification created a bit of distortion, but not enough that Smith couldn't immediately identify all of them as pros. Their long coats swept back almost in unison, displaying a glimpse of body armor as they pulled out American-made assault rifles. One of them seemed to be talking and his head moved in subtle, vaguely unnatural jerks. They were Merged up.

"Are the defense systems you used against us activated?"

Zellerbach nodded. "They're automatic."

Randi moved closer to the screen. "Is that the best you've got? Is there anything more deadly?"

"Deadly? No. Of course not."

"Call the police," Smith said as a turret rose from the ground and started firing paintballs at the man near the gate. "These kind of guys live and breathe anonymity. The sirens might scare them off."

"The police won't come. I have this sort of feud with some of my..." His voice faded when a man sprinted across the dying grass and disappeared into the same trap Randi had.

"One down," she said as two others started firing at the turret tracking them. The man by the gazebo went for the house and tripped the weapon Smith dreaded above all the others. A flounder rocketed out of a skeet launcher and caught him in the side of the face hard enough to knock him to the ground.

"Are there any more underground traps that we could funnel them toward?" Randi asked.

"No. Just the paintball guns, some flash grenades, and stink bombs. Oh, and a couple of pressure washers that I haven't really been able to get the targeting working on. It's a fluid dynamics issue. The force of the water is kind of unpredictable in the way it—"

"So you're telling us that in about thirty seconds, these guys are going to realize none of this crap can hurt them and come right for the front door," Smith said. "You've still got the Mace that shoots out there, though, right?"

Zellerbach shook his head miserably. "I got sued over it and one of the provisions of the settlement was that I had to disable it. Stupid Girl Scouts..."

"What about other weapons? Do you have any in the house?" Randi said, pulling out her Beretta. That and her ever-present blade were all they had. Once again, Smith had left the house unarmed.

"No."

"What about the back way out," Smith said. "Is that still there?"

Zellerbach seemed to be having trouble concentrating. He had an uncanny ability to apply laser-like focus to one thing at a time, but was easily overwhelmed. "Yes."

On screen, one of the men took fire and went down on the same slippery sheet of plastic that Smith had.

"Then get us the hell out of here, Marty."

Zellerbach grabbed something that looked like a television remote and they followed him into the bathroom, where he punched a sequence of commands into the device. A moment later, the bathtub started to rise and a trapdoor beneath slid open. Randi dropped into the crawl space first, followed by Zellerbach and then Smith. The hatch closed above them and emergency lights came on as they moved into an abandoned sewer pipe. It ran a few hundred meters before dead-ending into a ladder leading to another trapdoor.

They climbed quietly, exiting into the pitch-dark interior of a similar bungalow that Zellerbach owned on the next street. The lights snapped on and Smith was about to tell Zellerbach to shut them off again when he realized that his old friend wasn't responsible.

James Whitfield moved away from the switch holding a Colt in his right hand. A quick glance behind confirmed that Randi was similarly covered by two men with assault rifles.

"I've underestimated you in the past," Whitfield said. "But I think you'll find that I learn from my mistakes."

Randi was completely ignoring the retired marine, instead staring furiously at the red-haired man holding a gun on her. "So you've gone over to the other side, huh, Deuce?"

The young soldier frowned and gave a disappointed shake of his head. "What other side, Randi? We need the Merge and you're doing everything you can to screw that up. All the major wants is to make sure we're the best-equipped army in the world."

Whitfield activated an old-fashioned throat mike beneath the collar of his dress shirt. "We've got them. Pull back to defensive positions."

64

Near Washington Circle, District of Columbia
USA

Jon Smith watched Whitfield examine the wires connecting the disassembled Merge to Marty's Cray, then turned his attention to the two men guarding them.

Both had switched to pistols due to the close quarters and both had the slightly wandering gaze of Merge users—undoubtedly the military version he'd been developing. The man Randi called Deuce had bright red hair and a sunburned face that made him look less than intimidating despite his black garb and body armor. The fact that he'd gotten fairly close to her a number of times and she hadn't made a move, though, suggested that his appearance was deceptive.

The one standing next to him was older, probably pushing forty, with the look of someone who had risen through the ranks of the special forces and lost none of his edge to the passing years.

Smith had gone over every angle, every remote possibility, and concluded that there was no hope. Randi had been disarmed and these guys were serious players acting with a level of caution that suggested they were aware of what had happened to the team sent to Randi's cabin.

Another man who stank of former special forces came in and snapped to attention when Whitfield turned toward him.

"The premises are secure, sir."

"Police?" Whitfield asked.

"No calls from here have been received at the precinct. One neighbor made a complaint but it appears that these kinds of disturbances aren't unusual and the dispatcher suggested they pursue the problem in civil court."

Probably accurate, Smith knew. Despite the shabbiness of his home, Zellerbach was a multimillionaire with a battery of lawyers dedicated to keeping him out of jail. And one of their favorite strategies was orchestrating generous out-of-court settlements to the people he'd inconvenienced.

Whitfield dismissed the man and folded his arms across his chest. "What have you found, Martin?"

Zellerbach gave Smith a terrified, pleading glance but kept his mouth shut.

"Have you cracked Dresner's encryption? Do you have access to the operating system?"

"No," Zellerbach mumbled. "That's... That's impossible."

His voice wavered a little but it was hard to know if it was fear or if he was getting to the end of his medication cycle. What Smith didn't need was his old friend going manic in a situation this precarious.

On the other hand, maybe it didn't matter. It was unlikely that either Klein or the president knew anything about Whitfield's presence here, which meant that when he got the information he wanted, it would be a quiet burial for all three of them. He undoubtedly thought it would be easier to ask forgiveness than permission. And he was probably right.

There was a wild card, though. Despite Whitfield's likely plan for their demise, they were basically on the same side. Was it possible that the man didn't know anything about the hidden subsystem?

"Tell him," Smith said.

"What?"

"Go ahead, Marty. Tell him everything you told us."

Zellerbach just stood there, obviously wondering why his amazing mind couldn't immediately grasp the elaborate ruse that Smith was recruiting him for.

"This isn't a trick, Marty. He's a son of a bitch but, in a way, he's our son of a bitch. Answer all his questions completely and honestly."

The aging hacker's confusion deepened.

"He's serious," Randi said. "Do it."

"Okay," he said, drawing the word out as he watched his friends for some sign of what he was really supposed to do. "There's a hidden subsystem."

When Smith just gave him an encouraging nod, he continued.

"It's disguised as battery management and upgrade paths. No one's been able to figure out what they do."

"But you have?" Whitfield said, undoubtedly aware of the mysterious hardware from Smith's own reports.

"No. I figured out how to bypass the operating system and trigger it. But no one was wearing the Merge at the time so I don't know what it does."

While Whitfield's face gave away nothing, his silence spoke volumes. He *hadn't* known about this.

"How do we find out?"

Zellerbach licked his already wet lips. "The only way I can think of is to, uh, have someone try it."

Whitfield nodded and pointed to Smith. "Okay. Why don't we volunteer the colonel here."

With guns on him and his companions, there wasn't much choice.

"Jon..." Randi cautioned as he sat down at the terminal to calibrate the unit to his mind.

"We're dead anyway, Randi. Might as well exercise my curiosity."

He went through the familiar routine quickly and then stood, pointing to the chair. "Marty."

"But I don't know what it's going to *do*," he whined. "I don't want to."

To his credit, Whitfield didn't threaten or even get involved. A commander who knew when to step back was a rare and impressive thing. Unless he was your opponent.

"Just do it, Marty. Okay? We need to know, and this is the only way to find out."

Zellerbach reluctantly activated an icon on his screen and clicked it. Smith tensed as the screen flashed red and buzzers hooted through hidden speakers, but that was all. He waited eighteen seconds for the system to fully cycle but other than the adrenaline he was pretty sure he was generating himself, there was nothing.

Zellerbach glanced down at his feet for a moment and gave his lips another quick swipe with his tongue. It was then that Smith understood. He hadn't triggered it, instead using his computer to generate some impressive, but meaningless, displays.

Unfortunately Whitfield came to the same conclusion.

"I'm not stupid, Martin."

"I did it!" Zellerbach protested a little too energetically to be convincing. "Maybe I was wrong. Maybe it really is just an upgrade path. I could have the key wrong, too. I'm not a miracle worker!"

Whitfield glanced at his men, obviously trying to decide what to do. He'd be considering torture, of course. And putting a gun to Randi's head. But in the back of his mind, he'd know neither of those strategies led to certainty. Zellerbach was, by every measure, a genius in his area of expertise. And that area was computer trickery.

Smith thought he'd considered all of Whitfield's options and was shocked when the retired marine pulled Zellerbach from his chair and sat, starting to recalibrate the unit to his own mind.

When he was finished, he stood and shoved Zellerbach back in front of the terminal. "Do it."

"I...I don't think—"

"I didn't ask your opinion, son. Just do it."

Randi seemed happy with the turn of events and gave a short nod. "Go for it, Marty. Can't get any worse for us."

He pulled up an innocuous prompt, typing what looked like a nonsensical line of code into it. His finger hesitated over the return button for a moment, but then dropped obediently onto it.

This time, there were no alarms or flashing lights. A couple of seconds passed and Smith started to wonder if the system really didn't do anything when Whitfield suddenly grabbed his right arm and grimaced in pain. A moment later, he had collapsed to the floor.

"Shut it off!" Smith shouted, dropping to his knees beside the man.

"I can't. Once it's triggered, it runs off the internal battery."

Randi devised a typically inelegant but effective solution—grabbing a wrench and attacking the individual parts of the Merge on the table.

Smith ignored the men guarding them and felt Whitfield's neck for a pulse. Nothing. Based on everything Smith knew about the Merge technology, it was impossible. But impossible or not, the man was dead.

65

CHRISTIAN DRESNER SAT WATCHING a massive computer monitor on the wall. It was an irritatingly archaic technology, but transmitting a feed from someone else's Merge directly to the mind of another had turned out to be problematic. The complexities were slowly being ironed out but for now it did little more than create confusion as the brain struggled to differentiate its own experiences from the experiences of the person at the other end of the connection.

The image of Jon Smith performing CPR on Whitfield was coming in real time from Deuce Brennan and Dresner leaned forward, watching carefully. Russell was looking around, undoubtedly for a weapon, but her expression suggested she knew she'd be dead before she could use it. Zellerbach—a man whose genius he'd managed to completely overlook—was panicking, knocking things off his desk and tripping over them as he backed away.

The sweat was hot and slick in his palms, but Dresner

forced himself to remain calm. While the discovery of his subsystem so soon was a potential disaster, it appeared that control could be regained. In fact, he might one day look back at this moment as the day his mounting problems were resolved.

Dresner glanced at an icon hovering in his peripheral vision but instead of activating it, he stood and walked closer to the monitor. He'd experimented extensively with the effect of shutting down his subsystem after four seconds in order to simulate the experience of headsets being knocked off. The survival rate was twelve percent with no intervention and forty-nine percent with immediately administered CPR.

With implants and the full eighteen-second cycle, though, fatalities were nearly one hundred percent, even with medical intervention. Whitfield's situation—a shutdown halfway through the cycle—was something he hadn't considered. Could he be revived?

"You told me this couldn't hurt anyone," Randi Russell said over the speakers. "That even with a full battery discharge, it would only give you a little shock."

"It can't," Smith responded, sounding understandably perplexed as he continued to hammer the motionless man's chest. "I don't understand it. There's just not enough power."

While extremely intelligent—perhaps even borderline brilliant—Smith's thinking was too linear. A common failing of men who spent their lives in the confines of the military.

Dresner's curiosity was satisfied a moment later when Whitfield's eyes opened and he grabbed Smith's arm. Similar to the Koreans who were brought back, he seemed to suffer few ill effects. Not surprising. There had been nothing wrong with his heart.

Smith helped him to his feet and he managed to stand on his own, blinking at the people around him for a moment before speaking. "What happened?"

"It looks like it stopped your heart," Smith said.

Whitfield remained silent for a moment, but when he spoke again he had shaken off his confusion. "Deuce. Give the colonel back his phone. Jon, use it to tell your people what happened. We need to call a meeting with the president and the Joint Chiefs."

It was precisely what Dresner had wanted to hear. The implication was clear: All the people who knew of Zellerbach's discovery were in that room. What had been a potentially insurmountable problem now looked like a permanent solution.

There would be questions about their deaths, of course, but it was hard to imagine that they would lead to the rediscovery of his subsystem—particularly with the further precautions he intended to put in place. Once again, Castilla would want this to simply go away. To propagate his own power and the power of his country.

"Lieutenant. Did you hear me? Give Smith his phone back," Whitfield said.

So arrogant. So foolish to believe that he was in command.

Dresner activated an icon in his peripheral vision, opening a direct link to Deuce Brennan's Merge. "I think it's time we took control of this situation, Lieutenant."

66

Near Washington Circle, District of Columbia
USA

BY THE TIME SMITH HAD HELPED a shaky James Whitfield to his feet, both of the men guarding them had lowered their weapons. The red-haired one Randi had called Deuce reached toward his chest pocket—to retrieve the phone he'd been ordered to return, Smith assumed—but instead shot the man next to him in the side.

Smith froze at the quiet crack of the silenced pistol, unable to immediately process what had just happened. Randi was quicker and she lunged toward him with the wrench still in her hand.

"Not today, Randi," he said, swinging the pistol in her direction before she even got close. "Now back off, bitch."

She did as she was told, dropping the wrench while he followed her with his weapon, eyes sweeping smoothly around the room. Randi's deference appeared to be well founded. He was fast as hell and apparently completely unaffected by the fact that he'd just gunned down his teammate in cold blood. Not a man to roll the dice with.

"Lieutenant..." Whitfield said, not yet fully recovered

from being dead a few moments before. "What are you doing? You're a soldier. You—"

"No sir. The day I went to work for you, I left my oath of loyalty behind. I became a mercenary."

Whitfield continued to gain strength. "What the hell are you talking about? We do what we do to protect our country. To save the lives of the people you work with. How is that a mercenary?"

"Yeah, maybe I'm just rationalizing," he said, adjusting his aim to Whitfield. "And if Dresner had offered me a couple hundred grand, I'd have probably told him to screw off and reported it to you five minutes later. But he doesn't work in those kinds of numbers. So, while I regret having to kill all of you—and I really do—it might make you feel better to know I'm getting Learjet- and private-island-money to do it."

The quiet crack sounded again and Whitfield crumpled to the floor. This time, though, he wouldn't be getting back up.

Smith looked down at the bleeding hole in the man's chest, blinking hard as his focus seemed to waver. When he turned back toward Deuce, the gun was moving back to Randi, creating a colorful trail through the air that looked a little like a rainbow. Randi went for the soldier again, refusing to go down without a fight, but tripped over her own feet and sprawled on the floor.

* * *

Jon! Wake up now. Come on. Jon!"

Smith opened his eyes slowly, seeing nothing but a halo of light around something hovering over him. The image began to sharpen and he finally recognized it as Marty wearing a respirator with "Home Depot" stenciled on the side.

"What...What happened?" Smith said, the muffled sound of his voice suggesting that he was wearing a similar mask, which his numb face didn't register.

"The house's defenses don't end at my front door."

Smith managed to prop himself up on his elbows and Zellerbach grabbed him under the arm, dragging him to his feet. Once he'd regained enough balance to stand on his own, he looked over at Randi, who was lying partially on top of Deuce. No blood in evidence.

"Is she—"

"She's fine. He didn't have time to get off a shot."

"Didn't have time to get off a shot? Whitfield's dead. Why didn't you—"

"The gas is activated by my remote. I couldn't get to it until that Deuce jerk stopped paying attention to me. Now let's get out of here before he wakes up or those other people come back."

Smith staggered over to the two men and collected his phone and their guns, stuffing a Sig Sauer and Randi's Beretta down the back of his pants before handing the others to Marty.

"What do you want me to do with these?" he said as Smith struggled to get Randi into a fireman's carry. Zellerbach always had exactly one backup for everything—thus the fact that they were both wearing masks and she wasn't.

"Get rid of them," Smith said, inadvertently slamming Randi's head into the wall as he started toward the bathroom.

Zellerbach rushed to a massive metal cabinet and locked the guns in it before speed-walking awkwardly past him in the hall.

By the time Smith got to the bathroom, the tub was already on its edge and the trapdoor was sliding back.

"Does the tunnel get gased, too?" Smith said, remembering the man Whitfield had posted in it.

"Not just the tunnel. The house we come out in, too. I'm very thorough, you know. Very thorough."

It took some effort, but he managed to get Randi down the ladder without dropping her. She was starting to stir, which was good. What wasn't so good, was that so was the man Whitfield had left behind.

In fact, he was up on all fours by the time they reached him, shaking his head violently to clear the cobwebs. He made a move for his gun, but Smith swung a leg back and kicked him in the face hard enough to flip him on his back and send him sliding into the wall. He wouldn't be getting up anytime soon, if at all. But there was no telling how many more of them were out there.

Randi started to squirm and then struggle. He set her down and propped her near the ladder leading into Zellerbach's other house—grabbing her wrists so she couldn't attack him. "Randi! It's me, Jon."

Recognition came quickly and when it did, the adrenaline-fueled strength seemed to drain from her. He barely managed to catch her before she fell.

"What happened?"

"Not important. We're going up this ladder and then we're going to get the hell out of Dodge. Do you understand?"

A weak nod.

"I'll go first. Can you make it up on your own?"

Another nod—this one a bit less convincing.

He looked at Zellerbach. "Come up last. Make sure she doesn't fall."

"Okay. No problem. No problem. I can do that."

Smith ascended, feeling more steady every second. He opted for speed over subtlety, throwing open the trapdoor and going out gun-first.

The room was empty.

"Okay," he said. "We're clear."

Once they were all safely up, he ran from the room and found a window, opening it a crack as Randi stumbled up behind him. She gulped at the fresh air while he surveyed the dark street beyond. After only a few seconds, her eyes started to sharpen.

"Watch her," he whispered to Zellerbach and then pulled out his phone and initiated an encrypted call to Klein.

"Jon?" he said, answering on the first ring despite the late hour. "Are you all right?"

"No. Marty found something hidden in Dresner's system. Whitfield's dead. It—"

The unmistakable crash of a door being kicked in reverberated from the front of the house and Smith swore quietly.

"Jon?" Klein said. "What just—"

"Call you back."

He severed the connection and gave Randi back her Beretta before throwing the window fully open and shoving her through it. Apparently, it was higher than he thought, and he winced at the dull thud of her back hitting the ground. Zellerbach went out next and he followed, grabbing Randi by the arm.

Zellerbach managed to outpace them, which suggested that the gas was affecting him more than he'd thought. Smith pulled off his gas mask and tried to call him back but got no reaction. Either he hadn't heard or he was starting to panic. Probably the latter.

There was a flash about fifty meters to Smith's left accompanied by the bark of an unsilenced weapon. Zellerbach pitched forward into the street and Smith used the Sig Sauer he'd taken to fire a couple of rounds in the general direction of the shooter before shoving Randi into a clump of bushes.

"Stay!" he said before breaking out into the open and sprinting toward his old friend squirming in the street.

The shooter got off a burst on full automatic but the rounds went well behind him. The chance that he was just a lousy shot or didn't have a Merge to compensate for the darkness was fairly remote and when he looked back he saw exactly what he knew he would: Randi coming after him at about half her normal speed.

There was nothing he could do about her now, though, and he threw himself to the asphalt behind Zellerbach, pulling him closer to the curb. Randi landed a meter away, flattening herself on the ground as another volley chipped away at the edge of the concrete sidewalk.

"You think that's the only guy they have left?" she said, sounding like she was thinking clearly again.

"We're not that lucky. And unless I miss my guess, your friend Deuce is already back on his feet and looking for a weapon."

The next shot was followed by a scream from Marty. "I'm hit! I'm shot! Oh, my God, I'm shot."

While the curb was high enough to just cover Smith

and Randi, Zellerbach's bulbous behind was sticking up just enough for the shooter to graze it.

He looked like he was going to bolt and Smith grabbed his ankles while Randi held his shoulders and whispered soothingly to him.

Another shot created a second tear in the back of his pants and he screeched even louder this time. Neither wound was much more than a scratch, but they couldn't just lie there while Zellerbach was whittled down inch by inch. The curb they were pressed against would only protect them from a fairly distant attacker to the east. From any other sidewalk, street, yard, or driveway, they were sitting ducks.

A siren became audible, approaching fast from the north. Either the neighbors had finally convinced the police to come or they'd heard the shots themselves. Either way, it was looking like their only chance.

"Start scooting back, Randi," Smith said, flicking his gun out and shooting in the general direction of the man undoubtedly closing on them.

She did, dragging the whimpering hacker along with her. Smith slithered along behind, staying focused on the tall hedge they were closing on. It was thick enough to hide them even from a Merged-up soldier, but it didn't leave a lot of options for which direction to run.

When they got to cover, he pulled Zellerbach to his feet and held on to him as they crashed gracelessly through the hedge. It put them in the backyard of a modern home built almost entirely of glass. A light went on inside just as Randi was starting to climb the fence on the north side.

"You're next, Marty. Come on!"

"I've...I've lost too much blood, Jon. Just leave me. Just leave me here to die."

"Shut up," Smith said, wrapping his arms around the man's thighs and lifting him chest-high against the fence. Zellerbach had just gotten his hands on the top rail when someone behind them spoke.

"Stop! I have a gun."

Fortunately, it wasn't the confident demand of one of Whitfield's special forces men. It was the quavering voice of a homeowner who had heard the shots and seen three people run across his backyard. Smith glanced back and saw that the man was wearing a pink robe and speaking through a tiny gap in the bottom of one of the house's windows. Not someone looking for a fight.

Randi's hand appeared over the fence and grabbed Zellerbach by the collar as Smith vaulted over next to him. He tucked the Sig Sauer in the back of his pants and started immediately in the direction of the siren.

A swirling red-and-blue light became visible as they angled through an empty lot and ran out into the center of the road, waving desperately in the illumination of the cruiser's headlights.

It skidded to a stop and the driver threw open his door, ducking behind it for cover.

"They're shooting!" Randi yelled in a panicked voice. "Someone back there's shooting at people!"

Smith confirmed that the cop didn't have a partner in the car and followed her around to the side of it.

"Calm down, ma'am," the man said. "How many are—"

He fell silent when Smith put a gun to the side of his head and Randi deftly relieved him of his weapon.

"Marty, get in the passenger seat," Smith ordered as Randi forced the cop into the back and slid in next to him.

Zellerbach did as he was told but squealed in pain from his injured butt when Smith floored the car up the dark street.

"Are you crazy!" the policeman said while his cruiser crept up to eighty in a twenty-five-mile-an-hour zone. "You're never—"

"Shut up," Randi said. "We just saved your ass. If you'd come up against that shooter he'd have killed you. And now, instead of making your wife a widow, he's just going to disappear back into the woodwork."

"I'm dying, Jon," Zellerbach said. "I don't have much more time. I want you to know how much our friendship has meant—"

"You're not dying, Marty."

"This is your fault," he said, his mild schizophrenia flipping the switch from melodrama to anger. "Every time we get together something like this happens."

"You're exaggerating."

"I never want to see you again."

"Who the hell *are* you people?" the cop interjected.

Smith ignored him and dialed Klein again.

"Jon! Are you all right? What happened?"

"We've got problems and need a little of your magic."

"What kind of problems?"

"The good major sent people after us at Marty's house. We've got a lot of shots fired and a police response. Two bodies in the house, one man unconscious in the tunnel below the bathroom, and at least two men still fully operational."

"Understood. Are the three of you all right?"

"We'll live. But we're headed west out of DC in a stolen police cruiser."

"What happened to the cop?"

"That's a whole other problem. He's in the backseat with Randi."

67

Near Washington Circle, District of Columbia
USA

THE DARK COMPUTER MONITOR turned gray and then a hazy white as Christian Dresner moved hesitantly closer.

"Lieutenant!" he shouted, though he knew the man's Merge would automatically adjust the volume to a conversational level. "Wake up!"

Through Deuce Brennan's feed, he'd seen his orders carried out and Whitfield executed. But then the situation had devolved into chaos as Randi Russell attempted to attack and then collapsed for no apparent reason. Smith had fallen a moment later, followed by Brennan's feed losing cohesiveness and then going black despite a strong network connection.

There was little doubt that Zellerbach was responsible. He'd backed away in panic, as could be expected, but then picked up something. The playback wasn't entirely clear, but it looked like a television remote control.

Brennan's tooth mike was active again but the sounds

coming through it were badly distorted. The audio slowly sharpened, and after a few seconds was clear enough to decipher. Gunshots. And approaching sirens.

"Lieutenant!" Dresner shouted again. "*Get up!*"

The image on the monitor came into focus and then moved unsteadily from the blank white of the ceiling to Zellerbach's Cray, and finally the door leading to the hallway.

"Lieutenant!"

Finally, there was a response. "I'm here. What happened?"

"It doesn't matter. You need—"

"It was that goddamn computer geek and his half-assed security wasn't it? He must have had gas. Where are they?"

"Where do you think they are? They're gone!"

Brennan connected to the men outside. "Report. What's your situation?"

"Deuce!" a voice on the other end said. "We thought we'd lost you. The targets escaped in a police cruiser and we've got more cops on the way. The closest are less than a minute out. The three of you need to get the hell out of there."

"Whitfield and Eric are down."

There was a long pause as the man processed the news of his commanding officer's death. "There's nothing we can do for you, Deuce. I'm not shooting a cop. Now get your ass out of there."

"Understood."

The image shifted again as Brennan stood and began lurching toward the front door.

"They can't have gotten far," Dresner said as the dim

image of Zellerbach's front yard appeared on screen. "You can still track them."

"I can't do anything unless I get out of here first," he responded, barely avoiding a powerful jet of water from the property's automated defenses.

Dresner slammed a fist into the wall next to the monitor and turned away, activating an icon in his peripheral vision that displayed the current status of Merges worldwide. Eight hours to peak usage, with just over four million people online. Twenty-four percent of those people—972,000—had been marked for elimination by LayerCake.

He pulled up the "Security Breach" tab and activated the "US Military" subheading. Immediately a massive flow chart of interconnected names came to life in front of him. Overall U.S. military usage was within expected parameters, as was usage by the military's hierarchy. He switched to a tab labeled "Intel." Again, everything was within normal parameters. Utilization by the general intelligence complex was nominal and the directors of the CIA, NSA, and FBI were all connected through their personal Merges. Below their individual names was a family tree confirming that their close relatives were also using at normal levels. The "Political" tab showed a similar result. Congress was within normal ranges and while Castilla still hadn't adopted the technology, his wife was online with a headset, as was one of his children.

The data behind the "Networks" icon were equally reassuring. Internet service providers, cable companies, and phone companies showed no unusual outages.

Of course, there was no real purpose to looking at any of these numbers beyond the emotional reassurance he derived from seeing them. The moment any of the categories diverged from expected parameters, LayerCake would immediately notify him.

So either Smith hadn't yet notified his superiors of what he'd found or he had and they were still in the process of acting on that information. Either way, Dresner could no longer deny that he was losing control of the situation. Nine hundred and seventy-two thousand people. Would it be enough?

68

Near Tysons Corner, Virginia
USA

THE SUN WAS FINALLY UP and the crush of people heading to their jobs in DC had started in the oncoming lane. Westbound, though, traffic was light and Smith kept the police cruiser moving smoothly up the road. Constant glances in the rearview mirror provided no evidence of a tail, but did that really mean anything anymore? Using an actual car to track someone suddenly seemed so archaic.

"Yes sir," the police officer in the backseat said into his phone. "But they—"

He paused for a moment, face actually turning a bit red as Randi pressed his own gun into his ribs. Zellerbach was tilted up onto his uninjured butt cheek, head thrown back and eyes closed. The occasional moan was the only thing indicating he was still alive.

"I understand that, sir. But what I'm trying to tell you is—"

Finally, he just gave up, mumbling a submissive good-bye before severing the connection. When Smith glanced back, it looked like the top of his head was going to blow off.

"Everything smoothed over?"

"Yes," the man said through clenched teeth.

As requested, Klein had rolled out a few minor miracles, one being that this particular carjacking would be quickly forgotten. It was hard not to sympathize with their accidental hostage, though. He'd undoubtedly expected to have a chance to give the three of them a solid beating before sending them off to rot in prison. Now it was looking like he wouldn't even get a chance to pull out his Taser.

"There it is," Randi said tapping the glass separating them.

Gray and a little shopworn, the Honda was exactly what he'd asked for: the most innocuous vehicle on the planet. Smith pulled in behind it and hopped out, opening the back door as Zellerbach eased out of the passenger side with exaggerated slowness.

Randi tossed the cop's gun into the front seat and flashed him one of her award-winning smiles. "Have a nice day, Officer."

The keys were right where they were supposed to be and Smith eased back into the road while Zellerbach tried to find a comfortable position next to him.

"I need to go to the hospital. I need medical attention."

"I'm a doctor, Marty. In fact, I'm an army doctor. Who are you going to find at a suburban hospital that knows more about bullet wounds than me?"

"But you're not *doing* anything!"

"It's not even bleeding anymore," Smith said, dialing

Klein and putting the phone on the dash. "Just try not to think about it, okay?"

As was customary, there was only one ring before it was picked up. "Jon. Did you find the car?"

"We're in it now, sir. And you're on speaker with Randi and Marty in the car."

"Understood."

"Who is that?" Zellerbach said.

"General Davis," Smith responded, pulling a name off the top of his head. Zellerbach didn't know anything about Covert-One, so it would be easiest to just play Klein as his commanding officer.

"What happened?" Klein started. "Did you say that Whitfield's dead?"

"Yeah...Look, before we left, we sicced Marty on the Merge—asked him to see if he could find anything unusual. He called when we got back, saying he had." Smith paused, trying to put their actions in the best possible light. "We went to his house to make sure everything he'd discovered was wiped off his computer. While we were in the process of doing that, Whitfield showed up with his men."

"Uh-huh," Klein said, his tone suggesting that he wasn't so easily fooled, but was temporarily willing to overlook the fact that they had ignored a direct order. "And am I to understand that you killed the major?"

"No sir. But to tell that story we're going to have to dredge up an investigation that you've made clear is over."

There was a long silence before Klein spoke again. "Give me the broad overview and I'll decide if we need to go into more detail."

"Yes sir. One of Whitfield's men was on Christian Dresner's payroll."

"Deuce Brennan," Randi said from the backseat. The dripping hatred in her voice suggested that the man's life span could now be measured with a stopwatch. "He shot Whitfield and another one of his men."

"Why? What reason would Dresner have for ordering something like that?"

"To cover up the fact that he's hidden a subsystem in the Merge that's capable of killing its user."

Another long pause. "You told me it was impossible for the unit to directly injure someone. Something about a lack of power as I recall."

"That was the consensus. But it looks like the consensus was wrong."

"I want to be perfectly clear here, Colonel. You're telling me that, in your opinion, Christian Dresner intentionally created a mechanism to kill people."

"Oh, it was definitely intentional," Zellerbach chimed in, the pain from his injury fading a bit when talk turned to technology. "He went to *huge* lengths to hide it and to make it difficult to activate. Amazing stuff, really. The guy really is unbelievably—"

Smith ran a finger across his throat, cutting his old friend off. "Yes sir. You understand me correctly."

"So I'm to believe that a reclusive genius who's spent most of his career on things like childhood education, antibiotics, and helping the deaf is really bent on the mass murder of his customers?" Another pause. "Even if we accept what Eichmann told you about Dresner wanting to use the Merge to alter people's thought patterns, the goal was fundamentally altruistic. If a drug company came up with an antidepressant that did everything he was trying to achieve, it'd get approved and half the world would be on it a year later."

It was an incongruity that Smith had been pondering for the last hour. "But he *didn't* create that, sir. He failed."

"Your point?"

"I don't think he wants to kill *all* his customers. Just some of them."

"Do I hear a theory forming?" Randi said from the backseat.

"Think about where he came from," Smith continued. "His parents' time in the concentration camp. Their treatment by the Soviets. His experience in the East German orphanage. If there's anyone alive who's seen what powerful men are capable of, it's Christian Dresner."

"Go on," Klein said.

"The Merge is what everyone talks about, but Layer-Cake is really the cornerstone of his system—and one of its main functions is accurately judging people. Think about the weird focus of his apps when the system was released: They were for the financial people who got rich by bringing the world's economy down on top of the common man. They were for the increasingly corrupt and entrenched political class. And they were for the military, which keeps getting more and more efficient at killing."

Zellerbach's face was a mask of concentration. He was brilliant with technology but his illness made understanding the motivations of others more of a challenge. "So you're saying he's going to kill all the people he thinks are bad? People who make the world a worse place?"

"It makes a certain twisted sense," Randi admitted.

"I agree," Klein said. "And I'm going to take this to my superiors immediately. It—"

"I'm not sure that's a good idea," Zellerbach interrupted.

Smith looked over at him and he shrank a little, assuming he was going to be chastised again.

"Go ahead, Marty. Why not?"

"Because I *guarantee* that Dresner can activate that system over the network in a matter of seconds. And I *also* guarantee that he'll know if you start talking to people about it."

"Are you suggesting he can monitor people's minds?" Klein said. "What they're hearing and thinking?"

Zellerbach shook his head. "No. But he'd have known that there was a chance his subsystem could be found. And he's going to be watching."

"*How?*" Klein said, starting to sound a little exasperated. He wasn't used to dealing with Zellerbach directly.

"A million different ways. He'll look for unexplained network shutdowns. And LayerCake has those apps that evaluate news programs, right? I'll bet my PlayStation they're sifting everything being said about the Merge. But if it were me, I'd focus on individual people. He can see who's online and who isn't—that's easy. He'll be watching powerful people and their families. Let's say you went straight to the president. Everyone knows he doesn't use a Merge, but I'll bet his wife does. And can almost guarantee that his kids do. Do you think he's going to let them keep using it if you tell him? No way. And when LayerCake sees their usage—or other politicians', wealthy donors', friends', military guys'—start to drop below what his algorithm says is normal, he's gonna push the button."

It didn't take much reflection to recognize that Zellerbach was probably right. Because of his line of work, Smith was close to very few people—and even he was already considering how he could quietly get them to disconnect. If he'd had a wife and children, they'd have been his first call.

Klein's silence suggested that he had come to the same conclusion.

"It's actually an interesting idea," Zellerbach continued, getting uncomfortable in the silence.

"Marty, please…"

"Think about it, Jon. It's just a question of how you set up LayerCake's criteria. I'm guessing that if you had Dresner's password, you'd kill all the al-Qaeda guys pretty quick."

"They're murderers and terrorists," Randi said.

"Okay. But what about Iranian physicists? They're not murderers or terrorists. You just don't like what they're doing. The truth is that you don't object to Dresner's weapon. You just want to be the one aiming it."

Smith knew that Zellerbach had been taking some philosophy courses online and he had to admit that he'd made strides. But this was not the time to get bogged down in an existential debate.

"How do we stop him?"

"Do we know where he is?" Randi said.

"No," Klein responded. "We can try to locate him, but he's always been strangely difficult to track. Now I guess we know why."

"What would you do even if you *did* find him?" Zellerbach said. "Unless he's an idiot—and he's not—he's got it set up to automatically trigger if he's separated from his Merge or if it determines he's dead."

"Could we dart him? Keep him in an induced coma with his unit attached?" Smith said.

"I doubt it. The Merge monitors brain waves. If it were me, I'd have it set up to trigger if anything weird started going on with my head. I mean, even if you had a whole day—and I doubt you would—getting everyone on the planet to disconnect isn't exactly realistic. It'd be like showing everyone in the world incontrovertible proof that cell phones cause cancer. Half of 'em wouldn't listen."

"Okay," Randi said. "We can't kill him. We can't drug him. We can't shut down hundreds of thousands of networks all over the world at one time. And we can't allow critical people to stop using the system. Have I missed anything?"

"That he's going to be looking for us with the most sophisticated search engine on the planet and unlimited funds?"

"I just checked sales numbers," Klein interjected. "There are somewhere in the neighborhood of eight million Merges on the street."

"Jesus," Randi said. "Even if only a quarter of those people are targeted, that's two million people dead. Why hasn't he done it? He knows that we're going to try to stop him."

Smith nodded. "I don't know. Maybe he can't for some reason. Maybe he's having second thoughts. Hell, maybe he's just waiting for peak daily usage. But whatever the reason, it at least buys us some time."

Randi settled back into her seat. "Yeah. But time for what?"

69

Near Front Royal, Virginia
USA

I DON'T WANT TO HEAR THAT, Marty," Smith said, easing the car off the highway and onto an empty rural road. Best to stay away from civilization to the degree possible.

"Just forget shutting down the networks, Jon. Sure, you could pull down Afghanistan, because it's on military satellite. But you can't take down ATT, Verizon, and every little cellular carrier in America. And even if you did, how many of those people would be near a Wi-Fi hot spot that their Merge would immediately connect to? Killing all the networks at the same time in the U.S.—let alone worldwide—isn't technologically feasible. Believe me. If it was, someone like me would have done it. They'd be a legend forever. People would build statues to them. Write songs about—"

"What about the power grid?" Randi said, cutting him off before he could get lost in fantasies of hacker fame and fortune. With his meds back at the house, his mind was starting to loop a bit.

"No, no, *no*! Forget coordinated efforts. Right now

LayerCake is scouring the web, emails, forums, chat rooms, and probably half the secure servers on the planet for any hint of something like this. It's like Santa. It's watching everything, everybody. And you want to try to coordinate thousand of people and get every one to keep his mouth shut? You're thinking completely wrong. Not every problem can be solved with a huge hammer."

"If we're thinking wrong," Smith said. "Then help us think right."

"I'm bleeding again. Bleeding..."

His ability to focus was just going to get worse as his medication continued to wear off. They could stop and fill a prescription but then his mind would turn lethargic for the next couple of hours. Not something they could afford.

"You're fine, Marty. Now tell me what we're missing."

"You'll yell at me because you won't like it."

"I promise I won't yell at you."

"And you won't have someone shoot me again."

"Marty..."

"Fine. Electromagnetic pulse."

Randi actually laughed. "Are you suggesting we airburst a bunch of nukes and fry the world's grids?"

"Told you you wouldn't like it. Besides, I'm not sure it helps. With no power, how do you warn everyone to turn off their units before the lights come back on? Carrier pigeon?" His gaze turned far away. "How many birds would that take? Seven billion people in the world. Pigeons average about eighty kilometers per hour. What's the total land area of the earth? About a hundred and fifty million square kilometers, right?"

Fred Klein was still listening on the speakerphone and

weighed in while Zellerbach got lost in his math problem. "I'm afraid I have to agree, Jon. Even with the NSA fully behind you, it's not doable. And the process of getting the NSA behind you wouldn't escape Dresner's notice. All risk, no return."

Smith was suddenly reminded of a television show he'd once seen on the Rapture and how Dresner had, in his twisted way, taken on the role of God. Any minute now, millions of people could just collapse, leaving his innocents to stand in stunned silence.

And then what? Piles of rotting bodies. The destabilization of governments and economies across the globe. Mass graves. But would the seemingly inevitable chaos ensue? Or would all the potential creators of that chaos be dead?

His phone beeped with an incoming call and Smith looked at the screen, eyes widening. "I have an incoming call, sir. You're not going to believe this, but the ID says it's from Christian Dresner."

"Dresner?" Klein said, obviously equally surprised. "Go ahead and conference him in. He can't track me. I'm connected through a coffee shop in Cambodia."

Smith reached out, hesitating for a moment before picking up. "Hello?"

"I have to admit to an increasing respect for you, Dr. Smith. Or maybe 'wariness' is a more accurate word."

"The feeling's mutual."

"I assume that after what happened to the major, you've generated some theories about my plan?"

"You're going to murder millions of people whose life-styles you don't approve of," Randi said.

"Ah, Ms. Russell. A woman who doesn't mince words."

Smith glared at her in the rearview mirror. She flipped him off.

"And is Mr. Zellerbach there, too?"

"Yes," Marty said, looking more in awe than scared.

"My compliments to you. I identified thirty-nine people worldwide whom I believed had a chance at finding that subsystem and you weren't on the list. I apologize for underestimating your abilities."

"Uh, that's okay."

Dresner let out an incongruously warm laugh. "I see that you haven't informed anyone of consequence. I'm sure Mr. Zellerbach told you that I'd be watching all aspects of the network for unusual fluctuations."

"He did mention that," Smith said. "The message seems to be that if we do anything, an enormous number of people will drop dead."

"One million, seventeen thousand, six hundred and twelve as of this moment."

"As of this moment…" Smith said. The seemingly offhand phrase was the last piece of the puzzle he needed. "It's not enough for you."

"Once again, I'm impressed," Dresner said. "No, it's not enough. This isn't about vengeance or killing people who will be immediately replaced by others just as malignant. It's about fundamentally changing society. It's about making certain we survive long enough for someone to succeed where I've failed."

"In turning the Merge into something that perfects us as a species."

"Your phrasing is a bit melodramatic but it's substantially accurate."

"So if we try to stop you now, you'll murder just over

a million people. But if we don't, a few years from now, ten times that many will die."

"Closer to five times based on my projections. But these are people whose lives are about destruction, Jon. Hate. Greed. People who turn—"

"According to you."

"Not really true. You're ignoring the fact that one of LayerCake's main functions is to temper our judgments with facts. Whatever biases I have because of my life experiences are eradicated by the system. I think you'd be surprised at how many people I personally judge negatively that LayerCake doesn't. I'm not overriding a single one of those decisions. As you know, the system works. Extremely well."

It was true. The system *did* work. In Smith's extensive experience, LayerCake's judgments of people and things had proved almost preternaturally accurate. And to the degree it erred, it erred to the positive.

"Even your moderated biases, though, are *your* biases," Randi said. "Didn't Hitler believe he was right? Didn't Stalin? Didn't they believe that they were creating a Utopia?"

"I'm not trying to protect my own power, Ms. Russell. I'm not a racist or a sexist. I'm not promoting a political ideology. And my accusations are being vetted by the most unbiased judge ever created. If our species is going to survive to take the next logical step, something has to be done. The weak and the innocent have to be protected from men with access to technology that Hitler and Stalin only dreamed of."

"And so we should just accept that you've checkmated us," Smith said. "We should just stand by and do nothing."

"You think too small, Jon. That's not at all what I'm proposing. I believe that we should form an alliance."

"Excuse me?"

"The adoption of the Merge has been strongest in the United States for a number of reasons, including your undeniable talent at developing systems useful to your soldiers."

Smith felt the breath drain from him. Dresner was right. His confidence in the Merge's potential had handed Dresner a weapon that could decimate America's defenses in precisely eighteen seconds.

"Adoption by foreign militaries is fairly low still, largely due to the exclusivity agreement Whitfield insisted on. Penetration in Muslim countries like Pakistan, Afghanistan, and Iran is coming along, but is also still low—even with the upper class. In China, there's poor overall adoption because of the poverty in rural areas but also because of the limited effectiveness of the commercial unit in combat situations. Also, there's not a great deal of online information in those countries for LayerCake to base its judgments on."

Smith knew where this was going and wasn't happy about it. "So you have my country dead to rights. If you activate now, we're the ones who get hit the hardest."

"Overwhelmingly so," Dresner said. "But it doesn't have to be that way. Whitfield forced me into the exclusivity agreement. I propose a leak of the military operating system that would allow other countries full access. You'd see an immediate spike in adoption by your opponents and I'd stand by while you slow—but not reverse—the usage by the U.S. military. This would also give me more time to market to the Muslims and the ruling classes of Africa and Southeast Asia, whom I think you'd agree the world would be better without."

"So I'd be responsible for the deaths of millions of people."

"Terrorists, dictators, people involved in the Iranian and Pakistani nuclear efforts, criminals, military leaders in China, Russia—"

"And the men that I've led and fought with."

"LayerCake has no interest in killing a hundred thousand foot soldiers, Jon. In fact, I think you'd be surprised at how few of your military people have been selected. The system is interested less in people who fight wars than the people who court and promote them. Besides, you can't save them. For all intents and purposes, they're already dead."

Smith didn't respond.

"In the next fifty years, we'll be able to use the Merge to become what we've always aspired to be, Jon. Can you imagine what humanity could accomplish if we didn't spend so much of our time and energy looking for ways to destroy ourselves? Will my actions cause the deaths of millions of people? Yes. But how does that compare with the wars of the last century? The genocides? The countless massacres throughout history where the peaceful and defenseless were the first to die? How many innocent lives will my actions save? Humanity has a chance, Jon. A chance to survive. To thrive. Think about what role you want to play in that."

The connection went dead and there was silence in the car for a few moments.

"Thoughts?" Klein said finally.

"Talk about a Faustian bargain," Randi said.

"Yeah," Smith said. "What he's talking about doesn't save American lives so much as it takes foreign ones. I'm more patriotic than most, but that's a lot of blood on my hands."

"Agreed," Klein said over the phone. "We're not bargaining with this man. There has to be a way to stop him. We're just not coming up with it."

Smith glanced over at Marty, who was staring blankly out the window tapping his foot in a monotonous rhythm.

"Marty?"

He didn't answer.

"What about a virus, Marty? You write it and I'll get it into any network you want. You can crash the whole world."

Again he didn't answer.

"It won't crash," Zellerbach said. "It's won't, it won't, it won't."

Smith had seen him like this before. His mind was going a thousand miles an hour in a hundred different directions. His brilliance was unchained, but also spinning out of control. They were going to have to stop at a pharmacy.

"It's not about the networks," Zellerbach continued. "It's not."

Randi leaned up through the seats. "Then what *is* it about? How can we stop him from triggering it?"

"We can't."

"That's not acceptable," Klein said.

"LayerCake," Zellerbach said. "It's not about the networks. Or the grid. Or the Merge. It's about search. It's about Javier."

"Who's Javier?"

Zellerbach didn't answer, mumbling to himself and beginning to count something on his fingers.

"He may be talking about Javier de Galdiano," Klein said. "He's the main tech person behind LayerCake. He's why Dresner's search subsidiary is run out of a campus near Granada, Spain. De Galdiano doesn't like to leave home."

"Marty," Smith said. "Look at me."

He didn't seem to hear and Smith reached out to force his head around. When their gazes met, Zellerbach came back from the brink a bit.

"We . . . We can't stop him from triggering it, Jon. He'll have too many fail-safes. But maybe we could change the way LayerCake judges people."

"What do you mean?" Randi said.

"What if we could make it think everybody's great? Then he can trigger it all he wants. It won't do anything."

"Can you hack in, Marty? Rewrite the parameters?"

"No. There's no outside access. We'd have to be inside the building. And we'd have to have Javier's password."

"What do we know about him?" Randi said. "Dresner's security is notorious but we might be able to get to him somewhere else. Can we find the address of his home and a schematic of any security systems he has installed? How does he get to work? Does he drive himself? Does he have family or friends he visits? What about hobbies that would take him outside? Biking and skiing are big in that area."

"I can get that," Klein said. "It'll take some time, though."

"Jon," Zellerbach said, tugging on his sleeve.

"Just a second, Marty. We also need to start looking into the security at the campus. Even if we get to—"

"Jon!" Zellerbach repeated, this time grabbing Smith's shoulder and shaking him.

"What is it, Marty?"

"I know him."

"You know who?"

"Javier."

"You're friends? How close?"

Zellerbach's words came out in a breathless jumble. "I've never actually *met* him. He's an old hacker, like me. There are five of us who have a competition and we set up challenges and try to do them and get a trophy we pass around. Javier has it now. He broke into my system to get it. My system! He's so smart, Jon. So smart."

"Can you get in touch with him?"

"Yes. We have a private chat room. The five of us."

"Tell him you're coming to Spain and you want to meet."

"Face-to-face? We don't do that. He won't want to do that."

"You said he has the trophy right now," Klein interjected. "What if you won it and said you wanted to pick it up personally?"

"Yeah. That's in the rules. I could do that. But I haven't won it. He knows I haven't won it."

"What's the current challenge?" Randi said.

"To turn all the screensavers at the National Security Agency to gay porn."

Klein laughed. Probably not at the image but more at the fact that Zellerbach's contest happened to be very much within his sphere of influence. "That won't be a problem."

"No. It's hard. This challenge has been out there since

they repealed don't ask don't tell. The security is tough and getting it to hit all the computers at once is nearly impossible. No one's even close as far as I know."

"Trust me," Klein said. "Tell him you're coming to Granada and you want him to deliver the trophy personally."

70

North of Mitú
Colombia

THERE SHE IS," RANDI SAID, dropping her duffel on the dirt airstrip and pointing into the jungle.

The plane was a large turboprop but it was hard to tell the exact make through the modifications, rust, and camouflage paint. Smith approached a little hesitantly, looking at holes where rivets should have been and the cracked glass in at least a third of the windows. Zellerbach just stopped dead, suddenly forgetting the cloud of insects buzzing around him.

"This is it? This is the plane you told us about? What's wrong with the one we flew here?"

His alarm was understandable but there wasn't much they could do. Dresner had intelligence capabilities so cutting-edge that there was no way to anticipate them. While every effort had been made to ensure that the planes used by Covert-One were completely anonymous, it was impossible to guarantee in a post-Merge world. This plane, though—while maybe not entirely airworthy—could never be tracked back to Fred Klein or the president.

"It's better than it looks," Randi said, recruiting Smith to help pull the camo netting from the fuselage. "And my friend left a laptop with a satellite link inside. He says it's a super-fast connection."

"I'm not a child you can ply with candy."

"Suit yourself. Did you bring a magazine? Maybe you could just hang out in the sun and read."

Zellerbach looked around him at the jungle, at the old truck they'd driven there, at the mosquitoes.

"Come on, Marty," Smith said, yanking off the last of the netting and opening the door. "It's got air-conditioning."

Of course that was a lie—the heat billowing out of the plane felt like a kiln—but it did prompt the sweating hacker to inch closer.

Zellerbach peeked inside and crinkled his nose as Randi made her way to the cockpit. The seats had all been ripped out but, true to her word, there was a card table with a laptop on it near the back.

"There is *not* air-conditioning."

"Gotta start the engines first," Smith promised, lacing his fingers and offering Zellerbach a boost up.

He followed and closed the door, looking back to see Zellerbach on his knees examining something on the floor.

"Is this cocaine?" the hacker said, bringing his nose within a few inches before Smith grabbed him by the collar and dragged him to the table containing the laptop.

"Just dust from the insulation, Marty. Why don't you fire that thing up and see if you can get online."

It was another lie. The plane belonged to a Colombian acquaintance of Randi's who had helped her do away with a couple of Hamas guys looking to get into the drug trade. It had been a mutually beneficial operation—she got rid of two terrorists and he got rid of two potential competitors—that had gone smoothly enough to prompt them to stay loosely in touch.

Once Zellerbach was settled and had forgotten the coke in favor of the even more addictive glow of the computer screen, Smith went forward and took the copilot's seat.

"Nice rig," he shouted, putting on a headset as the props came up to speed. "You think it'll actually make it over the Atlantic?"

"Diego swears it's a cream puff."

She eased the throttles forward and the plane bumped its way to the makeshift runway.

"And you trust him?"

"Truth be told, he has a thing for me. And he's dying for me to go to work for him. Apparently, he has some other competitors he'd like retired."

"Good work if you can get it."

She grinned and twisted around to look through the tattered cockpit curtains. "Hang on, Marty!"

Despite its appearance, the plane felt solid as they lofted into the air and began to bank out over the jungle. Randi had an intense expression of concentration on her face and Smith remained silent. With her questionable skills and the unfamiliar aircraft, her focus was best left unmolested.

After a few minutes, they leveled out and she relaxed a little. The brief calm before it got dark and instrument-flying was required.

"What did Fred say?" she asked.

Smith had spoken with him on the way to South America, keeping his end of the conversation necessarily opaque due to Zellerbach.

"He talked to the president."

Randi winced. "Shit. I knew it. It's a bad call, Jon."

There was no denying that it was a risk. Klein wasn't willing to go completely off the books with this many lives at stake, though, and he'd been fairly certain he could convince the president that the risk to his family was limited.

"Yeah, but for now at least, Castilla's solid. And with the White House behind him, Fred has free rein to look into ways to mitigate the effect of Dresner pulling the trigger. They're using an anti-terrorism study on the vulnerabilities of the power grid to see how fast they could take it down. There's a chance that we could put most of the major cities on the East Coast in the dark over the course of a few seconds. And at the same time, we could pull the plug on the military networks."

"How much would that cut casualties?"

"Maybe thirty percent in the U.S."

"But everyone else in the world gets hammered."

"Yeah."

"And when they figure out that we knew and didn't warn them, how's that going to go over?"

Of course, she was right. But there was just no way to get the word out with Dresner watching. All it would take was one insignificant slip.

"That's not all they're looking at, Randi. Nothing's off the table."

"Including taking Dresner up on his offer to make a deal?"

It was an interesting question. Klein was strongly against it, but Castilla wasn't a spy, he was a politician.

"Probably, but there's no point in worrying about it. If they cut a backroom deal and we get called off this, then at least the pressure's off."

She nodded knowingly. If their plan went south—and it probably would—more than a million people could die.

They hit a thick layer of clouds and Randi turned her attention to climbing above them. When they were back out into the sunshine, she glanced over at him. "What if Castilla does make a deal? What if five years go by and suddenly twenty million just drop dead. Would you rebuild?"

"What do you mean?"

"The military. Fire back up the carrier groups and the tanks and the infantry. Sometimes, I think it all feels like a throwback to a different time. Now it's all about nukes and people who are willing to fight guerrilla wars for the next ten generations. But we've got all that stuff and we're used to it, so we perpetuate it."

"I don't know what I'd do," he said honestly. "What about you? The CIA completely missed the fall of the Soviet Union, the Arab Spring, and just about everything else that's happened in the world. Are you sure you're worth the money we spend on you?"

"Maybe not," she admitted. "What if the agency had never existed? Would the Soviets have invaded? Would al-Qaeda have destroyed us? I mean, I think we do a lot of good but if we had a clean slate, I'm not sure I'd set up the world the same way."

Smith leaned his head back and managed an exhausted

smile. "What would you and I do in a world full of peaceful happy people?"

"God," she said, actually shuddering. "Can you imagine? Everyone smiling and helping each other out? I'd have to—"

"Jon!" Zellerbach shouted from the back, cutting her off. "*Jon!* Come quick! Hurry!"

Smith leapt from his seat and ran back to where his friend was gesticulating wildly toward his computer. "What is it, Marty? Are you okay?"

"I'm a legend!" he said. "A god! And I didn't have to do *anything*!"

Smith looked down at the photo of a strategically pixilated naked man accompanying a report on CNN's homepage. The text beneath it told the story of an unknown hacker accessing the NSA computers and putting similar pictures on all the screensavers.

Once again, Fred Klein had come through.

71

Granada
Spain

Smith slowed his pace again, listening to Marty
Zellerbach huffing loudly as he crept up the endless set
of stairs. Below, the ancient city of Granada stretched
into the distance. He kept a watchful eye on the windows
in the whitewashed stone buildings on either side of the
steps and did his best to turn his face away from the occasional passing pedestrian. So far, things seemed to be
going smoothly, but that could all be an illusion. They
wouldn't know they'd been identified until the bullets
started flying.

Zellerbach limped up to him, still milking his bullet
scrapes, and then stopped in the shade of a fruit tree.
The early-afternoon sun had pushed temperatures into the
eighties and the forecast was promising another five degrees before sunset.

"You all right, Marty?"

He squinted through the green contacts Randi had
spent ten minutes getting into his eyes and scratched like
a flea-ridden dog at the fake beard covering much of his

face. Combined with the sweat-soaked dress shirt and high-water pants, the disguise gave him a bit of a deranged air.

Not that Smith looked much better. The baseball hat covering his hair had been padded in a way that made his head appear abnormally large and cotton stuffed into his cheeks caused them to bulge noticeably.

An often-ignored fact was that LayerCake constantly attempted to identify people in order to hone its facial recognition software. And while Dresner had been clear that the data collected was immediately purged, it seemed likely that he had the ability to use it for his own purposes. In all likelihood, every Merge on the planet was attempting to find their faces and send a GPS coordinate to their master.

Randi, already at the top of the hill, had gone with her old standby: Muslim. She wore a full headscarf, reflective sunglasses, and a long coat that gave the impression of thirty extra pounds—a configuration that he knew from his own testing confounded the system every time.

"Not much farther, Marty. Five more minutes and we're there."

The hacker scowled and gave his beard a few more scratches, but then started forward again. His trophy awaited.

They caught up to Randi on an empty cobblestone street and crossed over to a square lined with outdoor cafés. It was barely noon, so there were only a few scattered customers drinking coffee, reading magazines, and fawning over dogs they were taking a break from walking.

The restaurant they were looking for ran along the

back of the square and was the least inhabited. Only three chairs were taken—two by a young couple who could see only each other and the last by a thin, thirty-something man with shaggy black hair and clothes that seemed to have been pulled randomly from his laundry hamper.

"That's him. That's Javier," Zellerbach said. Randi immediately turned right, leading them on a circuitous route that would allow them to come up behind the Spaniard.

Not surprisingly, there was a Merge hanging on his belt. She deftly flipped the power switch before the three of them dropped into chairs around him.

"Eh!" he said, reaching behind him to turn it back on.

Smith grabbed his wrist. "We're going to leave that off for a little while, okay?"

De Galdiano used the near-perfect English he'd learned before dropping out of MIT. "Who the hell are you?"

Smith didn't answer but Zellerbach waved a hand manically to get the Spaniard's attention. "Javier! It's me!"

"Marty?" he said, trying to see through the beard and contacts.

"In all my luminous magnificence."

"Who are these people? Why did you bring them here?"

De Galdiano's tone had a nervous edge that wasn't surprising. He had a family, an incredibly high-paying job, and a respectable position in European society. The press and authorities thought he'd left his hacker life behind long ago, and being linked to a group competing to break into the NSA mainframe wouldn't exactly fit that image.

"They're my friends. Jon and Randi."

"Why are they *here*?"

"Don't worry. They know about the hack."

De Galdiano blanched a bit at that, immediately reaching for a bag at his feet and holding it out. "You were supposed to come alone, Marty. If you want people to know about this part of your life, that's your business. But these are your friends not mine. You had no right."

"Don't be mad," Zellerbach said, pulling out an enormous clown shoe and running a hand along it as though it were a holy relic. He seemed entirely mesmerized for a moment, but then a profound sadness seemed to come over him.

"I can't accept this."

"What? But I saw the report on CNN. You won."

Zellerbach shook his head. "I didn't do it. Jon did."

The Spaniard redirected his gaze to Smith. The wariness was apparent in his expression, but he was also clearly intrigued. "Do I know you? What name do you go by online? How did you access the system from the outside?"

"To take your questions in order: You don't know me. I go by the name Jon. And I didn't have to access the system from outside. I just called a friend and he told the NSA to load those screensavers."

It didn't take de Galdiano long to come to the most obvious conclusion: Zellerbach had sold him out. This was a sting and he was right at the center of it.

He tried to rise from his seat, but Randi grabbed his shoulder and shoved him back down. "Relax. We're not here to expose you or arrest you. We're here to ask for your help."

"It's true," Zellerbach said, leaning conspiratorially

across the table and scratching a little more at his beard. "They really *are* my friends. You can trust them."

De Galdiano's eyes flicked nervously back and forth— at them, at the square, at the sparsely populated tables. "What do you want?"

Smith nodded subtly toward Zellerbach. It would be better to let him talk.

"It's a problem with the Merge, Javier."

"What kind of problem?"

"You know all those weird upgrade paths?"

Smith watched him carefully, looking for any hint that would indicate he was in on Dresner's plan. Nothing.

"Yes."

"They're not upgrade paths at all. They're a hidden subsystem."

"A hidden…" His voice faded for a moment. "To what purpose?"

"Killing people. I figured out how to trigger it and it stopped a man's heart."

"Impossible."

The waitress approached and Randi spoke casually to her in Spanish. "Coffee for everyone. That's all."

"I wanted those chocolate churros," Zellerbach whined as she walked away.

"Focus, Marty."

De Galdiano tried to get up again and this time it was Smith who shoved him back into his seat.

"This is bullshit," the trapped Spaniard said in a harsh whisper. "I don't know who you people are but you look like you work for the American government. Two more paranoid spies who think everyone spends their days trying to think up ways to hurt you. Christian Dresner has given more to this world than anyone alive: His antibiotics are on their way to wiping out resistance worldwide, he's massively advanced childhood education and nutrition, he's all but cured deafness. And now he's handed us the most transformational technology since the printing press. Is it possible that you're just angry because you can't control it? Or maybe you don't like what LayerCake has to say about you and people like you."

"What Marty's telling you is true," Smith said.

"Oh, right. And I'm supposed to just take the word of two government agents and a crazy man?" He glanced apologetically at Zellerbach. "No offense."

"None taken."

"Even if it was technologically feasible," de Galdiano continued. "Why would Christian want to kill his own customers? He created this technology to *help* the people using it—to make us see things the way they are and not how our minds filter them. Beyond being psychotic, it would be counter to everything he's trying to accomplish."

"I have to admit that your system's ability to make subjective judgments about people is impressive," Smith said, deciding to adjust his approach.

"They aren't subjective," de Galdiano protested. "Not in the same sense as yours and mine. That's the point—to introduce reason and logic into..." His voice faded for a moment when he realized where Smith was leading him. "You think he's going to kill the people the system judges negatively."

"We spoke with him," Zellerbach said. "He admitted it. I heard."

"Maybe it wasn't him." De Galdiano indicated toward Randi and Smith. "Maybe they were tricking you."

"They're smart, Javier. But they're not that smart— particularly where technology is concerned. I'm telling you that Dresner purposely built a system that can kill its user. I'm *guaranteeing* you that. All you have to do is find the right combination of signals. I know because it took me almost two weeks to hit on it."

The Spaniard didn't answer immediately, his super-charged mind collating and assessing what he'd heard.

"It was you," he said finally. "You were the one pulling processing power from all over the world. You crashed Amazon."

"Twice," Zellerbach admitted. "With that many possibilities, I needed a lot of processing power."

Some of the skepticism drained from De Galdiano's expression and was replaced with confusion. He was slowly putting the pieces together and discovering that they all fit.

"I didn't tell you my last name, Javier. It's Smith. Colonel Jon Smith. Do you recognize it?"

He nodded numbly. "You're in charge of military development. But if you're telling the truth, where is everyone else? Why haven't you contacted my government? Why didn't you just kidnap me? Why aren't there black helicopters and a hundred CIA agents?"

"Because Dresner's watching every aspect of his system. He'd have early warning of anything out of the ordinary."

His face went blank in the same way Marty's did when he was working on a complex problem. Smith leaned back in his chair and watched the waitress approach with a tray full of coffee cups. He smiled politely as she doled them out but de Galdiano just stared straight ahead in what looked like the early stages of catatonia.

"Christian has made odd requests over the years," he said finally. "But he's a brilliant and eccentric man. I didn't think anything about them."

"They make sense now, though, don't they?" Randi said.

He nodded numbly. "LayerCake is much more than what the public—and even you, Colonel—sees. There's a core that processes enormous amounts of data that the public system doesn't have access to: credit scores, retail purchases, criminal and medical records, tax returns—"

"Data you hacked," Zellerbach said, not bothering to hide his admiration.

De Galdiano gave a nearly imperceptible nod. "It was never meant to be used in the public results. Christian just wanted to use it as a check and balance. When we found significant discrepancies between the core and public systems, we could fix it by hand and instantly see what went wrong with our algorithm. It's why the system is so accurate."

"And Dresner has access to that core," Randi said.

"He's linked directly to it. The judgments his Merge makes aren't based on the public data like everyone else's. I never understood why he wanted that—it was complicated to do and the differences in results aren't that significant."

"Unless the decision you're making is life or death," Smith said.

"Yes," he responded quietly. "Unless it's life or death."

"Then you'll you help us?" Zellerbach said.

De Galdiano met his eye. "Help you do what?"

"Stop him."

Despite everything, he seemed a little startled by the suggestion. "I've worked for Christian since I was in my twenties. I'd probably be in jail if it weren't for him and he's always been good to me and my family..."

"Look," Smith said. "What if we're lying to you? Hell, what if Marty has a bet with someone for another clown shoe and all this is just a big con. What's the worst that can happen? We shut down LayerCake and everyone has to go back to using Google for a few hours. You get fired and retire on the fortune you already have in the bank."

"And what about the best-case scenario?" Randi added. "That you save the lives of a million people."

De Galdiano didn't speak again for a long time. "What is it you want from me exactly?"

"Well, we have a few ideas," Smith said. "But the truth is, you're the expert. Is there any way to centrally deactivate every Merge in one shot?"

"No."

"What about a virus?"

"Impossible. You can't run so much as a single line of code on the Merge unless Christian personally approves it. And he's not going to approve a virus."

Depressing, but not unexpected. It was exactly what Zellerbach had told them.

"What about Dresner?" Randi said. "Can you help us get to him?"

"Personally? No. I can count the number of times I've met with him face-to-face on one hand—and he initiated all those meetings. We communicate entirely by email and videoconference."

Zellerbach had called that one too, but it had been worth asking.

"So what you're saying is that all we have to play with is LayerCake."

De Galdiano nodded. "I have root access to that system only. And even then, only from the terminal in my office."

Smith glanced at Zellerbach who gave a subtle thumbs-up indicating that the Spaniard's words rang true.

"Can you take down the system from there?"

"No. It's too diffuse. We have redundant processing centers all over the world. I set it up specifically to prevent someone from doing what you're asking. And if you're right about Christian watching, he would see it happening. This isn't like pulling the plug out of your PC."

"Okay," Smith said. "But you have access to the algorithms that LayerCake uses to make its judgments."

"Of course," de Galdiano said, starting to look a bit ill as he wrapped his mind around what was happening. "I wrote them."

"What about Dresner's judgments?"

"Christian uses data from the core but otherwise he's on the same system as everyone else. Obviously, it's customized to his values just like yours is customized to yours. What are you getting at? Do you have a plan?"

"Maybe," Smith said. "Can you get us into your office?"

"Security is heavy. That's something else that's always been strange. We're not talking about the normal . . . What do you call them? Rent-a-cops? These are very scary men with big guns."

"You must have people in and out of there," Randi said. "Consultants, reporters..."

"I can get you visitor badges. But after that, I can't guarantee anything. When I triggered the metal detector last year, I was one set of car keys away from getting a cavity search. And I run the place."

72

Outside Granada
Spain

THE BUILDING'S LOBBY was far more massive than it looked from outside. Serviced by a single broad set of stairs, the sweeping glass, concrete, and steel cavern was sunk a good ten meters into the ground. An enormous chrome mobile hung from the ceiling, swaying gently over a line of metal detectors and tables that had the look of a postmodern TSA checkpoint. Security guards were scattered throughout, mostly soft-looking Spanish locals pulling an hourly wage but also three of the men de Galdiano had warned them about—foreign, muscular, and sharp-eyed as they watched the light traffic of LayerCake employees flowing in and out.

They followed de Galdiano down the stars, with Smith and Randi taking up positions to either side of Marty Zellerbach. No one seemed to have badges and Smith assumed that they were using brain wave feeds from their Merges for identification. Dresner had included that function on the military operating system but they hadn't had time yet to delve into its obvious potential.

"I have three guests today," de Galdiano said to a guard behind a broad desk. "None of them is using a Merge. Can I get badges?"

The man eyed them and was undoubtedly scanning their faces for an ID. LayerCake would provide him their false identities but at a very low confidence rate since those identities had only just come into existence.

Still, the normal formalities were dispensed with. The guard's Merge uploaded their photos as well as collecting and collating the fictional information they'd planted on the web, making the customary forms and signatures redundant. In less than a minute, they had their badges.

De Galdiano went through the metal detectors first, with Randi right behind. She'd stripped herself of every piece of metal: jewelry, belt, shoes, purse. Nevertheless, Smith tensed when she stepped through. If the alarm went off, this would be over before it even started.

But there was only the sound of the piped-in music and the conversations of the people around them. As Randi began collecting her belongings on the other side, Smith pulled his powered-down Merge from his pocket and tossed it in a bin along with his wallet. A few moments later, they were all through and stepping into the elevator.

De Galdiano used a key to access the top floor and a few seconds later the doors opened onto a sea of cubicles inhabited by young programmers wearing everything from khakis and ties to pajamas. At the back, a massive office was visible through a glass wall that ran along the top of a meter-high stainless-steel band.

The Spaniard mumbled a few greetings as they waded

through the cubicles, but was visibly relieved when they got inside and closed the door behind them. The office was probably twenty meters square and looked a little like the dream bedroom of a grade-schooler. There were bicycles, vintage arcade games, and even a full-sized soccer goal full of balls. Video monitors along the ceiling, two terminals, and an enormous wet bar were the only things that hinted at adulthood.

De Galdiano went to the closest keyboard, and after he tapped in a quick command the glass wall turned smoky. Randi took a position next to it, looking out at the hazy image of the people outside.

"Can they see in as well as I can see out?"

De Galdiano shook his head. "They're just looking into a mirror now."

Randi pulled two guns from beneath her coat and tossed one to Smith. They were manufactured entirely from non-metal parts and worked a little like a semiautomatic flintlock rifle. A packet of gunpowder attached to a ceramic marble was projected into the back of the barrel by a carbon-fiber spring and then touched off by a spark when the trigger was pulled.

While entirely invisible to metal detectors, the design had significant drawbacks. The clip held only five rounds and the reload time hovered around fifteen minutes.

Zellerbach slipped past the Spaniard and took a seat in front of the terminal. "Can you get me in?"

De Galdiano entered his password and a graphic of a slowly spinning globe came on screen. Zellerbach pointed to the bright pinpoints of light dotted across it. "Are those the LayerCake server farms?"

"Yes."

"How many?"

"Hundreds."

"No problem. No problem. I'm on it."

De Galdiano walked across the room and sat behind the other terminal in the room. "Are you sending your Internet profile worm, Marty?"

"I'm connecting to the mainframe at my house now...Okay, it's on its way to you."

Zellerbach's profile worm was an incredibly sophisticated web bot that he'd originally designed to constantly search for mentions of him on the 'net and alter the pages to portray him as a particularly attractive combination of Abraham Lincoln, Albert Einstein, and Fabio. Later, he realized that it could also be used to get revenge on the people who had tormented him in high school. In fact, Smith occasionally still searched the names of a few of his football teammates when he needed a laugh. Last time he'd looked up a guy who had once given Zellerbach a very public wedgie, the web was wall-to-wall with reports of his arrest for shoplifting a box of extra-absorbent tampons from a 7-Eleven.

"Got it," de Galdiano said and then opened the program. A screen came up asking for the full name of the soon-to-be victim. He typed Christian Alphonse Dresner. A list of thirty-nine people by that name came up in the order of Google ranking. Not surprisingly, the man they were looking for was at the top.

"How does it work, Marty?"

Zellerbach was hammering away at his keyboard and it took a moment for him to answer. "There are a lot of different functions, but you just need the simplest. On the first screen, fill in the blank with words you want associated with him and the bot will start inserting them into web pages."

"Okay. But what are we going to say?"

"Something that will make him unique," Smith said.

"How about that he has a dachshund fetish?" Randi said, still gazing out the window into the cube farm beyond.

"Yeah, put that in," Smith said. "But I doubt that's going to make him completely unique. We need something else."

"He tried to drown his mother in Vegemite," Randi said.

This time they all turned to look at her.

"What? I've got a million of 'em."

"Go ahead," Smith said, feeling a surge of adrenaline twist at his stomach.

The Spaniard typed it in and then let his hand hover over the return key. "What if your suspicions about Dresner are right and this is something he's watching for? What if this is the trigger?"

It was a risk that they'd discussed at length with Fred Klein before getting the go-ahead to try this particular Hail Mary. It seemed unlikely that Dresner would tie a trigger to what was being said about him on the Internet—thousands of pages were active at any given time, portraying him as everything from the second coming to Satan. But unlikely was admittedly not the same as impossible.

"Randi," he said, pointing to a laptop sitting on a chair made of Legos. "Get on that and pull up a live video feed."

"What feed?"

"Anything that's got people in it."

She knelt in front of the keyboard and tapped in a few commands. "Okay. I've got a webcam in Times Square. What am I looking for?"

"People dropping dead," Smith said, reaching out and hitting the return button. A counter started scrolling on screen as Zellerbach's worm went to work modifying web pages with the terms they'd entered. A hundred records. A thousand. Ten thousand.

"Anything?" Smith said.

"Everybody looks okay."

Despite the powerful air-conditioning, a drop of sweat fell from his nose and splashed on De Galdiano's keyboard. He'd just pointed a gun at the heads of a million people and clicked on an empty chamber. But he wasn't done yet.

Unbidden, the Spaniard opened a window to LayerCake and typed "dachshund fetish drown mother vegemite."

There were too many hits to go through individually, but a quick survey of them suggested that all related to Christian Dresner.

"It worked," de Galdiano said. "He's unique in the world. For now."

"And you can access his personal search parameters?"

"They're stored in the same place as everyone else's."

"Okay. Type in the changes, but don't make them go live until I tell you to."

Smith took a step back and reached for the Merge on his belt. He hesitated for a moment but then flipped the power switch.

Beyond the fact that his teeth were clenched tight

enough that he could hear them grinding, there was nothing. Just the normal start-up counter and icons slowly populating his peripheral vision. Dresner would have no reason to expect that he would ever come online again and Smith had bet his life that he wouldn't be watching.

"You ready, Marty?"

"It would take a year for me to properly prepare."

"I know. But can we do enough to scare the hell out of him?"

"Oh, I'm going to put on a show. Marty Zellerbach always puts on a show."

73

Near Vientiane
Laos

We're following up on the cargo plane that took off from Colombia, but we haven't been able to track it or confirm that Smith and Russell were on board," Deuce Brennan said.

Dresner gripped the arms of his chair, feeling the pain of increasingly arthritic fingers. "So it would be fair to say you have nothing."

"I don't know much about Smith, sir, but I can tell you that Randi's no amateur. If she goes to ground, she's going to be damn hard to find."

"Keep me informed," Dresner said and then cut the connection.

He remained seated, looking around the nearly empty room—the white walls, the single terminal in the corner, the sliding door cutting him off from the rest of the world. What now?

It was possible that Smith and Russell had gone into hiding, correctly surmising that he was having them hunted. But it seemed unlikely. Had they informed their superiors about the hidden subsystem? About his plans? About his offer of a partnership? If so, he would expect to have been contacted—the Americans would want to negotiate the most favorable deal possible.

There was no choice now but to assume that they were going to attempt to stop him. But how? He was watching every network and power grid. Next-generation algorithms were tracking the Merge connections of every person of consequence on the planet, looking for any pattern that might suggest someone moving against him. The Internet and media were being constantly scoured for the vaguest hint that his plan had been discovered.

But there was nothing.

It would be easy to tell himself that he had planned for every eventuality, that they were acting entirely out of desperation. But Jon Smith was a more formidable opponent than that. If he was acting, he believed he had found an exploitable weakness.

Dresner activated his usage application and a set of graphs appeared in the air ahead of him. Units online were moving upward on their daily cycles and would peak in another few hours. Five and a half million people would be active at that point, approximately 1.3 million of whom were targeted by LayerCake. It wasn't enough—he was convinced of that. But could he afford to wait? Was it possible that Smith had found some flaw that he hadn't considered?

A quiet alarm began to sound, answering many of the questions and suspicions plaguing him. He rushed to the terminal against the wall, resenting having to use such a clumsy device, but forced to acknowledge his technology's inability to process complex inputs.

A screen displaying Merge networks came up and showed that the military's satellite links had all gone down simultaneously. There was little question that Smith was to blame, but why? Only about nineteen percent of America's soldiers were served by that network—mostly young, low-level infantry who wouldn't have been targeted by LayerCake anyway. What could he possibly hope to accomplish that would justify the risk he was taking?

The alarm varied in pitch and another window sprang to life on his monitor—this one showing some kind of virus attacking the servers in Canada. The system was rerouting traffic through excess capacity in Mexico but there was still a two percent slowdown worldwide. How could a virus have worked its way that deep into his system?

Another change in alarm pitch was accompanied by a screen showing a T-Mobile network in Southern Europe crashing, along with a number of independent Internet service providers throughout North America.

System security would be tracking the source of the disturbances and he pulled up the list, staring at it for a moment in disbelief. This wasn't a coordinated effort by the NSA and their foreign counterparts—the entire assault was coming from two terminals in Javier de Galdiano's office.

Dresner tried to shut them down, but found himself locked out as disturbances kept appearing all over the globe. Two cable companies went down in California, increasing the slowdown to twelve percent and disconnecting more than forty thousand users. A server farm in Kansas went offline as the power grid began pulsing beyond the capacity of its surge protectors. The temperature of a critical switch in Arizona suddenly went outside of parameters and began its shutdown sequence.

Dresner closed the windows on his monitor and brought up the videoconference software that connected him to de Galdiano. He didn't expect it to work and was surprised when the screen was immediately filled with the image of the man's office. In its center was Jon Smith, standing directly behind the Spaniard as he typed furiously on his keyboard. At the other terminal, working even more manically, was a bearded man whom he suspected was Martin Zellerbach. Standing at the nearly opaque glass wall was Randi Russell.

"Javier! What are you doing?"

He expected to see fear in the man's face—some hint that he was acting under threat—but there was none in evidence when he looked up at the camera. He was doing this voluntarily.

"They told me you're going to use my algorithm to kill people, Christian."

"And you believed them?"

"If they're lying then I've made a bad mistake and you should fire me. But they're not lying, are they?"

A server farm in Thailand was overwhelmed but the Canadian virus had been isolated and that capacity was coming back online for a net increase in bandwidth. Worldwide, the average slowdown was hovering just under thirty percent; total users were sixteen percent below nominal levels.

"No one screws with Marty Zellerbach!" the bearded man suddenly shouted. "I once key logged the computer of God himself!"

Wild-eyed and obviously mentally ill, Zellerbach was

nonetheless one of the best hackers in the world. With Javier's cooperation, could he really threaten the entire network?

Dresner moved to reset the servers in Thailand but found that the control system would now read out only in that language. Finally, he took a step back and used his Merge to connect to the head of the Granada campus's security detail.

"Yes sir, Mr. Dresner," the man said, obviously shocked to be contacted directly by the founder of the company he worked for. "What can I do for you?"

"There are people in Javier de Galdiano's office trying to sabotage LayerCake. It appears that Javier is working with them—or perhaps even leading them. I need you to take control of those terminals at any cost."

There was a disconcerting silence before the man responded. "I understand, sir. But the elevators have shut down and the locks on the doors leading to the stairs have frozen."

Dresner slammed a fist down next to his keyboard. Of course Javier would have access to the computer controlling the building.

"How long?"

"We're working on the locks now, sir. Less than five minutes to get a team to his floor."

"Five minutes?" Dresner repeated, taking another hesitant step backward. How much more damage would the system suffer in that time?

"Do it," he said and then shut down the connection.

When he looked at the computer screen again, Smith was staring directly at him through the camera in the ceiling.

"I'm almost there!" Zellerbach shouted, the spit flying from his mouth visible even with the marginal resolution of the image. "Once my new virus is uploaded, it's lights-out. I guarantee you, Dresner's never seen anything like it. No one has!"

The beginnings of a smile played at Smith's lips. And while it was nearly imperceptible, the look in his eyes was easy to read: *Victory*.

There was no way to deny what was happening any longer. Dresner had to face the fact that he wouldn't have the time necessary to change the world in the way that he'd dedicated his life to. A simple army physician had put an end to that dream. But he could still act. And he could pray that it was enough to give humanity a chance to save itself.

Dresner met his adversary's gaze, examining the smug expression for longer than he should have before expanding the icon that activated the Merge's concealed hardware.

"You have no idea what you've done, Colonel."

74

Granada
Spain

W E'VE GOT COMPANY!"

Smith turned toward Randi's voice and looked through the smoky glass at the armed detail pouring from the stairwell. Programmers appeared over the tops of their cubicles, watching the men with a mix of curiosity and fear.

"Everyone get down!" Smith shouted.

Javier had dealt with these men for years and was already way ahead of him—dragging his terminal to the floor and lying flat next to it with his hand hovering over the enter key.

Zellerbach, on the other hand, was lost in his own world—hammering away at his keyboard, muttering unintelligibly as he wreaked havoc in the world Dresner had created. Knowing that there was no point in trying to get his attention when he was like this, Smith ran at him and knocked him off his chair. The hacker squealed in protest, but was pacified when Smith moved the terminal to the floor in front of him.

Smith returned his attention to the guards and saw them fanning out to cover a man yanking on the locked door to the office. The programmers wisely started bolting for the exits.

"Any idea what kind of glass this is or how thick?" Randi said.

"I didn't build the place!" de Galdiano answered, flattening himself further on the carpet. "Talk to the architect."

She aimed her experimental pistol at the man trying to get through the door, lining up at an angle intended to keep a ricochet from bouncing back at her, then pulled the trigger.

It turned out to be regular tempered glass and not particularly thick. The ceramic projectile missed the man on the other side, but did succeed in collapsing the entire wall in a spectacular shower. With the opaque barrier gone, they were now fully visible to the ten or so security men on the other side. It took less than a second for them to open up with everything they had.

Randi dropped behind the meter-tall band of steel and Smith slithered across the floor to de Galdiano who, to his credit, seemed to be keeping it together. Randi aimed blindly over the wall and fired in the general direction of their attackers, but there wasn't much else she could do. Dents began appearing in the metal behind her and the air was filled with the deafening ring of impacts. The barrier held, though. Security hadn't brought anything designed to penetrate anything tougher than human flesh. Yet.

Smith was only a meter or two from de Galdiano when an intense ache enveloped his right arm. At first, he thought he might have been hit, but that was something he unfortunately had a great deal of experience with. This was completely different—something he'd never felt before.

"Javier!" he shouted, reaching for the switch on his Merge. "Now!"

De Galdiano didn't move and for a moment Smith thought he hadn't heard. Then he saw the bloodstain spreading out beneath the motionless man. With a million lives at stake, he abandoned his attempt to turn off his unit and went for the keyboard. The pain intensified and spread to his chest, strangling it in a vise-like grip as he crashed down on top of the dead man. It became impossible to breathe and his right arm felt paralyzed. He reached out with his left, vision starting to swim, and let it fall on top of the blood-splattered keyboard.

75

Near Vientiane
Laos

CHRISTIAN DRESNER BACKED AWAY from the screen depicting Smith crawling toward Javier de Galdiano, whom he clearly didn't yet realize was dead. Zellerbach was still on the other terminal carrying out his attack on individual components of a network that extended to every corner of the world. And Randi Russell had her back pressed to a low steel wall, occasionally shooting blindly over it in what was looking more and more like what it was: a last stand.

He turned toward a blank wall and activated his Merge's video capability, pulling up feeds from public webcams all over the world. They hovered in front of him bordered by two bar graphs, one in blue depicting the total number of people currently online and the other in red representing those targeted. He focused on an image of a busy street in the financial district of London, following the well-dressed people rushing along the sidewalks and the vehicles choking the street.

The confident stride of a man approaching a crosswalk

faltered and Dresner watched him grimace in pain and grab his right shoulder. A woman next to him reached out a helping hand but was unable to prevent him from collapsing to his knees. She started to call for help but then fell silent when she saw that the man she was hovering over was only one of many.

Cabs continued to move through the streets, their drivers not heavily targeted by LayerCake, but a bulky Mercedes in their midst suddenly swerved and jumped the curb, scattering people Dresner's system had determined were innocent.

He kept his breathing even, trying not to think of his failures, of Smith and Russell, of the future. The ramifications of what was happening were impossible to determine and would have to be allowed to unfold over the coming months and years.

For now, there was only this moment. A moment when people died, when children were orphaned, when industries, governments, and militaries wavered. A dangerous and solemn moment.

Another car veered toward the sidewalk but then managed to correct and roll safely to a stop. Dresner took a hesitant step forward, though the motion had no effect on the image being projected on his mind. The people lying on the concrete weren't moving but also didn't have the profound stillness of death. He'd watched this play out in the North Korean facility more times than he could remember and it always followed the same pattern. Something was wrong.

The red bar hovering to his right began to flicker and a moment later disappeared.

De Galdiano.

The Spaniard had full access to LayerCake and had used that access to modify the judgment criteria into something no one would match.

Dresner shut down the video feed and rushed to his terminal, but when he reached for it an intense pain in his right arm stopped him. The confusion he felt was quickly dispelled by a crushing tightness in his chest and a sudden inability to breathe.

De Galdiano hadn't changed the Merge's criteria to target no one, he realized. He'd changed it to target its creator.

The room began to swim around him and he reached for his Merge, fumbling the power button with a thumb quickly losing sensation. His legs gave out and he hit the floor, still clawing desperately at his unit.

The pain continued to grow and he abandoned his efforts in favor of trying to deactivate the subroutine. Unable to remain on his knees, he fell to his side, concentrating on the familiar human outline icon fading in and out of existence in his peripheral vision. The launch button he'd used only moments ago now glowed with the red letters "abort."

It pulsed irregularly, keeping time with his dying heart for a moment, and then went black.

76

Near Granada
Spain

Jon!" Randi screamed over the sound of bullets hammering the metal wall behind her.

De Galdiano was dead and Smith looked like he might be too, lying partially on top of the Spaniard with his hand on the keyboard.

A shot, louder than the rest, sounded and she threw herself forward as a round penetrated the steel and sprayed her back with shrapnel. It had just been a matter of time before security found something with enough heft to blast through the barrier, but she'd been hoping for a little more foot dragging on their part.

Randi looked at what was left of the windows on the far side of the room—not much more than a few loose shards clinging to the frame. A hot breeze blew through them, strong enough to swirl the smoke hanging in the air but not enough to dissipate the overwhelming stench of gunpowder. Zellerbach was lying on his stomach still absorbed by his keyboard, though there was little point to what he was doing anymore. Not that she saw any reason to tell him that. Better to just let him stay lost in his digital world until one of the Dresner's storm troopers got lucky and took his head off.

She scanned right again, finding it much harder than it should have been to look at Smith. His plan had been too convoluted from the start—an ungodly Hail Mary with a thousand paths to disaster and only one path to success. But they'd been in similar jams before and somehow always managed to walk away.

Not this time.

She stared at him for too long, eyes clouding with a sensation so unfamiliar that it took a moment for her to decipher it. Tears.

Pull it together, Randi!

She forced her left brain back into gear and calculated that she had only one round remaining. Options for survival were limited—but limited wasn't the same thing as nonexistent.

First order of business was to get Smith's gun—he still had a full clip. With his body stacked on top of de Galdiano's they would make a functional shield that she could drag along with her to the shattered windows. The building's facade was too featureless to climb, but it was possible she could shoot out the windows of the floor below and swing down.

Even if all that worked, her chances of getting out of the building alive were still slim. At least it would be a running fight, though. A hell of a lot better than lying around waiting to catch a bullet.

She felt uncharacteristically sluggish as she moved forward. It was easy to ignore the burning wounds in her back, but ignoring the image of Smith lying so still in front of her was less so. She'd lost friends and team members before. Why did this feel so different?

The steel behind her took another hit from the big-caliber weapon security had found and a pile of soccer balls in front of her burst and scattered around the room. The sudden chaotic motion created the illusion of Smith's head moving. Or maybe it wasn't the soccer balls at all—maybe she was just seeing what she wanted to see. Randi blinked hard, trying to clear her vision. Her mind wasn't normally prone to playing tricks and now wasn't the time for it to start.

But then his chest suddenly expanded and he rolled off de Galdiano onto the blood-soaked carpet. She froze, staring at him for a moment before looking up at the one surviving monitor bolted near the ceiling. It took a moment to make sense of the image made hazy by the smoke, but finally she managed to combine the shapes and colors into something coherent: Christian Dresner facedown on the floor.

Bullets continued to hiss overhead and security kept punching through the steel wall with their goddamn elephant gun, but all that seemed to fade away for a moment. Jon was alive and they'd done it. They'd actually pulled it off.

The moment of elation wasn't particularly well reasoned, she knew—her chances of survival had actually just taken a turn for the worse. After his partial heart attack, she'd be lucky if Smith could operate at half speed. And he was almost certainly going to frown on her plan to use him as a human shield. But why question the sudden surge in her mood? Better to just enjoy it while it lasted.

She slithered forward and rolled over de Galdiano's body, landing on her back next to a very confused Smith.

"You got him, Jon! Dresner's dead. But we will be too unless—"

A gun appeared over the steel wall and she aimed at it, waiting for the top of the guard's head to appear before firing her last round. It got close enough to make him drop behind cover again but confirmed her initial impression that the manufacturer had exaggerated the accuracy of her weapon.

She shoved Smith onto his stomach and pulled the pistol from his waistband, then started dragging him toward the empty window frames at the back of the room. There wasn't much time. If one of the security men had made it to the wall, the others weren't going to be far behind. And when they all got into position, they'd jump up in unison and spray the entire office. Game over.

"Marty!" she shouted as Smith came around enough to start providing some of his own propulsion. "Get off that damn computer and go to the windows. We're leaving!"

He ignored her and she swore under her breath, knowing that she'd have to go back for him. There was no time for this crap.

Smith's eyes had cleared by the time they made it to the windows and he grabbed her arm when she started back for Zellerbach. He didn't seem to be able to speak, and instead motioned toward the edge of the floor where it dropped to the parking lot below. She leaned out, careful not to cut herself on the glass still clinging to the frame, and immediately understood what he was trying to communicate. The building's facade was even smoother than she'd anticipated—making getting to the floor above or below unlikely for her and virtually impossible for the two men she was saddled with.

Another face appeared over the wall and she fired at it, but this time the man got a few rounds off first, taking out the leg of a pinball machine only inches from Zellerbach's head. Randi looked around for anything they could use, but there was nothing. With more time, they could probably string together some cables, but time was something they didn't have. She looked over at Smith, hoping for one of his inspired plans, but got just a smile and a shrug.

"I'm in!" Zellerbach shouted, and a moment later the sprinklers in the ceiling were dowsing them with frigid water.

"You get 'em, Marty," Randi said, appreciating the effort. With a little luck, a few of the sons of bitches who were about to kill them would go home with nasty colds.

"I have access to security's personnel files!"

She fired at a man sprinting for the barrier while Smith crawled toward a basketball goal and pulled it over, providing them with cover that was probably more psychological than real.

"Give 'em all a pay cut, Marty!" she said, opting not to bother with the few visible inches of a man's back as he ran from right to left across some cubicles.

"How many rounds left?" Smith said, speaking for the first time since he'd revived.

"Not many. Doesn't matter, though. Can't hit the broad side of a barn with this thing."

Randi tensed when someone shouted orders for the final assault, but instead of the rush of armed men she expected, everything just went silent.

She kept her gun leveled at the steel wall and Smith rolled to the edge of the basketball goal to spot for her. But there was nothing. No security forces pouring into the office, no barked orders, no gunshots. Just the sound of the wind coming through the empty window panes.

Zellerbach slid his keyboard away and stood, putting a hand up to block a sprinkler spraying in his face.

"Marty!" Smith shouted. "Get the hell down!"

He ignored the order and instead stepped gingerly through he broken glass at his feet. "I hate this place. Let's go home."

"Marty!" Randi cautioned, trying to cover the man, but still finding no targets.

"Don't be scared," Zellerbach said, heading for the door. "It turns out that the entire security detail loved dachshunds and *hated* their mothers."

EPILOGUE

Prince George's County, Maryland
USA

JON SMITH EASED THROUGH the gate of the Anacostia Yacht Club, enjoying the illusion of calm. Tiny snowflakes drifted through the empty branches of trees, the car he was driving was rented, not stolen, and Randi was sitting quietly in the passenger seat trying not to rip out the stitches he'd put in her back.

They came over a small rise and he leaned a little closer to the windshield, examining the car parked in front of Fred Klein's office: a 1968 Triumph.

He pulled up and stepped out, barely noticing the icy wind penetrating his jacket. It was stunning—a professional restoration that had virtually nothing in common with the hack job he'd done on the one Whitfield wrecked. Reluctant to touch the flawless paint and gleaming chrome, he crouched and looked through the side window at an equally stunning interior. A set of keys dangled from the ignition.

"Fred wanted to show his appreciation," Randi said,

coming up behind him. "He asked me what you would want and I figured this was it."

"He asked me the same thing about you," Smith said, going around to the front and admiring the reflection of the clouds in the hood.

"And what did you say?"

"Deuce Brennan."

A cruel smile spread across her lips. "You know me so well."

* * *

YOU DON'T LOOK TOO MUCH the worse for wear considering the incredible disaster you've created," Maggie said as they entered the office.

The comment hit Smith harder than was intended. He hadn't slept much since Granada and didn't expect to anytime soon. The toll of the plan he'd come up with had been terrible. And casualty estimates just kept climbing.

Klein appeared in the doorway. "I'm glad you're here. Come in."

He helped Randi with her chair before slipping behind his desk and lighting a pipe. Quiet fans started automatically, pulling the smoke into vents before it could drift out to the firmly anti-tobacco Maggie Templeton.

"So you're both all right?"

"Nothing permanent," Smith said. "The car's phenomenal, Fred. Thank you."

He gave a barely perceptible nod.

"How are *you* doing?" Randi said. "Damage control can't be easy on this."

"No, it's pretty much a catastrophe on every level."

"How many?" Smith asked.

"I don't think the number's importa—"

"How many, Fred?"

He frowned and took another pull on his pipe. Reports about what had happened were dominating virtually every news outlet on the planet but solid numbers were hard to come by.

"We've gone a little north of three thousand worldwide. Mostly people with preexisting heart conditions. You can't blame yourself for that, Jon. Without you, it would have been a hell of a lot worse."

It felt like a rationalization. Three thousand people were dead including nine members of Congress, four foreign leaders, and countless financial people. Ironically, the world's soldiers hadn't suffered too badly due to their higher-than-average level of fitness.

"Have you figured out how you're going to handle this thing?" Randi said.

Klein let out a long breath. "It's complicated. Dresner Industries has recalled all the Merges and is headed for bankruptcy. We'll support the buybacks and use LayerCake to find any units still out there. The goal is to account for every one but that's probably unrealistic. As far as a public story goes, we're still trying to come up with something credible enough to convince people that this was an accident. Fortunately, the media seem content to fan the hysteria and don't seem to be looking into the common thread connecting all the people who were killed. In the end, I think we'll be able to make it go away. But it isn't going to be easy."

"And the technology goes away, too," Randi said, not

bothering to hide her pleasure at the thought. "Permanently."

Klein didn't respond, deferring to Smith who had been put in charge of a highly classified task force studying that very question.

"The hardware is easy to replicate and while the public can't access LayerCake anymore, its core is still running in Spain. The key to the technology, though, is Dresner's algorithm—basically a Rosetta stone that translates machine code into the language of the mind. Without that, we can't make any of it work."

"Can you get to that algorithm?" Randi said.

"I don't think so. It all comes back to the same catch-22: In order to access Dresner's operating system, we need to know how Merge communicates with the brain—"

"And in order to figure out how the Merge communicates with the brain, you need access to Dresner's operating system," Randi said, finishing his thought.

"Exactly. It'd probably be easier to just reinvent the technology than to crack his encryption. So we're focusing on that—talking to the people involved in development, going through records. But it's going to take decades. And that's only if we can figure out how to get the North Koreans to cooperate."

"Which so far doesn't seem likely," Klein said.

Smith couldn't shake a deep sense of disappointment despite everything that had happened. "It was such an incredible technology. And if Dresner'd had another fifty years, he might have actually done it. He might have perfected humanity."

Klein dragged thoughtfully on his pipe. "The perfection of our species... It's an endless historical theme, isn't it? Eugenics, communism, fascism, genocide, and now this. Maybe we're not supposed to be perfect."

"I'll drink to that," Randi said. "What the hell would I do with my life if everyone spent their mornings dreaming up new ways to help their fellow man?" She winced in pain as she adjusted her position in the chair. "And speaking of what I'm going to do with my life, there's the matter of my reward for all the wonderful work I did on this."

Klein reached into his drawer and slid a thin manila envelope across the desk. "According to our sources, Brennan was recently seen in a small coastal town in Chile."

"Chile," she said, that disturbing smile playing at her lips again. "I could use a little sun."

ABOUT THE AUTHORS

ROBERT LUDLUM was the author of twenty-seven novels, each one a *New York Times* bestseller. There are more than 225 million of his books in print, and they have been translated into thirty-two languages. He is the author of *The Scarlatti Inheritance*, *The Chancellor Manuscript*, and the Jason Bourne series—*The Bourne Identity*, *The Bourne Supremacy*, and *The Bourne Ultimatum*—among others. Mr. Ludlum passed away in March 2001. To learn more, visit www.Robert-Ludlum.com.

KYLE MILLS is a *New York Times* bestselling author of over ten novels including *Rising Phoenix* and *Lords of Corruption*. He lives with his wife in Jackson Hole, Wyoming, where they spend their off-hours skiing, rock climbing, and mountain biking. Visit him at www.kylemills.com.